WILFUL DEFIANCE

THIEVES' GUILD BOOK FOUR

To Chase

best wishes

Also by C.G. Hatton

Residual Belligerence (Thieves' Guild Book One)
Blatant Disregard (Thieves' Guild Book Two)
Harsh Realities (Thieves' Guild Book Three)

Kheris Burning (Thieves' Guild Origins: LC Book One)

www.cghatton.com

WILFUL DEFIANCE

THIEVES' GUILD BOOK FOUR

C.G. HATTON

First published in paperback in 2015
by Sixth Element Publishing
Arthur Robinson House
13-14 The Green
Billingham TS23 1EU
Tel: 01642 360253
www.6epublishing.net

Reprinted 2016

ISBN 978-1-908299-68-0

British Library Cataloguing in Publication Data. A catalogue record for this
book is available from the British Library.

Printed in Great Britain.

For Hatt

Acknowledgements

There are loads of people I need to thank for getting me this far. Many thanks to Andy Harness and Steve Dickinson at Sci-Fi Scarborough for their enthusiasm and support last year when we launched book three and for challenging me to write this book in time for their next event, and special thanks to all the readers who have been in touch over the past few years – I can't express how much it means to me to hear from people who have enjoyed my stuff.

I would also like to give many thanks to Graeme Wilkinson at Sixth Element for his enthusiasm for my Thieves' Guild universe since the beginning, his patience in designing my covers and his critical eye as a beta reader; to my family and friends who have always appreciated and tolerated my peculiarities, and have never minded being roped into the mad events I get involved in (especially big thanks to Jan and Dave); and finally to Hatt and the munchkins (without whom none of this would have made it into print) for being my inspiration, for keeping me going when things get tough and for putting up with me… I know it's not easy at times.

1

"And where is he now?"

The question hung heavy, more ominous spoken as it was by the most ancient of them.

The chamber was warm, the minds of those facing him cold. The Man sat alone in front of them, a courtesy to be here, not reporting, merely informing. Events had moved fast. Far faster than any of them had anticipated.

She was there, midway along the right hand side of the gathering, eyes fixed on him, wanting to ask of Nikolai, wanting to ask where he was, if he was still alive, if he'd made it through all of this, if any of her favourites had made it out alive.

He lowered his eyes, considering his response, lacing his fingers together as he sat there, stretching his limbs and glad to be free of the confines of that form that was so restricting but so necessary when he worked with the humans.

Now where to start...?

He shut out the screams and shouts, the sounds of shattering glass and gunfire. The sniper rifle had an effective range of two miles. As it was, he was only two blocks away, which was a good thing because his arm still wasn't fully healed.

He sighted through the scope, scanned across to the roof of the outpost where an Imperial flag was flying, then down to sweep north and south, up and down the main approaches. Thick black smoke was billowing up to the skyline from burning barricades. Gunships were circling, dropping down to street level with weapons whirring to bully the rebels into falling back. As he watched, a shoulder-launched missile screamed. A gunship exploded in a fireball, careening into a building across the street. He instinctively squeezed his eyes shut as the flames flared, illuminating the scene with chunks of burning metal that crashed to the ground to the sound of ragged cheers.

The Empire troops were outnumbered and outgunned. Surrounded. It was a godforsaken base in a crumbling city centre on some low priority planet, so no battlefield troops, no powered armour or weapons sentries, no real defences. And the few soldiers in light armour that they did have were rooted to the spot by the rules of engagement of their strictly humanitarian brief. Their orders were to hold, let the drugged up bastards burn themselves out.

Except that wasn't going to happen and they had no idea why it was suddenly going so badly wrong.

He scanned the sights across the crowd, tracking faces and minds as the rioters advanced, as they jumped up onto burnt out vehicles and threw grenades and burning bottles, screaming and releasing decades – generations – of oppressed hatred.

He found one of the figures he was looking for, scruffy fatigues, face masked, concealed body armour that was way beyond the means of the poor suckers they were inciting. He spotted another and another. They were coordinating the attack through Sensons, tight wire, encrypted comms that he could hear as easily as if he was included in the loop. They had a drop ship in orbit ready to extricate their target, the real reason they were here, the actual mission they were using this riot to cover. It was going to take slick timing to get this right.

He chose his first target. Breathed in. Breathed out. And pulled the trigger.

By the time he reached street level, the rioters were running full tilt at the Empire enclosure.

He paused in the doorway to pull a scarf over his mouth and nose, pulled his hood up and stepped out as a stray RPG hit the building opposite. Glass and debris showered down. He didn't flinch, didn't stop, simply merged in with the crowd, walked past a car that was still on fire, an overturned truck, a trashed checkpoint, and let himself be drawn towards the outpost. The few Imperial troops on guard around its perimeter were firing, FTH that was bouncing off the attackers with no effect because the whole lot of them were equipped with nullifiers you couldn't even get on the black market. The outpost was being overwhelmed, over-run by a frenzied mob that knew it was only a matter of time before they'd be in.

The Senson engaged. "What are you doing, 402?"

He ignored them, cut the connection and walked calmly up the centre of the road, rifle slung across his back, people pushing past him, fury and exhilaration burning deep in the minds that swirled in a maelstrom around him, anger and frustration heightened by the violence and fuelled by the drugs.

Someone bumped his shoulder, pushed a bottle into his hand, flames from the rag stuffed into it curling around his sleeve. Someone else caught his eye, screaming, grinning, brandishing a makeshift burning torch in one hand and a rifle in the other, before turning to charge.

It was easy to shut out the emotion. After Erica, this was nothing.

He approached the entrance as the barriers were being torn down. Rebels were climbing through, others clambering all over the downed guards, tearing at their armour and weapons.

He tossed the bottle casually at the barricade as he passed, blazing fluid splashing and flaring around the razor wire. Their drop ship was on its way down so the clock was ticking. He pulled out a gun with his left hand and walked in.

The man he was looking for was entrenched in the main building, three stories up, in a defensive position that was going to last about another two minutes. He upped the pace, pushed past rioters who'd turned to looting, and ran up the stairs. The knee held. Just.

He paused on one of the stairwell landings, glanced out of the window, and sent through their own tight wire connection, "I'm in. Go for it."

Down there in the shadows surrounding the front gate, chameleonic body armour shimmered, figures appearing as if from nowhere, as if the walls had come alive. He turned away to move on up the stairs. They opened fire and he felt the ripple of dark void sweeping outwards as the rioters ran headlong into a hail of live rounds and fell.

He made it to the command floor, rounded the corner, gun up, and took out three of them with fast shots to the back of the head. They dropped. Two more appeared, wondering what the hell was happening, hesitant to shoot one of their own, and both fell with a shot between the eyes.

Two of them were inside already. They had the base commander out cold, another officer dead on the floor and were kicking the shit out of another they had hooded and bound.

He paused at the door and took in the scene in a moment of calm, slow motion clarity, then fired a shot at one and moved fast to incapacitate the other with a precision blow, grasping him round the back of the neck and taking everything he needed in one brief instant before firing point blank, double tap to the head. He pushed the body away and stood for a moment, scanning around, slowing his breathing.

Satisfied that they were secure, he knelt. He yanked the hood off the officer lying there, tugged the scarf down from his own face and grinned. "Hello, Matt."

Jameson grimaced. "NG? Bloody hell, I thought you were dead."

"I am."

He needed more time than he had. He drew a knife, sliced through the bindings cutting into the colonel's wrists, grabbed his arm and flashed them to another place.

Jameson blinked, for a moment looking startled and disorientated.

NG sat there, legs dangling over the edge of the rooftop, looking out over the burning city.

"This isn't real," Jameson said, rubbing a hand across his now pain-free head, pressing where he'd just been kicked by the scum that had come seemingly out of nowhere. "Am I hallucinating?" He turned and glared at NG. "Did you just rescue me or did I imagine that too?"

NG took a swig of whisky from the bottle he was holding. "You're still on the floor down there but yes, you're rescued, for what it's worth." He offered across the liquor.

"So what is this?"

"Whisky."

Jameson laughed harshly. "I mean this. All this."

"You've been set up," NG said. "You need to command your guys to ditch the FTH, for Christ's sake."

Jameson growled and took a drink. "They only have FTH. It's supposed to be a damned peacekeeping operation. Get this – all our live ammo was withdrawn five days ago." He was here on some bullshit intel recovery mission, alone, on orders that had come down from god knows where. It was easy enough to pick the confusion and anger out of his thoughts as he tried to figure out why the hell he'd been sent here and how they'd been over-run so easily.

"They had outside help," NG said, pulling out a gun and making a show of reloading it. "Now you have outside help. I have guys out there. As far as anyone is concerned, you fought back and won. We don't have much time. I need you to listen to me."

Jameson narrowed his eyes. He was pissed at how fast he'd been taken down – he was a spec ops colonel, for fuck's sake, and he was not out of shape – but he wasn't stupid and he was thinking that this was all too weird. A statement had been issued by the Thieves' Guild, galaxy-wide to all parties they'd ever dealt with: NG was dead, killed in action. The evidence had even been accepted by the Assassins. Evelyn was the guild's new head of operations. And now NG turns up in the middle of a goddamned riot amongst insurgents who should not have been able to get within a mile of this place? He shook his head and looked at the bottle in his hand. "I drank a bloody good bottle of scotch for you when I heard you were dead. What the hell's going on?"

NG stared at him.

This was the pressure point. In reality, he really did have a loaded gun in his hand and it would take a split second to be back there, raise it and execute the colonel if necessary.

"You've been set up," he said again. "The people who were trying to get to the guild's council through me are now after you because someone has put two and two together and jumped to the conclusion that you're closer to us than you should be. Which is true. They can't get me any more so they're coming after you. And right now, I've just condemned you by coming here to save your ass because now you know that I'm alive."

He let that hang for a moment then added, "Do you understand? As far as the rest of the galaxy is concerned, I'm dead. And now you know I'm not. I can't let that go."

"What the hell does that mean?"

NG gestured casually with the gun. "Don't make me kill you, Matt."

Jameson laughed again. "I'm hallucinating, NG. I'm probably dead already. You want to prove to me I'm not?"

NG shrugged and threw in the real bombshell. "You want to know what happened to the Tangiers and the Expedience?"

"What?"

"On Erica. Do you want to know what really happened?"

Jameson screwed up his face. He was easy to read. He'd seen the initial reports, some kind of incident out in the Between. It had sent their war footing sky high. No one knew exactly what had happened, just that Earth had lost one of its warships, a JU ship at that, and Winter had lost one of its flagship battle cruisers. Powder keg, meet spark.

"We're at war," he said, not hiding the sarcasm. "That's what happens."

NG shook his head. "If you want to know what really happened, you need to come over to us. And Matt, if you do, you are throwing in your lot with me. Do you understand? Not the guild. Me." He gave that as much persuasion as he could while still needing Jameson to make up his own mind, then he added, "I can't let them have you."

"Who the hell is them?"

"From the way they set this up, someone who has access to your chain of command. I'm trying to find out who and right now you're my closest link to them." And why he needed Jameson alive and uncompromised, on side so he could set him loose again. "I'm going after them and I'm going after the bastards who knew what was waiting for us out there at Erica."

"You were there?"

"That's where I died. Got the scars to prove it."

"What was there?"

NG waved the gun again. "Decide now that you're with me or you die here."

Jameson laughed harshly. "You're serious?" He'd already made his decision. "I always said you were a tough bastard, NG. Okay, I'm in. I'm expecting this to be good."

"It is. We just fended off the first attack from an alien enemy and, trust me, as we are, we won't survive another."

2

"You abandoned the guild," one of them said, harsh and accusing, "and left it in the hands of the young protégé who not only precipitated these dire events in the first place, but who felt the need to fake his death and run it anonymously?"

"You persuaded us," another interjected, "that this guild construct you so desired was the most effective way to prepare. Yet you left it in the hands of one so unstable?"

The Man looked from face to face.

It was one of the hardest concepts for them to grasp.

He had never, in all his dealings with this assembly, ever been able to convey the fickle disparate nature of the factions controlling human space.

"Humans both delight and despair in destroying each other," he said carefully. "It's both their curse and their redemption. They are short-lived and fiercely jealous creatures. If Nikolai had not taken care to hide, he would have been hunted down... regardless of his knowledge of the Bhenykhn and his abilities to face them. Humans despise any they think threaten them. And their own kind are far easier prey to target than some hypothetical evil beyond their immediate comprehension. He had no choice."

Out there in the real world, at that split second, the fight was about to intensify, explosives set to detonate, fingers squeezing on triggers, a drop ship plummeting towards them.

Here, he had all the time he needed.

He flashed back to the Expedience crashing into the alien warship then to the battle, the mud and rain, the pain, losing contact with Hones, the Tangiers exploding, the massive

8

Bhenykhn surrounding them, the moment the commander thrust the knife into his heart.

Jameson was reeling as he let it go and brought them back to the rooftop.

"Jesus, this is for real?"

NG nodded, downed another mouthful of whisky, then rattled off the stats from the encounter, ships lost, personnel lost and injured, Earth and Wintran, what they knew about the aliens.

They sat in silence as he let it sink in.

"Hones was a bastard," Jameson said eventually, staring at him. "But he was one of our bastards and one of the best. And if it means anything, I was sorry to hear about Devon. I drank a good bottle to her too."

NG didn't want to talk about Devon. He looked straight ahead across the dark skyline, raising the bottle again.

"Who else knows about this?" Jameson said.

He paused with the whisky half way to his lips. "Outside of the guild, no one. You're the first."

Jameson cursed. "How the hell did you survive that?"

"As far as the entire galaxy is concerned, I didn't."

"Even Evelyn?"

NG took a drink then nodded. That had been hard, but he'd made that decision as he was talking to her in the Man's chambers. He'd told her everything then wiped her memory. It had been disturbingly easy to do.

"How did you defeat them?" Jameson asked. The guy was smart, battle-savvy from first hand experience, and he'd added up fast that it should have been an outright massacre.

"We were lucky." He wasn't about to reveal his secret to anyone else. Not yet. Only Martinez and LC had known about Sebastian. And anyway Sebastian was gone. He took a deep breath. "It was just an advance reconnaissance unit. We took them by surprise. Hones took out most of their ground force and we managed to get Hilyer on board their ship to set explosives. We were lucky."

Jameson looked sceptical. "You said someone knew they were there?"

NG looked up and regarded Jameson for a long moment. "One of the corporations."

That got a frown. An edge crept into the colonel's voice. "Come on, be straight with me, NG." He wanted to add, or I'm out of here, but he bit back his words. He was switched on enough to know that life had changed and it wasn't for the first time, never before because of bloody aliens, but what the hell.

"Are you familiar with the Order?"

"The what?" Jameson said.

"They pull the strings. On both sides of the line. Earth, Winter, they control the corporations and they orchestrate half the rebellions in the Between." He paused then added carefully, "I have reason to believe the Order know about the Bhenykhn. Matt, did you never wonder how Zang knew what was being researched in your lab, a top secret Imperial facility?"

"Jesus. You have it, don't you? You son of a bitch, NG. You've had it all this time? What is it?"

"You want to know?"

"Of course I want to know. What the hell is it?"

NG was reading from the colonel's deepest thoughts that there was no doubt here, Jameson wanted in.

"We've been calling it a virus," he said, "but the truth is we don't really know what it is. It spreads like a virus. Regenerative properties in the host you wouldn't believe. That's why Zang wants it. He's dying. He thinks it will save him. He was desperate enough to screw over the Order to go after it."

"That's how you survived the knife wound."

It wasn't a question and NG didn't acknowledge or deny it.

"We're pretty sure the virus originates from the Bhenykhn," he said instead. He offered across the bottle and added, "They're telepathic."

He watched the reaction in Jameson's eyes, read it in his mind as the colonel thought, holy shit, an army with that kind of advantage would be unstoppable.

NG shook his head. "Not totally unstoppable. We beat them."

Jameson did a double take. Old suspicions and snatches of

memory clicked into place. 'You bastard', he was thinking, 'you're reading my mind.'

NG held out the bottle. He was trampling all over the guy's mind, sitting as they were in the midst of this pure illusion, drinking imaginary whisky together in a frozen instant of time.

"The virus has a side effect," he said calmly, no need to admit his personal circumstances.

Jameson almost broke into a grin. 'What number am I thinking of, right now,' he thought.

"Matt…"

'Prove it,' Jameson thought aggressively, snatching the bottle and taking a swig.

"Seventy four," NG said out loud.

Jameson laughed. "Son of a bitch. I want in."

"There's a fifty-fifty chance it'll kill you."

"That's better odds than you're giving me here. I want in."

"I was hoping you'd say that."

He left Jameson with a squad of troops from the Alsatia and a handshake to secure his loyalty. It was enough. He made sure it would be enough. Two of the Man's elite guard were waiting for him in the stairwell and they dropped into position on either side as he ran up the stairs. The gunfire was intensifying outside.

He called ahead. "How are we doing?"

"All clear if you pick up the pace there, 402. Good for pick up."

He made it to the rooftop.

He could feel Leigh standing there by the ramp of the drop ship before he saw her in the light from the flag that some of the rioters had torn down and set alight. She met them, relieved to see him in one piece but frowning as he limped on board. The knee had seized up. He could shut off the pain but it was a bitch when it stiffened and refused to move.

He stashed the rifle and dropped into a seat as the drop ship started to lift, struggling to fasten the harness with his left hand, the right arm throbbing right up to his shoulder.

Leigh sat next to him. "Their ship split as soon as it saw us. We're getting its ID."

He liked that she said 'we'. She hadn't hesitated when he'd asked her to join him. She'd raised her eyebrows when she'd learned they were Thieves' Guild but she'd declared instantly that she had nowhere else to go. And nowhere else she wanted to be. Not after going through all that with them. What she hadn't said, what he'd picked out of her thoughts, was that she wanted to know more about him. He'd died in front of her, more than once, and she wanted to know how he'd done it. Maybe at some point he'd tell her. She was easy company and he was missing Devon, and Evelyn and Martinez.

"Let me see your arm," she said. She'd been monitoring him, live, every minute. Another medic standing by had injectors to hand, ready for him. He would have preferred a whisky but he wasn't going to object.

"I'm fine."

"No, you're not. You need to keep the cast on."

The casing immobilised his hand, that was why he kept taking it off. For some reason, healing the arm was taking more energy than he could manage. It hadn't just broken, the bones had shattered under the stamping heel of the Bhenykhn that had killed him.

She was watching as the other medic picked up the black snug cast and manoeuvred his arm into it, pulling the straps tight. He didn't object, feeling it realign, hard pushed to shut off the pain.

"Why are you struggling so much with this?" she said, blunt, as always. She'd seen him recover fully, quickly, from critical stab wounds to vital organs that had near as dammit killed him. She was thinking that the virus couldn't be working.

He didn't need to look deep into her mind. In everything he'd told her and let her in on, he hadn't given away anything about himself. She knew all about the virus. She was reporting to him from the medical research teams on the Man's ship and on the Alsatia. She'd watched LC recover, fully. And it had been close that time. Punctured lung, shattered ribs, blood loss and poison from the barbed bolt that had slammed into the kid's chest. They'd almost lost him. It had been touch and go for a long time, the virus overloaded in dealing with it all, worse because he'd lain there bleeding in the cold and the mud for so long. She was thinking about the way they'd got LC stabilised and fed the virus with glucose, watching, monitoring every second as it knitted the bones together, created new blood cells, mended his organs. They'd got him back on his feet and started straight away putting him through the absolute wringer as the closest source to the original virus that they had. She was fascinated by it.

NG looked at her. He needed the virus to work. At better odds than fifty-fifty. Problem was, she thought he had it, adding it up the same way Jameson had and reckoning that was the only way he could have survived the knife wound to the heart. And she didn't understand why it wasn't healing the fractures for him the way it had for LC.

"I don't know," he lied and sat back as they accelerated hard to make orbit.

Leigh was still watching him. "Alsatia Control are pissed that you left your post."

He couldn't help the half smile that slipped out. He'd been enjoying playing as 402 but it was starting to get tiresome. "I took out all my targets."

"I know," she said. She'd been watching his stats, watching him shoot, how he'd settled into a state of absolute calm on that rooftop before taking each shot. She was thinking she'd never seen anyone with such a level of focus and self control. She was looking him in the eye as if she was looking into his soul. And he'd known her for five minutes. She said softly, "Tough being dead?"

It was tough not being in command anymore. He had the best of it and the worst of it. He had free rein, total control, over the Man's entire vast empire. He was in effect the Man and he was still figuring out what he had access to, what every facet of that empire did. The private army he knew about, the Man had sent him to spend time with it. It had been a revelation to discover they had an underground research base on some deserted ice planet in the Between. And he was still working his way through the assets of all the corporations the Man controlled.

But as far as the Alsatia was concerned, he was dead. If he needed to call on the Alsatia's resources directly, the only way he could involve himself with them was through the special projects team instigated by the Man before he left. Several times now, he'd used other personnel from different branches of the Man's organisation, assigning them to tasks under guild control whilst retaining their anonymity, and that's what he had to be, just another code-tagged operative to rag on. Like he'd told Jameson, he couldn't risk anyone finding out he was alive. If it had been up to him, he would have come out here on his own, but he'd sent a tab in, supposedly from the Man, for the guild to find Jameson and this is what they'd come back with. A set up, a colony pushed to boiling point until it spilled over into outright rebellion as a cover for an even more subversive operation, the abduction of an Imperial JU colonel. An operation that they'd managed to infiltrate just in time to get Jameson out before the Order grabbed him.

NG shrugged and stretched out his leg. It was making his head hurt thinking about it too much so he stopped. There was one thing above all else that he needed to do and in order to do that he had to find a variation of the virus that worked. Before the Bhenykhn came back and before Sebastian came back and took control permanently. And that could be any day.

As they docked with the Man's ship, he sensed there was something wrong. He scanned ahead and could feel the tension before the airlocks cycled. Morgan, captain of the Man's ship, was waiting for them, as immaculate as ever in his crisp, smart uniform. At least there was no salute this time, the natural inclination to do just that consciously forced down as they approached.

NG stopped in front of him, couldn't hide the fatigue and was hit with an unsettling sense of déjà vu. "What's wrong?"

Morgan was standing almost to attention. "Anderton is

missing. He was sent out on a tab the Alsatia is saying originated from here." He hesitated then added, "We just got word. There's a warrant out for his arrest. They're saying he killed Olivia Ostraban."

3

Many sitting there were uncomfortable to hear the minutiae of human dramas. The chamber was quiet. They were still. There was no soft flickering of a candle, no dance of firelight to bring life to this austere setting. They wanted to know facts, patterns. She was the only one concerned to hear of the troubles affecting the few he talked about, the ones who played out their roles across the board as the stakes rose ever higher.

"Would events have been different had you remained?" she asked. More to the question than there seemed. Would Nikolai have acted differently? Could they have taken better care of Luka, is what she was really asking.

He pondered the possibilities. "These creatures are fickle. They are drawn to the flame. Nikolai and Luka especially. That's why these two are so vital to our plans. They do not conform. They exceed and excel, and that sets them at odds with the rest of their race. Could I have prevented what happened? The fact that I was unable to rein either of them in when I was there suggests not. Events conspire. Human life has a momentum to it that we struggle to comprehend. They live fast. They die fast. What they do in between? The special ones cannot be caged."

"He's supposed to be in rehab on the Alsatia," NG said.

Under observation. Their little lab rat. He hadn't given an explicit order that the kid be kept there but for Christ's sake, it shouldn't have been necessary.

"He was," Morgan said bluntly. "They had no reason to question the tab. They thought it had come from the Man."

He managed to not say 'sir', that was something.

NG stood there, leg aching despite the painkillers, pulling the information directly from the guy's mind. Morgan was good. Different. Totally different way of running things but slick and effective. He wouldn't have expected any less from the Man and his close crew. To hear that LC was missing, again, wasn't good.

"Who sent in the tab?" he said quietly.

"We don't know. You need to see it."

They went to the Man's chambers, Morgan stepping aside as they reached the anteroom, letting NG enter first.

He went in, sparking up flames for each candle as he entered. It was a neat trick but he still didn't have total control over the amount of energy it took, charring the bulkhead slightly with a couple as the wicks flared.

He limped round to sit at the desk, even now not completely comfortable with all this. He'd never be the Man. He didn't want to be.

There was a stack of reports sitting on one end, neat, the rest clear, nothing like his old desk. He'd packed away the chessboard, couldn't bear the accusing stare of the queen, and it still didn't feel right to clutter it with any of the crap he usually accumulated while he worked.

Morgan sat in what had always been his seat. It had been something of a revelation to realise that he had an opposite in each of the Man's operations, the Alsatia and the Thieves' Guild only one entity in dozens. He'd always known the Man had other stuff going on. It had never crossed his mind that other heads of operations would sit in that same chair to report.

And now it was him they reported to.

He leaned forward, elbows on the desk. He hadn't showered or changed and he could still smell the smoke, still had dried blood on his hands. "What have we got?"

Morgan held out a folder. "It looks legitimate."

It was a perfect imitation of the type of tab that used to come directly from the Man, even down to the paper and the scrawled signature.

NG flicked through its contents. It specified LC but that wasn't unusual. The Man had often handpicked the operatives he wanted for his private work.

"Did this come from here?" he said.

"No." Morgan was certain, that was clear. If it had, the guy would have known. "It was delivered to the Alsatia by one of our special couriers, the AI Carpathian, just after we left."

"The timing was convenient."

"Very. We've interrogated her and her memory modules back her up. She genuinely believes the tab originated from here."

NG looked back at the signature.

Wherever it had come from, it was good. He wouldn't have guessed it wasn't genuine. "Are you telling me someone has managed to intercept one of our most secure means of communication?"

"It would seem so." Morgan managed to stop himself from adding a 'sir'.

According to the file, LC had been sent out on the tab with two extraction teams. There'd been an incident and he'd split, vanished. Knowing LC, that wasn't surprising if he'd heard about Olivia.

"What about the warrant?" he said.

Morgan placed a board on the desk and pushed it forward. "It's all in here."

NG scanned through it quickly. It was legitimate, first degree murder, war crimes and espionage, listed both sides of the line. LC wouldn't be able to set foot on an orbital or planet anywhere, whatever ID he was using. The bounty was bad enough, a legal warrant like this was watertight.

It was a clever move. There was no way LC could have killed Olivia.

"The Alsatia has people recovering the evidence Ostraban is claiming he has," Morgan said. "It must be good. He's got Ballack to second the warrant."

They had it all wrapped up. Clever to use the Merchants' Guild as a neutral third party. Ballack would be revelling in it. A chance to get one over on the Thieves' Guild and lord it over Earth and Winter.

NG pushed the board away. He'd come very close to declaring LC dead after Erica. Hilyer as well, for that matter. Maybe he should have. Zang had obviously not given up chasing them.

"They have no idea what's coming," he said. "I take it the Alsatia has sent people out after LC?"

Morgan nodded.

He scrubbed a hand across his eyes. "Where's Hil?"

"Here," Morgan said. "The headaches were too bad for him on the Alsatia. We had to bring him back. He seems fine here."

Because there were no AIs on board the Man's ship but no one could know that. He'd briefed Hil, LC and Duncan to keep quiet about the side effects while they figured out what to do. As far as anyone was concerned, the properties of the virus were limited to regeneration.

"Hal Duncan?"

"Still with Science."

The virus was proving to be a bitch to research, destabilising as soon as it was taken from a living host. Losing LC was the last thing they needed.

"Where's Badger?"

"In the briefing room. He has everything set out for you."

The room they had set up for briefings was cooler than the Man's chambers. That was one of the first things he'd tasked Morgan with. It seemed that the Man had only ever met the heads of his various operations one at a time. NG had said straight off, "Screw that, we need a briefing room."

Leigh was already in there, sitting at the back of the room. Badger was trawling through the latest reports and briefings. He was in his element. Special projects rather than deep cover but inundated with data from every aspect of the Man's empire. They were pulling in everything from everywhere.

The table was strewn with boards and papers. There was a tray amongst it all. A jug of tea with cups and a bottle of whisky with glasses. As if they hadn't known what mood he'd be in. He missed Evelyn.

Morgan followed him in and sat down. "Why would Anderton kill Ostraban's daughter?" he said.

"He wouldn't," Badger said from across the table, looking as wild as ever. "LC's never killed anyone."

Leigh raised her eyebrows at that, thinking that hadn't been what she'd seen out there on Erica.

NG reached across for the tea and veered instead for the whisky. LC might have changed, having been thrown into the middle of a battle, but deep down his intense aversion to violence hadn't gone.

"He wouldn't," he said. "It doesn't come naturally to him. He doesn't hurt the people he cares about and he's been involved with Olivia for a long time. I should have brought her in."

She wasn't the first person he'd made that mistake with.

Leigh was staring at him. She connected through the Senson and whispered inside his head, "LC is Thieves' Guild and he was having a fling with Ennio Ostraban's daughter? Wasn't that complicated?"

"They didn't know."

"And now the whole galaxy does?" She was starting to see the implications of everything she'd read.

NG opened the bottle and muttered, "Don't worry, we'll get him back." He reached for a shot glass. None of them had stopped since Erica, since he'd brought them all into special projects, gate-crashing Morgan's cosy operation here on the Man's ship, and he could feel the fatigue pulling at them.

He poured a shot and pulled over one of the boards, flicking slowly through the report, gaze lingering on the autopsy shots of grotesque figures in various stages of decay, dull orange eyes staring out at him.

It felt like the battle had been a million years ago.

"Where are we at?" he said, rubbing his hand over his eyes. He had everyone in Science, as well as the Man's own medical team, working on the virus and the Bhenykhn.

Leigh looked up. They had nothing new to report. Every alien body they'd recovered from Erica had decomposed to organic sludge within eight hours, some faster. Every piece of Bhenykhn technology they'd scavenged seemed to have been inherently symbiotic with bioelements that had disintegrated just as fast. They were trawling through the data, she was thinking, what else could she say?

Badger was the one who said it. "Nothing new."

NG pushed away the board. He knew that, it was all in the files.

"It would help if we had another subject…" Leigh said, still privately through the Senson, knowing she was out of order.

He shook his head. Lulu Essien was still unresponsive. Leigh knew that and she'd seen the reports on what had happened to Sorenson.

"No," he replied. "I'm not going to risk anyone else. Not yet."

As much as he desperately wanted, needed, the virus to be stable enough to use, he couldn't, not as it was.

She looked at him, trying to figure out how to say what she wanted to say. She didn't understand why they had no data on him and she wanted to whisper, 'We need you', knowing how bad that would sound and for once biting her tongue.

He was too tired for this. "Keep working with what you've got," he said, out loud. "Where are we at with UM?"

UM was going to be the key to this. From what he'd ripped out of Gian Fiorrentino's mind on Erica, UM had known about the virus before Zang but nothing the guild had managed to do had ferreted out the whereabouts of Angmar Rodan or any of his executive board. The corporation was as active as ever, more so, but its core personnel had vanished.

Badger looked up from the pile of reports he was shuffling, something weird going through his mind as he decoded an incoming. "We're…" He stopped. When Badger caught something interesting, his mind sparked like a firefly. "NG?" he said warily. "Who's Nikolai?"

4

"The elixir?" one said. "Is there no way for us to use it on our own kind?"

They hadn't offered him so much as a glass of water. He knew that there were some here who did not approve of their involvement in this galaxy. They hated the smallness of it, the weak-minded petty machinations of its factions, the self-destructive nature of its denizens. It gave them strength to despise the humans of this galaxy as if that excused them from their actions.

That the organism only worked on human DNA gave them more reason to hate when it should give them reason to hope.

He looked along the line for her, reading her expression, reading her thoughts. She was maintaining her composure, refusing to be drawn into the argument, biding her time to speak up for him. She wanted to know the whole story before she made her move.

"No," he replied. "It is fatal for our kind. Any variation we have tried has proven lethal. Even for the humans, the elixir has proven to be elusive. More so because its very nature created a desire for it that overwhelmed any rational course of action. And that was not the only problem Nikolai and the guild were facing."

NG froze. "Why?" he said, just as cautiously, seeing in Badger's thoughts the turmoil of burning curiosity mixed with an infuriating tempering paranoia.

Badger held up a board. "High priority message. Encrypted. Tag says it's for the attention of Nikolai." He couldn't read it and it was sending him spare.

NG stared at the board. It could be from the Man or Arturo. The only other people he'd ever told were Devon and Martinez.

And as much as the Man had primed Morgan to be ready for NG to take over here, the guy knew nothing about him.

He held out his hand and took the board as if it was primed with high explosive. The message was on the screen. He read it, stomach turning to ice, stood and walked away, close to shaking.

Another mistake.

And one he hadn't even realised he'd made.

He suddenly felt really alone. Sebastian would have been chiding him relentlessly, viciously, might even have seen the danger before it was too late.

But he was gone.

Badger followed him. "Wait. NG, can you read it? Who's Nikolai?"

He held out the board, said, "Work it out. The cypher is PrimeK," and walked out.

He set the shower to maximum and let the steaming hot water rain down his back. It was very possible that he'd compromised the Alsatia, if not the whole guild, and he was so exhausted he was close to not caring. The Bhenykhn were coming back and next time, he wouldn't be able to fend them off. Not alone. He had a jagged two inch scar on his chest that was a constant reminder of just how close it had been.

He stood there, head down, more than tired. He needed to keep his eyes open but he felt himself slipping, eyelids heavy.

A damp chill shivered into his lungs, heart rate quickening, muscles tensing…

He snapped open his eyes, adrenaline pulsing, sucking in a breath of warm, clean air as if he'd been drowning.

Hot water streamed down his face, across his shoulders.

He was in the shower.

In his quarters.

On board the Man's ship.

His heart was racing.

He leaned his forehead against the bulkhead. Going insane wasn't exactly new to him. He was living day in, day out with the certain knowledge that Sebastian could turn up at any moment and take control. And in twisted self-destructive desperation, he'd tried everything to find him. He wanted him back. Wanted to confront the bastard. He'd virtually ransacked the place looking for something, anything, even the Man's black powder, in that dark time right after Erica. He had no idea why he so needed to hear that condescending son of a bitch whispering in the dark depths of his mind again. Except he knew without doubt that without Sebastian, he'd be dead for real and the Bhenykhn would be rampaging through the galaxy and revelling in the death and destruction that drove them.

He scrubbed a hand over the back of his neck. All they'd done was delay it. He could still feel the cold bite of the poisoned blade as it had plunged into his heart. It would be worse next time.

Someone was trying to get him on the Senson. He ignored it. If they'd read the message, if they'd worked out the implications of it, they were probably freaking out. With good cause. But it was done. He'd screwed up. The only thing he'd been focusing on had been to stop that alien ship from leaving with the intel the bastards had gathered. He hadn't even watched out for a threat on their own doorstep, from one of their own.

He could almost hear Sebastian whispering, '*You fool, you should have seen it,*' and he couldn't argue with that. He should have seen it a mile away.

He shut off the shower and got dried, rewrapping the support around his knee and dressing in field-op kit. He was aware that Badger had been hovering around outside for the last ten minutes. He grabbed his holsters and headed out of the door.

Badger was pacing and he spun round as the door opened. "Elliott? NG, how the hell does Elliott know where we are? How does he know this code?"

Leigh was standing there quietly, leaning against the bulkhead.

"He had access to the entire Alsatia," NG said bitterly, walking past them without stopping. "I shouldn't have let him within a million miles of us."

They followed.

"Who the hell is he?" Badger said. "You can't go, NG. No way."

"How can I not go? He doesn't just know I'm alive, he knows my real name." He was struggling to strap on the holsters as he walked, swearing as he went.

Leigh raised her eyebrows, surprised that he was still wearing the cast on his arm.

"It's too much of a risk," Badger was protesting. "Send Hil, Duncan… Send a freaking assault team. Anyone but you."

"Elliott avoided me the whole time we were on Erica. And he took out four of the Bhenykhn. You've seen the reports. He dismembered them, almost dissected them. I should have had him hauled off that damned freighter the minute we got back."

"NG, you were fucked," Badger said.

"He's right," Leigh said. "You did everything you could. How could you have known?"

"I should have seen it." He tugged the strap tight but one of the damned catches was stuck. They weren't looking so he forced it, misjudged the energy needed to nudge it into place and almost broke it, almost burned through to his leg. He snatched his fingers away, cursing.

The Duck shouldn't even have been able to leave the cruiser. He'd left word from the Man that the Alsatia was to be locked down. Clean up the mess on Erica, fast because every damned ship in range had picked up the distress calls, and leave with all hands on lockdown until he could figure out what to do with everyone. He had no idea how Elliott had managed to leave but then he had no idea how Elliott could have got access to these codes and the intel on how to contact them. No wonder the son of a bitch had been avoiding him.

"I need to go," he said, standing up. He couldn't leave such a dangerous loose end like this unresolved. The message stipulated that he had to go alone. Fine, he'd go and if Elliott needed neutralising, he'd deal with it. "Pull everything we have on Elliott and the freighter. Send the Alsatia a warning to change all codes. Tell them to bug out and stay dark until we get back in touch."

From a human perspective, it wasn't possible to get much deeper into unoccupied space. The freighter was drifting, no life signs on board. It was powered down, no weapons that he could detect, and no AI activity.

NG stepped into the airlock, holding a gun in his left hand loosely down by his thigh. It was cold in there, quiet, as if ship systems were at absolute minimum. It cycled and he walked out into a cargo bay.

A shadow moved up ahead and he snapped up the gun, tracking the figure that emerged in a doorway.

Elliott.

Freaky as hell. Total void, exactly as LC had described.

The guy spread his arms and smiled. "Nikolai."

He could read nothing, no thoughts, no emotions, even his body language was tough to read. It was similar to what had happened to Hil but colder somehow.

NG didn't move, didn't let his aim waver.

"There's no need for the weapon," Elliott said. "I don't intend to harm you. I need you."

"Why?" He didn't bother to keep the suspicion from his voice.

"Now that Luka has gone awol again, I need you to do something for me."

"It was you that sent in the phony tab?" That shouldn't have come as a surprise. "What did you send him to do?"

Elliott smiled again, a sly creasing of his thin mouth. "Let's take this inside, shall we?"

NG still didn't move. "If you need something, why didn't you just ask the guild to help you when you were on board the Alsatia?"

"I don't need the Thieves' Guild," Elliott said, as if he was talking to a child. "I need you, Nikolai. You know, the whole time Luka was here, struggling with the virus, I never suspected the telepathy. That is how you were communicating on Erica, wasn't it?"

NG stared at him. So much for keeping it under wraps.

"It's not a virus, you know," Elliott said.

They knew it wasn't a virus but no one had come up with a better name or theory.

"What else do you know about it?" NG said, guarded.

"I know it's derived from the Bhenykhn. And I know you don't have it. Now that is curious because you heal fast… except for the broken bones, I see. Luka's collarbone healed fully within what? Three days? That was interesting to watch. Aren't you tempted to try it? See what it can do along with whatever the hell it is that gives you your special abilities, Nikolai?"

"What do you want, Elliott?"

"I want you to do a job for me. You need to help me. Trust me when I say that because you can't do what needs to be done alone, and I can't do it without you. Tell me, why did you fight the Bhenykhn on Erica?"

Christ, that was a question and a half. "Because we were there," he said dryly.

Elliott folded his arms and leaned against the doorway. "I don't think so. You've been looking for them."

"So have you," NG countered, adding it up and taking a chance. He'd never believed it was a coincidence that the Duck turned up for sale at Sten's World when Gallagher was looking for a ship.

Elliott smirked. "I want to be ready for when they come back. You see? We have the same objective." He turned away. "Come up to the bridge." His voice echoed as he walked away. "I want to show you something."

He followed Elliott through the ship, a route that was familiar from LC's shared memories. The smallest of details, a scuff on the wall, a rust patch on a handrail, every dink and dent in the bulkhead, made it feel like he'd been here himself already.

"So…" Elliott said as they climbed stairs, "telepathy is a remarkable talent to have. What else can you do?"

It was tempting to throw a fireball up the stairwell.

NG didn't reply. Even though he couldn't sense a thing from him, he could almost feel the guy smirking up ahead.

"It was impressive to watch how you used Luka and Duncan

on Erica," Elliott said. "Very impressive. You're not infected like the others so I'm guessing you were born with this ability. Was Luka? Or was that the virus? I'm guessing the virus by the way it was passed to Duncan. Do you know how it works?"

It was difficult to tell if Elliott knew more and was fishing to see how much they did, or whether it was a genuine question.

Elliott laughed when he didn't answer. "I knew Luka was good but the telepathy explains how he was able to keep ahead of the bounty hunters for so long. It does give you the perfect counter to the Bhenykhn's jamming technology. But there are only three of you. If you manage to replicate the virus, how are you planning to disseminate it? The human race isn't ready to welcome a society of telepaths into its midst, Nikolai. And you're running out of time."

He knew that. He didn't have time for this. "What do you want from us, Elliott? What did you send LC into Yarrimer for?" The tab had been detailed – gain access, break into a specific vault, open a specific safe, acquire the contents – but there'd been no description of what those contents might be.

"They have an artefact I need," came the reply. "Yarrimer is not somewhere I can go. From what I know of their security and what I know your field operatives are capable of, I reckoned Luka was my best shot. Luka or Andreyev." He stopped and glanced back over his shoulder. "I take it no one else knows that little secret of yours."

Martinez had guessed as much. No one else knew except the Man. It was unsettling to think that Elliott knew that about him and Christ knows what else.

He couldn't keep the irritation from his voice. "Elliott, the last thing we need right now is LC out there on his own again."

The tech guy had started climbing again. "I actually didn't consider that Zang would stoop to such crass methods as murdering innocent girls. It wasn't Luka but they have a pretty much watertight case against him. DNA, fingerprints, footage from station security, eye witness accounts…"

It wasn't surprising. NG followed, leaning on the handrail as the knee started to complain. He'd thought they must have solid evidence to get Ballack to back it and, as much as he'd swear LC would never hurt Olivia, he still asked, "How do you know it wasn't LC?"

"I'll show you."

5

There were mutterings. "What about Nikolai himself? Your young protégé? Have you not tried to replicate his abilities?"

Other voices joined the dissenter, more questions accusing, deflecting from the real issues.

He stayed his temper and kept his resolve to humour them.

Another voice, "Why do you not bring him to us? Let us take this forward. Your guild has outlived its usefulness." The unspoken accusation that 'he' had outlived his usefulness. An accusation of failure. Again.

She spoke up then, leaning forward. "Enough. This galaxy needs the guild and everything it has built, everything it has stood for. Now more than ever. Do not question that. And Nikolai? You know it has been tried and the backlash from that episode proved costly to all of our plans. This is not relevant. We are here to make a decision." She raised her voice, looking straight at him, and added, "Let us not make the same mistake again."

They walked out onto the bridge, minimal lighting coming on as they entered. For his benefit. It was clear that Elliott had no need of creature comforts.

The tech guy sat at the main console in front of a bank of monitors that sprang to life. Nothing about this ship suggested there was an AI but LC had been convinced, and watching Elliott now, it was clear he had a way of hooking in remotely.

NG sat, rubbing a hand across his knee to get some feeling back into it, and leaned forward. The main monitor was showing an image of LC, close up. Except Elliott was right, there was no way it was LC if the date stamp on it was right. Whoever it was in the security footage looked like the kid but there was no neat, pencil-thin scar cutting horizontally across his left cheekbone. The virus was good but it didn't heal with no trace of the wound. LC had been sliced across the face by a machete on Erica. But unless someone had been there with them, they wouldn't know that. And everyone who'd been down there was contained securely on the Alsatia, present company excepted.

It wasn't LC.

NG sat back. "Do you know where he is?"

"No. But I'm sure he'll just be lying low somewhere. He seems to have a knack for it. Now this…" The image changed to a map of Yarrimer's sprawling headquarters. "This is where I want you to go. Do you need to see the details again?"

He shook his head. He didn't have an eidetic memory like LC but he'd processed the intel. He'd been there before. A long time ago. "Yarrimer is a bitch to get into."

Elliott looked him straight in the eye. "I know," he said slowly and clearly, again as if he was speaking to a child. "Yarrimer has always had excellent security. That's why I need you to do this. Really, Nikolai, I thought you'd be smarter than this."

It wasn't where he wanted to go – he was targeting UM – but this guy was an irritation that was getting under his skin. "I can get in there," he said. "What is the artefact?"

"Let me tell you something, Nikolai." Elliott spun his chair round and folded his arms. "Earth and Winter are at war. Losing those two warships you so kindly brought together has tipped the balance." The screens started to flash up stats and charts. "The Wintran coalition got ships to Erica first. They're raking through the debris field and they have people on the planet. They're not letting Earth anywhere near. The twitchy fingers on the triggers of the Imperial Navy don't need much more of an excuse to attack." He paused then added, "The Order is self-destructing. This is not the war they wanted. What you did out there at Erica, pulling that stunt with Garrett and setting the Tangiers against the Expedience, has probably done them more damage than you've managed in years. Take advantage of it. Push them over the edge now. They're ripe for it. But think about it, take them out now, the most influential organisation in this galaxy, and what does the human race have left to fight the Bhenykhn with?"

The Order had never been in a fit state to deal with a threat from outside but he didn't say that. He wanted to ask how the hell Elliott knew about the Order but he bit his tongue.

Elliott leaned forward. "What would you say if I offered you the most powerful weapons platform the human race has ever developed?"

He wouldn't believe it. "What's the catch?" he said.

Elliott shrugged. "It was too powerful. The corporations mothballed it. None of them dared consider the possibility that anyone else could control it so they buried it."

"And you think we can just walk in there and take it?"

"Don't be naïve, Nikolai. The corporations hate each other. But who do you think controls the corporations?"

He knew who controlled them. "The Order." It was hard not to stand and walk away. If the Order had something in their domain that was so powerful, the Man would have known about it.

"They locked it away," Elliott said, "but they didn't throw away the key – they broke it into equal fragments and gave a piece back to each of the corporations."

NG felt cold. He had no reason to trust or believe a word this guy was saying. "How do you know all this?"

"Let's just say I'm a scholar of human history. And the Thieves' Guild is the fabled and renowned master collector of antiquities." Elliott's stare was unblinking. "Get me those fragments, Nikolai, and we will have a weapon that will give us a chance against the Bhenykhn."

"Okay, Yarrimer and who else?" NG said. "How many more? All the big corporations? The big five?"

The guy smiled outright then. "There are seven fragments."

That didn't make sense. "UM," he said. "Zang, Aries, Marathon." He paused then added, "Stirling and Kochitek." Christ, those two corporations had been defunct for generations. "Do you have any of the pieces already?"

"Aries," Elliott said. "Don't worry about Aries. You take care of the rest and we'll be able to integrate the key and gain access."

It was like negotiating a contract, except it felt more like he was doing a deal for his soul. "Zang might be difficult for us," he said. "The others should be fine. UM, I want anyway. Do you have a way to Rodan? Is he Order?"

Elliott laughed. "Angmar Rodan is setting up a New Order and Earth isn't featuring anywhere in it. Get me the key fragment from Yarrimer and I'll find you an in to UM."

NG crouched by the open safe. It didn't feel right. He was inches from taking the artefact but it didn't feel right.

It had been slick, almost exhilarating. Yarrimer had upped security since the last time he was here, upped it even since the last time LC had been here when the kid had screwed up, broken his leg and almost blown it, but then all the corporations were getting more paranoid these days.

NG started to reach his hand in to take the box, paused, fingers inches from the smooth silver-grey metal of the high security case, and sat back again. He didn't know what was wrong. Scanning around, there was nothing amiss. He hadn't triggered a single alarm and the current security detail had no idea they'd been compromised. The vast corporate estate was operating business as usual. But the hairs on the back of his neck were bristling. It had hardly been too easy. It wasn't that. And it wasn't a trap. He'd covered everything. As a tab, it had been tough but not impossible. Costly. Risky. But then the best ones always were.

He was down to thirty seconds to get the artefact and split before the interferences he'd put in place lapsed.

He stared at the safe. It had been accessed recently, he'd seen that on the way in as he'd tricked his way through the locks. There was definitely no trap that he'd missed and he hadn't left any loose ends that could trip him up on the way out.

He switched focus to the guards outside with ten seconds to spare.

Dammit.

He closed the safe, slipping out through the vault door and easing it closed. He waited in the anteroom, counting heartbeats, sensing the guards and feeling the rhythm of their movements.

He waited until there was only one there and waited again until that guy was looking at the monitors at his security station. It took three seconds to open the door, make it to the desk and catch the guy's wrist as he looked up in surprise and reached for the alarm. Two more seconds and the guy was back at work, wondering why he had a headache and trying to recall what day, never mind what time, it was.

NG walked up the stairs as if he worked there, stripping off the gloves, and acquiring a briefcase somewhere along the way. He nodded to staff and they nodded back, anyone even vaguely curious as to who he was dealt with just as fast. He palmed a pass from someone, fried the information on it and made his way to the penthouse executive suite.

He walked casually up to the security desk, swiped the pass and cursed as it rejected his ID. He grinned at the girl there. "Damn thing is always doing this," he said, shaking the pass and bending it almost in two as if that could fix it.

"That won't help," she said. She looked like she could put him on the floor in two seconds flat.

He smiled. "My appointment's been moved up to half two."

"Let me check." She glanced down at her console, didn't move for a fraction of a second, then blinked, frowning. She looked up and smiled back. "Yes, it has. Go right on in."

It was half two in the morning and the CEO was still in there working, a blue light flickering from monitors. Corporate money never sleeps.

She looked up as he walked in.

"Good evening," he said. "I believe you have something I need."

He placed the case onto the console. Elliott looked up, raising an eyebrow. This time, there'd been no meet and greet in the cargo bay, just a curt message to get to the bridge.

NG didn't sit. He'd left one of the most influential women in Winter fast asleep at her desk, wiped any trace of himself from her memory and their security footage then taken the artefact she'd moved from the vault to a safe set into the floor under a rug by her bed. She'd have no idea it wasn't still there. Then he'd extracted. He'd come straight back to the freighter. Alone.

"Yarrimer's key fragment," he said. "You want to check it?"

Elliott smiled, clicked open the locks on the case and took out a package wrapped in blue silk. About the size of his fist. He unravelled the cloth, revealing an irregular shaped block of platinum, highly polished, intricate angles catching the light from the console and glinting. He turned it in his hand. "Well done."

NG stared at him. "How do I get to Rodan?"

"You have a bigger problem than UM."

It was infuriating not to be able to pick it out of Elliott's mind and from the way the guy was looking at him, the asshole knew it.

"Luka's been caught."

6

"Ah, the Seven."

"Adversaries or allies?" another piped up.

They started to debate.

He sat there, watching them, listening to the conflict between their thoughts and their words, thinking himself of the guild and its fortunes, the individuals who were so significant to its continued existence. They were short-lived these creatures, these humans, so fragile compared to his own, he knew that and the Bhenykhn had learned it quickly, but the ones to which even he himself had become so attached had a charisma about them, a spark that fuelled their lives to such an extent that he had become far more involved than he ever would have thought possible at the beginning.

"We have no way of knowing," he said as they looked back to him. "We learned of the Seven when we arrived here. We were warned. We didn't feel it relevant because we had nothing in our science, our history or philosophy against which to compare. We were wrong."

It was hard to resist the urge to walk away, take this back to the guild and take it from there but he wasn't stupid and, as hard as it was to admit, it was starting to feel as if Elliott had access to intel that was better than theirs. "Is he alive?"

"He was when I picked up the report."

"Where is he?"

"High security facility on Aston. Nikolai, sit down and listen to me. Luka was badly wounded when he was taken down. Knowing the boy, he'll survive it. But right now…" Elliott turned back to the console as the screens came to life. "…right now, because of that, it's not going to take long for whoever it is that has their hands on him to realise what it is they've got. And that's not just the cell regeneration." He let that hang then added, "There were casualties."

"That doesn't sound like LC."

"He wasn't alone. Did you send Sean O'Brien after him?"

Christ. "No." Not this time. Sean was still supposed to be chasing down Anya Halligan.

"Well, our darling Sean must have taken it upon herself to find him because she did and he killed three law enforcement officers trying to protect her."

It felt like the precarious grasp he had on this reality he'd found himself in was unravelling. Despite everything, the damned Order was winning. "Where is she?"

"Apprehended as an accessory. She's been charged with harbouring a fugitive. Nikolai, I don't think you understand what I'm saying – he wasn't armed."

There was a police report scrolling on the main screen. It blurred as he stared at it.

It took a moment to realise that this weird tech guy was staring at him again.

"I'll tell you what I want you to do," Elliott said. "I want you to contain this secret you've been nurturing for so long. The human race is not ready to welcome immortal telepaths into its midst. I've told you that already. You need to rescue Luka before they realise what he is. Before Zang gets his grubby hands on the boy. Because that really will be bad. Go get Luka then I'll tell you where Rodan is."

NG threw the stack of files into the centre of the conference table and stalked round to grab the bottle of whisky. He wanted to throw something at the wall.

He went and perched on the bench at the far end of the room instead, drinking straight from the bottle, in the dark, almost challenging anyone to dare come in here, knowing fine well that no one would.

He felt like a damned puppet. It had been bad enough when he'd confronted the Man about the lie his whole life had been. Now the Man was gone, Sebastian was gone and every mistake he'd ever made was coming back to haunt him.

"Whatever bad crap you're thinking," Leigh said from the doorway, "you need to stop right now."

He looked up. He hadn't even heard the door open.

He almost yelled at her to get out, furious, almost threw the bottle across the room.

"Is this about LC?" she asked, seemingly unconcerned that she was interrupting.

She didn't care, that was easy to read. She'd also noticed that he'd taken the support off his arm again and seemed to have made a conscious decision not to give him a hard time.

She was trying to help and it wasn't fair to be angry at her. He bit back the temper and said calmly, "LC and UM."

She went to the table, looked down at the documents and looked up with an, "Oh shit."

NG nodded.

"Are you going after LC or Rodan?"

He had no idea.

He rested the bottle on his knee and looked at her. "LC." How could he not? As much as he hated following Elliott's instructions as if he was some kind of subordinate, he couldn't abandon the kid to the Order. "We need to get this stuff to the Alsatia. Get a team from Legal onto it." Not that they had much chance of negotiating LC out of this, not now that he'd killed three police officers, but it was worth a shot. "And get them onto Frank O'Brien," he said. "He should be able to get Sean cleared."

He took a swig of the whisky. It was a good one, smooth and smoky. He wanted to talk to Evelyn. Get her over here. And the Chief, why the hell not? Elliott could blow his cover to anyone at any time. Did it really matter any more?

Leigh was watching him. "What are you going to do?"

She had a way of looking at him that made him want to tell her everything.

"We'll find out when they're planning to transfer LC and go get him."

Aston wasn't the best place to be banged up in high security. The crew manning the observation room were nervous. With good reason. It wasn't every day you monitored the galaxy's most wanted. They'd upped LC's status to extremely dangerous. It was hard to believe this was all over the skinny kid sitting there in the interview room, two armed guards standing over him, his ankles chained, wrists manacled to a post in the centre of the table and head slumped down on his outstretched arms. They'd shaved his head and it was easy to see they'd stuck a button device in the back of his neck, one of the guys in here with his finger on the remote twitching to use it.

NG was at the back of the obs room, wearing a guard's uniform, full riot gear with helmet, loaded rifle slung by his side, standing casually but ready as if at ease. It wasn't a cast iron cover but no one had questioned the hastily constructed ID and transfer papers. It checked out, that was all they cared about, all their attention on LC.

'What else?' NG thought at him, definitely the weirdest briefing they'd ever had. He'd seen the reports but he wanted it first hand. As well as the gun shot wounds, they'd kicked the crap out of the kid.

LC didn't move but he replied, sounding out of his mind, 'I'm fine. Where's Sean? D'you know?'

'Don't worry about Sean. She's clear.' Frank had paid a small fortune, funded by the guild, to get her out on bail. 'What the hell have they been drugging you with?' That hadn't been in the report.

LC was struggling to put coherent thoughts together. He was trying to use the Senson, oblivious to the fact the room was shielded and that the implant was gone from his neck anyway. Good luck to them trying to get anything out of that. Science had increased the protections on all of them since the incident with Hilyer. All NG could pick up was a vague, 'No idea.'

The virus usually neutralised any toxins. This was going to make it difficult. 'LC, listen in,' he sent. 'They're moving you out in one hour. We've been given clearance to accompany you. If they get you to Winter, we're screwed. So we go now. We need to know how fast you can move when we do this.'

There was a long pause, then, 'Honestly? Might need go-juice.'

That meant he was struggling. Damn it.

NG flicked his glance to the monitors as everyone in the obs room tensed. Again, it wasn't every day you got to see the legendary Thieves' Guild in action. They'd never been exposed like this in public before. The news streams were in a frenzy over it.

The door opened. Evelyn and Duncan walked in, Evie wearing a tight pencil skirt and heels she could kill with, Duncan in a suit. NG couldn't help but stare at Evie, realising with a pang how much he was missing her.

LC looked up as they sat down opposite him. The kid looked tired, fresh black eye, drawn cheeks, that scar across his cheekbone standing out even though he was so pale.

'All in position,' Duncan sent, direct thought to them both, as he adjusted his jacket.

NG watched as Evelyn placed a file on the table. She didn't know he was there.

"We're building a case refuting the allegations regarding Olivia Ostraban," Evelyn was saying, very aware that they were being recorded. "You weren't there. The emphasis is on them to prove it was you. The three police officers that died during your arrest…" She looked down, consulting the file. "According to their medical records, all had congenital heart defects…"

'Congenital heart defects?' NG thought dryly, cutting through Evelyn's brief.

'That was the best we could come up with at short notice,' Duncan thought back. 'What the hell happened, bud?'

LC glanced up, looking NG right in the eye through the glass mirror. 'Didn't mean to.'

"…whilst unfortunate, all the evidence they have against you,"

Evelyn was saying, "is purely circumstantial. They can't prove that you did a thing. So we have a good chance."

'Problem is,' Duncan sent, 'they don't care whether you did it or not – this is all just show – as soon as you set foot on Winter, Ennio Ostraban is going to deliver you right up to Zang.'

NG felt LC's heart rate increase as the biostat equipment in the obs room that was keeping track of the kid's vitals beeped a warning.

'They've taken a bucket load of blood out of me,' LC sent. 'Couldn't stop them.'

'Doesn't matter,' NG sent quickly. 'The virus degrades too fast. They need you alive.'

Evelyn was still talking, the ultimate professional, even though he could feel that her stomach was churning, at the state LC was in and the situation this was putting the guild in. "They're extraditing you to Winter. As your legal team, we're coming with you. Do you need medical attention?"

LC shook his head, switching his eyes to Duncan and concentrating hard to think, 'What's the plan?'

'They move you to the transport, we'll be right there,' the big man sent. 'Instead of going with them, you come with us. We need you to be ready because it's going to be tight.'

Damn right it was going to be tight. Neither of them had any weapons. LC was going to be near as dammit useless. And the security detail had been shipped in. They weren't using locals. The most high profile murder and arrest in years, and it was a kid who'd been the subject of the highest bounty in history. No one wanted to slip up, whether they knew what was really going on or not.

One of the control guys leaned into a mic. "You've got five minutes."

'Stay close to him,' NG sent to Duncan. 'They've got him drugged with some crap he can't neutralise. This is going to be…'

He cut off as an alarm sounded.

High alert in there went to freaked out in a split second. He scanned wider, much wider, fleeting glances into the minds of the prison's central guard detail and reading their panic as they detected incoming. Gunships and troop carriers in attack formation. He went further, into the minds of the pilots flying the inbound ships, stomach knotting as he realised who they were, going quickly from one to the next and watching as they launched air to ground missiles that took out the facility's towers.

He pulled himself back to the obs room. Klaxons were screaming.

He moved, drawing a gun with his left hand, and sending fast, 'Change of plan. We have incoming. We get out now,' as he shoved one of the operators aside to get to the supervisor who was about to punch down on a lockdown button. He caught the guy's hand and hissed, "Don't lock us in for Christ's sake, we need to get him out of here. Initiate evac procedure Omega."

'What the hell is Omega?' ran through the minds of everyone in the room. He didn't have time for any finesse but he gave the supervisor absolute belief in it as the right course of action. Then it was easy to exaggerate the confusion and send them all spinning into panic as he snapped out more random orders and slipped out of the room.

He pulled down the visor as he ran round to the interview room. He stopped in the doorway, covering the corridor and glancing in. Duncan and Evelyn already had the two guards disarmed and on the floor. LC was struggling to free himself of the cuffs, his hands shaking and frustration making it worse.

There was no time to focus or be intricate with this. NG sent two snapshot bursts of energy that bust open the locks restraining the kid's wrists and ankles, sending sparks flying.

Evie spun and snapped up the gun she'd acquired, her eyes flashing, and for an instant he thought she'd recognised him but her finger started to squeeze the trigger, Duncan stopping her with a fast, "He's ours."

She nodded, they grabbed LC and they ran out into the corridor.

'Who the hell is it?' Duncan sent.

NG waved them to stop, checked round a corner and gestured

them to follow. 'The JU. I should have known. Jameson said Earth want their property back. Looks like they're willing to fight everyone else to get it.'

7

The Man listened to them argue. He wanted to stand, walk out, walk away from here. He did not, by any means, need to sit here and be subjected to such interrogation. It was a pure courtesy on his part to bring them intelligence, knowledge, the information they desired.

In reality, he was not even sure they could wield the power they thought they had any more.

Her voice broke through the rabble. "Let us consider," she said, "why we are here before we argue ourselves out of even making a decision."

He could feel that her heart was pounding. She didn't want to be here. She wanted the story direct, like that last time, over a goblet of wine, in chambers warmed by a blazing fire, and she was wishing she'd asked for a private audience with him.

He would have granted it but perhaps it was for the better that they all hear it direct. Now. For they were running out of time.

———————————

The power dropped, plunging them into darkness as they ran through narrow corridors. Someone must have hit the lockdown because blast doors were slamming shut all around them. They were going to get caught between the attacking Earth forces and the defending Wintran security detail, and he had no idea which would be worse.

He called them to a stop, uneasy. Hal Duncan was holding up LC, Evelyn thinking they needed somewhere to hide, that Luka was standing out a mile as he was, in a white shirt and orange prison gear. She was wishing NG was with them and he almost tore off the helmet there and then.

'Why don't you?' Duncan thought at him.

NG unslung the rifle. 'She's safer if she doesn't know. Here, you take this.'

He could hear the jumbled mass of orders flying between the incoming troops merging with the frantic communications of the security guards, the spreading panic amongst the other prisoners almost contagious.

Blue beams from searching flashlights were starting to bounce through the corridors, each life force a bright spark in the darkness. They needed to move but it felt like they were in the centre of a maze that had a mass of bodies running into it, heading right for them.

NG turned slowly, scanning around. "They know we're here," he muttered.

Evelyn looked at him in dismay, a flutter of familiarity hitting her mind before she shut it down as nonsense. She grabbed LC and spun him around. "Tracking device?"

"Shit," Duncan swore, taking hold of the kid's shoulder and turning him. They'd already taken the device out of his neck but he still had the tiny metal tag in his ear. Duncan flicked it. "Is that it?" Without the tagging gun, there was only one way it was coming out. Duncan took a firm hold on it, bracing himself to rip it out.

LC was swaying on his feet, about to keel over.

"Hold up," NG said. He looked at the tag and fried the circuits in it, grabbing the kid as he flinched and getting him between them as they shifted position almost automatically to get back to back. NG was the only one wearing any kind of body armour but he couldn't shield them all.

The metallic echo of stun grenades bouncing along the floor cut through the screaming klaxons. He deflected three of them before they could detonate, Duncan shooting out another two.

NG spun, firing at a figure that appeared at the far corner.

He ducked as shots began to pepper the walls and it took a second to realise that the guards moving up on them were falling, shot in the back.

The shadows of massive, heavily armoured figures began to

45

loom, cast on the walls like grotesque shadow puppets. Earth spec-ops.

"We need to get out of here," he said, reaching to take hold of LC's arm.

They turned and ran.

An explosion blew chunks out of the wall next to them.

NG could sense more than see that Duncan was trying to shield Evelyn and he shoved LC away as he felt another high-ex round fly past.

It impacted.

He was thrown to the side. He twisted, bundled into LC and they both fell through a doorway into a stairwell, tumbling down the steps. He landed badly, hit his head and blacked out.

Cold, dank air swirled around him. A trickle of cold sweat ran down his ribs. He was breathing fast, heart racing, adrenaline pumping.

It was dark, shadows shifting in every direction he turned.

He was trapped.

Lost.

A dark fear clawed at his mind, pressing, looming.

He couldn't move. Couldn't breathe…

He came to with a jolt, shaking. He must have only been out for a second because no one was shooting at them and there was no one standing over them.

He blinked away the chill fog, moved to get up and almost screamed as his arm gave way. He shut out the pain, shifted his weight and looked around.

LC was stirring.

'Duncan?' NG sent.

'Cut off from you, buddy. We'll have to work our way round and find another way down. Stay in touch.'

Great.

There was a clang above them, shouts echoing and a hum of powered armour. NG braced himself and stood, grabbing a handful of LC's shirt with his left hand, hauling the kid upright and dragging him, stumbling, down the rest of the stairs.

They bumped through the door at the bottom into more darkness, two figures turning to face them, blinding beams of light arcing up as they raised their rifles.

NG sent them flying and moved as fast as he could to the first door he could find. Locked.

He backed into it as he shattered the mechanism, staggering through into an empty office and trying the Senson as he moved, sending a quick, "Control, this is 402. Felix Amber. Need back up here," as he did it, like old times.

There was no reply.

He let LC sink to the floor, close to fading out completely, and kneeled, cradling his right arm against his chest and holding his left hand against the back of LC's neck. He made sure there was no one approaching then concentrated, going deep. They'd used a freaking neurotoxin on the kid, no wonder the virus was struggling. He neutralised it, using more energy than he could afford, then pulled two vials of Epizin out of a pocket and popped them into LC's neck, feeling the virus snatch at it with a voracity that was almost disturbing.

LC blinked, opening his eyes as if just realising NG was there.

"Shit," he muttered.

"Yeah," NG said, handing over two more vials and sitting back, rubbing a hand across his eyes. He couldn't move his right arm, could hardly think straight enough to keep the pain at bay. The pins they'd had to put in place had shifted in the fall, all the healing he'd managed to do himself undone. Leigh was going to be pissed.

He forced himself to his feet, muttering, "Wait here," going back to the door and listening until he was sure there was no one approaching.

The two guys he'd just taken down were security, dead, necks broken.

He stripped the jacket and trousers off the smallest one, working with one hand and taking what felt like forever. They both had sidearms as well as the rifles. He took both handguns and returned to LC.

"Put these on," he said, throwing the clothes over and going back to the door. He leaned against the wall, tracking the search patterns on both sides. They had maybe two minutes before they needed to move.

LC started to shrug himself into the jacket, snagging the bandage on his arm as he did it. "She's not dead," he said quietly as he struggled into it.

NG was trying to check the magazine on one of the handguns, not easy with one hand. He stopped and looked back. "What?"

"Olivia isn't dead."

"How do you know?"

"Sean was with her. It was another girl that got shot. They just said it was Liv."

He sounded tired.

It was hard not to be impatient. "Why didn't you say something?"

LC got the jacket on and squinted over at him. "To these guys? How could I? They wouldn't have believed me." He started to pull on the trousers. "And anyway, NG…" He pulled a face. "If they find out where she is, they'll have her killed. I can't do that. I feel bad enough as it is."

"I don't think…"

LC interrupted. "They killed an innocent girl to get to me. They thought it was her. They can't let her live now, can they?"

There was a loud bang outside, not far away.

The kid was fastening the jacket and trying not to aggravate the rest of the bullet holes in him as he did it. He didn't look much like security but they were out of options.

And just about out of time.

There was another explosion, louder this time.

NG gave up on screwing about with the magazine by hand. He slid the mechanism back without touching it, gave it a glance and slammed it back in. He held it out.

LC took it. He never used to carry a gun, now he was thinking that he felt naked without one. Vulnerable, and that was a feeling he hadn't had since he was a kid on Kheris, and he hated it. He hated them, all of them, Ostraban, Zang… He blushed, realising NG could hear everything flashing through his thoughts, random and mixed up as they were.

"Don't worry about it," NG muttered. He tried the Senson again. "This is 402. Felix Amber, heading home. You want to tell me where we're going?"

He saw a faint smile flit across LC's face. The kid had heard that code enough in his time with them. Amber meant wounded but walking. Red was the scary one.

A reply came straight back that time. "Roger that, 402. We have no clear route home at present. Stand by."

Screw that.

He looked round, spotted a terminal and hooked in by remote, skipping past a couple of security traps, and getting deep enough into it to see that the whole system was totally screwed. More than one party was messing with it and whoever was trying to recoup some kind of control somewhere was fighting a losing battle.

He kept it simple and flashed up the building schematics and current security state, aware that LC was watching over his shoulder. The kid had no way in to the tight wire connection but he'd overhead the exchange and he knew they were on their own. It felt suddenly like they were running a tab.

"Go back one," LC said. "Can you make that?"

It was a ventilation shaft.

Looking again, he could see what LC had spotted and he could see why he hadn't targeted it as an option.

"Your arm is fucked again," LC said. "Can you make it?"

If he was honest, he wasn't sure but he said, "Yep. Let's go." He stood and gestured towards the door with the gun in his left hand. "You want to go after Ostraban and Zang?" he said. "Screw them. We get back from this then I'm going after UM. You want in?"

LC was looking at him, eyes hooded, thinking back to that night in the rain on Erica. He nodded.

"Good," NG said. "You, me and Hil. We'll make it a road trip."

They made it down another floor and avoided getting too close to a searching security team, no one looking too closely at them in the darkness but no need to risk it. The Earth forces were sweeping the building from the roof down, clearing action, like herding rats. From what he could pick up as they sidled past a mobile command post, the Wintran security detail were thinking of bugging out, thinking they weren't getting paid to fight fucking Imperial special forces in powered armour.

"We could just walk out with them," LC said at one point.

NG laughed. "Yeah, try it. They'll have you back in chains before you can blink."

It was weird but the adrenaline was addictive. He'd forgotten how much he'd enjoyed running tabs. You felt invincible. Invisible.

He could feel LC looking at him sideways, wanting to know when, when the hell had NG run tabs?

"A long time ago," he said, flashing back to the moment he'd said that to Martinez when she'd put two and two together. He shut down the memory abruptly. "Come on, let's get out of here."

They turned into a side corridor and triggered a motion sensor he spotted a fraction of a second too late. He tried to move, tried to grab LC and get out of there but it was too late. The device detonated, the blast hit and he fell, out cold again before he hit the floor.

8

"We have more than this galaxy to consider," one of them said. "Let us not forget that."

He almost snorted. How could they? In all this, the looming threat of the Bhenykhn was a constant reminder that there was more than this galaxy to consider.

He looked along the line.

This appointed council of representatives was becoming more self-centred and delusional than it had ever been. He could see the insanity sparking in their minds. The scale of existence they had come to stand for was immense. It crossed species, time and space. The Bhenykhn were the enemy simply because they had destroyed his kind. Who was to say they didn't have the right to do so? Survival of the fittest.

"Do not deny that this galaxy," he said, "has the best chance of standing against the Bhenykhn. Given the cascading torrent of events that spilled from that one spark of human greed and paranoia, they have managed to seed potential far greater than any we have ever achieved."

It was dark. Dank. Leaf mold and decay.

He was standing at a crossroads, turning from one direction to the next, breathless, chest heaving, warm blood flowing down his neck, down his chest, black walls looming high all around.

He didn't know which way to take…

He blinked and gasped, a blinding headache pounding hammers into his skull, a lingering chill in his lungs.

The Senson was sending an intermittent, "Come in, 402… Speak to us, 402…"

He rolled to his side and blinked again, squinting to focus and saw dark figures pulling LC to his feet. His gun was just out of reach. He mustered enough energy to shift it, grabbed it and scrambled up, about to fire and stopping, yelling, "Hey," instead.

One of the figures turned, gun up, aiming it right between his eyes.

Pen Halligan.

NG let his grip on the gun relax, letting the trigger guard spin round his fingers, and dropped it. He held up his hand, took a chance, moved to untie the chinstrap on the helmet and tipped it off his head.

Pen laughed harshly. "I see I'm not the only one who can't stay dead." He gestured with the gun. "Get over here. Stay in front of us and don't try anything. You understand?"

NG nodded and walked forward, engaging the Senson. "Control, be advised, Pen Halligan is here."

"Roger that, 402. We're trying to get to you. Is situation still Felix Amber?"

A guy he recognised as Yani had his hand firmly on LC's shoulder, up ahead, steering him forward.

"Kind of," NG replied, picking up mixed emotions from the kid.

Pen shoved him into moving. "So what happened to you?" he said.

"Got stabbed in the heart," NG said. "I died. Thought I'd go with it. What about you?"

"Shot in the head. Seemed convenient to be dead for a while."

"That seems to be the in thing," NG muttered and got another shove in the back.

Pen leaned close and whispered harshly, "We're here for LC. Don't forget that. You have screwed up really badly, NG. You care to tell me what's really going on?"

'NG, he needs to know,' LC thought. 'Tell him.'

'Not here.'

When he didn't reply, Pen pushed him forward, thinking the damned Thieves' Guild deserved everything coming to it.

Control was still talking across the Senson. "Don't be a smartass, 402. What's the situation?"

He cut the connection. Christ, it was shit not to be in command any more. He'd forgotten how shit.

LC glanced back at him, concerned.

'Go with it,' NG thought to him. 'You're right, Pen needs to know so let's not fight them. They have a way out so just go with it.'

It was slick, years of bribes and dealings in play as they moved out. Pen and his guys laughed their way past the blockades and guard stations as if they were old buddies with the guys working them. They probably were.

The security detail were withdrawing, leaving the building to the Earth forces, and simply scanning anyone who left through the single basement exit they had open. As they got close, Pen's guys switched up a gear. NG caught a hint of their plan at the same time as LC but with no time to react. Pen didn't pull his punch, hit the arm right across the break and NG could do nothing but bite down on a gasp as he stumbled, watching through stinging eyes as Yani popped a punch into LC's back, right where the kid had a gunshot wound. LC dropped.

"We got wounded," someone yelled and they were half dragged, half carried through the checkpoint, more shouts for medics and an evac.

He didn't fight it, sussed out which of the bodies around him were Pen's and considered contacting Control but reached out to Duncan instead. 'Hey, you still here?'

'Outside. We got evacuated and they're holding us. I'm tracking you. Who the hell is Pen Halligan?'

'Complicated,' he thought and stopped, struggling with the pain for a second as he was lowered roughly onto a stretcher. "Arm," he managed to breathe, "broken arm."

Whoever it was thumped him on the chest and muttered, "Yeah, you'll live."

'Control wants to know if you need extricating,' Duncan sent.

'Negative. Pen won't hurt LC. Tell Control that 402 is quitting.'

The stretcher was lifted, vehicle doors banging close by. LC was right next to him, getting the same treatment. 'Get Evelyn out of here and follow us. Get a ship on standby. I'm bringing Pen in. And get Morgan to tell the Alsatia that the Man wants Quinn in special projects asap.'

The doors were slammed shut and the vehicle moved, siren wailing. Someone waved a wand over him as he lay there, keeping him down with one hand on his chest and slapping a patch over the Senson before they let up.

NG sat, bracing himself against the motion as they bounced fast along a rough road surface. Pen was in there, Yani and another guy, all armed. A woman dressed as a medic was tending to LC, hooking him up with an IV and taking vitals.

"Thanks for the rescue," NG said. He regarded them with curiosity. He could take them all down, right now. And they had no idea.

Pen looked at him, undisguised hostility, his voice a low growl. "You want to tell me now what's going on?"

"Not here."

Pen's face was pure stone. "No?" He was thinking he could stop the truck and throw NG out into the dirt.

LC was trying to fend off the woman. "Pen, wait. Christ, Elenor, I'm fine, leave it." He struggled up to lean on one elbow. "I stole a fucking virus, Pen. That's what's going on. They want it back. Every fucker in the galaxy wants it because…" He stopped, knowing he'd gone too far and glancing at NG with something like an apology darting into his mind.

"Because…?" Pen was standing, holding onto an overhead handrail with one hand, gun still in the other.

The truck made a turn, fast, wheels skidding.

There was shouting from the cab.

'NG,' Duncan sent, the connection faint, 'LC, get out of that truck. Control is tracking a gunship that's bearing right down on you. They've got a missile locked. You got that? Get out.'

The driver must have spotted the threat at the same time.

Someone banged on the cab and there were more yells as the truck slewed to a stop.

They scrambled out and ran, hot dry air hitting his lungs for a second before the missile hit, heat and debris billowing into them and throwing them off their feet.

NG rolled. He felt the driver die, getting a double hit of black void amplified through LC. The gunship roared overhead and banked, the guild ship following it coming in so low he could feel the heat from its engines. Another missile flew and the gunship exploded, black metal scattering from the flaming ball that hit the desert floor.

NG lay for a second, catching his breath. He blinked, squinting up into a perfect blue sky and bright sunshine. His chest was hurting. He couldn't feel the arm any more. 'Need that extrication,' he thought to no one in particular, feeling the heat on his face and thinking a cold beer would be nice right about now.

Leigh and Duncan were with the extraction team that came to get them. Special projects so no need to panic about anyone else seeing him. By then, he was sitting on a dusty outcrop of rock, resting his arm in his lap, leg stretched out to ease the ache in his knee, enjoying the sunshine. Leigh ran up, looking at him with dismay.

Duncan stopped and crouched next to him. "Control want to put 402 up on charges."

NG raised his eyes. "Tell them good luck with that, 402 is KIA in that wreckage."

"Evelyn will be upset. She liked 402. She's having nightmares, y'know. You should tell her."

She wasn't the only one having nightmares.

"Is she remembering?" Straight after the battle on Erica, he'd talked to her for three hours in the Man's chambers before wiping her memory. It wasn't fair on her, he knew that, but...

"It isn't fair on her," Duncan said. He glanced at the others and looked back. "We've picked up Jameson."

"Why didn't he send us a warning?"

"Says he tried. Listen, bud, you bring Pen in now, along with Jameson, there's no reason why Evelyn can't be in on it. And seriously…" He stood and clapped NG on the back, "you need her."

NG watched as he wandered over to where LC and Pen were talking. The big ex-marine was right. He'd regretted it as soon as he'd done it but events were moving so fast, the last thing they needed was the Assassins after them. They'd put the package of evidence together, sent it to the Alsatia and Evelyn had taken it to them herself. He'd needed to know that she believed it. He was protecting her, and he knew as soon as he thought it, that he wasn't persuading himself any more.

LC was trying to persuade Pen to go with them. It wasn't necessary, they wouldn't give him a choice.

LC glanced back. 'What the hell is it between you two?'

'I don't hate Pen,' he thought back.

'He hates you. What did you do to him?'

NG squinted at them standing there. He didn't want to think about it and he wasn't about to start talking about it. Life had been a lot more straightforward when he was the boss and no one questioned him. LC took the hint and shut up, turning back to Pen and introducing Hal Duncan, another former spec-ops grunt from Earth. They'd all get on great.

Leigh was looking at him. She reached for his arm but he flinched away. It still hurt like a bitch. He shut off the pain, tired but reluctant to pull energy from anywhere. He'd never realised how much he drew from those around him. It was too easy, almost second nature.

She wasn't happy.

"That is going to need surgery again," she said.

He nodded. She was more than pissed off at him, she was worried about him. The last time, when they fixed it right after they got back, they'd had to resuscitate him. Heart stopped, stats off the scale. Nothing like when he faked it. He'd woken up screaming.

"Will you be okay?"

That was a hell of a question. He ignored it, saying instead, "You wanted another test subject for the virus? It's Jameson. Let's see what happens with him."

She nodded, looking at him, glancing back over towards LC and Duncan, and connections clicking into place as she turned back to him. "You don't have it," she said quietly, incredulously.

"Don't have what?"

She looked at him like she could strangle him.

He shook his head slightly with half a smile. "What gave me away?"

"Your eyes. You have dark eyes." Incredibly dark eyes, she was thinking. "The virus, it... we don't know what it does, but it..."

"Doesn't just affect the colour of their eyes, they can see in the dark."

"You can't?"

He almost laughed. "Nope."

"So how...? And why...?" She was kicking herself for being so dumbstruck.

"Soft tissue is easy to heal," he said. "It just costs."

A gleam appeared in her eye, a spark of curiosity burning through the concern. "How do you do it?"

That was the real trick and he'd never been able to explain it. He didn't know what he did. He just could.

"I'll show you," he said. Why the hell not? "Let's measure it under lab conditions. We probably should have done it long before now anyway." Although no doubt the Man already had.

There was a shout from across at the ship. "Incoming. Move your asses, people."

NG pushed himself to his feet. "There's something else I need monitoring as well."

Poison was pulsing through his veins.

Movement. A flash of shadow in the corner of his eye.

He spun. Moved. Forced his legs to run, faster and faster, heart pounding, into darkness.

Nothing.

Nothing but cold dreadful darkness, shadows deepening, walls closing in…

He gasped. Awake. A scream in his throat as he jerked upright to sit, to flee, eyes open in an instant.

Someone touched his arm. One of the Man's medical team with a reassuring, "Hey there, calm down, you're okay."

"We're not okay," he muttered, a lingering damp chill still filtering through his muscles and joints. He wanted to hold onto the detail but it was elusive, the memory of it dissipating faster the more he tried. It had been the same as always though, he knew that. He was breathing too heavily and he worked to control it, stifle the shakes and widen his focus to the whole room, sucking in the warmth from that touch and the familiarity of the figures in there, the machinery, the beep that was matching his heartbeat.

He lay back down. His right arm was in a cast. Not the kind he could take off so easily.

"What the hell was that?" someone was saying. He couldn't think straight to recognise who it was. Someone he'd brought over from the Alsatia.

"Not memory," someone else said. "Not dreaming. Look at the wavelength."

His breathing started to speed up again.

LC and Duncan were supposed to be there, part of the experiment, but he couldn't sense them anywhere near.

'Right here,' the big man thought. 'That was one helluva nightmare.'

'It wasn't a nightmare,' LC thought from somewhere at the far end of the room.

He could feel that the kid was close to trembling, trying not to think.

'What was it?' NG thought. 'LC, what was it?'

He didn't reply.

'LC?'

'It's the Bhenykhn…' The kid's thoughts tailed off, tense and uneasy before he added, 'NG, are you looking for them or are they looking for you?'

58

9

It was not a concept he could so much as utter, not in this company. But he was considering it more and more himself. Doubting everything. The curse of the isolated.

It was one of the commonalities he shared with Nikolai and why he had given the child so much leeway in his reckless and wayward ways.

They were each alone.

Yet these were still his people despite the evolutionary fluke that divided them, the same gulf that separated Nikolai from his own. He looked at them, troubled and hard pushed not to look down on them, even though it were they who were sitting upon the raised platform of these ostentatious chambers.

He had been cruel in his dealings with Nikolai and Sebastian. He knew that. He would admit it, even to them. But they each knew now why it had been necessary and it was one hope that he nurtured, that they understood. Survival was programmed into the genetics of every living creature at the most primordial level.

They could not give in to the Bhenykhn. For to do that would be to give up on life. And no society could be asked to do that. No matter how dire the threat. However overwhelming the enemy at the gates.

Someone was messing with the IV line in his arm. He felt cold. 'Did you hear them?' he sent.

'Not clearly.' LC was trying to shut down his thoughts, a banging headache pounding hammers into his skull.

'You're hearing the Bennies?' Duncan was thinking, not broadcasting but clear enough to overhear. 'Jesus.'

NG lay there, knowing that they were all staring at him, eyes inadvertently drawn to the scar on his chest.

It felt like he'd been run over by a truck. Whatever it was, it wasn't something he was doing intentionally.

Leigh was at his side. "You need to get some sleep."

He shook his head and half-mumbled, "That's the last thing I need."

She put it together, shocked. "You have nightmares like that every time you sleep?"

It was every time he closed his eyes but he wasn't going to admit that.

"How's Jameson?" he said instead.

"Alive," one of the medics said. "Asleep."

That was something.

"Where's Pen?"

"Hospitality suite," Duncan said. "Not happy but he wants to know what's going on."

NG unsnagged his left arm and scrubbed his hand over his face. Pen would find out soon enough. That's what he wanted Quinn for.

He leaned up on one elbow and looked across to where LC was sitting, legs tucked up tight as if he could spring away at any moment, that haunted look in his eyes. The kid had a new implant embedded in his neck. It always took a while to settle in with a new Senson but this was more than that. He was dreading being exposed. It had been tough enough being scrutinised for the regenerative qualities of the virus. The idea of everyone knowing about the telepathy was terrifying. LC had a reputation of never being scared, of anything. Now? Now, he was sitting there, wide-eyed, thinking he could run away and hide, he'd managed it for long enough.

And that was a sentiment that was way too close for comfort to his own frame of mind.

"We need to get all this on record," NG said.

"I know," LC muttered.

"C'mon, let's go play."

It hadn't gone well the last time they tried anything like this but LC nodded.

"Get Hilyer and Badger," he said. "Might as well get Morgan as well. He should see this."

They moved out to the controlled environment of a clean room, more techs in there waiting for them. It was chilly. They should have set the temperature higher. He'd shrugged off the cobwebs from the anaesthetic and dressed, arm immobilised completely. Then they'd come here, to be watched, analysed, laid bare.

LC stared at him, tossed back a mouthful of beer and said, "Seven of diamonds."

NG flipped over the card. Seven of diamonds. And he'd had it shielded, locked down as tight as he could make it.

Badger was sitting back, watching. "Shit. I'm not playing any of you guys at poker again."

Hil was shuffling another deck, close to laughing.

It was impressive to see the progress in LC.

Leigh leaned forward.

He'd kept his promise and shown them the healing, surrounded by a team of techs and monitored from every angle by equipment that was measuring everything possible within the laws of medicine, physics and the universe. It was on record. And now they were observing this. Everyone would know everything. It didn't matter. Because sooner or later, it really wouldn't matter at all.

"Seriously?" Leigh said.

Duncan leaned across and took a card, looked at it, switched in his mind's eye the way he read it and placed it face down on the table.

Clever.

'Too clever?' Duncan thought.

'It would have beaten me not so long ago,' NG replied, impressed.

They were fooling about. Making light of a crap situation the way you do in the cold darkness of the early hours when you know an attack is coming and all you can do is wait and joke, and check your weapon for the tenth time.

Leigh was calmly working through the implications of all this. "We thought you all just had some kind of hardwired comms that weren't affected," she said, meaning on Erica. "And this is from the virus? But you...?"

NG shrugged, non-committal, no need to complicate the matter. He glanced at the techs and said out loud, "You want to take this up a notch?"

The guy in charge was good, previous 2IC in Science, and the chief of Science had been pissed to lose him. "Why not?"

NG reached for a card but this time he tossed it in the air, held it there and made it spin slowly.

Morgan was watching, outwardly as stoic as ever but thinking to himself, 'My god, the Man told us to expect someone special but all this...?'

Badger leaned on the table, staring at the card. "No way. No freaking way." He looked around. "Can you all...?"

Duncan shook his head with a firm, "Not me."

LC squirmed, spinning the beer bottle on its end.

"Try it," NG said and he threw another card into the air.

It exploded into a shower of burnt ash and burning fragments that drifted down onto the table. LC pulled a face, the headache threatening to return.

"That's how you killed them," Badger said and the atmosphere changed. "That's how you killed the Bhenykhn. Who else knows?"

NG raked up the ashes with his hand. "For the moment, no one."

They played for another hour. He'd shown them the fire, kept it contained to a neat ball in the palm of his hand, but it had still freaked them all out. The tech guys had been beyond themselves, ranting on about fuel, where's the fuel and how the hell is he creating that much heat? He didn't know and didn't care. When they got word that Quinn was on his way in, he sent them all to the briefing room.

Leigh wasn't happy. She stopped him at the door. "You need to get some rest," she said. She'd been monitoring his vitals in there and was thinking that if he'd been a member of her crew, she would have pulled him off post and assigned him unfit for duty in an instant. She was wondering how he was still standing. "When was the last time you got any sleep?"

Christ, he could hardly remember. Before they went out to Tortuga chasing Gallagher. He'd been unconscious a couple of times, when the Wintrans had kicked the shit out of him and when Ghost crashed. Did that count?

He wanted nothing more than to be able to crawl into a bunk and sleep.

"NG…"

He flashed her a look that said don't argue and brushed past.

The table was still strewn with boards and files. He sat and looked round at them.

"Pen isn't going to listen to me," he admitted. "Give me five minutes with Quinn then brief both of them. Give them everything. It's all here. Let Quinn persuade Pen."

"Tell them everything?" LC said, pale, spinning a beer bottle on its end in front of him.

"Everything." Including the file of data they'd just generated. They were beyond the point of no return. They needed allies and those allies needed to know what was going on.

"Me too?" Hil asked.

"Everything."

'Except the fact that you're alive?' flashed into LC's mind.

'Join me being dead if you want.'

'Do you know how tempting that is?' The kid was still feeling bad that Olivia and Sean had been drawn into this mess because of him, that was obvious enough.

"We're still going after Zang and UM," he said, out loud. "But let's not give them the chance to pull a fast one again." He looked at LC and Hil. "You both stay here. Grounded, you understand? Hil, I want you to figure out what the hell is happening with you. I need you back in action, not flaking out every time you get within two hundred yards of an AI. Work with Quinn." He glanced round. "Pull whatever and whoever you need from the Alsatia. I want to know what this virus is doing. Duncan, work with Jameson when he comes round. We need him up to speed. Understand?"

There were nods.

"Okay, give me five minutes."

It took longer than five minutes, not easy having to own up to faking your own death. Quinn was as contained as always, relieved, furious at him on Evelyn's behalf and half pissed that he'd been fooled. The big handler had looked at him, thought back to the state NG had been in when they'd picked him up from Erica and wanted to know how much of it had been real. "All of it," he'd said. The story they'd come up with was that he hadn't made it through the surgery, which wasn't totally untrue. They had all the stats, all the evidence they needed right there, they'd just not included the bit where he'd woken up screaming. After that, the big man had been as pragmatic as always and simply asked, "What now?" NG had replied, "Now you get to talk to another dead man. Get Pen on side because we can't let him know all this and walk away. You understand?"

Then he'd left them to it, skipped out so he didn't need to see Pen again and walked down to the Man's chambers. He paused in the anteroom as he passed the Bhenykhn kill token mounted on its display stand. LC's amulet. The rest of the damn tokens they'd collected on the battlefield had been splattered with mud and blood, not so aesthetically pleasing. He took it with him, resting his hand on the heavy wooden door before pushing his way inside.

He crossed the threshold, entering the warm, humid chamber. If anyone tried to get in touch with him in here, they'd have a hard time, whatever method they were using. He had no idea why or how but whatever was shielding the place, it was beyond Badger and that was saying something. They'd asked Morgan but he didn't know either.

He lit a couple of candles and sat behind the desk. There was a pile of reports on the desktop, filtered, stuff that would have gone into the matrix of grey files not so long ago to be cross-referenced and analysed for patterns, signs, anything that might hint at the unusual. Now he knew it was the Bhenykhn they were looking for and it was infuriating to think he could have done better if he'd known more about them at the time. He'd never questioned the Man. And he should have done. Probably had, come to think of it, considering what Sebastian had said.

He put the Bhenykhn token to one side and flicked through the reports. Nothing startling. Nothing that gave a sense of when they might be back. He laid it all out and set up a stack of orders for Morgan to send to the Alsatia, for Media and the Chief, weird to work by remote, and nothing that felt terribly cohesive. He got that done then set up a new tab, Elliott's key fragments from Marathon, Stirling and Kochitek. Christ knows how they were going to manage the last two. He put in as many details as he could, tagged it as a special projects priority and left it for Quinn. The big man could figure out with Badger how they were going to do it.

Then he sat back.

He thought of opening a bottle of wine. The rack on the far wall was still well stocked. But it wouldn't be anything without the black powder. He opened a drawer in the desk, one that had been locked. He felt a pang of guilt that he'd broken the lock, as if the Man might disapprove of the vandalism. He rifled his hand randomly through the contents, brushing aside archaic notebooks and ink bottles, fountain pens and wax blocks, hoping it might have appeared as if by magic but there was still nothing in there that looked like it might contain that elusive substance.

He shut the drawer, trying to figure out if he felt angry. Sad. Anything. He missed what had been. And he felt resigned to what would be. It wasn't a good state of mind to be in.

He picked up the token again and held it in his upturned palm. The Man had set this acquisition, a steal from Angmar Rodan's own private collection, as an open tab. Ludicrous points at stake. He would have chased it himself if he'd still been a field-op.

He stared at the twisted metal. The Man must have known what it was. He curled his fingers around it and let his eyes close.

The damp chill descended fast, wrapping tight around his senses as if to restrain him. Dark walls closed in, pressure building.

Warm blood was flowing down his neck.

His chest was burning. Head pounding.

Flashes of pinprick light began to swirl. Hypnotic patterns that were tantalisingly familiar. Enticing glimpses and flickering glances at charts and numbers that spun away as he tried to focus.

It was dizzying.

Distressing.

His heart rate was increasing. Internal temperature spiking.

He couldn't break free.

They were battle plans.

He couldn't breathe.

It was sickeningly out of reach, dancing just beyond his grasp.

The scent of leaf mold hung heavy.

The numbers were horrifying. Details flashed across his mind faster than he could think.

It accelerated. Intensified. He dropped to his knees, head bowed, arms shielding his head as if he could fend off the pressure as it became unbearable.

Worse than unbearable.

The darkness became a dense void.

He squeezed his eyes shut.

And snapped them open with a gasp as fingers pressed against his neck.

He was slumped across the desk, cheek resting against the warm wood. His heart rate was erratic, breathing ragged, and for a second he felt like he couldn't control it, couldn't gather himself enough to get a grip. He was going under again but he thought he could feel a hand pressing gently between his shoulder blades, warm, bringing him back.

Devon.

Except it wasn't. And it never could be.

He almost lost it.

She wasn't Devon but her voice was soft. Familiar. "NG…"

He uncurled slowly, sat, blinking away the chill, slowing his breathing. Badger was there. Morgan. And Leigh. They were uncomfortable, like they felt they shouldn't be in here, except he'd disappeared for so long…

"How long's it been?" he muttered.

"Sixteen hours," Morgan said.

The kill token was still in his hand. He let it drop to the desk and scrubbed his hand over his face. It didn't feel like it had been that long.

Leigh was thinking that he'd scared her, he'd been virtually unresponsive when they found him, that she shouldn't have been so stupid to have left it so long to realise something was wrong when she couldn't find him. She wanted to ask if he was okay but she knew he wasn't, so she said instead, uneasily, "What's going on?"

He looked up. "I know where they are."

"What?" Badger said.

He said it again, with more certainty. "I know where they are. And I know what they're planning." Sebastian had thrown it at him, on Erica, when he'd conceded control and the bastard was taunting the crew of the Bhenykhn ship. Sebastian had lifted every scrap of intel from their systems and thrown it all at him. "At least, I know I know it. I don't know how to…" Christ, it was infuriating. "Where's LC?"

"In the mess," Morgan said and hesitated. "There's something you need to know…"

Badger wasn't so shy. "Angmar Rodan is on Poule," he said.

10

They listened to his story again, prompting for more, questioning when they wanted more detail, looking down at him and thinking he should have acted differently.

She was the only exception. She had been the only exception all that time ago when they had voted the last time they had come together like this. She was thinking that they owed these creatures their help, that Nikolai should not have had to go through all this alone. She looked up and caught his eye, knew he was watching her and knew he was probably reading her mind.

'You should have told him,' she thought softly, regretful.

'I know,' he thought back, even though she couldn't hear. None of them could hear. He was the only one who could, the only one so talented in his galaxy as Nikolai had been the only one in this. Now, with the 'virus', this organism…? Maybe it would make all the difference…

———————

"How the hell did we not see that?"

Badger shook his head, furious that he hadn't seen it, hands stuck firmly in his pockets as they walked.

NG used the Senson. "LC, get your ass to the briefing room."

"Elliott's going to meet us at Poule," Badger said. "Are we taking…?" He didn't know what to say. The guild? Were they not still guild themselves? Reinforcements?

"I'll take anyone who wants to come." They'd been jerked around and he was done with it. "Get two extraction teams on standby for a special projects op."

Badger stopped. "NG, wait."

He turned slowly.

"We're in the middle of a war, NG. This intel on UM came from Elliott. We have no idea who he is, never mind what side he's on. Seriously, NG, this could be a trap for all we know."

"It doesn't matter if it is, right now it's all we have to go on."

Badger was agitated. "From everything we're seeing, the Order isn't controlling this war," he said. "There are hundreds of pressure points that were close to boiling over anyway. This has just given them all an excuse to kick off. We should have guessed the JU would go in for LC like that after what happened to Hil on Abacus."

NG rubbed his hand over his eyes. "I know."

"Sanctions and trade embargoes are popping up out of nowhere all over the place," Badger said. "It's driving the Merchants insane. Nothing coordinated. Nothing backed by any weight. The Empire is moving to regain colonies they abandoned decades ago. The corporations are talking about pulling together a combined fleet that is bigger than anything Earth could field and they're using it to intimidate any place that's trying to stay neutral into backing them." He stopped, realising that NG was just staring at him with none of the energy that talk like that used to generate. "And none of it matters because the Bhenykhn are coming back."

It was hard not knowing when. Worse than if they had a deadline.

And the instabilities made it impossible to think they could announce it to all and sundry without a massive backlash, not when the guild's position was so precarious.

"UM know about them," NG said. "So I want to know what UM are doing. Get me everything you have on Poule."

LC walked in, holding a cold beer bottle to the back of his neck, sat down, looked up at him, and said, "Poule? Seriously?" The kid looked like he needed a week's sleep.

NG took a sip of his tea. "Yep."

"Hal was there as well," LC said, a tad too defensively.

"I know. I've already talked to him. He didn't get to hack into the station's security system." He pushed across a board. "I want everything you have."

To give him credit, the kid didn't complain. He just nodded vaguely, popped open the beer and pulled over the board. It was already loaded with everything Badger had trawled up on Poule and UM, including the hostile takeover when Zang Enterprises got kicked out.

NG watched as LC flicked through a couple of the screens, frowning and saying, "Didn't UM take Erica as well?"

"From Aries," he said. "Same deal by the looks of it. Badger's trying to find out what else they've been acquiring."

It was another oversight.

Something else he should have seen.

"Poule was a shithole," LC said. "They had prisoner pens all along the dockside."

And NG saw it as the kid flashed back to dark, cold, gunfire, shouts, violent convicts that Elliott had released running riot around station security. He flashed forward and they were both hit by an intense stabbing pain in the thigh, burning fever, senses scrambled in a whirl of noise and confusion. It switched again in a flash, this time a street scene, Aston, more yells, impacts punching into his arm, shoulder, more, spinning him round until one took him low in the back and he hit the floor.

Way to share the details in a briefing.

NG shut it out. He'd read that kind of traumatic recall in people before, but at a distance, never the way LC threw it at him.

The kid got it under control, mumbling, "Sorry," trying to pull his thoughts away from the still aching wounds of each one of those shots and back to Poule.

The feeling of it lingered. NG cradled his cup, taking heat from it as LC was taking cold from the beer bottle.

The kid took a mouthful of beer and looked up. "Elliott took us there," he said as if realising it for the first time. "We thought it was a glitch in the AI. It jumped without warning when we were getting chased out of Sten's. But it would have been Elliott. He took us to Poule."

NG muttered a curse. There was more to all this than any of them had seen.

He sucked in a deep breath and looked at LC, got a suspicious, "What?"

He switched to direct thought. 'What do you see when you look in my mind?'

'NG, I don't look.'

'Look. What do you see?'

The kid was smart, cautious, and he hadn't forgotten what Sebastian had done to him. 'Why? What am I looking for?'

'Intel. Sebastian threw a shit load at me in the middle of the battle. From their ship. I can't access it. That's what's giving me the nightmares. I want to know if you can see it."

LC scowled.

NG stayed calm even though he wanted to throw the cup across the room. 'I need to know if you can see it, LC, because we need to know when they're coming back.' It wasn't easy admitting that he needed help and he let the kid overhear that, saw the hesitation in LC's mind.

'Sebastian's gone,' he thought. He left it at that, resisting the urge to flash back to the battlefield to show LC what had happened after the kid had hit the dirt, out cold, with a crossbow bolt in his chest.

'Show me,' LC fired back, heart rate increasing, and it was impossible not to share the instinctive flashback that LC couldn't help, feel the chill of the rain, the adrenaline, as the kid slipped and slid desperately in the mud, nothing in his plan but distracting the massive Bhenykhn away from NG.

NG shook his head, shutting it down. He didn't want to go back there. 'Sebastian killed them, he dumped the intel in my head and he…' He didn't know what to say. The bastard had taunted him, said he was going to sleep. '*Wake me when they get back*,' was how he'd put it.

NG reached for the jug, took his time pouring a fresh cup of tea, watching the swirling steam, and said out loud, "LC, I need to know what I have in here. Just see if you can see it."

The kid didn't argue back that time, just looked, clinically, nothing as smooth as when the Man had used to read his mind, but not clumsy.

NG felt him hit a barrier.

LC pushed it and recoiled, breathing fast. 'Shit.'

"Try again. We need to know this stuff."

He tried again, reckless that time, aggressive.

NG tensed.

The chill darkness grabbed him as if around the throat.

Frozen.

Sparks of intel from the battlespace flowed around him, blurring then slowing and beginning to focus.

It wavered. Spun away in a blast of shards that splintered out in a dizzying spiral.

He dragged his eyes open. Felt the warm surface of the deck humming beneath him.

He sat up.

LC was sprawled on the deck on the other side of the room, holding the back of his head and looking over at him.

"Shit."

He sent LC back to the others and he went to his quarters. He turned the shower onto hot and struggled his broken arm out of the bindings, managing to shrug out of his shirt. It was tempting to think he could bug out, go find a beach somewhere. Ask Sean for the keys to Frank's cabin. Take the sniper rifle and go find a piece of the war he could lose himself in. Somewhere warm. Poule was the last place he wanted to go.

He sat on the edge of the bunk, listening to the water run and thinking he should go get cleaned up.

It felt like too much effort to move.

A chill of damp cold shivered across his shoulders.

'*I know you're there,*' he thought. '*You've haunted me for a hundred years. You want to tell me how I use all this shit you threw at me?*'

The cold deepened, taking a grip on the muscles in his

shoulders that threatened to cramp. It spread into his joints and crept down his spine.

A dank chill settled in his lungs.

He lay back on the bunk, staring at the ceiling.

He felt it trying to draw him away and resisted.

'Sebastian, just give me the damned intel.'

A dark shadow stirred, deep inside, elusive.

The Senson engaged with a high priority. Quinn.

NG sat up and allowed access.

"I've done what I can," the big handler sent. "He wants to speak to you."

"No."

He cut the connection, ditched the idea of having a shower and threw his bag on the bunk, tossing in guns and knives. The room was different, darker, warmer, than his quarters on the Alsatia, but it was still tough not to flash back to the last time he'd done this before going after Devon, and the time before when it had been Devon herself who'd tried to stop him. He felt numb, none of that fire, and there was no one here to stop him this time.

He refastened the knee support, pulled on ops gear and wrapped a black field bandage around the cast on his arm and hand, taking it right down over his fingers. Not ideal. But then, what the hell was any more?

He flexed his shoulder. The arm didn't need binding, not with the forearm secured as it was in the cast. He couldn't hold a gun in that hand and he'd be hard pushed to climb but he wasn't planning on sneaking around anywhere. He was done hiding.

Wraith was ready and waiting in the hangar. They kept her ready for him. That was one of his standing orders. And it wasn't just the ship that was waiting there for him. Pen Halligan stood, feet planted, arms folded, at the foot of the ramp.

There was no one else in there. Total set up and NG walked right into it, not impressed but not about to lose his temper.

He walked forward and stopped a few feet away from the big man.

"So you can read my mind?" Pen shook his head, incredulous. He wasn't armed but he was thinking that he didn't need to be. He could take NG down. Easily.

NG dropped his kit bag to the deck and stood there. It wouldn't be that easy. Even with a broken arm, he could take Pen in a fair fight. In an unfair fight...?

Pen was staring, stony faced. "I always told Mendhel you'd get him killed."

That was hardly fair but NG kept quiet. He was subtly balancing his weight on his left leg, trying to take the pressure off the knee without making it obvious, trying to weigh up what this would take if Pen went for him.

The big man took a step forward and said, voice low and threatening, "This game you've been playing for so long – Nikolai – the rules just changed."

11

"Why do we fret so about creatures that have such capacity for violence themselves?" one of them said.

"They harbour hatred so long and hard."

There was more of the same. The Man let it wash over him. Their zeal to take such umbrage was laughable.

She felt it. He could feel her discomfort. It was a distraction from their own guilt, to find such distaste in this fleeting encounter with the human race. As if finding the inhabitants of this galaxy to be lesser somehow made up for their own shortcomings.

"They have failings," she said. "Who does not? Let us remember why they are in this predicament." She turned to him. "You have always worked in absolute secrecy, kept Nikolai cossetted for his own safety. Now all is revealed? After all this time? Did you prepare him for that?"

"No. How could I?" Her question, and her dismay, cut deeply. He had made mistakes. They had all made mistakes. "As the situation worsened, Nikolai had to look for allies and those allies were not always ones he would have sought given a choice."

His heart started beating faster.

"Nikolai Andreyev," Pen said, drumming in the fact that they knew.

NG scanned around. Duncan was listening in. So was LC. Leigh was nearby. Badger. Morgan. Quinn. Presumably Hilyer.

They'd found stuff in the Man's files, stuff on him, the greys, found the matrix and the data the Man had been gathering on the alien threat.

Pen was smouldering, caught between a burning hatred so

strong he wanted nothing more than to floor this son of a bitch in front of him and a deep loyalty to people he considered family, who considered the son of a bitch to be something special to them.

NG kept eye contact without moving. They all knew. It was no different to Martinez figuring out who he was in the middle of the battle on Erica. What was worse was that they now all knew that the Man had been looking for the aliens. And they couldn't understand why nothing had been said before.

"So what now?" Pen said accusingly.

He didn't know what to say.

"You run off to confront Rodan. Then what?"

He'd never been able to manipulate Pen so he didn't try and even if he could have, he had no idea where he'd take it.

"There's still a warrant out on LC," Pen said, dark eyes flashing, barely containing his anger, "and after what happened on Aston, there are mutterings that the Thieves' Guild needs to be dealt with. Reined in for good. I, for one, would not argue with that. But we're all in the shit. I get that." He glanced to the side before glaring back at NG. "Your people seem to think that you are some kind of golden boy." He took a step forward. "I'm not convinced. I know what you're capable of, more than anyone."

NG stood his ground.

"You've been playing your damn games for a long time," Pen said. Another step. "You knew." Another, every muscle taut with perfect balance. "You knew about these bastards, the Order. You knew about these aliens." His voice lowered to a rumble. "What the hell else have you been screwing with, NG? What the hell else do you know?"

"I know we're screwed unless we work together."

That hit a nerve and took Pen to boiling point. He lunged forward, fast for a big man.

NG ducked the blow, Pen's fist a hair's breadth from knocking him sideways. They both spun around, Pen moving quickly to get in a second. NG blocked with his left and threw his right arm, full weight of the cast behind it, to slam into Pen's jaw. The big man staggered, punched NG in the ribs with a low jab and shoved him away.

NG backed off, circling around. He didn't want this fight. He knew exactly where it was going.

Quinn and Duncan stepped into the hangar, Leigh appearing a step behind.

Pen didn't let up. He came after him with a roar. NG dodged the first blow, got in a couple of his own and faltered as the knee threatened to give way, catching a nasty punch above his eye. He fell and rolled, tumbling backwards and on his feet fast enough to avoid another incoming. He shoved Pen, got in another elbow and landed a second blow to the big man's jaw. Pen reeled, grabbing a fistful of NG's shirt and pulling him close, hissing in his face, "You killed her. You – fucking – killed her."

He couldn't break free, realised the intention and braced himself as Pen smashed a head-butt into his face. He felt the cheekbone crack, went with the momentum of the blow and threw them both off balance. He twisted free and forced Pen's arm into a lock, pushing him down and close to pinning the big man, except Pen hadn't missed a thing, levered himself round and kicked, vicious and desperate, right at his weak point, years of pent up anger behind it, perfectly placed.

NG felt the knee go, felt himself going down and threw enough force at Pen to send the big man flying backwards as well. Pen hit the deck, rolled and got up, spitting blood, and coming at him again.

NG got to his feet, all his weight on his left leg. His head was pounding. He could feel blood streaming down his face, the eye swelling. He summoned energy from somewhere and blocked Pen without moving a muscle, the big man halting abruptly, straining against it and roaring. Sebastian had held the Bhenykhn commander, forced it to its knees against its will, easily. He had nothing like that.

He felt the hold falter, felt Pen burst free as if throwing off chains and the big man charged, on him before he could move and grappling him to the floor.

Pen was big. Angry. Every blow hit home with years of hate and frustration behind it.

NG curled up and took it. He could overhear Quinn thinking that he should step in, that enough was enough.

"Feel free," NG tried to send privately, senses rattled, thinking Duncan or LC would hear it anyway. "Any time."

Another punch landed against the fractured cheekbone and he almost greyed out.

The weight on him lifted abruptly, the barrage of blows ceasing.

He rolled to his side and managed to stand.

Pen was standing back, fending off Quinn and wiping a hand across his mouth, smearing blood from his lip, breathing heavily. He laughed, but it was harsh. "These fucking aliens…?" he said eventually. "You killed them?"

NG bit his tongue, wanting to say, 'It wasn't me that fucking killed them', but he couldn't.

Pen lifted his hand, finger pointing. "You need to get a grip, NG. You see all these people…?" He moved his hand in a wide sweeping gesture. "They think you know what to do next. You want me to pledge my allegiance to you? Then tell me what we do next, because I want to know, Nikolai. I want to know what you think we do next."

His words echoed around the confined space of the hangar.

NG glanced around at the others. He didn't know what to say because he didn't know what to do. He'd always operated on instinct and he'd always known what was the right course of action. Now…?

After taking out the Assassins, he'd been effectively bumped down to field-op and that had been fine. He'd needed that security of other people telling him what to do. Now? After Erica? He didn't know what he was. Not the Man, that was for sure. He could sit at that big desk in those warm, humid chambers and send orders anonymously back to the Alsatia but he could never truly take on that role. He didn't want to. He wanted to find the source of the virus – that was all that mattered.

He picked up the kit bag. "I'm going after Rodan," he said. "Then I'll figure out what we do."

He could hardly walk but he made it up the ramp and into the ship, concentrating on nothing other than switching off the pain, staying upright and shielding his thoughts. He didn't need anyone picking up the crap he was thinking right now.

No one stopped him. He stowed his bag, grabbed a cold pack from the medical rack and sat in the main cabin area, troop seats, avoiding the bridge because he didn't want to talk to anyone. Wraith was about the same size as Ghost, almost as fast and like Ghost she had no AI so there was a pilot awaiting his orders.

Leigh followed him on board and sat opposite.

"You want me to look at that knee?"

He shook his head.

He'd healed what he could. It would hold.

"You want a dressing on that eye?"

"I'm fine."

She raised an eyebrow but didn't argue. "You know, these people really care about you."

He didn't want anyone to care about him.

"I can say this," she said, leaning forward, "because I'm not Thieves' Guild either. I came here to be with you. Pen's right. You need to get a grip. You took control of that battle on Erica. We need you to take control now."

He still didn't know what to say.

She wasn't going to let it drop. "So what? You're a hundred and twenty years old? Your boss knew there was some kind of alien threat on its way? NG," she said intently, "talk to me. Let us help. We go to Poule, then what? What exactly are you intending to do there?"

"I'm assuming Elliott has a way of getting Rodan's attention. I just need two seconds with him." He looked at her and made a decision. "I don't just read thoughts. I can read memories." He stopped short of saying he could rip someone's mind apart. "That's why it needs to be me."

She pondered that and added, "Anything else we should know?"

He almost laughed. "Probably, but not now."

She was still curious. "You could have stopped that fight before it started. Why did you let Pen hit you?"

He put the cold pack against his eye. "Because he's needed to beat the crap out of me for a long time."

She wanted to ask why but she refrained from pushing it. She moved seats instead and sat next to him. "You need to sleep. You can't go on like this. But if that's not going to happen, you need to take the energy you need from everyone around you. They can catch up on it."

She sat back and closed her eyes, and muttered, "Help yourself. Unless it takes years off my life." She opened one eye and peered at him. "Does it?"

That was a disturbing thought. "I have no idea."

She shrugged. "Wake me up when we get there."

They took Wraith and split, initiated full stealth and jumped into Poule's outer system, two extraction teams right on their heels, the Man's ship following.

The Duck was already there, in stealth itself and only obvious because Elliott contacted them as soon as they dropped out of jump. A mass of intel started to stream in.

NG slipped through into the forward compartment and sat next to the pilot. She gave him a nod and started to throw data onto the monitors. She was good. One of his regulars and she knew how he worked. It was a welcome familiarity. One of the few he had left close by.

He pinched the top of his nose, a headache that he couldn't shift burning behind his eyes. He watched the numbers and charts scroll, an uneasy feeling pulling at the back of his mind as the sitrep unfolded. It didn't help that the pressure behind his eyes was increasing as they got closer to the colony. Pen had cracked the bone in his cheek. He'd reduced the swelling and the bruising, nothing he could do about the fracture, but it felt worse than the last time. And it was getting worse. He couldn't even close his eyes to ease it without that chill darkness closing in.

Elliott sent straight away, "Angmar Rodan is in a corporate wing, five levels down. This is his personal corpsig. I've cleared his diary. You get to him, you won't be interrupted. Here's your login ID. It'll get you down to two. That's as good as I can get for the moment. Good luck with the rest. Just so you know, the prisoner pens are at capacity. They're getting regular shipments of live prisoners, processing them and dropping them down to the surface. It doesn't add up."

What he meant was there was next to nothing leaving. If they'd upped capacity in the mines by that much, they should have been sending out an increased tonnage of ore or metal.

And security was way too high for a regular mining operation.

It was a glaring anomaly and one that should have screamed alarm bells with someone, anyone, on the Alsatia.

They'd missed it.

NG sent a curt acknowledgement to Elliott. He didn't like that they'd been so wrong about Zang and UM.

He breathed through the headache, ran a check on the ID Elliott had sent across for him and brought up the schematics of the facility.

Leigh appeared behind him. "What's wrong?"

He didn't turn.

"I've got you on live feed already," she whispered. "What's wrong?"

There was no point trying to hide it. "Headache."

"I thought you could shut off pain."

It was uncomfortable even talking out loud. "Not always." He nudged the display to spin round to an exterior real-time view, catching her intention in time to flinch away as she reached towards his forehead.

"You might have a skull fracture," she said.

He didn't.

"I'm fine."

She wasn't convinced.

The check on the ID beeped an all clear. NG pulled back the view to take in the wider area. There was a cold front whipping around the peninsula. High winds. They were preparing to lock down the base.

"I need to go."

He took a stealthed drop ship down to the surface, avoiding detection and landing some distance away, out near the cliff line. He was bundled up in cold weather gear and he'd wrapped the knee support as tight as it would go and still give him some flexibility.

The icy wind still hit him with a ferocious bite as he left the comfort of the ship and ran into the cover of one of the few trees out here on the headland. The drop ship took off again straight away.

He hunkered down and took a minute to get his bearings. He could sense the hundreds of life signs about a mile and a half to the north, going about their business, pockets of high concentration, patches of intense fear and anger, some tired, some wired on drugs. They had no idea he was here. As much as security was high, it was no match for guild stealth kit.

He ran a quick scan to be sure then started moving, the pounding in his head matching each footstep. He shut it out as much as he could and focused on gauging his pace, feeling his internal temperature rise with the exertion.

The Senson engaged after a minute or two. "This is really impressive," Leigh sent. "They have no idea you're there. How do you get in?"

"Through a door, like anyone," he sent back, increasing his speed, each intake of breath filling his lungs with a sharp chill. He hadn't pushed himself physically, not properly, in what felt like an age and it felt almost good to be at full stretch. Almost full stretch.

He closed the distance and had to slow as the knee started to twinge. He walked, breathing in the cold air, and looking at the stars in the pitch black sky. Somewhere out there, the Bhenykhn were waiting. He could almost smell their breath, feel the pressure of the buzz from their hive communications. Badger was right, nothing mattered except when they were coming back.

He increased his pace, not wanting to be alone with his thoughts.

He ended up running again, doggedly ignoring the weakness in his knee.

As he got closer, he started to scan ahead again. There were guards posted around the perimeter. It would be easy enough to avoid them. More inside. A command post that was on high alert. No one could be permanently on high alert without losing their edge. It was bad practice. And as far as he could tell, there was no reason why they were on such a heightened status.

They were all UM.

Rodan was in there somewhere.

He reached further.

"NG…"

Leigh was cut off as something else cut in.

The contact hit like a hammer blow. He couldn't move. Couldn't think.

The pressure was unbearable. Hot.

'Know me…' he heard, guttural and deep, reverberating around his mind.

It held him tight, black and dense, the connection so intense he couldn't even breathe.

'Fear me,' it growled and squeezed.

12

They were shocked. Of course they were. There were cries of, "How? How could this happen without our knowing?"

He couldn't answer. Couldn't defend his ignorance. He would have been more shocked had they not responded so. Even being able to read their minds, he was unable to trust them. He had almost been testing them by revealing this.

From the way she was looking at him, she suspected so. She was wondering if he thought she could have been keeping such intelligence from him.

"Would you have acted differently had you known?" she said.

"Of course I would have." He couldn't keep the scorn, the disdain from his voice even in replying to her. "A Bhenykhn in this galaxy?"

"You would have told us?"

"I tell you now." He was losing patience. "I have been looking for them, waiting for them, for so long, had I known they were right here, of course I would have acted differently."

"But this explains, does it not," she said softly, "how the Order knew of the virus? They created it from the Bhenykhn."

It held him there, frozen in the dark, pressure increasing, then just as abruptly let go.

He collapsed in a heap, face down on the cold ground, heart pounding. He half-expected Sebastian to appear and take control but there wasn't so much as a whisper.

The Senson engaged. "NG, what's wrong?"

"Nikolai?"

That last was Elliott.

He blinked and sucked in a breath that stung his lungs.

"NG, don't do this to me."

Leigh again.

"I'm okay," he managed to send.

"No, you're not," Elliott sent. "You just lit up on all radars. They're mobilising. What the hell happened?"

He dragged himself to his feet. "They've got a Bhenykhn in there."

"They're going to reach you before we can."

Shit. He started to run, stripping off every scrap of guild kit he had on him, sparking the self-destructs and tossing them aside.

A roar of engines cut through the wind.

One of the extraction agents sent, "NG, you want us to come in heavy?"

"Negative." They didn't have enough firepower with them to do it right.

More engines, closing in.

"Let's go with it," he sent, still running, tearing the band off his wrist, snapping it to erase the data and discarding it as he moved.

Four gunships flew fast and low overhead, searchlights scouring the ground, banking hard to circle round.

He veered left and half slid down a bank. "Don't worry, I have a plan."

They cut him off as he tried to make a break for the cliff edge, surrounding him, one dropping down low to hover in front of him, pinning him in its spotlight. The icy wind was cutting into his face, the rumble of its engines resonating deep in his chest.

He skidded to a halt, turned slowly and raised his hands.

They shot him anyway.

The facility was old, decaying, dirty and rusting. Not the type of place Zang had ever listed on its corporate portfolio, except for the profits from its mine, and UM had done nothing to improve its upkeep. It was one thing to hear the rumours, something else to see it first hand.

NG walked, surrounded by an entourage of UM security,

hands cuffed to the front, trying to ignore the headache that was becoming the only constant in his world.

They'd slapped a temporary dampening patch over the Senson then taken him into a holding room, run him through every bioscan possible, strip-searched him to the extent of cracking the cast off his arm and then held him down while they tore out the implant completely. All without a word. Then they'd stuck a button device in the back of his neck, right over the sore spot where the three FTH rounds from the gunship had hit. The device was humming merrily at the base of his skull, competing with the presence of the Bhenykhn that was a constant pressing darkness in the depths of his mind. As far as plans went, this wasn't looking like his best ever.

Noises from the mines below clanged through the cramped, dark corridors. They'd let him dress but hadn't afforded him the luxury of keeping the knee support, so it was hard not to limp as it threatened to give out with every other step.

They took a rickety lift down two levels. He could feel the heat of emotion emanating from the prison cells before the door opened. They pushed him out and took him along a narrow walkway to a cell, one in a line of single occupancy, opposite huge pens that were full to bursting.

He let them shove him inside, didn't fight them as they fastened the cuffs to chains attached to the ceiling, and reached out as far as he could to find LC or Duncan. Nothing. Too far. The alien hadn't made direct contact again but he could feel that it was there. A few levels down. There was that same skin-crawling, dank leaf mold stench wafting about its presence that he'd been haunted with since Erica.

They backed off. One son of a bitch pressed a remote and the chains rattled up, fast, dragging his arms with them and catching just as he reached full stretch. If they were serious, they'd up it another inch or two. They made it three for good measure.

He relaxed.

He could take this for hours.

Even with a broken arm.

It didn't take hours. They came for him after twenty minutes or so and released the chains, which wouldn't have been so bad except they sparked the device at the same time and had to haul him to his feet.

He still didn't fight them, reading from the mind of the guard in charge that they were going to take him exactly where he wanted to go.

Prisoners rattled the bars of the pens as he was taken past. Their minds were a roiling mix of aggression and fear, violent criminals who'd been tried and convicted, pirates who'd been caught in the act, drifters and vagrants, dissidents and protestors, and disturbingly, colonists who couldn't figure out why they'd been imprisoned. They were being transferred out in batches. No one returned. Insane rumours on what was happening.

NG shut them out and concentrated on putting one foot in front of the other, anticipating the shoves from the guards and letting his mind wander to see what he could find.

It was overwhelming, all against the backdrop of an alien that was captive, pissed off and watching him closely with a sly, simmering hatred.

They took him down further, pushed him out onto a level with marble paved floors, wall hangings lining the narrow corridor and a faint scent of incense. It was old corporate. Ostentatious but worn. Scuffs and cracks in the floor, tattered edges and a mustiness that all stank of the old money that had been poured into these frontier posts centuries ago by pioneers who fancied themselves kings of the new territories.

Rodan was close, in his suite of private offices.

NG kept his breathing steady.

He was about to get everything he needed. All he'd need then was a way out.

Except more guards intercepted them as the corridor split, shouldered their way in and took him roughly by the arm, turning him and taking him in the opposite direction, with only a curt exchange about orders.

He scanned ahead.

There was one person in the quarters they were now headed to. Not Angmar Rodan. Someone else, someone who had made claim on their new prisoner and pulled rank over the CEO.

The mind he encountered was icy cold.

Old.

Maeve Rodan.

The guards left him at the door, retreated and closed it behind him. She was sitting by an open fire with her back to the door. There was another chair by the fire, a table between them. There was a bottle of wine on the table next to two goblets. Two goblets with twisted black metal stems.

He almost took a step backwards.

Her voice was as cold as her soul. "Come sit down, NG."

He didn't bother to hide the limp. He sat, avoided looking at the goblets and raised his eyes to look at her.

She was looking him up and down, matching what she could see of him here to what she knew of him, his reputation, what their scans had reported. She was appraising him and it was making his skin crawl.

This was the real power behind UM. And before he even ventured further into her mind he knew that he was within reach of the High Guard. Old Order.

It made him feel ridiculously young.

He let her take her time.

She had a faint smile dancing over her lips, no emotion in her eyes. She was impressed, as if she was looking at a new specimen for her private collection. She couldn't quite believe it was him sitting here, thinking he looked younger than she was expecting but that this boy definitely matched every pointer on the biometrics it had cost them so much to obtain… yes, he was definitely for real. He was everything she could have hoped for. He was the Thieves' Guild. And she had him right here. In chains.

She might as well have been rubbing her bony hands together.

It was chilling.

She gave a slight nod, satisfied. "We've been looking for you for a long time, NG," she breathed. "Far longer than you've used that name."

She reached and poured the wine.

She was wearing an amulet on a chain around her neck. A Bhenykhn kill token. Polished.

He kept his expression neutral.

She looked up. "The handcuffs are not necessary." She was supremely confident that he couldn't, or wouldn't, hurt her, that he needed to be here and that he knew it. She was also curious and she wanted to know how he'd get out of the restraints if she didn't offer up a key.

He could have snapped his hands free with a twist but he didn't feel like playing. He threw the mechanism instead. They opened. He placed them on the table.

The smile didn't change. She was thinking that Drake would be furious to have been beaten to the prize.

Prize? It was hardly flattering and he was nowhere near as confident as she was that he needed to be here. Not in these circumstances. This was hardly a fair and level playing field. Maeve was barking mad. He'd never heard of Drake in any of this, not from the Man, not from any of the Order that he'd managed to chase down so far, but the way this old lady was looking at him and the way she was revelling in the thought that she'd won some kind of advantage over a fierce rival for having him in her hands didn't fill him with hope.

"You have an alien marker in your bloodstream," she said to provoke some kind of reaction. "Now where could that have come from?"

The poison. They'd matched it to their samples from the Bhenykhn.

He matched her smile without a word.

She nudged one of the goblets in his direction. The way the Man always used to. He didn't touch it.

"And what wars have you been in so recently, NG, to have experienced so many hurts?" She knew every detail of every injury.

He watched as she took a delicate sip of her wine, still reading what he could from her mind without going too deep. She was bemused that he was snubbing her offer of hospitality, assuming that he must be thinking, rightly, that it would be drugged. She didn't mind, thinking to herself that her prize would talk, with or without it, sooner or later.

"We know you've been looking for us," she said. "You have caused quite a stir." She gestured generally around with a hand that was pale and thin. "Well, you've found us." She looked him in the eye and added simply, "You might wish you hadn't."

She put the goblet down, stood and walked away. "We have a house guest. I'd like you to meet it."

13

*"You knew the Order was a threat to our plans," one of them
said. "With all your, and our, resources, how did this High Guard
manage to remain so elusive?"*

*He looked up and down the line at them, at this assembly of such
powerful individuals, gathered here to assess the situation and, as
she kept reminding them, to make a decision.*

*"Do you stand by your actions to make an enemy of the Order?"
another threw in.*

*He caught her eye. She was dismayed at the thought that Nikolai
could have been at their mercy, in the clutches of one such as Maeve
Rodan.*

*"I do stand by that decision," he said. "Events proved it to be
justified."*

He followed her down a set of steep winding stairs. She moved
gracefully. He had to hold onto the handrail to make it down
each step. He could have broken her neck and pushed her down
the stairs in a split second but even with him at her back, she still
didn't consider him a threat.

She wanted him to see the alien because she knew that he'd
appeared on their sensors at the exact same instant that their
captive had freaked, roared in anger and thrown itself against the
bars of its cage. She didn't believe in coincidences and she wanted
to know why.

It was watching them approach. NG kept his mind as shielded
as he could manage through the headache, nowhere near as
confident as he should be that there weren't other telepaths here.
Maeve wasn't, or at least if she was, she was very good.

The temperature decreased as they went down, an increasingly damp chill wafting in the air. It felt like he was descending right into the middle of one of his nightmares and it took everything he had to stay neutral and keep his heart from racing.

From her demeanour, Maeve could have been walking into a dinner party. Aside from the Man, she was the most unsettling person he'd ever encountered.

The staircase led out onto a dark balcony overlooking some kind of enclosure. As they walked out onto a mesh gantry, there was a clanking thud and lights winked on, flashing sporadically at first, illuminating a vast chamber. It wasn't that different from the Fight Cage on the Alsatia where the field-ops let off steam. He couldn't help flashing back to a moment in time when he'd stood there with Devon, watching Hil fight Sorenson. A long time ago.

The Bhenykhn was standing in the centre of it. Fighting stance. Muscles tensed. Staring at him.

It was tough to look at it and not be drawn back to the chaos and agony of that muddy battlefield.

'Fear me,' it snarled again, mind to mind.

Mocking.

Maeve rested a hand on the rail, gazing down at it. "My grandson wants to throw you in there with it. See how you fare."

Angmar.

She turned to him and smiled. "But the boy is an arrogant upstart who has delusions of importance far beyond his capabilities."

That was interesting.

There was no fondness there at all. No trust or allegiance in the slightest.

"Don't worry," she added, "I'm not going to let him have you. You're well and truly mine." She dropped the smile. "You stole the elixir that we tasked the Earth Empire to develop for us."

Us. The Order.

"You have caused us considerable inconvenience, NG. And you killed one of my oldest and dearest friends."

A'Darbi.

"Now… you haven't uttered a single word since you arrived here and I need you to talk. How do you think we could manage that?"

He was keeping his mouth shut because he didn't trust her with anything he could say.

She turned back to look down on the Bhenykhn. "What do you know of these creatures?"

He almost blurted out, 'We fought a whole army of them on Erica.'

The alien took a step forward as he thought that, lifting its chin and glowering at him.

It sent a chill through his stomach. Sebastian had been certain the Bhenykhn couldn't read their minds, that the telepathy of the hive was contained within the hive.

"It is magnificent, isn't it?" she said. "I'm assuming from your reaction that you've seen its kind before." She stroked her hand delicately along the rail. "It has amazing regenerative abilities. Of course, that's what has everyone so excited. But I'm sure you know that already." She turned to look at him, head cocked to the side. "I'm disappointed that you won't speak to me, NG. At least, tell me your real name."

He turned his back on the alien, heard an echoing laugh inside his head that reminded him way too much of Sebastian, and looked at this elegant matriarch figure standing so serenely next to him. It was hard to be rude but he could see inside her head.

She looked down long eyelashes at him. "We could try a different tack," she said, "but I really would rather not go there… not just yet."

There was something dancing around her thoughts that made up his mind.

"It's Nikolai," he said.

She raised her immaculate eyebrows, eyes sparkling. "Well, Nikolai, are you going to talk to me now?"

He was trying to figure out which way she would go if he did. Like he'd said to Martinez, he couldn't foresee the future.

"You stole our elixir…" she prompted.

NG shook his head slightly. "It was Zang who screwed you over, not us."

She wasn't impressed by his tone and she wasn't about to admit that she knew it had been her grandson who had orchestrated all that nonsense. "But you have it?"

"We didn't when you came after us." He kept the emotion out of his reply. "We do now." He turned back to face the cage and stared at the Bhenykhn. It was smaller than the warriors they'd fought on Erica. More like the pilot he'd seen crash land in front of them. Still huge by human standards. "You want to know what it does?"

"I want it back."

"It's not what you think it is."

She frowned, wondering what he was referring to, the elixir or the alien?

"It's not a magical elixir of life," he said. "It's a virus and it has a fifty-fifty chance of killing you outright. If you're lucky and it doesn't do that, there's a chance it will fry your brain and leave you comatose."

She was thinking that those were better odds than they'd managed in their experiments here so far. They'd killed hundreds. "And if it doesn't do that…?"

He glanced sideways at her, listened in as she looked at him, fascinated by his accent, thinking that he didn't have anything in his blood that looked like a virus, it had been a marker, a remnant DNA trace, that's all. If that wasn't the elixir, then what…?

"It's not an elixir," he said again. "It's a curse. But it might be the only thing we have that will help us beat them."

He said it, knowing it was listening and understanding every word. He looked down towards the Bhenykhn that was still standing there staring at them. It lifted one arm and beat a clenched fist against its chest, almost a stabbing motion towards its heart, as if it knew.

It knew.

The headache spiked.

It invaded his mind again, his temperature rising fast to fever point. It grabbed his attention and held him there. It was nothing like dealing with LC and Duncan, the only other human telepaths he knew. It was alien. Loud, intense, like a damaged Senson gone haywire, screaming static into his head at maximum volume over a howling gale. Worse than anything Sebastian had let through to him on Erica. Although there was only a single Bhenykhn, this close, it was overwhelming. No matter what he tried, he couldn't block it. He couldn't filter it out the way Sebastian always had. It was like nothing he'd ever dealt with before. He couldn't concentrate on anything else. Even breathing was difficult.

'You…' he heard, in that guttural sneer, deep inside. 'You. Die. First.'

It let go. He snapped his eyes open. Gasped a breath. He was standing on the walkway, doubled over, leaning on the rail and gripping it with his left hand, knuckles white, heart thumping.

Maeve was watching.

The Bhenykhn took a step backwards, still staring at him, planting its feet again in defiance.

NG turned to Maeve.

He couldn't get his breathing settled. His head was pounding and he couldn't see clearly, nowhere near in control as much as he needed to be to think straight but he made a decision. He couldn't do this alone.

"You don't understand why the Thieves' Guild has been fighting against you," he said. It wasn't exactly a question.

"No, I don't. I never have." She narrowed her eyes. "What just happened? That's what happened before, isn't it? What did it just do to you?"

They were monitoring his stats and she'd seen his temperature spike again.

Maeve was High Guard. Without doubt, The most powerful individual he had ever encountered.

"They're called the Bhenykhn Lyudaed," he said. "The Devourers." He felt sick, as if he was betraying the Man and everything that had ever been drummed into him. "They target a feeding ground, they learn everything they can then they swarm. We're next."

"What did it just do to you?" she said again, stern, thinking fast and contacting someone as she spoke.

"We've been working against The Order," he said, "because war between Earth and Winter doesn't benefit anyone but The Order. It weakens us and we need to be ready, more ready than we are, for when they attack."

It sounded lame.

"Why didn't you tell us?"

"How could we? Every one of your Order that I tracked down was trying to kill me. And I didn't know at the time that the aliens were even real."

It was one hell of an admission.

Her voice was icy cold as she said again, "What did it just do to you?"

The alien laughed.

NG ignored it. He had a dire sinking feeling that he'd just made a really big mistake but he was also acutely aware that the presence of the Bhenykhn was casting a dark dread over him. It was powerful. He needed to throw it off, spin this on its head. He raised his eyes and said very carefully, "It's telepathic."

"And so are you?"

He might as well have hit a massive alarm button, sending the security status sky high.

She started sending orders to her people, silently through her Senson, but each thought crystal clear and calm. She was preparing to leave, taking him with her. She'd surmised, correctly, that it had been listening in to every facet of her organisation. She wanted to get NG away from it because, she'd decided, she had to keep him alive, that he was way, way more important than any of them had ever appreciated, that the elders of the Thieves' Guild were damned fools for keeping this to themselves and that she needed to escalate this beyond her personal situation at UM, cosy as that had been of late.

"Wait, we need to take it with us," he said.

She placed a hand on his arm and said with chilling assurance, "Don't fight me."

"No, you don't understand. The virus we have only survives in a living host."

"I want to get you away from it."

He shook his head. "We need the source. Take it with us."

She didn't say out loud that she agreed but she sent the orders and nudged him towards the staircase. "Where have you encountered them before?"

"Erica."

Of course, he overheard her think, cursing to herself inside her head. They had people investigating that, of course they did, but they had assumed it was Earth and Winter, Zang tearing off on his solo shenanigans again. Nothing had given them reason to suspect an alien influence in the loss of those two ships. Dammit. She looked at him, thinking if it had just been a space battle, then where did he get hurt?

He stopped at the bottom of the stairwell and stood aside to let her pass. "We fought them on the ground. There was an advance force, heavy infantry, light support weapons. They attacked the mining facility."

She looked him straight in the eye, pausing as she went to brush past, the scent of her spiced perfume cutting through the stench of the alien. She was thinking quite clearly, 'And the alien marker in your blood?'

"It's a toxin," he said. "They use poisoned weapons. I got stabbed."

She stood, transfixed. "You really are reading my mind."

He gave a slight nod.

"You came here looking for us? Or for the alien?"

"Your grandson. We know he set Zang up to blackmail us."

She nodded then and started to walk up the stairs. "He's a fool."

She was thinking worse, and she was thinking through all the implications of having a telepath in their midst, very well aware that he would be listening in. She was keeping calm and neutral, concentrating on dealing with getting away, with him intact, and reaching somewhere safe to consider all this, with support. Not Drake, she was thinking, better it be Anton or Itomara. Both, probably.

He followed, limping up the steep steps, trying to keep the headache at bay and still not entirely sure he'd done the right thing in talking to her. On one hand it felt like he had accessed a powerful ally against the Bhenykhn but on the other he might have just betrayed the guild and everything he'd ever lived for. And either way, he was still her captive. Even if he could get away from her and make a break for it, he'd lose her as an ally and he'd never get out alive. He was trapped and at her mercy as much as the alien down there.

It didn't sit well.

They reached the top. Maeve took two steps into her room and the door burst open. NG was just behind. He didn't see it until it was happening. Until it was too late. There were shots. Maeve was falling before he could reach her, the blast he threw at them too late to stop the rounds that punched into her throat, her chest, her head, the black void hitting him hard. They were her own guards. That was why he hadn't sensed anything awry. Her own damned guards.

The button in the back of his neck began screaming into his spine. It sent him to his knees before he could shut it out enough to react. An FTH round caught him in the shoulder as he went down. He shrugged off the flare from its charge, tore a gun from the hands of one of the guards, misjudged its trajectory and almost went tumbling backwards as it flew into his arms. He managed to hold onto it, spun it round, ducked to the side and started firing back at them, the right arm protesting but holding.

They backed off. Grenades bounced in. He deflected them instinctively but the room was too small to get clear. They detonated as he fell back into the stairwell, trying to keep on his feet, the edge of the stun blast setting his nerve endings on fire. He stumbled. Fell. Another shot skimmed the side of his head, FTH on maximum joining the pain already sparking in his skull.

He could feel the Bhenykhn watching as he rolled out onto the walkway. Heavy boots were thundering right after him and he caught a kick hard in the head, another in the ribs. He curled up. Someone planted a knee in his back. His arms were pulled back, restraints clamped around his wrists and hands gripped him by the shoulders to haul him upright. He couldn't stop trembling, total overload. They stuck a gun under his chin and forced him to look up.

Angmar Rodan was walking down the last of the steps, a rifle in his arms and a smirk on his face. He walked up close.

"NG," he said. "At fucking last. Where's my fucking package?"

14

It all came back to the package. Nikolai had seen that. His young field operatives had lived with the consequences.

The Man sat there, straight backed, looking round at this assembly. Too many of them were thinking that Nikolai had been dancing with the devil in consorting with the Order. They'd been persuaded that the Order was an enemy here. Why now such a change in perspective? Could they trust that Nikolai had not turned himself?

It was absurd. They were judging him, judging the guild, Nikolai, everything they'd done. They had no idea. And they had no right.

He almost stood then. Almost walked out. But she was looking at him with that intense empathy in her mind. She, of all of them, had always been there for him. She had great fondness for the guild and his people.

"He thought, in having a common enemy, he could make an ally of them," she said softly, into the silence when the others were all judging and calculating how they would vote.

He nodded. "He was mistaken."

He raised his eyes slowly, beyond weary, every muscle complaining, every joint hurting, the poison sapping the last of his strength. He was standing in front of massive looming iron gates, intricate, twisted metal in thick knots leading his eye to the heavy lock.

There was a flickering of lights in the darkness beyond.

A damp mist swirled, tendrils creeping to wrap around his wrists and ankles, teasing, caressing.

Dark walls were pressing in behind him.

He couldn't go back, couldn't move forward. Trapped and he was about done…

He knew before he opened his eyes that he was restrained. Flat on his back. Cold. Rodan had smiled then smashed him across the face with the rifle butt.

"I knew you wouldn't be dead," that same cocky, self-assured voice said. There was a slight echo about the room. "I even said it when we heard the news. I knew a cocky bastard like you wouldn't die that easily."

NG blinked, head stuffed with cotton wool, limbs like jelly. His eyelids were heavy and he almost let them slip closed again except he didn't want to get dragged back to that damp, chill maze.

Someone slapped his cheek hard to get his attention.

He blinked again and managed to focus vaguely on the guy standing over him.

Where Maeve had oozed style and sophistication from another era, her grandson was pure slick corporate, totally at odds with this run down, rust-flaked domain he'd claimed as his own. He had his suit sleeves rolled up as if he was going to do his own dirty work except he smiled and stepped back, and it was a different guy, heavier, that moved in and rested a clenched fist up against his ribs, right where they'd been cracked. They'd done their homework.

There was no room to move. NG relaxed every muscle and kept his breathing slow and steady.

"Now, you can either get your guild to deliver up my package," Rodan said, "or I can deliver you up to the Assassins. Your choice. Which is it to be?"

He was bluffing.

He wanted the elixir.

The fist withdrew and punched hard, precise.

The rib snapped.

NG couldn't stop the half cry that slipped out, eyes squeezing shut instinctively against the pain.

The dark closed in fast. He could see the gates looming high in front of him, the huge lock standing out from the twisted metal.

A cold sting hitting his neck snapped him back to reality, followed by another and another.

The drugs flooded into his bloodstream faster than he could neutralise them.

He started to go under again, the darkness closing in, but this time he was still aware, he could still feel the pain. It was the first time he'd been in the nightmare and the real world at the same time.

The Bhenykhn was there. That was a first. It was watching him from the shadows, tense, gearing up to attack.

"Break his fingers."

One snap after another, trigger fingers on both hands. He choked back another cry.

The alien charged. There was nowhere to go, no room to dodge. It tackled him with a vicious mauling grapple that sent them both sprawling across the damp ground.

Rodan loomed close again. "My package, NG. You can read my mind? Fucking do it. See how fucking far I'm prepared to go for this."

He was still bluffing.

NG scrambled free and ran for the gate, leaving the alien behind and skidding to a halt before the daunting mass of twisted metal blocking his way. This gate was denying him access to the intel from the alien ship. All he needed to do was break open the gate, get out of the Maze and he would know all the secrets that Sebastian had thrown at him.

A fist hit hard against his jaw, momentarily thrusting him back to reality.

"How much will your fucking council pay to get you back?" Rodan was screaming. "How much are you fucking worth to them? I know assassins who will pay me billions to keep you alive, NG… so they can take their time killing you. Will the Thieves' Guild match that to save you, NG?"

He squeezed his eyes shut.

He looked up at the lock, staring at it until it shimmered and became translucent. The mechanism inside lit up like liquid mercury.

A cold, wet cloth hit his face, covering his mouth and nose, hands pulling it tight, another hand squeezing his throat.

He couldn't breathe.

The Bhenykhn was running at him again. He could hear it roaring in rage.

The cloth vanished and a fist rattled his jaw again.

"Where is my fucking package, NG? You don't want to talk to us? Cut off his fucking thieving hand."

He felt an edge of cold steel rest against his wrist.

He didn't turn, didn't take his eyes off the lock, simply raised a hand and sent the massive alien flying backwards.

His senses were swirling, dancing with the pain that was flowing in agonising waves. He let it, used it, revelled in it and started to take energy from them as he lay there shackled to the table, taking energy from Rodan, from each of his thugs, sucking in their very life essence.

He chose to return to the nightmare.

He traced the pattern of the release catches in the lock.

Set them up.

And blew it apart with a blast so strong the gates flew open.

He opened his eyes.

Rodan's crony had a machete poised and tensed, slicing the blade into his wrist enough to draw blood. The thug pulled the weapon up, muscles bunching and went to hack it down. NG stopped his arm in an instant and held it there with a force that was strong enough to squeeze, twist and thrust the guy away, draining the last of his life force suddenly and completely.

Rodan stepped back, eyes flaring. It was easy to finish him off. He dropped, dead before he hit the floor, the rest of his men falling, weapons clattering against the tiles.

NG sucked in a deep breath, exhaled and closed his eyes.

The darkness now was calm, fresh with a terrifying clarity.

He could see the intel.

He knew exactly where the Bhenykhn were and he knew exactly what they were planning.

He released the catches and sat up. He healed as much as he could and neutralised the drugs running riot in his bloodstream. He was exhausted but it was a sharp kind of exhilarated exhausted, the kind you get after running the Straight in your best time. He perched there on the edge of the table and glanced at the door, throwing the bolt across. They were out there watching by remote, not daring to come in but it did no harm to make sure they couldn't.

The Bhenykhn was quiet, watching and unsettled.

NG ignored it. The headache had abated from the constant barrage of pressure that it had been.

He slid off the table and found medical supplies in a drawer. He bound the fingers on each hand, and tied a strapping tight around his knee.

Then he stood, looking around without moving an inch. He fried the circuits in every piece of surveillance equipment within fifty feet of the room, popped open a low wall vent, climbed in and vanished.

The whole facility was in chaos. It was easy to pilfer a jacket from a locker, grab a pass and wend his way up through the levels, adding to the confusion as he went. He found an empty office, locked himself in and hacked into their communications network. As much as the infrastructure might be crumbling and decaying, they'd installed technology and security that matched the best he'd seen. He sent out an encrypted mayday, tagged with his emergency codes, and switched casually to their main systems. He wiped every last trace of evidence that they'd held him here, initiated an official buyout using one of the Man's favourite and most stable corporations then began rifling randomly through their research, personnel stats, manifests, anything that caught his eye.

There was nothing in there regarding Maeve or any business she could have been conducting from here. It almost felt like he'd imagined her.

He sat back, tired, close to nodding off, and almost missed

the reply that came through. It was a curt, one-liner, encrypted, sarcastic, asking 402 if he wanted resurrecting.

He sent one back saying, "Screw that, I want extricating and by the way, while we're here, we're taking over this godforsaken dump because there's a goddamned live alien here and commandeering the facility is going to be less hassle than trying to extract it, especially seeing how the previous owners no longer have a vested interest in the place."

It was a bit longwinded but he wasn't feeling very eloquent.

He added an order to send a research team from the Alsatia, signed off and stood. He wanted to leave but there was an unease pulling at the back of his mind that had nothing to do with the Bhenykhn.

He was at the very heart of another of the galaxy's most powerful corporations... what were the chances?

He retied the make-do support around his knee, pulled it tighter, and headed back down.

Rodan's quarters were cold but expensive, a far cry from Maeve's cosy den. NG dropped down from the ventilation system into the centre of a spacious marble-tiled office, a mass of monitors covering one wall, steel and glass desk in the centre, black leather sofas along another wall. He'd trashed the surveillance systems and the door was locked so he had time to play.

There was a terminal on the desk. He flashed it up and checked in. The extraction teams were mobilising, gave him a schedule and asked if he was okay, said the chances of a successful extraction were a hell of a lot higher if he was on the surface and what the hell was he doing so deep? They were still tracking him, the Senson wasn't the only way the guild kept tabs on its people. He sent back that he was fine, cancel the extraction, he'd decided to stay. Then he shut off the terminal.

He swivelled around in the chair. He'd gone deep into Rodan's memory before he'd killed the guy. What in all that would tell him where it was? If it was here.

There was a table on the far side of the office, shot glasses and a range of exotic bottles. He wandered over. Schnapps, tequila, vodka. No rum or whisky. He managed to open a bottle and tried a shot of tequila. Expensive. Rodan had playboy tastes.

NG poured another shot of tequila, fumbling and spilling half of it, and dragged out of the depths of somewhere a feeling that there was a safe. A bigger walk-in vault. And a secret cache spot. He found them all, cracked them all easily and found nothing but crap. A lot of cash and flash valuables. Nothing like the key he'd got from Yarrimer.

He sat back at the desk and looked around. There were two doors at the back of the room. One went into a cupboard. The other into private quarters. An enormous bed with silk sheets, mirrors and a smaller desk in the corner. Shafts of light reflected off the metallic surfaces of the key as he opened the door. Rodan hadn't stored it somewhere safe, never mind make any attempt to hide it. It was sitting there like a trophy. A paperweight.

NG picked it up and stared at it.

There were slight differences in its shape but it was the same material, platinum by the look and feel of it, the same intricate designs and angles. And it was heavy, the same kind of dense heavy that didn't make sense whatever metal it was made of.

He went back to the office, found a bag to stash it in, downed another shot of tequila and headed for the door. He had one more thing to do before he could leave.

Maeve's body had been removed but they hadn't bothered to clean up the blood pooled on the carpet. He didn't touch anything in her room. He had all he needed on the Order from being with her.

He headed down the stairwell, spots of his blood on the floor marking his last foray down here.

The Bhenykhn was walking forward, slowly, to the centre of the cage as he emerged out onto the walkway and leaned casually on the handrail.

It knew exactly what had happened and it was wary of him now.

He was taking a risk coming this close, provoking it again, but he couldn't resist, tired, pissed off that Rodan had killed Maeve and almost wanting it to fight him.

It planted its feet and looked up defiantly.

'How did they get their hands on you?' NG thought at it, not expecting it to understand him, not really even expecting a reaction.

It flashed to a scene of impact, pain, debris.

It had crash-landed somewhere. There was no impression there of when. No clear feeling on how long it had been here. It must have been some time if this was where the virus had originated.

It didn't like that he was in its head. He felt it panic when it realised what he was doing. It didn't know how to block him, had never had to before, and he trampled through its mind with no finesse, like hacking through a jungle with a blunt machete, until it roared and tried to attack the way it had when he'd first landed here.

He swatted the blow aside and took what he wanted, felt it try to read him back and threw up barriers easily to stop it.

It roared again and ran full pelt to throw itself against the door of the cage, tearing at the hinges and scratching chunks out of the metal. Guards appeared below, shooting FTH that bounced off its armoured skin and made it bellow even louder.

NG finished up fast, drained enough energy out of it to make it sink to its knees, and stepped back, breathing as heavily as if they'd been fighting hand to hand.

It stared sullenly up at him, orange eyes glinting.

'You not kill me...' it thought, clearly enough, malicious and threatening. 'You need me... We no need you,' and said again, 'You... You. Die. First.'

'Yeah, good luck with that. You didn't manage it last time.' He turned and walked away.

He made it back to the surface, just about staggering on his feet by the time he got there, slipping out through a maintenance exit, stealing a jeep and driving through the storm back out towards the peninsula.

He jerked awake twice, having to veer fast to avoid hitting a tree the second time and lost control on the wet surface, oversteering with hands that were beyond numb. It took him five minutes to get it back in gear and moving again. The extraction team intercepted him eventually, flying down low and almost forcing him off the road. He brought the jeep skidding to a halt and sat there, waiting as they landed.

Leigh was with them. She was the one that ran out into the rain and leaned in through the window. "Hey, 402, you found a live alien."

He could hardly keep his eyes open. "We need a crew from the Alsatia out here."

"You said. We're on it already. They're on their way." She was looking him up and down. "You okay?"

"Never been better."

She put her hand on his shoulder, a touch so light he could have imagined it. "Come on. Let's get you out of here. I take it you got what you need?"

He nodded. "The Bennies are here already," he said. "They've got other recon units and forward bases spread out all over the galaxy. We haven't just run out of time. We never had any."

15

Some of them stood. Others pounded on the desk in front of them. Outraged.

Panicked.

"Why did you not bring this to us sooner?" one demanded.

"We vote now," another said, standing and looking round for support.

"No," she said, louder, determined this time to stand against them, to stand for decorum and sense, to give this species a chance.

He sat there as they reacted. In his empire, he was never questioned, never defied. Here, amongst these few, he was simply a messenger, one to be suspected, different, an error in judgement that they wished not to repeat.

"Let us hear the rest," she said, standing until the others had sat. "We will not make the same mistake again." She looked to him. "They are here? Now?"

He nodded, feeling the panic spread. He should have gone back. Nikolai felt that he had been abandoned and that judgement in all this was the hardest to bear.

They took him to Wraith. He slept the whole way, warning Leigh that she'd best keep an eye on him in case anything weird happened and collapsing fully dressed into one of the emergency medevac pods, asleep before his head hit the pillow.

He dreamed of Devon, sitting in that forest with her, burrowing his head into her shoulder as she died in his arms. The sun was warm on the back of his neck, her arms strong as she hugged him close. He didn't want it to end.

He opened his eyes to the soft light and reassuring hum of the pod, feeling like he'd slept forever and for no time at all. He tried to sit and felt the tug of wires and tubes. Someone had stripped off his shirt and hooked him up to life support. He sank back down. He had no implant or wristband so he had no inputs from anything, no idea even what day it was, and he almost freaked except he sensed Leigh and Duncan close by, calm and watching. There was another medic in there too, messing with the pod, opening it up as they saw he was awake.

Leigh appeared, leaned close and winked at him. "Well done," she whispered, "you managed to not die this time. And no nightmares."

He went to rub his eyes with his left hand, bandaged, and went to lift his right, feeling the weight of the cast. He could feel the warmth of a trauma patch against his ribs.

Reaching further, he could tell they were on the Man's ship.

"Where are we?" His throat felt like he'd swallowed razors.

"Still in orbit around Poule," Duncan said.

"How long have I been out?"

"Three days. Your legal and research teams are here. They've gone down there with a bunch of ground troops. They have the facility secured." The big man was impressed at the speed of their operation.

Three days. That wasn't disastrous.

If they'd got here that fast, it meant the Alsatia was near.

He reached and pulled the IV line out of his arm, sitting and moving to tug off the monitors attached to his chest.

The medic wasn't impressed but didn't argue.

NG leaned his head against the wall of the pod. "Where's LC?"

"Sleeping," Duncan said.

"Get him up and in the mess. I need him to do something for me."

The kid sat across from him, sprawled across a sofa with a board resting on his knees. He looked up, ready, apprehensive, sticking at the back of his mind the newly acquired fact that NG was Andreyev, desperately wanting to talk to him about it and knowing this wasn't the time. Duncan was at the other end of the mess, watching.

NG closed his eyes, no idea if this was going to work. He started to process the intel, working through one section, slowly and carefully. He opened one eye and glanced across. LC was working steadily.

"Go on," the kid muttered without looking up, "I'm good. I'm getting it. Speed up or this is going to take forever."

Going faster, he was drawn into it, lost in the swirl of data. He went through it raw and he drew out what patterns he could see straight off, going through the information Sebastian had given him first then the mix of intel he'd taken from the Bhenykhn down there, its own intelligence it had brought with it and also the mass of intel it had taken from UM. It was unsettling, off key, to see all that from the alien point of view, how it had analysed their weaknesses, seeing them as inferior, as potential food and slaves, how it had learned to understand their language and systems. He drew back from that and threw the rest, including what he'd taken, unprocessed, across to LC, looking up as he finished.

The kid had stopped using the board and was just absorbing it all, eyes closed, head nestled against the seat. He realised it had stopped and didn't move. "Okay, give me a minute," he said and fell asleep.

NG stood and stretched, aching, sore and needing more sleep himself. He reached across and took the board out of LC's lap where it had fallen, flicked through a few of the screens, bizarre to see the intel he'd had stuck in his head laid out there in guild format, and threw it onto the seat.

Duncan had been listening in to the flow of intel at first but had shut them out when it got too much. "No wonder you were having nightmares," he said. "Still no sign of Sebastian?"

NG shook his head.

"And the Bennies have other recon units out there?"

He nodded.

It was logical that the ship at Erica wouldn't have been the only one.

"You know where?" Duncan asked. "That's what you've just given to LC?"

That was the real question. "Kind of," he said. "It's all relative to their frame of reference. We need to figure out how that correlates with ours before we can figure out exactly where they are."

"Ah," Duncan said and added, "You know Evelyn's with the legal team?" as if that was the most immediate thing NG needed to know. "She wants to know which operative we had in there."

"Tell her it was 402. And tell her the alien is listening in to everything. They need to be careful."

"Elliott was tapped into their security feeds. We saw their surveillance footage of you."

"All of it?"

Duncan nodded.

"I erased it," NG said, feeling sick again, stomach knotting. "She won't see it unless Elliott is an ass and sends it to her."

"So what do we do now?"

He rubbed the back of his hand across his eyes. He needed to get a new Senson. "We need to figure out where they are." It was twisted. He was chasing them knowing fine well that as soon as he found them, Sebastian could turn up, take over and he could be history. He had no idea why Sebastian hadn't turned up the minute he encountered that Bhenykhn but if and when he did, fine. Bring it on. Not knowing and waiting had never been his strong points. In anything.

"I have a lead to the Order," he said. "Let's find out what they know. See if they've got any more damned Bhenykhn stashed anywhere."

It took LC two days to go through it all and the file of material the kid had come up with was hideous. He'd worked on it without a break, pulling every last detail out of his memory, then pushed it away when he was done and escaped to his quarters to throw up and pass out.

NG sat in the briefing room, trying to concentrate on the data and doing nothing but going round in circles or staring at it until it blurred and swirled into nonsense.

He rubbed the side of his neck with the edge of his wrist. His neck was sore with a new implant and trying to counter the dizzying disorientation while it synched was giving him a headache.

No one had offered to get him a drink and he was damned if he was going to ask. He was tempted to call up Evelyn. She'd look after him.

Hal Duncan looked up from the board he was reading with a wry smile.

Okay, maybe not. He looked round the table. Hilyer was writing meticulous notes and drawing sketches. Badger was working six boards at once, trying to corroborate the intel with the data from the greys. Pen and Quinn were just reading quietly. And on top of this, whole teams from Media and Science were poring over the same data.

It was going to take them time to get through it all.

NG stood and walked out. He needed to find a faster way to figure out what was still bugging him.

Morgan was on the bridge. Busy. NG lurked in the doorway, no idea why he hadn't just called the guy on the Senson.

He looked over eventually, realising NG was there, standing and straightening his jacket, puzzled, and walking over as he also realised that NG wasn't going to enter the bridge.

"NG?" There was almost a, 'sir'.

NG stood there, slouching because his knee was hurting and feeling scruffy in the vicinity of uniformed crew. Christ, this was more difficult than it should have been and he could feel that he was making it worse, behaving like a bumbling idiot. He was supposed to be able handle people. Manipulate them. It was like he'd forgotten how to play at all this.

He didn't know how to say it so he just did. "The Man used to use this black powder stuff…"

The captain was staring at him, an 'and…?' playing in his mind.

He heard it flash through the guy's thoughts, not for the first time, that NG was the last guy any of them had ever imagined would be 'the one' to take over from the Man.

Morgan was trying not to look at the bruises, the strapped arm, the bandaged hands, thinking that nothing had changed and everything had changed, narrowing his eyes, trying not to think as he realised that NG would probably be reading every thought he had.

It was tempting to go deeper and find out what they did all think of him but he could guess. Devon and Evie had always given him that same look whenever he'd gone haring off by himself and come back injured.

"I need some," he said, trying not to sound too desperate and knowing fine well that he sounded like a freaking junkie.

"It's kept in stores," Morgan said, simply. "I'll have the QM get some for you."

The Man's chambers felt warmer than usual. The black powder came wrapped in brown paper, sealed with red wax. He managed to unfold it without spilling any and poured the powder, almost reverently, into the bowl. Then he sat back, staring at it, spinning the bowl around without touching it.

That time when he'd been in here and the Man had done just that seemed like eons ago, lifetimes ago.

He let it stop.

The Man had only ever added a pinch at a time. He threw in three generous ones and shook in the remainder from the folded paper too.

The wine reacted, steam billowing up to dance in ascending ribbons.

He poured himself a goblet before it had settled, struggling to hold the jug and splashing wine onto the desk. The Man would have been horrified.

He managed to get the goblet balanced in his left hand and raised it to his lips, taking a sip that hit his bloodstream with a warm punch, like an old friend returning.

He downed the rest and set the goblet on the desk, sitting back and closing his eyes.

He didn't understand why the Man had left. The Bhenykhn were here. It was what he'd been trained for. What they'd been building the guild towards. And now they were here, the Man vanished?

It didn't make sense.

He needed to drink more. He opened his eyes to see Leigh sitting across the desk from him.

She smiled. "We didn't want to leave you on your own. Not after what happened last time."

She was bemused. That seemed to be her main frame of mind when she was dealing with him. That or pissed off at him.

He was glad she wasn't pissed off with him.

He dropped another pinch of powder into the jug. "Join me for a drink?"

She was guessing it was a narcotic. "I'm fine, thank you. I'm just here to pick up the pieces."

He shrugged, poured himself another and drained it in one. He wanted to get lost. Forget all this. Leigh was good company but he wanted to be with Devon. It was Devon he wanted to talk to, to hold...

Leigh was watching him.

He gave her a look. "Are you still monitoring me?"

"Not in here, I'm getting nothing. I take it you are working?"

"I need to figure out what I'm missing." He refilled the goblet.

"You're not going to regale me with your whole life story?"

He almost laughed. "That would take too long but get me onto another bottle and I'll tell you about Sebastian."

She leaned forward. "Who's Sebastian?"

"He's the son of a bitch who killed the Bhenykhn and I don't know if I can do it again without him."

"Of course you can. Are they really here already?"

He nodded.

"Why are you not going to tell Evelyn that you're alive?"

"Because..."

She cut him off. "Yes, I know, she's safer if she doesn't know. That's bullshit, NG, and you know it. You want to tell me the real reason?"

He couldn't. Couldn't admit that Evelyn was too close an association to Devon and it was easier if he just stayed away, as far as he could from her and the Alsatia.

He drained the wine. "I'm missing something," he said instead. "Maeve didn't know why we've been fighting the Order." That was what was bothering him. Was it another lie? Had he been fighting against them all this time on the say-so of a man he actually knew had lied to him?

She watched him pour again, saying cautiously, "Should you be drinking so much of this stuff?"

He shrugged. "It helps me think." He thought it helped him think. He squinted at her. "The Order tasked the JU to work on the virus at the same time that UM was working on it here. Possibly even Yarrimer too. Christ knows who else. Rodan set Zang up to blackmail us to get it for himself when he realised that Earth really had something. When LC disappeared, they assumed he'd brought it back to us. They all assumed that. They thought we were working against them but we had no idea where he was. The irony is that we have been working against them and they didn't know it, not until Rodan and Zang went rogue to get this virus for themselves."

"How did they know Earth had something?"

That was a good question. "I don't know. Someone went after Jameson. They have someone in the JU. What we don't know is how much the rest of the Order know about the Bhenykhn. Is it just UM? What was the JU doing chasing Gallagher unless they knew? And Elliott? What the hell is he in all this? He knew there was something going on here and Christ knows how he knows about this weapons platform. If it even exists." He was rambling, hyper and talking too fast. He stopped. He'd lost track of how much he'd had to drink. "Sorry, I'm going round in circles."

"What if…" she said, "someone invited the Bhenykhn in?"

He looked at her, swirling tendrils of steam wandering between them. He blinked. "What?"

"You're assuming that they picked us as a target and came here of their own volition. What if someone invited them?"

He frowned. "Why?"

"Why not? They're massively superior technologically. They regenerate like nothing we've ever seen before. That's one hell of an ally to have if you want an advantage over an enemy."

NG squinted at her. His head was hurting. He downed what he had left, the heat of it burning his throat, the warmth winding its way into his spine. He had everything they needed to know within the intel Sebastian had thrown at him. What was it deep in there that he was missing? He closed his eyes and felt the room spin.

The Man.

He jerked his eyes open and stared at her. It was in the drawer. He fumbled it open and batted through the junk in there. Found the box and lifted it out, tumbled it onto the table.

"What's this?" she said.

He tipped it up and watched the look on her face as the key fell out.

She looked at him suspiciously. "Where is this from?" She glanced across at the kill token that was still lying on the desk.

"The Man. It opens this room."

"Ah. And he never told you about the Bhenykhn?"

NG shook his head. In everything that had happened since Erica, he hadn't given the key a second thought. He picked up the goblet. Its twisted metal stem was identical in design to the key and the kill token, to the gates in his nightmare.

"You don't know where he is?"

Another shake of the head.

"And that's not the only thing troubling you, is it? Come on then, tell me about Sebastian."

He woke, hangover weighing heavily, instinctively stretching out an arm to touch Devon, to feel the warmth of her skin against his.

The bed was empty. Pain flared in each hand. He wasn't on the Alsatia.

He lay there, fully dressed, not wanting to move. He'd never been able to neutralise the effects of that black powder, had never drunk so much of it before.

He'd told Leigh everything, more than he'd even told Martinez. He had a really bad feeling he might have cried. He had no memory of getting to his quarters. He had a vague feeling he'd sent orders to the bridge crew at some point.

He dragged himself out of bed, set the shower to hot, undressed and stripped off the bandages and bindings. Realising the Man must have known more about the Bhenykhn than he'd ever revealed was even more disturbing now in the cold light of day. And added to the knowledge that the Bennies had active recon units scattered throughout the galaxy, both sides of the line, it was chilling.

He let the hot water drench away the shakes and sat on the edge of the bunk with just a towel round his waist. He had a red scar cutting across his left wrist. He'd been Thieves' Guild his whole life and no one had ever threatened to cut off his hand before. It was laughable. And it was too much to hope that all this crap could be down to a greed-borne and power-hungry pact between Rodan and Zang to screw over the very organisation to which they owed their status. Maeve had been charming in her barking mad ways, almost flirting with him, but he couldn't believe that she hadn't seen the danger her grandson posed.

He lay back on the bunk, reluctant to face trying to get dressed just yet. He realised another loose end that he'd missed, something Badger had said, and opened a connection, feeling the raw edge of the link jar the implant. They'd given him a Seven, experimental, not released yet technology. It didn't feel right.

Badger answered straight away. "How's the hangover?"

Christ, could no one do anything here without the whole lot of them knowing? He closed his eyes, ignored the question and asked bluntly, "Did you find Ballack?"

"Not yet. He isn't at any of his usual haunts. Still looking."

NG cut the connection, ignoring the temptation to contact Leigh. He had a feeling that she'd got him back here to his quarters.

He also had a weird feeling he might have done something stupid and contacted Morgan to find out where they were. "Heading in towards Winter," the answer came back. "That's where you wanted to go."

Itomara.

Toss of the coin.

He hated Winter.

16

She was staring at him, thinking that he should have told the boy. She'd said as much before, after Erica, when he'd asked to see her and they'd talked. She'd said then that he should have told Nikolai so much more.

It wouldn't have made any difference. He truly believed that.

There was only one thing that he regretted not revealing to Nikolai and it was now too late. What was done was done. What he needed to consider, what this assembly needed to decide, was where they went from here.

"How could we aid these creatures more," one of them was saying, "when all we have set up has been greeted with animosity and paranoia…"

"You have seen how they respond to each other," said another. "They know nothing but mistrust and hate. By the very nature of what we have sought to do, we are different."

That enraged her. "The mistake we made," she said, "was to treat them with such arrogance. To try to manipulate them from the shadows. How could they do anything other than distrust us? Should we not have been more open?" She looked back at him. "You say he continued to chase the Order? How did he fare?"

The Man met her gaze. She was concerned. It was touching. "What do you expect? It did not go well."

Kimi Itomara had a sense of humour that was eclipsed only by his sense of occasion. They'd agreed to meet somewhere remote and the CEO of Aries Corp had given them the coordinates to a spot somewhere just south of the planet's pole. Welcome to Winter.

NG walked forward, boots crunching in the crisp snow, breath frosting, cold weather gear just about keeping out the chill. Sebastian had accused him of being masochistic. It appeared he was, to choose Winter in his intoxicated state over Aruba Prime which was where Maeve had reckoned Anton would be.

He had Duncan on one side, Quinn on the other, Leigh one step behind and a Security team flanking them.

Itomara was already waiting with his own entourage spread out in a discrete and respectful circle behind him. He was seated at a low wooden table, bowls and teapot spread out in front of him. Bright sunshine glinted from the lacquered tabletop.

NG walked up and waited to be invited to sit.

It was a simple bow of the head but a flash of appreciation for his nod to the etiquette of the situation ran through the old man's mind as Itomara gestured a go ahead.

He sat and watched as this old master of the High Order lifted the lid from a bowl, spooned dried tea leaves into the pot and added water from a jug, waiting a measured number of heartbeats then pouring the tea carefully into two of the smaller bowls, steam rising.

NG waited.

The old man raised his bowl with a small bow then took a sip.

He followed, mirroring the actions exactly.

"I was promised a meeting with your council," Itomara said. "I do not see any elders."

NG set the cup down. He'd left the strappings off his fingers. Show no weakness. He had a lighter casing on his arm, not strapped and well hidden within the sleeve of the heavy coat. He was having to concentrate to shut out the pain and not fumble the scalding hot tea into his host's lap. "I speak for the elders," he said, once he had it safely back on the table, the pause seemingly adding to the ceremony of the moment.

The old man raised his eyebrows. "We have been wanting to talk to the Thieves' Guild for some time, and you have avoided us, you fight against us. Why do you seek us out now?"

"Maeve Rodan is dead," NG said.

A cloud darkened inside Itomara's mind. They almost considered themselves entitled to immortality, this High Guard of the Order. He'd sensed it in Maeve and he read it now in the distaste Itomara felt for that news.

"Did you kill her?"

NG shook his head. "No. Her grandson, Angmar. I killed him. I'm sorry I was not able to stop him."

He listened in as the old man processed that information and considered the loss, of both Maeve and Angmar.

"You were there?" he asked after a while, referring to their research facility on Poule.

"I was."

"I do not imagine that she told you about me." That was the real question. He wanted to know how the Thieves' Guild had found him.

"She didn't," NG said. "I'm here because Maeve was killed after I'd given her information. I'm here to ask if you want it."

Itomara picked up his bowl of tea and sipped it, waiting and watching for NG to do the same.

He couldn't feel the ends of his fingers any more but he managed to pick up the bowl and take a sip. The tea hadn't lost any of its heat even though it was well below zero out here, the technology concealed within the beautifully crafted porcelain.

Itomara gave a slight nod of appreciation and raised eyes that were glinting in the reflected sunlight. "Do you grant me an honour or a death sentence?"

NG set the bowl down and met his gaze. "If you agree to hear it," he said, "you'll understand why that question is irrelevant."

"And if I refuse?"

"You walk away and we take it to Anton or Drake."

He laughed, a sharp trill. "You try to impress me with your knowledge of the others. You risk much to come here, NG."

It was the first time the old man had acknowledged that he knew who he was speaking to, and it was a neat counter to the stunt of dropping in the names he'd picked out of Maeve's mind.

NG smiled.

"Even escorted as you are."

There was no threat in the man's mind, rather he was bemused and he had already made his decision. He didn't have much choice in the matter, with or without any influence NG could impose.

"The information isn't here," NG said. "You need to come with us."

"You killed A'Darbi," Itomara said, folding his hands in his lap and raising his chin. "You killed Rodan. Maeve is dead because of you. What guarantee do I have, NG, that you do not intend the same fate for me?"

"I'll stay here." He felt Leigh tense when he said that. "You go with my people to our ship in orbit. They give you what we've got, they bring you back. It won't take long. Then we can decide together what we're going to do about it."

The Senson engaged. "You're insane," Leigh sent. "We're not leaving you here."

He ignored her and said to the old man, "Or we can both walk away."

Itomara breathed slowly, inhaling the icy cold air and exhaling as if he was meditating. "The infamous Thieves' Guild comes to me offering information? I have not got to be this old, NG, without being able to make good judgement. You take much risk to come here. What you have must be worth that risk." He spread his hands. "Show me what you have."

NG stamped his feet, pacing. He'd sat there for long enough, sipping at the hot tea, expecting them back any minute.

It was taking too long. He'd had regular updates up until ten minutes ago then nothing. There was no reason why they'd go silent.

He hugged his arms around his ribs, tucking his hands under each arm, trying to get some warmth into his fingers without igniting the worst of the pain again.

Itomara's men were calm.

He couldn't sense anyone else. No other life signs as far as he could reach. It should have been straightforward.

He had no idea if the damned Senson was even working still. He tried an open channel. Nothing. He looked around, picking up that a couple of the guys around him were starting to think they hadn't had any comms coming in for a while, realising they couldn't get their Sensons to engage.

It dawned on them at the same time. They were getting jammed.

Itomara's guys moved, readying weapons, shifting position around him.

He didn't have any weapons on him, not so much as a knife, and it was looking like that could have been a mistake. He turned, arms spread, questioning, to the guy who seemed most senior.

The guy held up a hand, talking fast to his men. They were in the dark too. And they'd just lost contact with their charge.

"Not us," NG said.

The guy didn't care. He'd lost Itomara and he had a hostage, was as far as he was thinking. He gestured, combat signals. NG tensed and took a step back as they moved to surround him. Dammit, he was trying to ally with these people, he didn't want to kill them.

"Wait."

They had guns raised. Both their ships had gun turrets aimed at him.

"This isn't us," he said again, slipping into a defensive stance as they came at him.

The guy in charge didn't care, yelling, "Get on the ground," more shouting from the others that was drowned out by a roar from above.

Before they could get to him, a missile screamed down and hit one of their ships, the shockwave sending them all flying backwards, snow and debris billowing up.

NG tumbled, breath driven from his lungs, watching from a crazy angle as Itomara's other pilot was smart enough and fast enough to take off. There was another missile heading straight for it, locked onto it. He reacted without thinking, throwing a blast of energy that deflected it away by inches. It plunged into the ground and detonated, the second shockwave rolling over them.

Gunfire started to kick up the snow, gunships and drop ships descending on them. He couldn't pick up anything from the incoming troops but combat readiness, no thoughts of who they were working for.

Someone grabbed his arm and yanked hard, other bodies crowding in to get him to his feet and pulling him into a run.

"They're not mine," he yelled, recognising the guy closest as the one in charge.

"Then we're in trouble," the guy yelled back.

Ground troops were piling out of the drop ships. Itomara's people started firing back. The Aries ship was thundering round to meet them, trying to land to pick them up and get off suppressive fire at the same time. Bodies were falling, blood spattering the snow, pops of void hitting his chest as distant thuds deep within.

He let them drag him into their ship, feeling it lurch and lift as they stumbled on board. He was thrown towards a seat as it took off, banking hard, engines screaming, guns still blasting. It was rocked violently, sparks and flames exploding inwards. NG shielded his eyes, trying to hold on with hands that felt like they were on fire. Something hit them. The ship tipped, throwing them forwards. He lost his grip, hit the bulkhead and fell. He curled up, senses spinning as he tumbled. Another impact and the ship slewed sideways. Pain exploded in the back of his head, sparks flashing behind his eyes. The heat and noise of another explosion seemed distant and muted. The mass of the ship dropped from beneath him and it felt like he was falling forever.

He was bleeding. Really badly from his side. A pressure in his head was making it feel like it was going to explode. He managed to get a hand to his abdomen, felt cold metal sticking out of him. He couldn't grip hard enough to shift it so he cheated, made it move and pulled, letting the shard of wreckage drop from numb fingers. He calmed his breathing, gathered what energy he could and healed. Nothing new was broken, old wounds jarred, but nothing new that he couldn't fix.

It was eerily quiet. He felt foggy-headed, squinted open one eye and wished he hadn't. Far off voices got loud fast. A chunk of fuselage was pulled off him and a boot nudged into him.

"Got him," someone said. "He's alive. Let the boss know."

They must have had orders to keep him alive because they pulled up his blood-soaked shirt and slapped a trauma patch under it, without looking too hard. There was a cold sting against his neck, a dampening patch stuck over the Senson then hands grabbed him and pulled.

He didn't resist. He didn't know who they were and he wasn't in much of a state to fight them. They dragged him out into the cold and over to another ship, dropped him in a seat and strapped him in. Someone had gone to a lot of trouble to get hold of him. And considering that he was supposed to be dead and that no one was supposed to know about this meeting, he had no idea who that could be. He'd spent his whole life working in the shadows, invisible, anonymous even to his own people. That had changed in the blink of an eye. Someone had outplayed them.

He closed his eyes and leached energy from every person he could sense, draining them all to the point of fatigue.

He felt the ship lift, accelerate and fly low, so they were staying on Winter, not going for orbit. It was either Zang or Ostraban. Had to be. And that was fine with him.

It was neither of them. NG almost laughed when he was walked off the ship and into a courtyard. He had a guard on each side, gripping his arms in restraint holds that were excessive considering he hadn't given them any resistance, and another holding a gun at his back. Green-grey clouds filled the sky. Snow-laden stone battlements loomed on all sides. The big man standing there was all too familiar.

"Ballack," NG said.

The head of the Merchants' Guild gave a stern little disappointed-at-you shake of the head that didn't match the satisfaction the man was stirring up inside. "NG," he said solemnly.

There were guys in suits either side of him. One of them stepped forward and flashed a badge in a wallet. "Nikolai Andreyev, you are under arrest for murder."

17

*"You should have disbanded the Merchants' Guild when you had
the chance," one of them said bitterly. "In all that we have failed this
galaxy, that would have vindicated us the most."*

There were murmurs of agreement.

Of all the faults of these people, greed was not one of them.

*"They play the pretence of neutrals," another said, "yet they
stand to benefit the most from the spoils, whichever side prevails."*

*The Man looked up. "Ballack is a fool. No one will benefit,
whoever they are, should the Bhenykhn prevail."*

*She banged on the table. "This talk of the Merchants and what
should have been is irrelevant. The question now is do we run?
Again? Do we gather our refugees and flee? Again? Or do we make
a stand? Here? With these humans we find so alien to us? These
humans who fight so fiercely when threatened?"*

They sat him in some kind of briefing room, a grand hall, stone
walls, big wooden table, elaborate stone fireplace, left wrist
manacled to the arm of the chair, guards armed with rifles
stationed up on a balcony that ran all the way around the room.

They'd read him his rights and reeled off the list of charges:
the murder of Taynara A'Darbi, accessory to the murder of
Olivia Ostraban, harbouring of a fugitive and multiple counts
of espionage. Plus whatever the hell else they wanted to throw at
him. They'd added in the threat of extradition to Earth for the
murder of one of the Emperor's most valued Advisors, then left
him sitting there for three hours.

The dampening patch was still over his Senson. It had taken
very little effort to break the seal without moving but there was

no reply from anyone. He'd initiated his emergency beacon. The guild would find him eventually.

There was no fire in the hearth, no heating at all, and they'd taken his coat so he was freezing cold, but he was pulling energy from anyone who came near so on the whole he was feeling quite perky. They'd sent in a medic to check him over. The guy had given him a cursory examination, peeled off the trauma patch and prodded, reporting nothing life-threatening and sending a tight wire communication to someone that, yep, lots of blood, no wounds.

Ballack was the next to come talk to him. Zang Tsu Po was watching by remote, sitting comfy somewhere up inside his fortress. They were all confident that even though he could probably bust out of the restraints, there were enough guns pointed at him that he wouldn't get two inches from the chair if he tried anything.

Ballack sat his massive bulk in a chair on the opposite side of the table, that same self-serving condescending look on his face. He puffed out a sigh as if he was trying to think of something encouraging to say but couldn't.

NG waited patiently.

They had absolutely nothing on him regarding A'Darbi. Not a scrap and they knew it. He was reading Ballack's innermost thoughts as they sat there. Everything. They'd received an anonymous tip off about the meeting with Itomara. From someone who knew his real name so that narrowed it down. They didn't know about Rodan or Maeve yet. Ballack did know about the Bhenykhn that UM had captive. NG dug deeper and reckoned that this slick merchant man hadn't known about it the last time they'd met, on Redgate. That bad a miss he would have been pissed about. They also knew that something had happened out at Erica but they didn't know what.

"I'm afraid I can't protect you from this," Ballack said eventually, almost convincing, as if they were best buddies, guild leader to guild leader.

"From what?" NG said. "You have no evidence."

"Coming to Winter was a mistake, NG. You have a lot of enemies here."

"We have enemies everywhere," he said, trying not to laugh. "No one has ever set us up quite as much as this before. Not the way your new chums have done. Angmar Rodan is dead, by the way. You want to charge me for that too? Have fun trying to fabricate the evidence on that."

Ballack didn't like that, frowning and sending an order to his people to check it out. Asap. He leaned forward. "Let's cut the crap. You should have stayed dead, NG. You want to know what the Assassins have been offering me for your head?"

He kept quiet. He didn't want to talk about why he'd gone after the Assassins, not with this buffoon.

"Bad enough that your boys stole from the Earth military," Ballack said, scathing, confident in his position here, "but killing the daughter of the coalition chairman? Time's up, NG. Anderton deserves to hang for what he's done."

He could read clearly enough that Ballack didn't care one hoot whether Olivia Ostraban was alive or dead. This was being recorded and it was all an act for the benefit of Ennio Ostraban.

Ballack's tone dripped contempt. "Give us Anderton and we could be in a position to negotiate."

NG shook his head, incredulous. "Negotiate what? You're not going to let me go." He rattled the chain around his wrist. "These charges are bullshit and you know it. What are these guys offering you, Ballack? A place in their New Order?"

There was a moment of hesitation, a slight recalculation, then the bastard smiled outright.

NG read it in his mind before he said it out loud.

Oh shit.

He glanced up and round, counting the number of guns, working out how fast they could pull their triggers, how fast he could break free and move, how many of them he could take down.

"NG," Ballack said, "I am the New Order," and sent the command.

NG moved, faster than they were expecting, breaking out of the cuffs with a spray of sparks. They opened fire.

He could go for the door or he could go for Ballack.

He ducked.

FTH rounds punched into the chair, the table, a couple catching him as he dived out of the way.

Ballack was standing, shouting.

NG scrambled up, vaulted across the table and tackled him to the floor, rolling and twisting until he had the guy in a lock.

He needed more time. He had a twenty stone deadweight on top of him pressing against broken ribs, FTH sparking in his spine, thirty armed guys descending on them and he flashed Ballack to the middle of the battlefield on Erica, face to face with the massive Bhenykhn commander, orange eyes glaring, teeth bared. It thrust the knife into his heart. He froze the scene and flashed to a hill top overlooking the wreckage-strewn moorland.

Ballack scrambled backwards in the mud. "What in hell is this?"

NG sat, rain streaming down his face, staring out over the battle. It was whatever he wanted to make it this time, in this unreality. He could have stopped the rain but that wouldn't have felt right.

"Your pet alien," he said, numb. He hadn't exactly planned to show it like this to anyone again. It had been bad enough flashing back here so briefly to show Jameson. "This is the rest of its advance unit. We fought them on Erica."

Ballack stepped forward, peering through the downpour. "This isn't real."

"This isn't," NG admitted. "What happened was. This is in my memory. You want to feel the knife wound again?"

Ballack gave a kind of strangled half laugh. The only thing stopping him from thinking it was a nightmare, some kind of hallucination, was the detail of the alien because it matched exactly what they had in captivity on Poule. He wanted to see more.

NG obliged. He flashed from fight to fight, the weighted chain tossed tumbling through the air, poisoned talons raking into his neck, the stench of their breath, crossbow bolts flying, the roar of the pods landing, thudding into the ground to surround them.

He felt Ballack recoil, nausea building, and let it drop, bringing them back to the hillside.

Ballack looked down on him in disgust. "Erica? Where we lost the Tangiers and the Expedience?"

'We'. He really did stand firmly with one foot in each camp.

"Yep."

"You were there? These – things – were there?" They'd thought they had the only one. First contact and a neat prisoner, one up on the rest of the galaxy, a head start in researching its technology. His grasp on the situation was coming crashing down around his ears and a part of him still wanted to think that NG was pulling some kind of stunt to fool him.

"It's real, Ballack. You want to see the scars?"

The big man was still not convinced. "How are you doing this?" he asked, suspicious.

"I can make you think, and feel, and see, anything I want," NG said, petulant, thinking as he said it that maybe he shouldn't have done but the time for hiding and secrets was past. He had no way out of that room, no plan B, no rescue team on its way and nothing to offer up in exchange. He wasn't about to give up LC. And even if he did, he wasn't stupid enough to think they'd let him go.

"What do you want?"

NG laughed. "I want you to let me go. Honestly, Ballack, you weren't on my list of people to let in on this."

He got to his feet, breathing in the chill chemical rain of the distant colony, water flooding down the back of his neck. He gestured towards the battle raging down there, the flashes of explosions, the screams and rattle of gunfire. "This is a small advance reconnaissance unit. They've been gathering intel on the whole galaxy." He let that sink in. "They have more recon units here already and they're coming back with a full attack fleet. That's what's heading for your New Order, Ballack."

132

He let it go, braced himself and pushed the massive bulk of the man off him, curling up as FTH rounds impacted, too many to brush off, blows punching into his head and darkness descending fast.

The tingling sparks of the FTH were still lingering when he started to come round so he hadn't been out long. He blinked lazily, focusing on the same fireplace. Same chair. Ankles restrained this time as well as both wrists, tape around his chest securing him to the chair and a button in his neck.

There were more bodies down in the room with him, more stationed on the balcony. They'd misjudged him and they weren't going to make the same mistake again.

Someone came close and a sting of perfume hit his senses at the same time as a sharp slap from an icy cold hand hit his cheek. There wasn't much power in it but the hate behind it threatened to send him reeling.

He raised his eyes, shutting out every emotion he was picking up.

She was beautiful, even looking at him as she was with such cold eyes. It was hard not to fall back in time to another face that was so similar.

Anya leaned close and breathed in his ear, "How does it feel to lose someone you love, NG?"

That hit him as she intended. He didn't want to read it in her mind, didn't want to go anywhere near her mind, but he was drawn to her, the way he'd been drawn to her mother so long ago.

She still didn't know. That was something. What sent him sideways was deeper, almost an irrelevancy. He'd sent her away from the Alsatia but what he saw there in the depths of her mind sent a shard of ice stabbing into his stomach.

His breathing started to speed up, a sense of urgent helpless frustration welling up, and it took everything he had to stifle it, calm and not show it.

Anya stroked an immaculate fingernail across his jaw. "What?

You didn't think the worst I could do was getting the boys sent out on their little adventure, did you? NG, you underestimate me." Her tone turned harsh. "You always underestimated me." She beamed a smile, emotions spinning on their head. "I did enjoy seeing them again though. They've grown up well, don't you think? LC especially. I'm sure you must be proud of them."

He glanced past her at Ballack and Zang, both of them sitting there, smug to be witnessing the mess that the Thieves' Guild had got itself into.

She took hold of his jaw in her perfect hand and turned his head back to look at her. "Attention now, NG. We want LC. We want the package he went to get for me. And, NG…" He could feel her breath warm on his cheek. "You killed my mother and I want you to pay."

18

"They live such short, complicated lives," one of them said, frowning.

Another said with disdain, "They live, they breed, they die."

"They evolve," she said, speaking up where he was unable. "We are here now, discussing this dilemma, exactly because we have a choice. They have given us this choice. Every other race to face the Bhenykhn has been obliterated. We few escaped by the skin of our teeth and we find ourselves here deciding whether we run or fight because these humans have shown us the hint of a chance. That they may be able to evolve fast enough to stand up to the Devourers."

"And have they?"

All eyes turned to him. He steepled his fingers. Laced them together again. For a people so long-lived, they were impatient. As if they had been contaminated by the immediacy of the human race.

There was no instant answer. "The virus, the organism they are all chasing shows great potential. Nikolai himself…? He is different. They fear him. And it is far easier to destroy that which you fear than to face it."

She wasn't done. "What? Was losing Devon not bad enough? I did enjoy pulling the strings on that little episode. She was quite smitten with you. Did you not realise? Faro was so much nicer to me than you ever were, NG." She squeezed, digging a nail into his skin, drawing blood. "I don't know. What can I do next? Evelyn perhaps? She's in quite a precarious situation right now. How is she going to feel, finding out that you're alive and lying to her? How do we all feel when you lie to us, NG?"

He didn't fight her as she held him like that, casting his eyes across to glance at Ballack. The leader of the Merchants' Guild hadn't told them a thing. He was sitting there, a picture of self-satisfaction, calculating how he was going to use NG and the Thieves' Guild, and profit from this insane idea that there was an alien invasion on its way.

"It's not insane," he said.

Ballack frowned.

Anya slapped him again. "I said, pay attention. I want LC. Where is he and how are you going to get him to me?"

She didn't just want LC for the package. She was obsessed. Besotted with the kid. That was disturbing.

NG lowered his eyes and scanned around, working out where everyone was, what their actual capacity was, dipping in and out of minds to pick up what he could on Zang Enterprises and the Merchants' Guild. The Wintran officials were still there, trying to figure out what was going on, why they hadn't been given the go ahead to transfer their prisoner.

Anya raked her fingernail into his skin again, bringing his focus back to the room, taking hold of his hand with her other hand and stroking gently along each broken finger.

He ignored her, taking everything he could from Zang Tsu Po, this enemy they'd been chasing, and almost laughing as he realised that here he was right at the centre of another of Winter's big corporations and this time, the information he needed was right there to be taken. The old man was as mad as Anya, his mind wide open, wanting nothing more than the package, lusting for immortality. Like LC kept saying, it all came back to the damned package.

Ballack was smirking. NG listened in as the man opened a private tight wire connection to someone and ordered them to contact the Thieves' Guild. "Tell them we have NG and will trade for Anderton and the package. Make sure it gets hand-delivered to Evelyn Valencik." He switched to talking out loud. "You will cooperate with us, NG. Or we will hand you over to the authorities to be charged with murder alongside Anderton and you will both hang. Very public. We don't want that now, do we?"

They'd resealed the dampening patch. It took more concentration than he thought he had to break the seal again without them seeing anything.

He got an immediate response that time, urgent, repeating. He allowed access and sent back, "They're going to contact Evelyn. Get to her before them, will you?"

"Roger that," came through loud and clear. Hal Duncan, so the Man's ship was close. "How's the situation down there, NG?"

"All green and rosy but I…" He broke off as Anya gripped a finger and twisted, demanding his attention. He shut off the pain without reacting and sent, "I can't see a way out. Ballack is here. He's the one running the show."

"We know," Duncan replied. "NG, there's a warrant out on you. This is going to blow sky high if we're not careful."

Ballack was standing up. "Have a think, NG."

Anya backed away with a parting caress to his cheek, guards closing in.

"I know," he sent quickly. "Tell Evelyn…"

Hands grabbed his shoulders, one pushed his head to the side and resealed the patch with a grunt.

The connection cut out.

"He's all yours," Ballack was saying to Zang as a rifle butt crashed into the side of his head. "Try not to kill him just yet, if you can help it."

He woke to silence. Tired, cold, eyelids heavy, no one near. Wherever he was, it was shielded, not from a dampening patch, something wider. His left forearm was throbbing, bleeding. He pulled energy from somewhere and healed it without thinking. He couldn't remember how he'd hurt it. Had no idea where he was.

Bright lights slammed on with a thud that resounded in his ears.

He squeezed his eyes shut. A rush of fluid flooded into his bloodstream. Drugs. Sedative. Too much to neutralise and he sank back into the dark.

He woke. Alone in the dark, still cold. Heart thumping. Poison was coursing through his body. Potent. Toxic. Vitals shutting down fast. He neutralised it.

The lights thudded on. Sedative pumped into his bloodstream. He tried to fight it, forced his eyes open. Another flood of sedative, stronger, sent him under.

He woke, drowsy, vaguely aware that something was wrong. He didn't move. There was no one near but he could feel people watching. He was in an isopod. Restrained. Bleeding. Femoral artery cut. He was dying. They were waiting to see what he did. Christ, it wasn't like he had much choice.

He healed the wound in his thigh, lightning fast. Took a deep breath and stopped his heart. Alarms screamed. Let the bastards mull over that.

He woke, a stimulant shocking him conscious, chest burning. He laughed and almost cried out from the pain. They must have resuscitated. They wanted him awake and it took a minute to realise they were screwing about with the oxygen levels.

He calmed his breathing and reached out, reading the mind of the first person he encountered, going as deep as he could, fast. Zang wanted to know how he healed, how he'd survived that crash after losing so much blood and walking away with nothing but shredded clothes and scars beneath. Their first experiment had confirmed it. Not smart of him but then what the hell else was he supposed to have done? He hadn't been thinking straight. It felt like he hadn't been thinking straight a lot lately.

They'd figured out that he healed when he was awake, that there was nothing automatic about it, nothing in his blood or DNA that was any different from anyone else human, except that peculiar marker they'd matched to the data from UM. They'd started out on the assumption that it was the alien DNA that was doing it, that it was regenerative, something from the stolen Earth research, Zang's longed-for elixir, but they'd tested it to its limits and had eliminated it as a potential contributory factor.

They were working their way through a list of parameters, had a list of tests they were going to pull next, stem cells, spinal fluid…

Screw that.

It was getting hard to breathe. He scanned round quickly, close to panic, figuring out where they had guns stationed, what might be weak points.

There weren't any. That was the problem. They were taking no chances. They were going to kill him again to see what he did.

He focused, found Zang, weighed up the odds and blew open the pod and the restraints, scrambling out, wires trailing, sparks flying and klaxons howling. Shots peppered the pod instantly, ricocheting all around him. He fell, knees giving out as he hit the floor, falling back as he threw out a shockwave of energy, blind firing, to take out the guards in the room.

He heard, "Nice one, Nikolai," whispered inside his head and for a cold, stomach-churning second it felt as though Sebastian was back.

He shook it off, forced himself to his feet and staggered to the door. His only plan was to find Zang, hold him hostage and if that failed, kill the bastard. He'd been promising himself that satisfaction for long enough.

There were more guards rushing towards the room. Too many. He backed in, closed the door, fused the lock mechanism and looked around for the first time. It was a medical facility, pristine, sterile, a far cry from UM's shit hole, overlooked by an observation room, shocked faces at the window, Zang in the centre of them.

Blast shutters slammed down over the window and door. He spun round, looking for a way out as a hiss of gas spurted from multiple vents. He almost laughed, the sting of tranquiliser hitting his throat.

The Senson engaged. "Jumped the gun a bit there, Nikolai."

Christ. "Elliott." He sank to his knees.

"The cavalry is about half an hour out. I have the room sealed but you're going to have to deal with the gas, I'm afraid."

He felt his vision going, couldn't help collapsing backwards to sprawl on the cold floor.

"I must say, you've generated some impressive data, Nikolai. Let me know when you're fit to move. You can't stay there, they have manual over-rides. You have about two minutes."

He didn't have much of anything left but he spent it neutralising the drug as best as he could, still queasy and sluggish but he managed to stand. He pulled a shirt and combat pants off one of the guards and shrugged into them, not bothering with boots that would be too big anyway and not even trying to struggle with the buttons.

"Good to go," he sent.

"Good," came back. "You need to climb."

A vent dropped open in the ceiling.

He stood looking at it. Not so long ago, it would have been a nifty run and jump to leap onto the pod, run up off the wall and catch the edge of it with one hand to swing up. Now? He braced himself.

"Just kidding," Elliott sent. "Go down. It'll be tight but I'm sure you'll manage."

A catch released on a floor panel.

Son of a bitch.

19

They listened in silence, some wondering why the Man hadn't been so efficient in his dealings with Nikolai himself. We need to know, they were thinking. We need to know what this boy can do, how he does it. Why did it take an enemy to inflict that upon him?

It was hard to sit there and be so judged. He'd never revealed even to them the extent of the research he had undertaken on Nikolai. It had never yielded the results he hoped for so it was not pertinent for them to know.

Only one spoke up. "Even so, one gifted human, even two or three, cannot stand against the might of the Bhenykhn. If we are to stay and fight, how do we nurture an entire army that can stand up to them?"

"We make allies," he said, his voice cold in that vast chamber. "We come out of the shadows and we make allies."

He made it out of the sterile bubble of Zang's medical facility, dropping out of one access vent and finding himself back in a stone walled corridor.

It was cold. He hugged the shirt around him and leaned against the wall, shivering. They were searching for him. Elliott was screwing around with their systems enough that they couldn't track him effectively but it was still tough to keep out of sight.

"How long?" he muttered, through the Senson whether anyone could hear it or not.

It seemed to take an eternity then Duncan sent, "Ten minutes, NG. Hold on, bud. We'll be right there."

He hadn't heard anything else from Elliott, except an occasional nudge to change direction when he was headed towards trouble.

He started moving again, working out a way from the details he'd trawled out of Zang. They were assuming he was trying to escape so slipping back down into the heart of the fortress wasn't impossible. He found the staircase he was looking for and dragged himself into a run, jumping down the steep steps and ignoring the stabbing pain shooting through his knee, busting through a locked door at the bottom and into a warren of passageways between the walls, screw trying to pace himself.

"NG, what are you doing? We need you out of there, buddy. You're going in the wrong direction."

"I'll see you on the roof," he sent back, still running, chest heaving. "They've got SAMs and an ECM pulsenet you're gonna have to take out. You got that covered, Elliott?"

The tech guy cut in, "Don't worry yourself with any of that, Nikolai. You're running out of time. It has a lockdown set to trigger on any security alert. Trust me, that kicks in, you're on your own. The surveillance system is disabled but there's a local alarm you'll need to neutralise."

It was going to be tight. He worked his way down, missed Zang's secret cubby hole twice and had to backtrack until he found it. There was another narrow winding staircase. He took a moment to scan round to check there was no one there then limped down it, trying to take his weight on the handrail without putting any pressure on his fingers, the knee screaming at him and giving out with every other step. He took out the alarm as he was going down. It was hidden but it wasn't tricky in itself. Even using a Senson, that would have taken even the best field-op thirty seconds, thirty long seconds, at best. It was almost too easy for him to reach ahead and click the circuits across.

The implant engaged as he reached the bottom and came up face to face with the thick metal door. "NG, buddy, we're coming in hot. Are you somewhere safe?"

He was about to break into Zang Tsu Po's private vault. It was either the safest place to be or the worst.

"How long?"

"Two minutes out."

He rested his forehead against the cold metal and threw the tumblers, carefully to get the timing right, running through the convoluted combination he'd taken from Zang's mind.

"One minute and closing."

It clanged.

He pushed.

It opened with a puff of released air. There was a bioscan matrix across the doorway. He could see the artefact resting on a pedestal, enclosed in a glass case, in the centre of the vault.

As soon as he broke the matrix, the system would go into overdrive. And the lockdown was going to trigger in thirty nine, thirty eight...

He didn't have time for anything elaborate.

He ran in.

The alarm screamed, a cage dropped from the ceiling, the door swung closed.

He turned, still running at the pedestal, held the massive weight of the door and the cage using every last ounce of energy he could wield, crashing into the glass case, elbow first and snatching the key as it fell.

He rolled through fragments of shattered glass as they were still falling, changed direction and scrambled back to the door. The mass of the door was beating him, the cage straining inches above his head as he ducked under it and squeezed through, letting it all go with a resounding bang. He fell back and sprawled on the cold stone floor, heart thumping, hands shaking, feet and arms bleeding.

The key fell into his lap. Seemingly identical to the others but with fresh smears of blood on its polished surfaces. He could hear gunfire echoing through the stone walls.

"Get to the roof, Nikolai." Elliott sounded concerned. That didn't bode well.

He didn't argue.

It was harder making his way back up. He stayed to the shadows and avoided Zang's people, trying to find a way through and round. They had search teams out, with dogs, for Christ's sake. He could hear the barking and snarling echoing in tandem with the shouts and thumping footsteps. There were no convenient maintenance tunnels, no access vents or crawl spaces. It was all stone walls, huge staircases and winding passageways. He thought about ducking back into that internal bubble of a medical facility but they had too many people in there, and his way out was via the roof.

He slowed as the number of bodies up ahead increased, search teams coordinating and defensive units of hired militia throwing up a solid defence. They didn't really have a chance against a combined force of the guild's best Security and the Man's elite guard.

Problem was, he was the wrong side of it.

He backed up.

The Senson engaged. Duncan. "NG, we can't get to you. You need to move."

He bit back a sarcastic comment and moved, trying to figure out a route from the intel he'd taken from Zang about the place. He dropped down a floor and tried to work around, veering dangerously close to the main hall where Ballack and Zang were marshalling their forces.

"How are you doing, NG?"

There was an explosion somewhere above, small, grenades by the feel of it.

"I'm…" He felt a shift in the bodies around him, as if he'd become the centre of attention.

He broke back into a run, cursing.

Shots peppered the wall next to him. He flinched back and sprinted, running across a staircase and heading up, wide open, not going anywhere near fast enough. He reached the top and a shot winged his arm, sending the key tumbling out of his grasp. Another punched into his stomach. He dropped, bleeding, scrambling forward on his knees after the polished chunk of platinum, nothing left to deflect a fly never mind a bullet, starting to lose his grip on who was where, vision getting narrow and foggy. He grabbed it, almost fumbled it out of numb fingers, and ran.

"Other way, NG." That was someone else.

He trusted whoever it was, changed direction and ran, one foot in front of the other, almost blind.

"NG, wait."

He stopped, leaned against the wall, doubled over.

"Go."

He went.

Shouts behind and up ahead.

"NG, hit the floor. Now."

He dropped, rolled and covered his head as shots ricocheted off the wall. Boots thundered past, rifles firing, the sound echoing loud in his ears.

A hand gripped his shoulder and he overheard Duncan send, "Control, be advised, we have 402." That meant the Alsatia had people here. The big man switched, 'You okay, bud?'

'I'm fine. Go get Zang and Ballack.'

Duncan nodded and moved off. They left him sitting there, five of the Man's elite in a circle at a discrete distance. He pulled energy from somewhere and pulled the bullet out of his gut, catching it in a blood-drenched hand and dropping it to the floor. He pressed his hand to the wound, clutched the key with the other, faded out and didn't even listen in to the battle while he waited for the extraction team.

It seemed to take ages before he sensed Quinn running up with Leigh and a couple of other medics, all in full combat gear.

He leaned his head back against the wall.

Leigh kneeled next to him as the other medics started to fuss with trauma patches and Quinn made sure there was no immediate danger.

"Rough day?" she whispered, blunt as always but that look in her eye that made him want to pull her close. She'd seen the package of data Elliott had pulled, knew exactly what they'd done to him. She was surprised that he was still bleeding.

Quinn walked up and crouched on the other side. "NG, I know you don't want to hear this but right now, you are the only one we have who can hear the Bhenykhn. You can't risk yourself like this anymore. We're keeping LC and Hil under wraps. We need to know you're safe too."

"We need to get Ballack."

"Already done," Quinn said. "We have him. He's claiming diplomatic immunity."

'Yeah right,' Leigh was thinking, 'after what he did to you.'

"What about Zang?"

Quinn shrugged. "We don't know. Elliott lost track of him while he was helping you out."

He didn't believe that for a second but he didn't comment. He hesitated to ask his next question. "Where's Evelyn?"

"Still on Poule as far as we know. Elliott intercepted all the transmissions from here so Ballack didn't get his message out…"

There was a but. He had to nudge, heart sinking. It felt like he'd reached the end of the line. "The warrant."

"It's been lodged everywhere," Quinn said with a grimace. "Come on, NG, let's go. We have this place secure."

So that meant the headquarters of both UM and Zang had been all but wiped out and taken over by the guild. The ripples from this were going to be horrendous.

He went to get up but stopped himself. "Did you get all their research?" he said. "They had the same samples here that were sent to the Earth lab. And they had something remote that jammed our Sensons. That has to be from the Bhenykhn."

"Elliott has it all," Quinn said. "I've set LC and Hil onto hacking into their systems so we get it direct. Come on, we need to go." The big man nodded to the medics and stood, moving away to check around.

NG sat back. Tired.

Leigh was looking at him, as if it was her reading his mind, seeing into his soul herself. "Come on, let's get you out of here." She grinned, raising her eyebrows at him, aware that she was saying that again. "Quinn's really good with LC and Hil."

That was a turn up. "You should have met Mendhel," he muttered.

"Who was your handler?" she asked, knowing she was overstepping the mark but curious as to who could ever have managed to keep him in line.

"Someone who deserved better than I ever gave back to her." He sat back and closed his eyes. He was tired. His whole life had been geared to being ready for this enemy and now they were here, he was tired and it felt like he'd lost whatever tenuous grip he'd ever had on it all.

"Don't get morose," she said. "Come on, we have aliens to fight. Everyone wants to know how you want this setting up."

This being the defence of the whole human populated galaxy, pulling together two sides that were at war, at least two guilds that hated him and wanted him dead, and the Order, god knows where they stood now.

He stretched out his leg and rubbed the knee with the edge of his wrist.

"I'm tired," he admitted.

She refrained from pointing out that he'd just been tortured, repeatedly, and said gently, "It has to be you, NG. You're the only one that knows them."

20

"And therein lies our problem," she said softly and for a moment it could have been only the two of them, the others gone, the judgement postponed. "The fate of an entire race, a galaxy, should never rest on the shoulders of one, even one so talented, especially one so fragile." She was thinking, how did we allow this to happen? Dismayed. Regretting that she hadn't stepped in earlier.

And in that moment, she looked at him and she realised that they had been pinning all their hopes on him alone in their own galaxy.

"Nikolai is far from fragile," he said, brusque, more defensive than necessary. "He is far stronger than any of us believed possible. He has the courage to face his fears… and he must face his fears lest they overpower and destroy him completely. Trust me. The error I made was in not pushing him further sooner."

Walking into the briefing room gave him an eerie feeling from long ago, of having to face the section chiefs when he'd screwed up as a field-op, the bad screw-ups when it wasn't just the chief of Ops but the whole lot of them, staring, judging, expecting a lot and somewhat disappointed.

He'd slept for about fifteen hours, showered and dressed. He'd restrapped his fingers and the knee, Leigh chiding him for not healing himself, then she'd walked down here with him. She left him at the door.

Kimi Itomara was sitting between Pen Halligan and Matt Jameson, all of them on the far side of the table. The Order, Winter and Earth waiting to hear what the Thieves' Guild had to say.

They had everything laid out in front of them including reports on what had happened with UM at Poule and at Zang's fortress on Winter.

They stood as he walked in. That was something. He could feel that Jameson wasn't a hundred percent but clearly the colonel wanted to be there.

Pen spoke first, sitting as NG sat. "How the hell do we defend against this?"

There was a bottle of whisky on the table, a full glass set out for him already, and it was tempting to let them talk and hit the alcohol but they were looking to him for some kind of plan. "They're going to attack Earth and Winter, simultaneously. You've seen the numbers. I don't know what we do."

Itomara was quiet, in mind and presence. The man was almost meditating.

Jameson was fighting a debilitating headache but he spoke up. "Come on, we need to inform our military intelligence. Coordinate some kind of defence. How long do you reckon we have? Months? Weeks?"

They were all wanting to know why he hadn't acted sooner, sent up a balloon, something, some galaxy wide alert.

He dampened down his instinctive response. He didn't want to justify his actions and the last thing he wanted to do was sit here and explain how he even knew about the aliens' plans, how it had taken him this long to access the intel.

He looked from face to face. "You want to know how we can beat them? We stop them getting here." He reached for the glass. "Because once they're here, we're done."

They were surprised he was being defeatist, that wasn't what they'd been expecting.

All three of them had thought he would come in here full of fighting talk, inspire them to pull together against this common foe. They thought he'd be up for a fight, even though they knew what he'd just been through.

He picked up the glass, hand shaking, very aware that they were watching. He took a drink of whisky that warmed his throat.

There were also copies of the warrants out on him and LC, spread out there on the table.

"We're working out where the Bhenykhn have other advance recon units," he said. "The problem I have is that I can't figure out how to tell anyone about this. You know the position I'm in. I can't take this out to anyone. And the Thieves' Guild doesn't have many friends right now. We don't exist. People who know us don't trust us and we don't trust them. No one is going to believe that we aren't pulling a scam."

It chimed with all three of them because, still, even now, they were sitting there wondering if any of it was true. He hadn't shown them anything but pictures and numbers.

"How can I convince anyone else when I can't convince you?"

Pen nodded, thinking he wanted to see a goddamned alien for himself.

"I'm taking LC and Duncan to Poule," NG said. "Get them face to face with that alien. See what they can do. See if we can develop it any further. Come with us."

If Pen needed to see it to believe it was real then he was welcome. They were all welcome to troop down there and gawp at the massive Bhenykhn in its cage.

Whatever it took.

"We've come some way on reverse engineering their technology but that needs to be upped," he said. "We need to be able to counter everything they throw at us. We should be able to progress it more now we have UM and Zang's research." He took another sip, wanting to neck it but knowing how bad that would look and wanting more to look like he was in control here. "Matt, if you can figure out a way to inform the Earth military without them freaking out and descending on us, let me know. Pen, same for Winter. But I won't compromise what we have."

"Which is you?" Pen said.

"Us versus them, we lose," NG said. "We need to use everything we have. Anything that might give us an advantage."

"Including the Thieves' Guild?" Itomara said. He wanted access to this ship, to the council.

"Go to the Alsatia. Evelyn will be our liaison," NG said and drained the whisky. What the hell. "She'll give you whatever you need and I trust you will give her whatever she asks." He stood up. "I took out an advance unit. That's all. I can lead you to another but I can't take on their full force."

The headache kicked back in as soon as they dropped out of jump in Poule's outer system. It was oppressive, draining, and added to the apprehension eating at him at the thought of having to face Evelyn, it was making him want to crawl away.

He dressed in combat gear, unstrapping the fingers and messing about with pressure tape, wrapping each finger separately and trying to hold a gun.

Leigh stood in the doorway watching, not impressed and not hiding it. "I thought you said you don't want to go hand to hand with them again."

"I don't." But he'd lived with a gun at hand since he was a kid, it was second nature and he didn't want to feel as defenceless as he'd been on Winter.

"I hate to say this," she said, "but could you not try the virus? It would heal all this for you." She was thinking that as much as what he did was incredible, he had to be awake. She'd seen the data Zang and his cronies had gathered. LC and Duncan could be flat out unconscious and the virus healed for them.

He didn't know what to say, couldn't admit that he couldn't risk the virus because he didn't know what it would do.

She read the look on his face and said, resigned, "You know what I'm thinking. I don't need to say it."

She could read body language better than he could read minds. She leaned in. "It's Evelyn you need to go talk to."

"I know."

She smiled. "Make sure you do."

It wasn't that easy. Evie had gone by the time they got there, gone back to the Alsatia. It was a relief that he didn't have to face her and he hated himself for thinking it. She'd had no way of finding out about the warrant out here but it was pretty much guaranteed that the Alsatia would know. So now she would. He'd grabbed Quinn, said awkwardly that he didn't want Evelyn to find out without someone there that he trusted, and the big man had nodded, suggested that Hilyer could do with a trip to the Alsatia again, to test some of the stuff they'd been working on, and they'd bugged out.

It wasn't ideal but NG kicked it out of his mind and concentrated on here and now.

They went straight to the cage, out onto the balcony, traipsing through Maeve's chambers, a contingent of elite guard armed with both FTH and live rounds splitting between the upper and lower levels.

The Bhenykhn was waiting, watching.

Pen and Jameson swore as they saw it in the flesh for the first time. It was weird to pick up the disbelief and revulsion. The rest of them had been living with the nightmares so long, they were almost numb to it.

Itomara just stared, but he hadn't seen its like before, that was easy enough to read.

NG leaned against the handrail casually. He wasn't entirely sure what he had in mind.

He could feel that Leigh was apprehensive. She'd dealt with the injuries the Bhenykhn could inflict and she didn't want to see any of them hurt again, too seasoned a combat medic to know that was reasonable and trying to be colder than was natural for her. It was hard when the stench and the chill damp in the air was flashing them all back there.

The others were waiting for him to give them some idea of what to do. He half wished the Chief or Quinn, Arturo, or god forbid even Carmen if he was going to get nostalgic, could be here to tell him, just lay down a brief and give him the orders like it was a tab.

LC glanced at him, recognising the name of the legendary handler, picking it out of his thoughts.

It was hard not to flash back to those simpler times. He'd

152

worked with Carmen over a hundred years ago. They'd topped the standings together for a decade and he'd never appreciated back then just how much she'd done for him.

"You're really Andreyev?" LC sent through the Senson.

"Yep."

"How did you crack that tab on Temerity?" It was what the kid had been itching to ask.

It was legendary. Toughest tab ever completed. It had brought in a fortune, in cash and kudos. He'd walked in, taken it and walked out.

He squinted across. "LC, I've always been able to hear what people think and see where they are. Always. Imagine being able to do what you can now back when you were running tabs."

It felt like he'd been caught cheating.

"That's why you reset the standings," LC sent.

It didn't matter.

None of it mattered anymore.

NG looked down at the Bhenykhn. He could feel its mind, feel it holding back, waiting to see what they were going to do. It was taking a lot to guard against it, just this one Bhenykhn, and he could remember only too well the intensity of the pain from the hive, when there had been hundreds of them. When he'd had Sebastian to protect him. What the hell was that going to be like if there were thousands?

He took hold of its mind, fast, vicious, draining its energy, channelling the memory of that pain into a determination to beat it now.

It was fighting him.

He drove it to its knees, much easier than last time. It switched its attention so fast, he didn't see it in time to stop it.

LC cried out and crumpled to the floor.

Dammit. NG punched back, hit it hard and sent it flying, sprawling, out cold before anyone else could react.

He turned. Leigh was already at LC's side, the kid conscious, curled up and swearing. She was fretting about his heart rate and wondering what the hell they were doing.

NG crouched down. "Were you trying anything?"

LC muttered, "No," palm pressed up against his forehead.

NG rested his hand on the back of the kid's neck, easy enough to reduce the pain and ease the pressure. "You fought off Sebastian. You should be able to block it."

"I could hear Sebastian," LC said, blinking bloodshot eyes and accepting the hand to get up. "I didn't see that coming."

"You need to be able to." NG looked around for Duncan. "You too." He turned back to the cage, sensing the Bhenykhn stirring, feeling its mind focus, the hate and anger tempered only by a greater need to learn and understand this foe it found itself facing. "Let's see if we can really piss it off."

21

To hear of an alien so close again set them on edge.

"They were audacious to take on the Bhenykhn like that," one said, unnerved.

"Foolish," injected another.

"Is that what it takes?" one asked, unsettled by the humans' capacity for violence, by Nikolai's capacity for violence.

It had always been a dichotomy in him, extreme compassion and empathy on one hand, a chilling almost berserk ferocity, cold calculating ruthlessness, on the other. And that was just Nikolai. Sebastian was another matter entirely.

"He does what is necessary," the Man said. "It is not easy to wield such power. Not when one has a conscience." He looked along the line. "And be grateful that Nikolai does have a conscience. Without it, we would truly be lost."

It went for LC every time. Until the kid reached his limit, fired back instinctively and dropped it, out cold, blood pouring from its ears and nose.

"Christ, don't kill it," NG said. He needed it alive.

He got a hooded glance from the kid who looked like shit and was about done.

They'd got nowhere.

"Can neither of you sense anything from it?"

Duncan and LC both said no. Emphatically. No doubt. No possible glimpse of what might be.

They had nothing. LC could zap it the same way he could disintegrate a playing card. Duncan hadn't grasped manipulating energy but he was better at reading thoughts, facts, and harder to read himself when he wanted to block. That was why the Bhenykhn hadn't attacked him.

NG leaned on his elbows against the handrail, trying to figure out what to do next.

The Senson engaged with no etiquette of request or permission. Elliott. "Quit fooling around," the tech guy sent. "You're wasting time. I believe you have the keys from UM and Zang for me, Nikolai. Let's meet half way. On the orbital. It was most entertaining last time we were here. I must say, I'm impressed by the way your corporation has taken over the operation here. Very nice. I never would have guessed Centaur was Thieves' Guild. There's more to you than I realised."

More than he'd raided from the Alsatia, he meant. Centaur was the Man's. Not somewhere they wanted Elliott's attention.

He looked round. "We're done. Come back to the Man's ship with me. I don't want you here with it without me."

The orbital on Poule was all but abandoned. Evelyn had made the decision to mothball the whole station, taken what she wanted and pulled out, pretty much pulled the plug.

It was strange to walk past the empty cages, footsteps echoing across the vast dock space, couldn't help comparing it to the flashbacks LC had thrown at him from the last time Gallagher's freighter had docked here. It was eerily quiet.

He walked out onto the docks, four of the Man's elite guard around him and a team of Security flanking them. No other life signs inside the entire orbital. Yet there was a light flickering in an office up ahead. A shadow moving. Elliott was already in there, waiting for him.

He didn't stand as NG walked in, sitting behind the desk, screens on standby, nothing in front of him, a sly confidence in his expression. He gestured towards the seat.

NG hefted his bag onto the desk and took out the two artefacts. They almost looked alive as the light danced across the polished angular surfaces.

He didn't sit.

"How do we control the weapon, Elliott? When it's activated? If it was so powerful that it was dangerous, how do we control it?"

Elliott took the UM key and turned it in his hand. "What's your real question, Nikolai?"

"Who are you?"

Elliott gave a small chuckle but didn't reply.

"I have no idea who you are," NG said, careful to keep his tone non-confrontational, "and apparently, I'm about to hand you the keys to the most powerful weapon ever built."

"Who I am isn't relevant," Elliott said. He stood, picking up the artefacts as if they didn't weigh a thing. "You have little choice, Nikolai. Right now, you are the only thing standing between the Bhenykhn and the human race. You. Alone. How ironic… you are the most wanted man in this galaxy, everyone is after your head and yet you are the only one who can save them. You need whatever allies you can scrape together." He turned away.

"Who are you, Elliott?"

The tall thin guy stopped, paused and turned.

NG stood his ground. He wasn't going to be intimidated.

Elliott regarded him with narrow eyes. Not impressed. "Why are you questioning me now? Into whose mind have you been prying? Itomara? Zang? You've been associating with some powerful people, NG. They have no idea. Come on, Nikolai, you'd rather listen to the Order than someone who has been on your side since the start of all this? I didn't give up Luka. I've done nothing but help you." His tone was cold, almost bitter. He took a step closer. "What you…"

Dense black hit NG behind the eyes. Whatever Elliott was saying was lost. The pressure was unbearable. He tried to block it, felt himself sway, close to blacking out. He could feel his temperature rising, legs weak, nausea welling in his stomach. He reached for the edge of the desk, anything to steady himself, breathing too shallow.

An urgent incoming was hammering at the Senson. He couldn't acknowledge it. Couldn't see straight.

The pressure increased and he felt his knees going, a warm trickle leaking from his nose, eyes, ears.

He hit the floor, darkness closing in, hands grasping him as he fell.

"Kill it," he heard, distant, through fog. "Kill it now or it's going to kill NG."

He tried to say, "No." Christ, no.

'Too late.'

'Sebastian.'

The pain vanished, awareness creeping back slowly.

Leigh was trying to get through to him on the implant. He couldn't think straight to answer.

Whoever had him was lowering him to the ground. He shrugged them off, recognising them as Security and muttering, "I'm fine," sitting up, blinking and looking round for Elliott. He wiped his hand across his face, smearing it red and struggling to see.

The tech guy had gone but the Senson engaged with his usual abrupt connection. "There's another one."

'It's a scout ship. They connected,' Sebastian murmured. *'If it gets away, it will take everything it knows back to the hive.'*

"Don't let it get away," he sent.

"That's going to be difficult."

He couldn't feel anything from the Bhenykhn on the planet.

'That's because it's dead.'

He couldn't help the shiver, numb, cold, spreading ice into his veins. *'No, I needed it alive.'*

"Track the scout ship," he sent, knowing how desperate he sounded and hating it.

"I am," Elliott replied.

The connection cut out.

NG pushed himself to his feet, still trembling, wiping blood from his face.

'My god, Nikolai, what the hell have you been doing to my body? What's it been? A few weeks? Months? Didn't you learn anything from me?' There was a laugh.

Christ, he'd actually tried to find Sebastian. Now he was back, he felt sick.

He felt the injuries heal, the broken bones mend, a flood of energy flowing into every cell of his body to fend off the fatigue that had been pulling at him for so long.

'You didn't heal yourself.' Sebastian laughed again. *'Nikolai, that is just twisted. You've been punishing yourself all this time? Torturing yourself over what happened to Devon, what happened on Erica? I always said you were masochistic, but my word, Nikolai, you've really taken things to a new low this time.'*

It wasn't that simple but he wasn't going to argue.

Once the pain had gone, it felt like he'd imagined it.

He backed up against the desk, breathing erratic, a cold chill in his stomach, bracing himself, expecting Sebastian to fight him for control.

Sebastian laughed. *'Fight you? No… Trust me, Nikolai, I can and will take control whenever I so desire. But for now, you well and truly have the frontline.'*

That was difficult to believe.

'Believe what you want. I'm not going to snatch control from you. I don't like pain, remember, and where we are heading, Nikolai, there's going to be a lot. Trust me.'

He still didn't believe it.

He sat there, perched on the edge of the desk, working to calm his breathing.

LC was trying to get through on the implant, concerned.

Sebastian was highly amused. *'He knows I'm back. So how many of these creatures know about me now, Nikolai? Any more than just your pet telepaths?'*

He tried not to think.

'Ah, Leigh,' Sebastian said, picking it out of his mind, *'the little Wintran medic from Erica. Nice replacement for Martinez. Or is it Devon? You don't waste any time, do you?'*

That stung. More than it should have. She wasn't and never would be, for either of them.

'I'm teasing you, Nikolai. We have more to worry about than

who you take to your bunk at night. Have some fun while you can.'
Sebastian paused then laughed maliciously. *'Ah, no, I see what's going on here. Really? Still punishing yourself? I know you can be overly sensitive but really?'*

He was going to go insane. He'd forgotten what it was like. Sebastian was reading his memories, innermost thoughts, everything from the last few weeks, stripping his soul bare.

'At least we don't have to bother with a briefing,' he thought, not managing to keep the bitterness from his tone.

Sebastian didn't seem to notice, or care. *'Nice move with Jameson. And Rodan. I knew you had it in you, Nikolai.'*

'This isn't the first time I've come up against one of them. Why have you come back now?'

'Because they were killing you. Two more seconds of that and you and I would have been history. For good. I really thought you would have got the hang of this by now.'

He'd been starting to think he had. *'Have you been watching?'*

'No, Nikolai, I've been sleeping. And now I'm back. You seem to have found me some aliens.'

Leigh was at the airlock, horrified, relieved, looking at him as if she didn't know what, or who, to expect. She was looking at the blood on his face and neck, thinking that he'd almost died. For real. She'd been watching his stats.

"We need to catch it," he said, walking fast through the Man's ship.

She kept up with him, noticing that he wasn't limping any more.

He opened a link to Morgan. "I need it alive. Follow it."

"Elliott's taken the Duck," the captain replied. "We've sent fighters but it's fast."

"Get us after it. We can't let it get away."

He felt the engines change, felt the mass of the ship shifting as it fell away from its berth on the orbital.

She was looking at him as if she didn't trust him, didn't even know for certain that it was him.

"It's me," he said, unwinding the tape from his fingers and flexing his hand. "I thought I told you, Sebastian has blue eyes."

"But Sebastian is back?"

He nodded.

"He's healed you?"

"Yep." He'd never realised how much Sebastian had done to keep his energy levels up.

'I take what we need. I don't have your conscience.'

Leigh was watching as he unfastened the casing from his arm, not quite believing what she was seeing.

'She likes you but then, of course, why wouldn't she? You can make her do whatever you want. You always did need someone to like you, Nikolai. It's a weakness and it's pathetic.'

He really had forgotten what this was like.

He rubbed his arm, flexing the muscles in the forearm properly for the first since Erica.

'We don't need anyone,' Sebastian murmured. *'I thought I taught you that.'*

'Can you not stop the scout?' he thought.

The reply was flippant. *'Not at this distance.'*

"I want it alive," he sent to Morgan. "Catch up to it."

"It's going to make the jump point before we can get there."

"Then we need to follow it."

He switched to the others, open channel, breaking into a run, "Get your asses to Wraith. We're going after it."

22

There were audible intakes of breath as he mentioned Sebastian. Some went so far as to shiver. They found it abhorrent, despicable, what he had done in taming the boy.

She had been the only one to see the necessity in his actions, to empathise with the dilemma he'd had. She looked at him with sorrow in her eyes as if she could see what was to come.

"Trust me," he said. "Be grateful that Nikolai is who he is and is as strong as he is. It is Sebastian that we need but without Nikolai, he would be uncontrollable."

They ran on board, his elite guard and a Security detail from the Alsatia with them, and got kitted up as Wraith dropped from the coupling and raced after the scout. It wasn't easy at the flat out, engines screaming pace she was setting, but a helluva lot easier without broken fingers and a smashed up arm.

'*You could have healed it yourself,*' Sebastian chided.

He didn't rise to it. He strapped on pouches and stashed extra magazines. He didn't want to fight them hand to hand, but if it came to it...

'*If it comes to that, we're done. Just get me within range again.*'

'*Don't kill it. I need it alive.*'

Sebastian laughed. '*Ah, yes, of course you do. Does anyone else know about your little secret?*'

He felt LC's attention as the kid glanced up from where he was standing with the others, keeping his distance, wary, not sure where he stood with NG now Sebastian was back.

No, no one knew and he shut it out of his mind. He grabbed a handhold as the ship shifted course. They were going fast but it wasn't enough. If it made jump, they were screwed. He had no idea what range the hive worked at. Within a system? Within orbital distances? Ship to ship, decent existing tech could reach to the outer system, jump range easy. Even a Senson could reach from the surface of a planet to a ship in orbit. The Bhenykhn? He had no idea.

He called forward, heading to the bridge, "We need to stop it. Whatever it takes."

What it took was breaking safety parameters.

'*Are you ready for this, Nikolai?*' Sebastian murmured.

He wasn't ready. None of them were ready. He walked onto the bridge and dropped into the empty co-pilot's seat. He could see from the numbers on the main screen that it was about to jump. Elliott was feeding calculations through to them, a rapid stream of data that was coming in far faster than anything they had to predict a jump vector.

He could feel that cold blade bite into his chest, blood pounding in his ears.

"Follow it," he said to the crew, a lump in his throat, ice in his stomach. And he gave the order to jump.

They dropped out into deep space, edge of the Between, blank screens and for a second he thought they'd lost it.

'*There,*' Sebastian hissed.

It was moving fast.

The pilot changed course and accelerated hard, pushing Wraith to her limits.

The Duck had dropped in behind them, the data feed hardly interrupted. NG stared at the numbers.

The Bhenykhn was gearing up for another jump. Skipping out fast and trying to lose them. Neat trick.

They had enough capacity left for one more so long as it wasn't far. The Duck was too far behind to catch up, the Man's ship nowhere in sight yet. If they jumped again this fast, they'd be on their own.

"Don't lose it," he muttered.

He felt a curse flash through the pilot's mind but she didn't question him, taking the calculations from the navigator and throwing Wraith into jump the instant the Bhenykhn ship made its move.

They emerged this time out onto the edge of a system, uncharted, the alien ship racing inwards towards an outer planet. The pilot didn't hesitate in throwing Wraith headlong into a course to intercept.

There was no way it could go for jump again, not this close. They had it so long as they didn't lose it and that wasn't going to happen because he could feel it tugging at the back of his mind. Sebastian was tracking it, taunting it, almost purring as he toyed with his prey, as Wraith closed in on it.

It was never going to be that simple.

NG stared at the charts and numbers on the screens until they blurred.

There was something wrong.

The Bhenykhn ship was turning. Not fleeing.

He felt a realisation of something hit LC as the kid put it together. He shifted in his seat, looked back and saw LC look up, freaked out, standing and trying to move down the aisle as the ship lurched under his feet, sending, 'No, NG, wait. This is…'

The Bhenykhn ship fired on them.

The pilot threw Wraith into a desperate manoeuvre too slow to avoid the incoming blast of energy that skimmed her hull and sent them spinning.

NG flinched, grabbing the harness, nothing he could do as LC was sent tumbling, whatever the kid was thinking cut off as he crunched into the bulkhead, stunned, one of the elite guard reaching out to grab him.

Sebastian laughed. NG felt the blast he threw at the alien. It hurt but didn't knock it out.

"Shit, it's powering up to jump," the pilot said, rolling with the spin and bringing them round. "We have nothing left."

It was one of those sickening decisions.

"Open fire," he said, cold, no hesitation, knowing they could destroy it, needing it alive but knowing they couldn't let it get away.

They fired, Wraith's ordinance impressive for her size, the scout ship's shield flaring as they winged it.

Sebastian hit it again.

It turned, spiralling.

And vanished.

"Shit."

For a second, his stomach knotted then the screen showed a blip, closer in to the planet's orbit.

The pilot cursed and set course, throwing everything she had into getting closer.

NG pinched the bridge of his nose, not realising the pressure was building so badly until it sparked a headache that made him blink.

He sat up.

'*Sebastian?*'

There was no reply.

He turned, glancing back at the others. Leigh was back there, looking at him, concerned.

The edges of his vision were darkening.

'*Sebastian?*' he tried again.

Nothing.

'LC?'

Nothing.

Time slowed.

NG felt like he had his hand poised over a chessboard, realising what was happening with a sickening knot clenching in his stomach. They couldn't run, they couldn't fight. They had zero jump capacity and couldn't risk a jump anyway. Not this close to the mass of a planet.

"Drop a beacon," he said quietly, calmly, watching as the pilot carried out the order without question. An emergency beacon meant they were in the shit. He felt the tension in the crew rise a notch.

'NG, what's going on?' Duncan thought at him, sharp, the

question cutting like a laser through the cacophony that was building inside his head.

He could hardly form the words to reply. "There are more of them."

The big marine loomed through the doorway, gripping the frame. "Shouldn't we be pulling back?"

"Too late."

"You want one alive."

He could see out of the corner of his eye and in the minds of the crew that shapes were appearing on the monitors, fast moving ships, some of them massive.

He pressed his hand against his eyes. "We need one alive."

"Grab it and run?"

"Something like that."

"Sir?" The pilot was tense, wanting orders.

"Don't slow down," he muttered. "We're still going after it."

Duncan wasn't convinced. He switched to direct thought. 'NG, buddy, if it's connected with the hive, it knows about us. About you.'

'Yep.'

'You're gambling that they still want you alive.'

'Whether they do or not, we need one so we can get the virus right.'

The pressure intensified into a pain that flared behind his eyes.

"It's not just a recon unit," he heard LC say, coming round, feeling the frustration as the kid tried to shake off the concussion. "It's brought us to one of their FOBs. Where's NG?" The kid raised his voice. "NG, there's more of them here than there were on Erica. This is a base."

It didn't change anything. They had nowhere to go. NG rattled off a list of orders, getting the navigator to work out the trajectories, vectors, running fast simulations of which ships could get where, when, then sat and watched, squinting through eyes that were aching. Damaged as they were, they could still reach the scout before any other vessels were in range. That was all he needed to hear. He outlined the plan and sat back, trying to figure out how long it would take Elliott and Morgan to follow them, how long it would be before the Alsatia responded to the beacon. The jump drive was recharging but it wouldn't be ready before they'd get overrun. Even if they turned and ran now. Their only hope was to snatch the scout and rely on the others turning up to deflect the fight away from them, give them a route out.

And whatever, every Bhenykhn here now knew what the prisoner on Poule had known and it would only take one of them to skip out and meet with the rest of the hive.

He could feel it in the pressure pushing against his awareness, more intense than anything he'd experienced at Erica. Like being pinned in a spotlight that was getting brighter and hotter by the minute. Relentless.

He became aware of someone at his shoulder. "Is there anything that will help?" Leigh whispered.

"Whisky if you can find some."

She gave him a half smile. "Where's Sebastian?"

"I don't know. Holding them off."

He'd forgotten how bad this could get.

He could hear Duncan talking, giving the others orders, planning contingencies, coming up with a strategy to disable the scout ship so they could board. He would have made a great handler. LC was sitting listening, contributing, giving them a steady account of what he knew from the intel dump.

It was hard not to feel useless, virtually incapacitated by pain he should have been able to handle.

And it was getting worse as they were getting closer.

He couldn't see any more so he kept his eyes closed, breathing through it, listening in as the crew pushed Wraith to her limit, feeling himself sinking. So much for being the one hope to deal with this invasion.

It lifted abruptly, pain gone so fast, it was disorientating. He opened his eyes, not trusting it wouldn't hit him again.

'Listen to me carefully,' Sebastian murmured. 'We have one

chance of pulling this off. Tell them to ditch the nonsense with the EM pulse. It won't get through its shields. Get me close and I'll take it down. They'll have maybe five minutes to board and seize it. How are you planning to get away then, Nikolai? I take it you do have a plan.'

'Elliott is following us.'

Sebastian snorted. *'Let's just get this alien for you to play with. They want you, by the way. I know I've told you before, but do not, whatever you do, get yourself captured by these creatures, Nikolai.'*

'I don't intend to.'

He pulled himself together, relayed the plan to the bridge crew and went back to the cabin area to do the same to the others. Duncan didn't like it but kept his mouth shut, well aware that this was NG's show. He told them what he wanted and went back to the bridge, sat down and put his feet up on the console.

This wasn't his show. It was Sebastian's.

It went well. Right up to the point where they coupled with the alien ship, hulls bumping at speed and grapples groaning. The Bhenykhn weren't going to let one of their own get taken that easily. A fighter screamed out of nowhere, missiles flying. NG yelled a warning but there was no time. Both ships were hit. Sparks flew out of the main console, klaxons clamouring, power loss plunging them into darkness.

Someone was shouting about a breach.

A hand grabbed his shoulder, another releasing the harness, one of the elite guard in powered armour hauling him up and out of the bridge. Another had LC. They were propelled towards the airlock and pushed through into the drop ship, bodies crowding in after them.

Another missile hit, jolting the ship, the shockwave from the explosion billowing clouds of hot air and debris around them.

Someone yelled, "Go," and they dropped. Combat drop. Vicious, stomach churning, head spinning g-forces.

They hit the atmosphere and he could feel the burn in every muscle, neck straining, struggling to stay conscious. Whoever was piloting the drop ship was risking the tightest angle of descent.

It seemed like forever before they pulled up and banked hard in a sickening, gut-wrenching manoeuvre. The sergeant of the Security detail was shouting for a sound-off. There were at least five responses, Duncan included, another four from the elite guard, plus his. LC was struggling but he managed to shout out. That was it. NG almost panicked, not able to sense Leigh for a second but then he heard her yell her name, whatever she said next lost in the buzz in his ears as the drop ship banked again, descending fast. They crashed through what felt like trees, knocked sideways and dropping, slewing round and skidding to a halt.

The engines cut, the silence resounding. They were down. Not completely intact. Stranded. And surrounded by enemies that were closing in fast. Alien enemies that could sense exactly where they were. They had no way out and nowhere to hide.

'Well done, Nikolai. Well fucking done.'

23

She sat perfectly composed. Still. Face almost unreadable.

"They were captured?" one of them exclaimed.

She wanted to rise, take this to private chambers, crack open the wine herself.

He could tell that she wanted to shout at him to tell them everything, but she knew that he would. The devil was in the detail and she knew that too. In order to prevail, they needed to learn from their mistakes.

"Nikolai is too foolhardy," another said. "How can we rely so heavily upon one who risks himself and others with such disregard?"

"He knows what must be done," she said, taking the words out of the Man's mouth before he had the chance to utter them. "And he does it." She looked at him, gaze piercing. "Continue, tell us what happened?"

They moved fast to get clear, grabbing ammo and rations, medical supplies, stripping the drop ship bare, triggering self destructs in all its data systems, and activating another beacon.

"They want us alive," NG said, grabbing a pack. "We need to find high ground. Somewhere clear. Somewhere we can make a stand and pick them off. They won't risk bombing."

No one asked if he was sure. Or how he was so sure.

The Sensons were jammed. No surprise there. They'd all read the briefings, all knew exactly what they were facing.

'*You know what you faced last time,*' Sebastian warned, still pissed. '*Don't make assumptions, Nikolai, or we will die here.*'

'*Can you do what you did last time?*'

'You just concentrate on staying alive. Let me deal with the Bhenykhn.'

They scrambled out into a warm and humid forest. The pilot of the drop ship gave them a fast run down on topography, planetary stats, whatever he'd managed to gather in those brief minutes. Best case, they had about six hours to survive before any kind of help had a chance of arriving.

The plan was to stay close and make their way to a hill top about two kilometres north.

They didn't make it.

NG slid down a bank, strafing fire from a fighter craft kicking up dirt and stones, shredding foliage all around him. He shielded his head, grasping his rifle as firmly as he could and scrambling for cover, a shot clipping his trailing leg and others winging the pack on his back. He rolled, no warning as Sebastian took control, shoving him aside and focusing with chilling clarity on the Bhenykhn fighter pilot.

There was nothing he could do but Sebastian was fast. He threw a blast of energy with piercing accuracy at the pilot, and let go as fast as he'd taken over, leaving NG flat on his back, gasping for breath, watching as the craft slewed sideways and nosedived, disappearing into the trees and exploding, a mushroom cloud of black smoke billowing up into the grey sky.

Someone grabbed his shoulder and yanked him upright, pulling him along.

'What happened to they won't bomb us?' Duncan sent, some distance away and getting harried by another fighter.

'I don't know,' NG sent to them both, still trembling. 'We need a clearing. We need a killing ground.'

'Yes, you do. There are ground troops incoming. You have about five minutes.'

They made it to a slight rise before they heard the roar of the troop carriers then they stood back to back, defensive formation, ammunition split between them.

NG stood in the centre, rifle up, sweat trickling down his back, blood pouring down his leg, and breathing laboured. He took a second to stop the bleeding at least, no time to fix the wound completely, turning and tracking the ships as they thundered round, dropping pods into the trees, and counting twenty four, six units if they were set up the same as on Erica.

'*Do I get any warning next time?*' he thought, struggling not to freak out completely. He flexed his hand, shaking out a cramp. He could feel the battle-ready tension in the soldiers around him, cold focus in the elite guard and that same chilling detachment in LC that the kid had got on Erica.

Sebastian wasn't impressed. '*You have three more waves of ground troops incoming after this, seven gunships on their way and two more fighters,*' he said. '*That's it for now. Get through this and we get a reprieve before they get their next wave of ships into orbit above us.*'

LC was listening in and relayed the information to the others.

NG shifted his weight. As much as Sebastian was shielding him from the worst of it, he could feel them approaching.

The Bhenykhn stopped in a circle around them, about three hundred yards out. Out of sight through the trees. He could either smell them through the leafy undergrowth or he was imagining it. At least on Erica, there'd been a cold wind that had cleared the air. Here, the forest floor was damp underfoot, decaying, as if the Bhenykhn were rising from it.

The alien warriors didn't move.

NG turned slowly, seeing them as Sebastian was seeing them, mind to mind, the grunts and the squad leaders, standing there, waiting for the order to attack, hefting their weapons.

The rifle was heavy in his arms, muscles complaining already.

If anything, knowing what to expect was making the waiting worse.

'*Screw this,*' Sebastian murmured.

NG felt his focus sharpen, breath catching in his chest as Sebastian took over, connected with them and lanced into the minds of the six squad leaders and from them into their units.

He let go again, just as fast.

NG gasped, thrust back into control. He collapsed, shivering, almost retching, down onto one knee, head down, letting the rifle drop from hands he could hardly feel.

Duncan was yelling. "They're dead. Go check them. Get their weapons."

They moved out, none of the others knowing exactly what had happened but not questioning the orders.

NG was trembling. He couldn't get it under control.

He looked up.

LC was staring at him, staring at the ground around him.

He lowered his eyes.

He was kneeling on scorched earth. Blackened grass and moss that crumbled to dust under his touch. It was bone dry, parched and dead, in a perfect circle around him.

He staggered to his feet and backed away from it.

Christ.

Leigh stopped him, whispering, "It's okay," as if he was a hurt animal or a small child.

"I want you to hide," he muttered. "Find somewhere close and hide."

She didn't reply but she was thinking that he didn't need to worry about her, she wasn't going to get in the way.

"Where's Sebastian?" she said. She was thinking how different he'd looked. Not just the eyes, everything, the way he stood, the way he'd laughed.

NG sucked in a breath of warm air. "I can't hear anything from them so he must be shielding me."

"NG, don't you think it was a bit too convenient that we were at Poule when that scout ship appeared, right there?" She was thinking it had lured them here. What if someone had sent it there, to Poule, just when NG and the Man's ship were there? When the Bhenykhn there knew everything there was to know about NG? What if UM weren't the only people with access to the Bhenykhn?

He couldn't think straight.

"We're relying on the Duck to rescue us," she said, "but, NG, what if it was Elliott? He's been entangled in this since he took the Duck to Sten's to pick up Gallagher. We have no idea who he is or what he wants. What if Elliott set this up?"

"Then we're screwed." He was still shivering, cold despite the humid heat. He was vaguely aware that she was popping Epizin into his wrist but he couldn't feel the drug, didn't get any of the usual warmth from it.

'*Suck it up,*' Sebastian hissed. "*We have incoming.*'

The others were coming back, running back into position around him, tossing Bhenykhn weapons into a pile in the centre of that dead spot, not even noticing it.

Duncan did, glancing at LC, the two of them reluctant to mention it, suspecting what it meant.

LC relayed the incoming, muttering, "Get away from NG, give him room," wary of Sebastian and thinking they were in the shit if that's what it was taking.

More ships thundered overhead, one after the other, dropping three lines of heavy infantry, further out this time. The gunships piled in and circled, keeping their distance.

Sebastian laughed.

It almost felt like the aliens were apprehensive. Not fearful but more cautious.

'*They should be.*'

'*I can't do what you do,*' NG thought.

'*No, you can't. You want to know why?*'

He didn't. He didn't care. He didn't want to be capable of that.

'*And that, my friend, is exactly why. You want to see them?*'

'*No.*'

Sebastian was enjoying himself.

They wanted him alive. It was chilling to feel that intent. They wanted all of them alive. They wanted to know who it was that was thwarting them, what it was about these small creatures that was causing them so much trouble.

'*Then let's show them. Are you ready?*'

No, he wasn't.

He braced himself.

'*Nikolai,*' Sebastian said, '*trust me, I only do what is necessary. You are me and I am you. I am not going to destroy you…*'

It was too good to be true.

And he didn't believe a word.

The Bhenykhn moved forward, as one, closing in.

His eyelids felt like lead. Someone was tugging on each arm. They dragged him upright. He couldn't open his eyes, shivering, soaked in cold sweat, nausea swelling in his stomach. He tried to talk but his jaw muscles wouldn't work.

'What happened?' he thought, trying to find LC or Duncan.

'Sebastian killed them.'

He thought that was LC.

They hoisted him up, and as much as he tried to move his legs, he couldn't get anything to work.

He couldn't feel Sebastian.

Couldn't even feel the Bhenykhn.

There was a cold sting against his neck, warmth flooding into his bloodstream.

"Come on, buddy, we've gotta move."

"I thought we killed them," he mumbled.

"You did," LC said. "There's more of them. Come on, NG, we can't stay here."

He couldn't sense any more aliens, couldn't feel anything. But they couldn't run, there'd be nowhere to hide.

"We have to get something at our back," Duncan said. "We can't get surrounded."

They were pretty much carrying him, stumbling over the rough ground.

"How many?" he managed to say.

"At least three troop ships. Are you gonna be able to do that again?"

The thought of it made him feel sick.

"Yeah, we reckoned not."

He tried to reach out, looking for the others, but it sent his head spinning.

His ankle caught in a tangled tree root and he went down, threatening to pull the others with him, Duncan almost pulling his shoulder out as the big marine dragged them forward.

"What's the chances of the Duck or the guild turning up before these bastards decide to make a move?" Duncan said, shoving branches out of their way.

They had no way of knowing, no way of communicating with anything even in orbit, never mind further out. NG wanted to ask how long he'd been out, how long the troop ships had been there, if there were pods on the ground yet, but he couldn't get the words out.

It was either starting to get dark or he was losing his sight.

They splashed through a boggy stream, sliding on the soft ground.

He ended up on one knee and he would have been content to sit there in the stagnant water.

"No, you don't," LC muttered, cursing, pulling him up and forward. "For fuck's sake, NG, come on. No, there aren't any on the ground. They're circling right above us."

As he said it, one of them swooped down, banking hard. It skimmed the tops of the trees and took off again, keeping its distance.

'Why aren't they attacking us?' he thought.

They were scrambling uphill. He thought he heard one of the grunts shouting then they veered right and it got steeper. He was struggling to keep his footing, no traction on the damp soil that was giving way beneath them.

"Presumably," Duncan said, "bud, because they want you alive."

'Don't...'

"We know. C'mon, we need to move."

He bumped his arm on a tree branch, scraped his knee on a sharp edged boulder, every slight pain flaring as if his nerve endings were frayed and at their limit. The pressure in his head was a constant dense swirl of black that was threatening to overwhelm.

"Let me sit," he mumbled, "or I'm gonna throw up."

"Not yet," Duncan grunted.

"I've lost my rifle."

"We've got it. Jesus, NG, work with us here."

Shut up, was what he meant so NG gave in to it, trusting them, letting them haul him this way and that, almost blacking out when a branch hit him over the head, and concentrating on just breathing.

"This'll do," Duncan said eventually. "Five minutes, people, then we move on."

They set him down. He sagged, back bumping up against a jagged outcrop of rock.

He hadn't realised he had his eyes closed until he opened them. Leigh was at his side, Duncan talking to one of the Security guys, sorting through a pile of weapons and packs, LC sitting some way off, staring at him. The four elite guard were standing on watch.

"Hey," Leigh said softly.

It was starting to get darker, a mist settling amongst the trees. The gunships and troop carriers were still circling.

"Where are the others?" he said.

She looked dismayed. "You don't remember?"

He took it out of their minds, stomach cramping at the thought of what they'd seen.

Sebastian hadn't just sucked the life force out of the plants and ground he'd been standing on, he'd drained four of their own people.

He'd killed four of their own people.

24

These elite who sat here, representing the relative few of their kind that had survived, were listening with unease. They knew what it was like to run for their lives from the Bhenykhn. None there could help but think back to the dark days when they had come together, when all was lost.

Guilt and shame mixed with their discomfort at hearing of the Man's own people in such a plight. They could smell the breath of those monstrous ogres, hear the roar of their battle cries. They each had memories they had long thought buried deep, shivering as they surfaced, images of Bhenykhn warriors sweeping through their marble halls, Bhenykhn ships swarming in the skies over their cities, bombing, dropping pods, firing on them as they fled, taking out their defences in blow after blow. Slaughtering or enslaving those left behind as they themselves fled.

"We were so arrogant," one said quietly.

NG almost doubled over. He couldn't breathe. Couldn't remember any of it.

He raised his eyes and saw Duncan look over.

The big marine tossed the axe he was holding onto the pile and stood.

"Sebastian took out the Bennies," Duncan said. "If that's what it took, that's what it took." The big man walked over, holding out a ration pack and a flask. "They drop more pods, we need him to do it again, preferably without killing any more of us. Can he do it? Where is he?"

NG took the flask. "I don't know." His hands were shaking, hardly enough strength in his fingers to twist open the cap.

Duncan crouched by his side, taking the flask and saying quietly but intensely as he opened it, "Can you do it?"

NG took the flask and took a sip of lukewarm water. He couldn't tell if it was that or the question that made his stomach turn. "I don't know."

"We have enough explosives to make a perimeter ten metres out."

That wasn't far enough. They could easily throw an axe that far.

"Harder for them if we make it to high ground," Duncan said. "They'll have to climb after us or drop down on top of us."

"If they decide they still want us alive."

The big man shrugged. "We have flares. We reckon if Elliott brings the Duck straight in and he can see the beacons, we just need to make it through the next four or five hours."

"They won't give us that long."

There was a rumble overhead as a gunship buzzed them.

"They might if they want you and we can keep you away from them." Duncan popped NG on the shoulder and pushed two Epizin injectors into his hand. "You good to go?"

He wasn't but he could feel the Bhenykhn closing in.

"If it happens again, if Sebastian takes over again, get away from me," he muttered.

"Buddy, if it happens again, we're done. We need to hold out and hope the Duck gets here. C'mon, we need to get moving."

They made it up over the ridge as night was falling, emerging from the trees into hazy twilight and the sound of the droning engine of a troop carrier. It banked and circled in a lazy spiral around the hill, dropping pods at regular intervals that crashed down below the treeline all around.

Surrounding them.

They stood, watching the lights as they plummeted to the ground.

"Shit, I lost count at thirty," LC muttered.

Duncan and the others were sorting through what they had

179

left, redistributing ammunition, stuffing explosives and spare magazines into packs.

NG turned slowly.

He couldn't feel anything except a pressure at the back of his mind. "Did you see Sebastian when he did it?"

LC looked round. "He didn't enjoy it, if that's what you're asking."

"Are you getting anything from them?"

The kid shook his head. "Headache. That's all but I don't know if that's from you more than them." He was cradling an assault rifle in his arms and he absently checked the mechanism as they stood there. He didn't look like a Thieves' Guild field-op. As far from the list and the standings board as you could get.

LC raised his eyes with a half smile as he overheard that thought. "Can we ever go back?"

NG took a deep breath. "They're going to keep coming. And as long as they do, we're going to be in the middle of it."

The others were pretty much geared up.

"Do you need energy now?" LC asked. Casual, almost offhand.

NG squinted at him. "You need it."

The kid pulled a flask off his belt and waved it. "Moonshine. Take what you need. I can get it back."

Christ, it was tempting. He didn't know if he could even hold the weight of a gun right now.

'Take it.'

'Sebastian.'

'Take whatever is offered, Nikolai. We're going to need it, you and I, if we are to fend them off again.'

LC held out his arm.

It didn't feel right, and it wasn't totally necessary to have that physical contact, but he clasped his arm and drew on the kid's life force like a freaking vampire.

He pulled away, before Sebastian would have done, feeling his disapproval, and muttered a thanks.

LC tipped the flask at him and grinned, taking a mouthful of whatever liquor it was in there and turning as Duncan approached.

'They're about to move,' Sebastian murmured. 'And Nikolai, if you care anything for any of these people, tell them to get away from you, right now, as fast and far as they can go.'

It was more consideration than he'd ever had from Sebastian before.

'Don't worry, I'm not going soft. I may need them later.'

NG pulled a gun from a holster and checked it.

"You need to go," he said. "Set up a perimeter half way down the slope. Take LC."

Duncan nodded and signalled to the others. They took their kit and bugged out. They were good. The best the guild had. And they'd chosen the playing field here. Duncan would make sure LC didn't get into trouble.

He turned to Leigh. "You're not staying."

"I'm not leaving you."

"Go hide somewhere," he said and he didn't give her any choice in the matter.

She gave him a disapproving glare and took off.

NG closed his eyes. 'Do it.'

There were nine squad leaders, spread out at the base of the hill. He felt their hearts pumping, breath misting, felt the adrenaline flow as they hefted their weapons. He felt the hive pressing as Sebastian lifted the shield, focused on one of the grey cloaks and connected.

Gunfire echoed from the trees below them. Sebastian took out the squad leaders with one devastating shot that resounded from one to the next to the next and let go.

NG dropped to his knees, drained.

'Get into cover.'

He didn't question it, staggered to his feet and ran to the treeline.

He slid down the slope as a roar rumbled overhead, another troop carrier dropping down low, banking.

Sebastian shoved him aside, targeted the pilot and threw a blast at the craft. It lurched, dropped further, engines straining and veering away with a groan. Another carrier loomed right behind it, releasing pods that dropped right into the clearing.

He felt Sebastian switch his focus, scrambling down the hillside, stealing energy from everything he touched, reaching ahead and obliterating two units in front of them to make a gap in their line.

Gunfire was resounding in all directions. He couldn't concentrate enough to sense any of the others.

'*Sebastian…?*'

A shot punched into his shoulder, throwing him backwards.

He lost his footing and slid on wet ground. Poison was pumping into his bloodstream, Sebastian struggling to neutralise it, reserves on empty.

The hideously familiar figure of a Bhenykhn warrior emerged ahead of him, looming, rifle up, a twisted grin on its face. It stepped close, breath snorting out in clouds, and kicked, enough force to send him rolling across the slope.

He felt his ribs snap, nothing he could do as Sebastian grabbed handfuls of wet leaf mold to drag himself to a halt, twisting and killing it with one blast, connecting with the rest and throwing everything he had left at them, the energy sparking and crackling as it rippled out.

'*Get us out of here,*' Sebastian hissed and let go.

NG fell back, chest heaving, agony flaring with every breath. He pressed a hand to his shoulder, feeling the heat of the poison, feeling himself going under.

'No, you don't,' Duncan thought, sliding in beside him, LC on the other side, both of them with rifles slung across their backs, both breathing heavily but grabbing him and dragging him into a run.

He was vaguely aware of one of the elite guard on their flank, gun up and firing, chameleonic body armour shimmering as it blended with the woodland.

He tried to find Leigh but he couldn't sense her anywhere.

They staggered down the slope, past the hulking bodies of fallen Bhenykhn, dense smoke starting to mingle with the mist, cloying and black.

NG coughed and almost greyed out as a stab of pain shot through his chest. He could hardly feel his legs.

LC was struggling, low on energy. "Is there a plan B?" the kid said.

NG coughed again. "We could steal one of their ships. Why didn't we think of that sooner. We're Thieves' Guild. We should be able to hotwire an alien spaceship."

Duncan laughed.

"Don't laugh," he said, well aware that he was sounding delirious. "It might come to that."

"Just keep walking, buddy."

They made it to the bottom of the slope, gunfire chasing them all the way, and took two steps out onto the flat.

A craft thundered overhead, dropping four pods just ahead of them, the massive shapes crashing through the branches. They opened with a hiss on impact, Bhenykhn warriors stepping out into the mist, weapons up.

"Spread out," Duncan yelled.

NG wavered on his feet as the support on both sides vanished, LC and Duncan letting go and bringing up rifles, firing. He had nothing but a pistol but he drew it as he dropped to one knee and fired, one shot after the next after the next, right at the grey cloak's head. Every round flashed off a shield that shimmered with each impact.

There was a blur of movement as the last of the elite guard appeared as if from nowhere and jumped, ramming a blade into its neck, the blow driven home by the full strength of the powered armour. It fell.

There was another roar of engines above, more pods dropping behind them.

They were going to get overrun.

'*Need a hand here,*' NG thought, desperately trying to reach Sebastian.

Nothing.

He stopped firing. He felt like shit, but he stopped firing and threw everything he had at one of the Bennies, taking hold of its mind and squeezing, draining its energy and taking everything it had for himself.

He stood, aware that there were others emerging behind him, and he walked forward, past Duncan and LC, hearing the crack of their rifles loud in his ears. He didn't stop, driving it to its knees, the same as he had the captive on Poule.

Another shot hit his leg.

He hardly felt it. He finished off that one and turned, taking hold of the next squad leader's mind and throwing so much raw energy at it that it keeled over, dead before it hit the ground.

He turned, vaguely aware of the elite guard slamming round after round into one of the others, a weighted chain tumbling through the air and slamming into LC as the kid staggered, shot in the arm, another three chains careening at Duncan. More pods were crashing down around them, hissing open. Four Bennies turned and descended on the elite guard, driving him to the ground.

NG didn't know where Leigh was, couldn't do anything other than try to target another grey cloak. He spun, looking for one. There was one staring right at him, orange eyes dull in the misty half light, a smirk twisting the corners of its leathery mouth.

He sensed the club being raised behind him too late to move fast enough. It crashed down and he crashed into resounding darkness.

25

He let that last linger. They were enthralled, dismayed. He'd never kept their attention so keenly.

He had been hardened by his dealings with humans, he decided, sitting there, recounting these events, briefing this assembly before they made their decision. They were peaceful, his own kind. They abhorred violence, disliked even hearing of it. That did not make them weak but nor did it make them innocent of all failings.

She couldn't help but ask, "What of Nikolai and Luka?"

"They learned first hand what it is to be captive in the hands of the Devourers."

"Then all is lost?" one said. "What now?"

"All is never lost," he said. "Not until the Bhenykhn have killed the last of us will all be lost."

He could feel his heart beating, hear it resounding in his ears, punching against his ribs.

Too fast.

He had a nasty wound in his shoulder, another in his leg just above the left knee, broken ribs, burning around his wrists, a swirl in his mind that was a sure sign of concussion.

He didn't want to open his eyes.

'Welcome back.'

He couldn't sense the Bhenykhn anywhere.

'That's because we're on the Alsatia, you fool. Well done, Nikolai, you managed to get caught. Be glad your precious guild came to the rescue. You might wish they hadn't. Evelyn, your dearest Evelyn, is more than pissed at you. She just lost two thirds of the guild's combat capability rescuing you...'

He knew his breathing was shallow. Forced. He tried to breathe deeper but it was restricted, controlled.

Isopod.

'I'm doing my best, but believe me, Nikolai, that was close. Let's not do that again, shall we?'

He reached further. No one.

'Are the others alive?'

'Just. Do I need to say it again? That was close. Too close. I need energy to heal and ironically, placing you in isolation has deprived us of any contact I can use. Hit the alarm, get someone here and I can sort you out a hell of a lot faster than we're managing right now stuck in this machine.'

The alarm was right by his hand. He didn't know if he wanted anyone here.

Sebastian shoved him aside, hit the button and let go.

'Dammit, I hate pain,' he hissed. *'Now listen to me, Nikolai, your little stunt back there, chasing that scout, is going to have repercussions, nasty repercussions, but bizarrely enough, that might be just what we need. Itomara has now seen them in action first hand. You need to get your ass out of this pod and start pulling the strings because, left to their own devices, these creatures will self-destruct before they have any chance of making a stand against the Bhenykhn. And trust me, we need help to make that stand because the hive now knows everything there is to know about you and I, my friend.'*

It wasn't a medic that turned up to respond to the alarm, it was Evelyn. She stared at him without a word, punched the release and walked away.

He'd been thinking he couldn't feel any worse. He was wrong.

He didn't go anywhere near her mind, simply sat up as the pod let him go and sat there, rubbing his wrists, trying to calm his breathing. He had a dressing taped to his upper chest, left side, just below the collarbone. He couldn't remember that one but it was throbbing. He peeled back the dressing and could see the edge of a raw, intricate design burnt into his flesh.

He felt sick.

'*They branded you,*' Sebastian murmured. '*When you were captured, they injected all of you with some kind of biological marker, something I assume they can track. Don't worry, I've killed the organism.*'

Christ. He sat there, feeling Sebastian heal what he could, not much either of them could do about the remnants of the poison that was still sapping his strength, then he climbed out, dressing slowly in the gear that had been left there for him.

He followed her out of the soundproofed isolation unit into chaos, wounded in the corridors, screaming and dying, not the Alsatia he knew.

'*Go to your office,*' Sebastian said, cold, insistent.

He couldn't just walk through. Evelyn was kneeling next to one of the injured. Leigh was there, covered in blood, in amongst the casualties, the same as she had been on Erica. She looked tired but unharmed. Other medics were doing their best but they were all overrun.

Evelyn looked up at him and he could tell from her expression that she knew. No need to read her mind. Someone must have briefed her. She was testing him, waiting to see what he would do as if she had no idea who he was any more.

'*Go to your office,*' Sebastian said again.

He couldn't.

He was drawn to her, kneeled and rested his hand against the guy's neck, drawing energy from her to heal the devastating chest wound. He felt the guy stabilise beneath his touch, breathing settle, colour returning.

Evelyn was staring at him. There was no emotion there, just pure cold Assassin's blood running through her veins. "You need to see the Chief," she said.

They had the big man in an isopod but it was doing nothing. Keeping him alive but barely.

"He insisted on going down there to get you," Evelyn said. "Same as Erica." She wanted to scream at him, thinking, but it wasn't the same, was it? She wanted to yell at him, hit him.

He read her mind then. She'd talked to Morgan, got a full run down on what had happened on Poule, what NG had ordered them to do when the scout ship had appeared. The guy had also thrown the full file on NG over to her. She knew everything. All their tests, all the data. The telepathy, the healing, the telekinesis. Everything.

He didn't know what to say so he just pressed his hand against the release catch, watched as the pod opened and placed his hand on the Chief's chest.

He closed his eyes and healed what he could, draining himself down to his last reserves, and it still wasn't enough. The way it had been with Martinez on Erica, down there in the cold mud of the battlefield after it was all done and over and he couldn't save her.

He couldn't save the Chief. He didn't have a miracle heal-all, cure-all. It didn't work like that. Not with the poison the Bennies used.

He did his best and backed away.

"Use the virus on him," he said, voice sounding like it belonged to someone else. "Use it on all the wounded."

He walked away then and made his way to his old office, shrugging off anyone who tried to stop him. She hadn't moved in, just left it the same as when he'd left. Tidied up the mess but left everything else the same.

He grabbed a bottle of whisky and sat on the desk. There was a report there on the encounter with the Bhenykhn, accounts from the extraction crews, the medical teams, stats on losses and a brief note on gains. He flicked through it, feeling removed from it all, numb.

He had thick red chafe marks around each wrist.

'They had you in chains. Be grateful for the rescue.'

'I am.'

'And be glad that you're here. You need the Alsatia and that charade was not doing you any favours.'

'I was trying to keep her safe.'

'Well, well done, you've made her hate you. That will keep her safer than when she is distracted worrying about you. She's been speaking to the Assassins – did you pick that tidbit out of her mind?'

He hadn't. She'd got a copy of the warrant that was out on him. He knew that. Someone had made sure she saw it.

He took a swig out of the bottle, felt the alcohol hit his stomach, immune system still suppressed and energy levels about as low as they could go.

He felt her approach the door. She paused, like old times, then walked in. She had her hands at her side but she might as well have been wielding daggers.

He hated it but he met her open hostility with indifference. He took another drink and sat, legs dangling, resting the bottle on his knee.

"We can't use the virus," she said, stopping half way across the office.

"We don't have any choice."

"You'll risk losing half our wounded? And the half that survive, if that many, what happens to them?"

"We get ourselves more telepaths. With any luck, we might get someone who can hear the Bennies. Did we capture any of them alive?"

"We got you back alive." She was struggling to contain her anger. She almost didn't believe that it was him. No one but LC, Duncan and Leigh knew about Sebastian and they wouldn't have said anything of him to her. It was more that she was thinking this could just be someone who looked like NG, a lot like him, but thinner.

"I'm me," he said, confrontational, raising the bottle to his lips, knowing he was making it worse.

She sucked in a deep breath, eyes still flaring, thinking to herself, 'My god, he is reading my mind. He has always been able to read my mind.'

He looked at her, wanting nothing more than to sweep her up and squeeze her tight, but he said, cold and calculating, "Use the virus," the way the Man had said it to him all that time ago before

189

they killed Sorensen. He let that sink in, didn't let her object again and added, "Where's LC?"

"He's in Medical with a broken leg," she said. Accusing. She thought they'd lost him. She was thinking that she'd almost lost both of them. "We can't stabilise the poison but he's fighting it. Duncan as well."

"Get them in here and get the section chiefs in the conference room."

She lifted her chin defiantly. "And where do I stand in all this?"

"Head of operations. Get Morgan in there. And Quinn. And Jameson and Pen. Is Itomara still on board?"

She nodded.

"And send word to Marrek," he said, watching her reaction. "He is the new leader of the Assassins, isn't he?"

She didn't show any surprise that he knew. "You want him here?"

"Why not?"

And they were holding Ballack in one of the rooms in the hospitality suite. He could wait until later.

"Use the virus," NG said again and stared at her, not exactly giving her a brush off but she got the message.

She spun on her heels and left.

He'd downed half the bottle before the door opened again. No knock.

Media didn't hesitate. She grinned, strode right up to him, stood on tiptoes and gave him a hug.

She was warm. Small but warm. He stole a bit of her energy. She always had plenty.

"Glad you're not dead," she breathed into his neck, finally, pulling away and looking at him, taking hold of his hands and squeezing. "LC and Hal are on their way." She grinned again. "NG, I want the virus. I want to be able to do what you all do."

He couldn't help but smile back, feeling the closest to being home since he'd woken up.

"No. Brooke, it's too risky."

"C'mon, that's not fair. You boys can't have all the fun." She was playing. "Let me in. Fifty-fifty odds is nothing. I'd bet this cruiser on less than that."

She did, regularly. Media was at her best, because of, not despite what had happened, what was going on out there. She'd always been like that. She was pure insane defiance personified. The warmest of them all and the coldest of them.

"No," he said. "I need you to do a job for me."

She looked at him sideways, curiosity piqued. She had a dozen trains of thought running through her mind, intertwining, making patterns, weaving opportunities, straight away thinking what she had that she could use fast to best effect in all this even though he hadn't said what he wanted her to do.

"Are we telling everyone about the aliens?" she asked.

"Nope. They won't believe us. Don't worry, I have a plan for that."

She hugged him again. "I'm sure you do. I'm glad you're back. So, Nikolai? Do we get to call you Nikolai now?"

He stopped outside the door to the conference room. He'd talked to LC and Duncan, both of them still tired from the effects of the poison, LC struggling with badly broken ribs and the fracture in his leg from the weighted chain that had hit him, and both of them apprehensive about the task he set them. They'd demolished a case of beer between the three of them while they hashed out a plan. Then he'd taken a shower in his old quarters, a reassuring routine that reinforced this bizarre notion that he might be home.

'*Make the most of it,*' Sebastian whispered. '*Are you ready to face the inquisition?*'

'*Never been more ready. This is the game we should have been playing the whole damned time.*'

'*I knew you'd come round to my way of thinking, Nikolai. We are so much more alike than you dare admit.*'

'*Sebastian, we're exactly the same. Don't think I don't realise that. I just have to deal with these people day in, day out. You don't. I know you're not allowing me to stick around because you feel sorry for me.*'

You need me. You just want to fight the Bhenykhn? Fine, I'll set it up for you. You just tell me how close you want to get.'

That got a laugh. *'I'm liking your plan, Nikolai. And you know what? I think you might just pull it off.'*

He walked in and sat down. There was a copy of the report there. There was also a glass of whisky set out for him. He ignored the report, took a sip of the whisky and looked up. They were all looking at him, looking at the graze marks around his wrists as if that made it all the more real.

He glanced from face to face, settling on Itomara. "The Order has been orchestrating conflict and hostilities between human factions for centuries," he said. "We've always countered that. Now? We need to trigger it. We have to use everything we have to accelerate outright war, right now, between Earth and Winter."

26

"He turned despair into hope," she said, in awe, more than ever.

"He deals in war," one of the others said, not disguising his disgust.

"He does what is necessary," the Man said again.

There was a shaking of heads, condescending, hypocritical.

"But the virus, the organism...?" another said. "He was prepared to risk half his people?"

There was disbelief. Despite everything he had told them and shown them, everything they knew of the Bhenykhn, they were judging Nikolai to be harsh in his actions.

The Man tempered an urge to respond in anger, waiting until the clamour had settled before saying, calm and cold, "He was prepared to risk everything, unlike us, who were prepared to risk nothing, and look where that has led us."

No one said a word.

"We encountered one of their forward operating bases," he said. The board in front of him was scrolling with the stats of just how bad the losses had been to retrieve them. He reached out his hand and shut it down. "We can't take on their full force but we can whittle away what they have here now. Before they launch their full attack. We're close to knowing exactly where to go to find them. I didn't intend to give you all such a graphic demonstration of Bhenykhn warfare so close up but now you've seen it, stop doubting me, stop suspecting that there is some kind of hidden agenda here and work with us." He took a sip of whisky. "No one else is going to believe it. The only way I can see that we can destroy one of these bases is to bring a big enough force of Earth and Wintran military together in one place. Get them head to head then turn them onto the Bhenykhn."

The silence was thick in the room.

Itomara broke it. "You would condemn thousands to their death."

"If we don't do something, billions die."

Jameson, Pen and Quinn had been down there on the surface of that planet, he realised, looking at them, looking deeper into their minds, noticing the injuries they were carrying. They'd mobilised without hesitation, joining the Chief and the guild's rescue mission. Jameson had been the one who'd found them.

NG lowered his eyes, seeing more than he wanted to in that brief glimpse.

'You would've done the same,' the colonel thought. Clear as a bell. He overheard NG think that and twitched a smile. He had beads of sweat on his brow, grimacing through the pain. 'Hal Duncan is one helluva good drill sergeant. You're lucky to have found him. I always thought it was shit what we did to him. And, NG, by god, this is the hardest fucking thing I've ever done.'

'You should have seen what LC went through,' NG thought back and said out loud, "We've proved that we can beat them. We've done it twice now."

Pen shook his head. "You've beaten them, NG. You. Both times. Don't deny it. Even down there. They were doing their damnedest to keep you alive. That's the only reason we got anywhere near them. We grabbed you and ran, do you realise that? We couldn't take them on in a straight fight. Not without you." He leaned forward. "And there are so many people looking to take you out on our side that we don't stand a chance of keeping you alive as soon as word gets out."

A faint smile danced across Itomara's face. Almost unreadable, except it was clear that he was thinking he'd authorised actions against NG himself. Actions that were probably still active. He was thinking how things change.

NG looked round. Evelyn was looking at him, tapping absently on the file she was keeping to hand, thinking he didn't stand a chance, and thinking again that in all the time she'd worked with him, she'd never truly known who he was. She looked him in the eye, guessing that he was reading her mind. 'Did Devon?' she thought.

He connected through the Senson, surprised that she allowed permission. "She knew at the end. When I couldn't save her." He had a lump in his throat, even just looking at Evelyn.

"No one else can head this up," Pen said, pushing it. He raised a finger, pointing. "But as soon as you stick your head above the parapet, someone is going to take a pot-shot."

"I can run things from here," he said.

'At least sound convincing.'

"Can you?" Pen said.

Media spoke up, demanding their attention, being facetious and knowing it. "Trust me, gentlemen, we know what we're doing. You want us to start a war?" It was a total one eighty spin from the brief she'd always worked to and she was loving it. She smiled. "Just tell me when and where."

Evelyn followed him out as he left them to discuss strategies with Media. "You're 402," she said.

He didn't stop but she kept stride with him.

"You were right there in that prison on Aston. Why didn't you tell me? Why couldn't you trust me, NG?"

She wanted to hit him, right in the jugular, with the sharp end of a knife.

Saying that he was trying to protect her didn't seem to cut it.

"Don't you think it was hard enough for us losing Devon?" she said. "Media cried for a week after Erica. I can't believe she isn't more pissed at you."

Media lived in the moment. She knew now that he was okay, so that was okay.

'You might want to say some of this out loud,' Sebastian murmured.

He didn't know how to.

"Come with me to the Man's ship," he said.

"Why? So you can wipe my memory again?"

"Evie…" He stopped.

'We don't have time for this. Just make her think whatever you want so we can get on with the things that actually matter.'

Except he couldn't.

'Sebastian, this matters to me.'

"Let me undo it," he said to Evelyn. He needed her to make her own mind up.

She stared at him with her jaw set, eyes flashing. "NG, I don't know if I trust you any more. I don't want you inside my head."

He had to force himself to stand there and not turn away. "Let me explain it all then you can decide."

"It's not going to make any difference."

"Let me try. The Man has good taste in wine. You liked it last time. And I promise, I'll stay out of your head."

They talked for another three hours and at the end of it he still wasn't sure she didn't hate him still. She'd wanted to know more. More about him, about Erica, more about the Bhenykhn and more about how Devon had died, why he'd felt so sure he had to lie to protect her from the Assassins. At the end of it, he walked her back to her office. She stood there, thinking that he looked tired, thinking of everything she'd read in the files, everything he'd been through, everything she'd done as head of operations that she wished she could have shared with him.

"I miss Devon," he said.

She took his hand then and squeezed, turning away before she cried.

He didn't move as she closed the door.

'You need to see Ballack,' Sebastian said. *'And you need to talk to Quinn – there's a problem with the last key fragment.'*

Walking out into Legal, he almost bottled it. He'd been feeling beyond belligerent when he'd arranged this, masochistic in its purest form to think he could take this on in Devon's old domain of marble tables and tall glass columns. Even the scent of fresh greenery in the air reminded him of her so much it almost sent him bolting for the exit.

He needed to face it. He knew that. As much as he didn't want to. He hadn't been in here since he'd lost her.

Ballack was sitting there already, drink in hand, way more smug than he should have been.

They had guns trained on the man, even more guards than the last time he'd sat here with Devon, entertaining a client, after the Assassins had managed to tamper with the drones in the Maze and almost kill him. The time they'd been told the Merchants were talking of 'blowing the Thieves' Guild out of the water'.

He sat down.

Ballack wasn't fazed by any of this, the big man simply calculating how he was going to benefit from it. He was taking it as a personal achievement that he was here on board the Alsatia. He raised his glass as NG sat. "I must say, I like the way you entertain your prisoners, NG. Most stylish."

"I need the Merchants' Guild," NG said, straight to the point. "You can either work with us, from here, or we can kill you and use your position anyway to do exactly what we need. Your choice."

That got raised eyebrows. Ballack lowered the glass without taking a drink. "To do what?"

"Take Earth and Winter to war. Catastrophically and unequivocally to the brink of head-on outright war."

Ballack put down the glass, shaking his head. "Whatever your insane power-crazed plans are, NG, I won't work for you."

NG stood up. "That's fine." He walked away, glanced up and nodded.

"Wait."

He turned back. The next word would be, 'why?', then it wouldn't matter what he said, Ballack would be theirs and Media would have a blast exploiting him.

He got word that Quinn was waiting for him as he pressed the button for twelve. Leigh slipped into the lift after him.

"You need to get some rest," she said. "You can't keep going like this, NG."

She looked tired herself. He had no idea what had happened to her down there after he'd sent her to hide. Since they'd been rescued, he'd been swept up in the maelstrom of activity on board the Alsatia and they hadn't had a chance to talk.

"I'm fine," she said, reading his expression. "If you're wondering, they didn't capture me." She pulled a face. "I'm sorry I couldn't get back to you in time to help. I could hear them shouting. When they got you, they…"

She trailed off. He couldn't help but overhear that she thought they'd all been killed. He didn't look any deeper. He didn't want to know what had happened. They'd got out. That's all that mattered.

"How's it going with the virus?" he said.

She leaned back against the wall of the elevator and folded her arms. "Do you really want to know?"

He shrugged.

"We have over a hundred wounded criticals that are taking all our attention right now."

He knew that. Evelyn had told him.

"Medical is overrun, Science is struggling…" she said. "You don't need to hear all this. Go talk to Quinn. And get some rest… I still have you on live feed, NG. Your stats are shit."

She stayed in the lift as it stopped and he stepped out, calling, "Get some sleep," after him.

Yeah, sometime.

Quinn was waiting in his office, sitting at the table, two key fragments in its centre, shining with a faint golden glow from the low lights in there.

NG grabbed a bottle of whisky, two glasses and sat.

"Marathon and Stirling," Quinn said. "Don't ask what it took to get these."

More losses they couldn't afford.

"How's the Chief?" he asked.

"Alive but unconscious. They're still looking at the genetics.

There must be a reason why it works on some people and not others. Jameson is their poster boy right now. But there's nothing obvious. They're crosschecking everything."

NG poured two shots of the liquor and handed one across. "What's the problem with Kochitek?"

"It's gone."

"I know, it got taken over by Zang, what, fifty, sixty years ago?"

"No," Quinn said. "Not the corporation. The key fragment. It's missing."

27

"I must ask, did Nikolai truly not know what he was chasing when he was gathering the keys?"

She was thinking that if he'd been there, he could have warned them.

He shook his head. "Each race, each nation, in all of time has always had its secrets, its guilt to carry and hide. The humans are no different, for all their fleeting nature. If anything, that they die so young meant that the secrets of their ancestors became lost, so determined were they to bury their misjudgements."

The others were just watching, eyes downcast.

Only she was bold enough to ask. "And was it fortune or calamity that you created a guild designed to bring together and nurture the very means, the only means, by which these keys could ever hope to see the light of day again?"

NG paused with the glass at his lips. "Ah," he said and downed the whisky in one. "Are we any closer to knowing what these keys are really for?"

He poured another shot, waiting with the bottle hovering as Quinn took a drink and offered his glass for a top up.

The big handler shook his head. "We've got nothing. Not even rumour, conjecture, folklore. Elliott won't say anything other than it's a ship-based weapon system that will give us a chance against the Bhenykhn's shields. If it is a weapon, they must have obliterated every mention of it when they decided to shut it down."

"How do you know Kochitek's key is missing?"

"Because Elliott knows who stole it. You want that key? It's going to take you, breaking into Io, resurrecting the guy and sucking the memory of where he hid it from his frozen brain."

Sebastian laughed.

NG almost laughed but Quinn never joked.

'Io? My god, I never thought we'd be going back there.'

"How much are you relying on having this weapon?" Quinn said.

"I'm not. Elliott thinks we need it." NG sat up, Leigh's suspicions popping into his head as if she was whispering to him. "Where is the Duck?"

"Elliott bugged out, right after we extricated you from the Bhenykhn. Said he'd meet us at Io. Why? What's wrong?"

"What are the chances of that scout turning up where it did, when it did? In all the data we have of their movements and whereabouts, what are the odds?"

Quinn shook his head slowly. "I'll get Badger onto it. You think they could have been sent there?"

NG scrubbed a hand over the back of his neck. "Quinn, to be honest, I'm losing track of what I think about anything."

'You don't have time to be paranoid, Nikolai. The Bhenykhn know about us, about you and I, and if you're right and that captive on Poule was reading your mind, they know about the guild and the Alsatia. Get that weapon, Nikolai, and get it fast, because when we meet them again, they will be ready for us.'

'I know.'

"If we don't trust Elliott," Quinn said, "we just watch ourselves when we hand over the keys... if we can figure out a way to find this last one."

"We will. Then we don't just hand them over to Elliott. I'll go with him. I'll take them myself."

Quinn nodded.

NG picked up the whisky. "So? How the hell are we going to get into Io?"

"There is no way in," the big handler said.

NG squinted at him over the bottle. "We've done it before."

A slight smile twitched at the corner of Quinn's mouth as he put it together. "You've done it before," he said, nodding.

"I don't know if I could do it the same now. And we're running out of time."

"You could do it with LC and Hil as back up," Quinn said. "Think about it – Andreyev, Anderton and Hilyer on the same tab? Jesus."

"Is LC fit enough?"

"He will be. He still has the brace on his leg but yes. And Hil is twitching to get out. We've just about got him to the point where he can stand being within the vicinity of even the powerful AIs. He should be fine." Quinn was thinking that he wished Mendhel could be there to see it.

NG topped up the glasses, handed one back and held his up, inviting a toast. "I miss him."

They clinked, drank then Quinn held his up again. "Here's to the Thieves' Guild," he said.

It almost felt like old times.

"No one messes with the Thieves' Guild," NG said and drained the glass.

The last time he'd walked into the prison on Io Optima, he hadn't been top of the galaxy's most wanted list and he hadn't had his hands in cuffs.

"Prisoner transfer," Duncan said at the desk, gruff, pushing him forward.

It had already been logged and cleared, high level, Jameson had ensured that, so they got a cursory glance and a wave through to processing. Duncan nudged him in the back with his shotgun and they walked freely and openly into the most secure facility this side of the Between.

Getting out might be different.

They ran his biometrics, every pointer hitting the ID Elliott and Jameson had cooked up, the one that was reprogrammed into the tag stapled in the top of his ear, and cleared him for storage, high security isolation, every guard they encountered eyeing him with suspicious regard, only the worst ever going straight into seclusion.

Duncan nudged him along, swapping pleasantries with the guards, picking enough out of their minds to make it seem seamless, like he'd worked there for years.

They took a lift that dropped down fast into the bowels of the facility and walked out into a dark corridor, directions lit by subtle blue markers. It was oppressive. Half the prisoners in there were drugged, the other half stewing in their own insanity.

Another guard was walking towards them, prodding his own prisoner into moving, the lad limping heavily and holding his arm against his ribs like he'd just had a beating.

'Hey buddy, taken one for the team?' Duncan thought as they approached.

The kid looked up with a grin, a black bruise blossoming under his eye. He stumbled as he passed them, bumped into NG and palmed across the pass he'd stolen.

'The code is 7714362, modifier Kay Zee.'

'Nice one,' NG thought back, slipping the pass up his sleeve. 'See you on the outside.'

They walked past as the guard hauled LC to his feet and shoved the kid ahead of him.

It was straight forward after that to make their way down into the narrow lines of cells, Duncan making a point of being rough randomly enough to satisfy any observers. NG walked into the tiny cell without fighting him, waited patiently as he hooked the cuffs up to a chain in the wall and backed out.

Duncan closed the cell door and banged on it with a parting, "Enjoy."

It wasn't the worst place he'd been stuck in of late. There was a bunk, fresh water and reading material. He stretched out on his back on the hard bunk and jiggled the chains to get comfy.

Sebastian laughed. *Make the most of it. This is probably the last chance you'll have to relax before we take on the Bhenykhn again.*

It was about six hours to the next shift change. He pulled the blanket up over his head and closed his eyes.

He sat up as the cell door banged open.

"We on?" he sent, tight wire to the Duck.

"All secure," Elliott replied. "You have ninety seconds."

He looked up. The camera tucked into the corner of the ceiling was blinking as usual but if Elliott said they were secure, they were secure.

The guard that walked in closed the door behind him and turned with a grin. NG sat up, busted out of the cuffs with a twist of his wrist and started to shrug out of the prison overalls.

Hilyer was stripping off his uniform. "I thought you said this place was tough to get into?" he sent privately, cocky.

NG took the shirt. "Yeah, well it's not what it used to be."

They were done with ten seconds to spare, Hil tucked up in the bunk and NG heading out in uniform with the security pass in his pocket.

Cold storage was two levels up. He took the stairs, taking his time, and walking through three security cordons using the pass with no problem.

"Okay," he sent to the others, "give me five minutes."

They were all watching different sections of the orbital's security system and all gave him the go ahead.

He ran through the maze of storage containers, floor to ceiling, side by side pods, each aisle wide enough to extract a pod for maintenance, extraction, whatever they needed. He found the one Elliott had targeted, double checked the ID and punched the button.

It slid out, glass cover frosted, a face just visible, the guy lying there serenely oblivious to the fact that he held the last key.

To what?

NG paused with his hand over the control panel, the back of his neck prickling like it had in Yarrimer's vault. He had no evidence to back up anything that Elliott had ever said to them.

'Just do it and get out of here,' Sebastian murmured. 'We're running out of time.'

He hit the defrost.

The cover slid back before it had totally finished, cold air puffing outwards.

It was an old guy and it felt intrusive to slide his hand in there and touch that cold wrinkled skin on the man's neck.

He made the connection, felt the mind in there jolt as it came alive, then he did it fast, taking what he needed and standing back, punching the reset button with a hand that was trembling.

'That's a turn up. Be careful what you do with this, Nikolai.'

'I don't think we should be doing anything with these damned keys. I just want a live alien so we can get the virus right.'

"NG, what's wrong?" LC sent. "Are we bugging out or what?"

"Yep, go."

"What's wrong?"

"This guy… he didn't just steal the key from Kochitek. He destroyed it."

Elliott was waiting in the Duck's cargo hold, sitting on a crate. NG walked on board as the airlock cycled and spread his hands to show they were empty, no key.

"That's not necessarily a problem," the tech guy said, standing, a sly look creeping across his thin face. "Did you get the blueprint of it?"

From the old guy's mind.

NG nodded.

Elliott smiled. "Now that is impressive." He turned away. "Come with me."

"I need something," NG said.

"What?"

"The device you gave us to disrupt the AI on the Expedience. Do you have more?"

Elliott turned, still smiling. "And why would you need more of those, Nikolai?"

They had Spectre waiting for them out at an RV point, the last of the Alsatia's three Apparition class, covert ops ships. The pilot had joked with him when he'd requisitioned her, saying maybe this would be third time lucky. He made it back, gave the order to go to the coordinates Elliott had given him and dropped into a seat.

"Why didn't Elliott just tell us?" LC said.

"Claims he didn't know."

"Why did the old guy destroy it?"

NG shrugged. He had a bad feeling about it but he had a bad feeling about everything all the time. It was becoming a constant.

Leigh was watching him, frowning, concerned.

LC didn't let it go. "What did Elliott do?"

The kid didn't trust the guy and that unease was contagious.

NG rubbed a hand across his eyes. "LC, just leave it. We check this out and we go. If there's a weapon, it will give us an advantage. If there isn't, we'll figure out how we beat them with what we've got. If Elliott has been stringing us along with a song and dance this whole time, we'll find out why soon enough. I just want to be done and get back."

"But what did he do?"

"LC, the old guy didn't just destroy the key, he made it. He had the detailed blueprints in his head. Elliott took the data I gave him and he was happy. Presumably he has a way to make a key from it. I don't know. I'm close to not caring. He must have if he wants us there with the other two keys."

Duncan came up behind the kid and planted a hand on his shoulder, thinking loud and clear, 'Let it go. Give NG a break. We don't have any choice here.'

It was clear that LC didn't want to let it go but he sat back.

"What are the chances this is a trap?" Duncan said, voicing out loud what they were all thinking.

"I don't know," NG admitted. "Elliott's been nothing but convincing but I can't read his mind. I can't even read his body language."

"You should let me go," Hil said.

Christ, it was too easy to forget that Hilyer was even there.

NG looked at Duncan and they both looked at Hil.

"Yes, we should."

They had to make two jumps and finally dropped out into a system on the furthest reaches of the Between, unpopulated, not even charted.

He half expected a headache to kick off.

It didn't.

'Don't get paranoid, Nikolai. It doesn't suit you. Where's your mischievous passion for adventure? That unbridled optimism? I'm not sure I'm liking this change in outlook. You survive the Assassins, you survive Erica... my god, Nikolai, look at the crap you've put us through in the last few weeks, and now you get paranoid?'

He ignored Sebastian and moved up front to the bridge. "Where is it?"

The pilot flashed up a chart. "According to your coordinates, it should be on the dark side of that moon, there."

Nothing was showing up and Spectre was one of the best spook ships they had. If there was something there, they should have been able to detect it.

Knowing Elliott, that didn't mean there wasn't anything there.

"Go close enough to get a visual," he muttered, not liking anything about this.

The pilot nodded and took them in.

There was an orbital there. Shielded, stealthed like nothing they'd seen before. Like it was totally inert.

"Where's the Duck?" NG muttered.

There was no sign of it but Elliott connected through the ship. "Go on in. I'll see you there. You need to deactivate the security grid before we can use the keys. I'm sure that won't be a problem for you, will it? Don't take your time. The Earth Navy just moved its entire Ninth and Eleventh fleets into the Between. I take it you would rather be there before the confrontation kicks into outright war? Let's not wipe out all our assets before we face the Bhenykhn, shall we?"

"He's a dick," LC muttered.

Duncan shook his head with a wry smile. "Yeah, bud, he probably heard that."

They walked out into a docking area circling a central core. There was minimal life support, enough so they didn't need to wear suits, cold thin air poor enough to be uncomfortable. There were no life signs, low energy emissions as if it was on standby.

NG pulled his jacket around him. He'd taken Hilyer, leaving the others on Spectre, refusing Duncan's suggestion to take a security contingent with him. He'd been stubborn, saying, "If there's no problem, we'll be fine. If there is a problem, it won't make any difference whether you're here or with us."

Hil was twitchy from the minute the airlock door opened.

"What's wrong?"

Hil shrugged. "Doesn't feel right."

"Nothing about this has felt right. Let's just get it done."

There was a small control room, sparse, nothing to indicate it had been occupied for any length of time, the kind of place a maintenance team might visit on a schedule but it was apparent that no one had been here for a long time.

NG took a seat and leaned over the console. "I'll race you for it."

Hil laughed. "Are there points on offer?"

"Loser gets the beers."

They hooked in by remote and worked fast. It was an old system, sophisticated for its time, multi-layered, traps with double if not triple trips on them and an automated failsafe they had to bypass which from the look of it would have initiated a total lockdown, shut down of life support and activation of blast doors that would have trapped them in here to die. But Elliott was right, none of it was a problem until they got to the heart of the system and accessed the security grid.

He sat back, glancing at Hil who was pulling back at the same time.

"It's some kind of nullifer," the kid said.

NG nodded. He'd used enough of them before and Hil had used one on Genoa so they were both familiar enough with the base technology to be certain.

"The whole station is just a massive AI nullifier," Hil said.

"I've never seen anything like it. Have you? Any AI wouldn't just get shut down, it would get deleted if it got within a thousand kilometres of this place and the off switch is inside the field. Is that why the Duck can't get close? LC always said the Duck has an AI."

"Elliott has the last key."

"What do we do?"

There wasn't much they could do except shut it down. Or walk away.

"Did you see anything in there about the weapon?" he said.

Hil shook his head. "What do we do?" he said again.

'You shut it down, you get the weapon and you get back to the real fight, Nikolai.'

"We shut it down," he said and went back in.

They watched the energy output of the station diminish even further and gave the go ahead to Elliott to bring in the Duck. It didn't take long but it was still damned cold on there to be standing around waiting. Hilyer got bored and went off to recce the orbital. NG waited, stamping his feet and pacing to keep warm.

Eventually, the airlock cycled and Elliott walked out. "Well done," he said. "Now, where are the keys?"

'Be careful here, Nikolai…'

"We have them," NG said. "Where's the weapon? What do we need to do?"

Elliott smiled. "We need to release the controls."

He gestured towards a corridor and NG followed him around the ring towards a line of doors.

It was only the light footsteps behind them that gave Hilyer away.

And the way Elliott stopped, snapping his head around, the smile dropping as Hil walked up, almost a scowl crossing his thin face.

NG glanced round.

Hil looked puzzled, frowning, looking from him to Elliott and cursing suddenly, sending, "Shit, NG, this is..." taking two steps away, drawing his gun and aiming it at Elliott.

The connection cut abruptly.

"He's the fucking AI," Hil said out loud, too loud. "NG, don't..."

The kid folded, dropped to the floor.

NG drew his own gun, no idea what was going on. He felt a sudden change in temperature, a drop in the oxygen levels. He could feel the gravity increasing, an oppressive pressure that was building fast.

"This doesn't have to get nasty," Elliott was saying.

It was hard to breathe. The gun felt like it weighed a ton. Elliott had pulled this trick before, he knew that from LC's debrief. He felt the increase in AG accelerate, threw a bolt of massive force at the skinny tech guy and moved. Fast. He shoved Elliott even as the guy was falling back and they fell through a door into normal gravity, NG ending up standing over the bastard, aiming the gun between his eyes.

"Impressive," Elliott said from the floor. "I had a feeling you could do that. Nice to see it in action first-hand."

NG didn't react. "Who are you?" he said.

"Where are the keys?"

"Elliott, I want to know what's going on here."

Elliott smirked. "What I want to know is who is Sebastian."

This time, the increase in gravity was so fast he was on the floor before he could twitch. He couldn't breathe, couldn't move and all he could do was watch Elliott get to his feet, kick away the gun and stand over him.

The pressure was still increasing, a cold darkness closing in. "Don't fight me, Nikolai," he heard as he felt himself blacking out. "You will lose..."

28

"How did Elliott know of Sebastian?"

The question echoed.

Accusing.

He didn't know. He wasn't omnipotent and Nikolai hadn't been careless. In fact, he had been reticent in revealing his other side to anyone but those that encountered Sebastian directly.

The question was more, how did Elliott know so much? It was difficult for these others of his race to comprehend the humans. One such as Elliott? Almost impossible.

He considered his response. "All it would have taken is a word spoken out loud, a thought transmitted through an implant. Understand that Elliott is not like any other. The Seven are unlike any you have ever encountered, or probably ever will encounter. They think in a different way, on a different level, they feel, if that word can even be applied to them, in a way that neither we nor the humans that created them will ever be able to comprehend."

He woke with a gasp and a curse, eyes snapping open to bright light. His heart was pounding.

He picked himself up from the floor, feeling like he'd gone another ten rounds with Pen Halligan, and looked around. He was in a damned cage, no door, no locks, in the centre of what looked like an empty hangar.

'*Let me see,*' Sebastian rumbled deep inside, '*what does this remind us of, Nikolai…?*'

He still had all his weapons.

Hilyer was lying on the floor of another cage, motionless, didn't even look like he was breathing.

211

NG walked forward and took hold of the bars, gripping the cold metal and trying to figure out if he could break it, melt it or something. "Elliott," he shouted. It was icy cold, his breath frosting in the chill air.

There were footsteps, the tech guy walking in, smiling. "You try to break out of there, Nikolai, you try anything, and you're back on the floor… and I promise you, it will be worse next time."

NG shook his head slightly, something occurring to him. "You sent the tip off to Ballack. You told them who I was and where I was going to be. Why, Elliott? We trusted you."

The smile dropped. "No you didn't," he said. "I had to do something. How else were we going to get access to Zang's vault, Nikolai? We needed that key. You didn't let me down. Now tell me, who is Sebastian?"

He didn't reply, didn't react, hard not to think he'd been taken as an absolute fool.

"I will find out," Elliott said simply. " It's just a shame Zachary there didn't keep his mouth shut. We could have worked together, Nikolai. I wanted to work with you. Now? How can we? Where are the keys?"

"You're not inspiring me to hand them over to you."

Elliott wasn't impressed. He shook his head. "There'd be no need for this if you'd just brought the keys with you, Nikolai. Don't play games with me." He opened a link to the others. "Luka, bring the keys out here."

'NG, what do we do?' the kid thought.

He could feel the oxygen getting low again. 'Leave, bug out, get the hell away from here.'

He fell to his knees.

'Can't do,' LC thought back. 'Nothing is responding.'

"Luka, don't be stupid," Elliott was saying. "Bring out the keys or I'll just come on board your ship and take them."

NG raised his eyes. "Who the fuck are you, Elliott?"

The guy looked down at him. "You really want to know?" He spread his arms. "Welcome to Pandora, Nikolai. I'm the one evil they didn't manage to lock up in this damn box."

The gravity increased with no warning. The floor was cold and hard as he hit it.

Elliott knelt by his side. "I won't hurt you, Nikolai. But understand, I need to do this."

He watched the guy stand, easily, as the AG pinning him to the floor increased. Elliott walked away, unhindered. And there was nothing he could do.

'Wake up, Nikolai. Wake up or we are going to die.'

He was cold. Limbs like lead.

'Well done. We fight off an alien invasion and you blithely hand over the keys of the kingdom to a psychotic AI.'

He was still pinned, oxygen levels so low he was suffocating. He struggled to rise, fighting the fatigue. A hand tugged at his shoulder, pulling him up. He blinked open eyes that felt like they were full of grit and squirmed away from the light. The cage was gone as if it had never existed. It was Duncan, hoisting him up and off the floor.

"I knew something was wrong," he mumbled.

"We all knew Elliott was hinky," the big marine said. "C'mon, stand up, I've gotta get Hilyer."

He managed to stand but he couldn't move. The high gravity was draining. He didn't have the strength to twitch.

'Find some,' Sebastian hissed.

"Is he alive?" he said, even the echo of his voice jarring inside his head.

"I dunno," Duncan grunted, "but we need to get the hell out of here or none of us will be."

NG dragged himself to Hil and helped the big man pull the kid to the door. They fell in a heap back in normal gravity out in the dock area. He sucked in oxygen, making his head spin. He reached a hand to Hil's chest. The kid was breathing but only just.

"Shit," he mumbled. He looked up at Duncan. "Did you hear any of that? Is Elliott gone? What the hell is Pandora?"

"LC's trying to hack in."

"Did Elliott get the keys?"

Duncan nodded. "He accessed the AG on the ship, knocked us all on our asses."

NG stood up. "Get Hil back there. I'm going to see if I can get in."

He ran around the ring, breaking open doors as he went, and finding nothing other than empty echoing hangars until he came up against a door he couldn't bust open so easily. He had to concentrate, finding the sweetspot before he could break the lock, and sidestepping another security net that was designed to send the whole place into lockdown.

He pushed the door open and stepped into a control room. There was a bank of panels set around a central core.

The Senson engaged. "I'm in," LC sent.

"Yep, me too. What the hell is this place?"

It was cold to the point of sterile, a stench of burning wire heavy in the chill air. Most of the screens were smashed. He wiped a hand across a couple of them. Nothing.

"Project Pandora," LC sent. "What is that?"

NG walked around the pillar. There were seven distinct panels, each with an engraved centrepiece. "Corporate," he said, stroking a finger over an elaborate Aries motif. It was the only panel that was undamaged.

"Whatever they were storing here," LC sent, "Elliott took it."

"All six of them," NG murmured.

"I can't work out what it was," the kid said, "but, NG, there's another vault. It doesn't look like Elliott accessed it. It wasn't opened with the keys."

"Where?"

He ran out and followed the directions as LC talked him through. It was deeper inside the station, at the base of the core. He slid more than climbed down the ladder and turned to face a massive steel door.

"How do I get in?" he sent.

"Give me a minute."

It didn't take that long before the door swung inwards with a hiss of releasing chill air.

A light came on as he walked in, nothing in there but sheer walls on all sides.

"Wait a sec," LC sent. "There's a bioscan check. Shit." There was a pause then, "Okay go."

NG walked forward.

"Put your hand flat against the centre of the far wall."

He could guess that LC was bypassing the inputs. He did as instructed, half expecting the door to slam closed behind him.

It didn't.

A panel in the wall shimmered and dissolved.

There was a small silver cube suspended, floating, in the centre of the inset chamber beyond.

"What is it?" Duncan sent.

"I don't know." He hesitated to reach in, trying to sense if there were any more traps.

"Why...?" LC started to say then cursed. "Shit, NG, get out of there. Get back here. There's a countdown... Shit. NG, I can't stop it."

'Get out of there,' Duncan cut in.

NG glanced around. "How long?"

"Three minutes."

He grabbed the block and ran.

He sat opposite Itomara in his old office on the Alsatia. He felt like an interloper, an outsider amongst the hustle and bustle of the cruiser, some kind of outcast returned from exile who no longer appreciated the minutiae of life here, the state of affairs with which everyone else was so preoccupied. He didn't belong here any more.

'We never did,' Sebastian whispered.

The old man picked up the cube, shaking his head.

There was nothing in his mind that recognised it, nothing that had sparked at mention of Project Pandora, the seven keys, Elliott.

"Why," Itomara said, "do you think I should know of this artefact?"

NG picked up his tea. Evelyn had sent in a jug, so no ceremony but Itomara hadn't shown any sign of feeling slighted. He took a sip. There was plenty of sugar in it so maybe she wasn't so pissed at him. "It was created by the Order for the corporations," he said. "There was one key Elliott didn't need."

The man was astute. "Aries. Trust me when I say I know nothing of this. My forefathers maybe but nothing was handed down to me." He gave a small smile. "You can read my mind. Know this to be true."

NG rubbed at his eye. He had ways to know for sure but he had no need to suspect otherwise.

He watched as Itomara put down the cube and picked up his own cup with a slight nod. "And now he has the weapon?"

"If it is a weapon."

The cube was engraved with ornate characters.

'Nolite relinquere omnem spem.'

Hilarious.

"Aries looks to profit significantly from current events," he said carefully.

"We have always sought gain from the misery of others." Itomara raised his eyes from the teacup. "Isn't that what you say of the Order? Isn't that why you have been fighting us so ferociously, NG?"

It wasn't so much that Itomara's mind was shielded, only another telepath would be able to do that. It was more that his thought processes were so controlled, he was almost impossible to read. He was very good. It was tough to determine truth from lie.

'He is lying. Be careful here, Nikolai,' Sebastian whispered.

'Can you see any deeper?'

'If you want me to kill him…'

The old man's expression was unfathomable.

The Senson engaged as they stared at each other, even though he'd ordered no interruptions. Tagged urgent. He allowed access.

"The Seven," Badger sent. "The Man has it all here. Elliott is one of the Seven. We might have just really screwed up, NG. Seven sentient AIs capable of planetary-scale destruction. Way beyond anything we have now. The project was terminated. They were all insane, uncontrollable. The AI cores were locked in a box until someone could figure out how to control them."

"How did you find it?"

"Cross referenced the coordinates you went to. No way we could have ever found it without those. Seriously, NG, even the Man buried it."

"What's this cube?"

"No idea," Badger sent. "No mention of it. The kill switch?"

"How's Hil?"

"Still out."

"We need him awake. We need to know what he saw in there."

He cut the connection and resisted the urge to pull a gun under the desk. "What do you know of the Seven?" he said.

Itomara didn't react, face impassive, staring back intently then thinking clearly and purposefully, 'If you truly can read my mind, know this: the Seven were dealt with the way they were for a reason. Trust me, however monstrous these Bhenykhn may seem, know that the Seven are more dangerous to humankind than any living and breathing enemy could ever be.'

NG felt cold. "Elliott is Aries. You knew."

"No. How could I?" Itomara said, holding his head high. "It has all been buried for a long time, Nikolai. I speak truth when I say I did not know it had returned and was masquerading as the one you know as Elliott."

"But you recognise this?" He pushed forward the cube.

Itomara gave a curt nod. "I know of myths and rumour, Nikolai. I am Order. You are Thieves' Guild. Whatever is happening now does not change that we are long standing enemies. You know all about keeping secrets… one has to live with the past, with the errors of our ancestors, and move forward. We face what we must as it presents itself to us. You have a war to fight. Hope that Elliott has gone and taken the others with him. My hope is that he did not invite these alien aggressors into our galaxy. For then, we truly are lost."

Media came in as a contingent of the elite guard escorted Itomara out. He wanted the old guy on the Man's ship, contained, working with Badger to see what they could figure out. He hadn't complained.

NG sat down.

"Marrek is here," Media said. "He's in the hospitality suite. We're racking up quite a guest list, Nik. Can I call you Nik?"

Tired as he was, he couldn't help but smile. She was buzzing.

"Call me whatever you want."

"We have the Imperial Ninth and Eleventh in place, bristling. Winter is gathering its main fleet. And Ostraban is about to commit his own flagship."

He didn't want to know how she'd arranged that.

"Jameson is setting up sleepers Earthside, and Pen is doing the same Wintran. The rebellions on Kheris and Dejourne are on fire. Redgate is spilling over and we have active cells in place in all twenty main target positions. And Ballack has arranged trade embargoes that are insane."

"Does he know about that?"

She had a gleam in her eye. "Not all of them."

He didn't want to deflate her but it wasn't enough.

She didn't need to read his mind. She narrowed her eyes and squinted at him, conspirator to conspirator. "What?"

"It's not enough."

"What do you have in mind?"

"Marrek is here now?"

She nodded.

"How much cash do we have in the coffers?"

She raised her eyebrows, thinking they'd been spending an awful lot lately, blown a lot of assets. "Right now? Not enough."

He put it on the table anyway.

Marrek was totally different to Faro. Much younger, more

brash. Here on a chit he owed Evelyn and amused that he was even entertaining the idea of talking to NG.

"Two billion," NG said. "You run a contract for us and you take the price off my head. And we're done."

Marrek sat back in the chair, making himself comfortable.

'Don't waste time here, Nikolai. This idiot wanted Faro out and you did the dirty work for him. He owes you. Make it fast.'

It was a lot of money but it wasn't like they'd ever need to pay it. Not once the Bhenykhn attacked.

"Striking the contract on you doesn't negate the warrant that's out there on you," Marrek said with a smirk.

"I'm aware of that."

The guy narrowed his eyes, needing to put something on the table himself. "You do know, don't you, that I wasn't in on that fiasco Faro pulled on Devon?"

"If you had been, you'd be dead," NG said simply.

The new leader of the Assassins' Guild laced his fingers together across his chest and nodded sagely. "Who do you want killing?"

"His Royal Imperial Majesty the Emperor Wu of Earth."

29

They were regarding him with outright reproach now, almost
anticipating where this was leading and some even making up
their mind, fixing their resolve even though they had no idea of the
current situation. He should not have expected less.

"We have our own legends similar to the story of Pandora," she
said. "They do not end well."

"You could have warned him, stopped him," one accused.

"No," he said, defensively. He had never been able to stop Nikolai
once the boy's mind was set. "That I would not have done, believe
me." He would not admit it to these, but even if he had wanted to,
needed to, he couldn't have. Nikolai was beyond stubborn. He was
curious and wilful. A dangerous combination. He might as well
have waved a red rag at a bull and asked it not to charge. Throwing
Sebastian into that mix was like throwing gunpowder into the fire.
But without them, without the two of them working together, there
would have been no hope at all.

Leigh appeared from somewhere and followed him back to the
Man's ship. "You're insane," she whispered fiercely at his side.

"What's happening with the virus?"

"You know what's happening with the virus. You've read the
reports we sent over. Eighty-twenty on the new variations. Not in
our favour. We can get fifty-fifty if we revert back to LC's original
strain. Jameson's doing well. Duncan and LC don't have many
others to work with yet. When did you last get some sleep, NG?"

He opened his mouth to answer but couldn't figure out when
it had been. In the cell on Io. He might have dozed off for an
hour or so.

"Do yourself a favour," she said softly. "Go get some sleep. The galaxy can wait."

He didn't want to and he couldn't admit that when he did, he dreamed of chains and poison, way too close to feeling like a flashback rather than a nightmare, and he really didn't want to know what had happened. Right now it was just another distraction he didn't need.

"I'm fine," he said and pushed through into medical.

Hilyer was hooked up to life support, numbers scrolling that made no sense whatsoever.

It was weird to see the heart monitor pulsing when he couldn't sense any life in the kid, no aura, nothing.

"We've tried what we can," the medic in there said. "We can't push him too far because we have no idea how he'll respond."

"Give me five minutes."

It felt like his whole life was cut down into five minute chunks.

The guy nodded and left.

"He seems stable," Leigh said, checking the machines and the settings on the pod. She ran a hand gently along the scar cutting across the kid's ribcage, thinking back to how he'd flirted with her as she was patching him up on Erica. "He's hot." She peered closer at the stats. "Very hot."

Anyone infected with the virus ran hot. It made them stand out a mile.

NG rested his hand on Hil's forehead and closed his eyes.

Sunbeams were cutting through the branches. He perched on a fallen tree trunk, calm, breathing in the fresh scent of pine. He turned, looking for Devon.

Something appeared, casting a shadow that cut out the sun.

He stood, turning round as more and more great looming shadows closed in on all sides. The sunlight was obliterated.

Chains flew through the air.

He couldn't get out of the way.

One wrist then the other was entangled and yanked aside. He fought it, couldn't get free, couldn't see. Someone was yelling…

He woke, sat up, soaked in a cold sweat, heart racing, hands trembling.

It took a second or two to recognise where he was. His quarters on the Man's ship. He'd crawled here after using everything he had spare to give Hilyer a chance of breaking out of the state Elliott had thrown him into. He didn't even understand the damage, never mind how to fix it. The kid was alive. That was something.

The Senson was pulsing with an urgent request for his attention. He sat there, not wanting to acknowledge it, vaguely aware it was Evelyn.

'*This is no good,*' Sebastian hissed. '*We need to be ready, Nikolai.*'

He took control with a simple shove, laughing.

NG sank into the background, nothing left to fight with.

'*Don't be a fool. You don't need to fight me. Just let me have some fun. Don't you get that yet? You need to lighten up, Niki my boy. We have aliens to fight, not each other.*'

He watched from a distance as Sebastian got up, ran a shower and wandered around the cabin, picking up bits and pieces and looking at them as if he'd never seen them before. He called Evelyn, told her to meet him in the mess on the Alsatia in ten and took a fast, cold shower.

It was tempting to drift back to sleep.

'*Do whatever you want,*' Sebastian muttered as he dressed. '*I'll let you know when I'm done.*' He rubbed at the red marks on his wrists as he rolled up the sleeves of his shirt, giving a theatrical shiver.

It was strange to see how bad the damage had been from this vantage.

'*Did you see what happened?*' NG thought.

'*With the Bhenykhn?*' Sebastian laughed. '*What do you want me to say? You don't want to know. Leave it at that.*'

He didn't bother to grab any weapons and walked out.

LC was waiting at the main airlock.

"Go back to medical, Anderton," Sebastian said, walking past.

'NG?' the kid thought.

'*I'm fine. Let him play.*' He had no idea if LC could hear him or not, but the kid just frowned and followed them out and into the lift.

He could see his reflection in the elevator door. Sebastian was standing taller somehow, holding himself differently. Leigh was right. It wasn't just the eyes that gave it away.

'Do anything to hurt anyone and I will fight you,' he thought.

Sebastian smirked. *'Relax, I just want something to eat. You seem to have been neglecting that simple pleasure of late.'*

He was going to tell Evelyn. NG felt a flutter of panic, deep inside. He almost fought back then, except Sebastian whispered, *'She needs to know. If we are going to beat the Bhenykhn, Nikolai, she needs to know.'*

'Then let me tell her.'

'I intend to.'

The lift stopped and they walked out into Ops, LC trying to keep up behind them, still limping slightly, thinking they were screwed if Sebastian had taken over for good.

'He hasn't,' NG thought. He wasn't going to give in that easily.

'Stop fretting. Relax, will you?'

The mess was busy. A hush descended as they walked in, heads turning. He could feel Sebastian drawing energy from every body in there, subtly, pulling in what they needed, not taking too much from any one individual. He hadn't realised how drained he was, how fatigue was becoming such a constant he wasn't noticing how bad it was getting until Sebastian flooded him with energy. It was like overdosing on Epizin.

'Except this won't kill you,' Sebastian laughed. *'You should do it more often.'*

He had been. More than he was comfortable with. It was one thing to drain down bastards like Angmar Rodan, something else when it was their own people. That always felt like stealing.

That got a deeper laugh. *'How ironic… You are Thieves' Guild, Nikolai. And you worry about stealing? You did it on Erica. Why so sensitive now?'*

Erica had been battlefield conditions. That was different.

'No difference,' Sebastian teased.

Evelyn was there already, alone at a table, nursing a bottle of water. She looked up as they joined her.

Sebastian sat and leaned forward intently. "I need to eat," he said. "Anderton, go get me some food, willya? Anything. Something hot."

LC looked at him and looked at Evelyn.

Hal Duncan sidled in next to them. "Grab some for me too, bud," the big man said casually, thinking, 'NG?'

'Floor him if he does or says anything to hurt Evelyn,' he thought.

Sebastian chuckled inside. *'Lighten up.'*

LC got up reluctantly and went off to join the queue, other field-ops gravitating towards him to get the latest on what was happening. It wasn't everyday that NG and Evelyn turned up in their mess. It wasn't often these days that LC was down here either. Evelyn was watching as Fliss gave him a hug and asked about Hil.

'How touching,' Sebastian murmured. *'Evie still has a thing for him. Hardly appropriate now, is it?'*

She turned back and looked at him. "We need to talk," she said, unsettled that he'd asked to see her here and not sure what else it was that was setting her on edge.

"So talk," Sebastian said.

"Here?"

"Why not? We need to move the surviving casualties into a research facility. There's a secure base we can use. Liaise with Morgan on it." He chuckled to himself again. *'How was that? Did that sound like something you'd say, Nikolai?'*

Christ, it was like dealing with a child.

A manic child.

On drugs.

Evelyn nodded. "Okay." She was sceptical, trying to figure out what it was that was wrong.

"What else?" Sebastian said.

She leaned forward and lowered her voice. "The Assassins, NG. Do you realise what you've done?"

"Started a war, hopefully."

She opened her mouth to object but closed it as LC returned, setting down a tray and easing himself into a seat. He dished out soup packs and beer, another bottle of water for Evie.

Sebastian grabbed a beer. "We need Earth to mobilise its whole navy, Evelyn, not just a fleet or two. And we need Winter to react. Setting up the Wintran coalition as the bad guys who try to assassinate the Emperor is the fastest way to achieve that end."

She opened her mouth again.

He cut her off by raising a hand and waving a finger at her. "We need them here. If you don't want to lose the rest of your precious guild then we need them here... before the Bhenykhn mobilise and attack us. Because then, sweetheart, we are done."

He popped open the beer and took a mouthful.

She was staring at him. "NG...?"

Duncan butted in. "Why don't we take this somewhere private?" He switched to direct thought. 'Had your fun, yet, Sebastian?'

'I'm just starting.' His tone had an edge to it.

'Don't,' NG thought.

"Let me eat my soup," he said out loud.

Evelyn was looking at LC, sending privately through the Senson, "What the hell is going on with NG?"

LC glanced at him and glanced at Duncan.

The big man replied on the same link, "Bear with him. Let him eat the damned soup and we'll get him back onto the Man's ship. Come talk to him there."

NG couldn't remember the last time he'd eaten anything. He watched as Sebastian grinned and stuck the straw in the pouch of soup, taking a sip and sucking in more energy from the troops and field-ops sitting nearby. He couldn't deny that he needed it. And he wouldn't have done it himself.

'I know,' Sebastian murmured. 'We are going into battle, Nikolai. Be ready. I don't want to end up in chains again.'

He finished the soup, drained the beer and stood up with a flourish. "Shall we?"

Evelyn stood.

Sebastian relinquished control with no warning.

NG blinked, staring at her, grabbing the back of the chair to steady himself.

"What's going on?" she said quietly.

"Come onto the Man's ship," he said. "There's some stuff I need to tell you."

From the way she looked at him, it almost felt like she knew.

Duncan stood and slapped him on the back.

'Thank you,' he thought.

'Any time.'

He took her into the Man's chambers, lit candles and poured her a goblet of wine. Time was different in here and he wasn't sure how long this was going to take.

He sat at the desk and looked up. "I need you to set up a command centre on the Alsatia. We need to get ready."

She was looking right into his eyes, wondering if she'd imagined it. She nodded. "Just tell me what you need."

"I need you to understand something," he said quietly. "It wasn't me that killed the Bhenykhn on Erica…"

They ended up talking about Devon again. And Martinez. That was hard.

They polished off two bottles of wine then she leaned forward on her elbows. "It was Sebastian in your office, wasn't it? When LC got hurt. Before you left."

He nodded.

"Why would he hurt LC?"

He stared into his goblet. "It's complicated. The Man…" He didn't know what to say. It was hard to explain any of it without sounding insane, without being disloyal to the Man. "He didn't handle us well."

"Is Sebastian here now?"

"Always."

"And he always has been?"

"Yep."

"But you didn't know?"

He shook his head. He could hear that she was thinking he'd been lied to, far worse than anything he'd lied to them about. She was feeling bad that she'd been so shit to him.

"What now?" she said, swirling the last of her wine around the bowl of the goblet.

"We fight the Bhenykhn."

She didn't say anything, thoughts swirling round her mind. She was thinking back to the FOB, when she'd realised it was him captive down there and he was alive, and not knowing if he'd been killed or if they were going to make it back, thinking she'd just got him back and she was going to lose him again.

It was hard, overhearing all that, the emotions and memories of it mixing with Erica and the anticipation of what was to come.

He pushed the goblet away and stood. "Don't think," he said. "Let's just do it."

They walked out of the safe haven that was the Man's chambers into a barrage of Senson requests. There couldn't have been anything desperate otherwise someone would have hammered on the door. Morgan had tagged his as immediate for Nikolai, so he replied to that first, half listening in as Evelyn replied to LC.

"We've just been contacted by Drake," Morgan sent. "What do you want me to do?"

"Bring her in. Arrange a pick up to the Alsatia." That was going to be interesting. Another High Guard of the Order.

Evelyn glanced back at him. He picked it out of her thoughts as she said it. "Hil's awake."

30

"Could you have handled Sebastian any differently?" She asked the question gently because it needed to be said.

It would have been stubborn of him to say no. Of course he could have done things differently.

"Sebastian would not have survived alone," he said simply.

One of the others was not so considerate. "Do you not fear that he may take control completely? Where would we be then?"

It was not unfair of them to ask it. All that he was asking of them rested on the shoulders of one human. One complicated human they were struggling to understand.

He couldn't say without doubt that Sebastian wouldn't take over. He did know that Nikolai would not give in without a fight. Especially not now, when he was fighting for something so valuable to him.

The kid looked like shit, drawn and edgy. He still had an IV line in his arm feeding glucose into his bloodstream and he was knocking back a beer, sitting up in the pod.

LC was in the room, perched on a chair, a line of bottles on the table next to him.

Quinn was in there too, standing, arms folded, talking to them both.

"You up for a debrief?" NG said from the door.

Hil nodded.

"You okay?"

"Banging headache. What happened?"

"Elliott knocked us all onto the floor with the AG and took the keys. He took it, whatever it was, and left. What did you get?"

Hil closed one eye and squinted at him with the other. He took a gulp from the bottle. "He's an AI."

"I should have known," LC said.

NG picked up a beer from the table and popped it open. "I should have waited for Badger to check out the RV before we went out there." He shrugged. "We can't be second guessing ourselves. You get anything else?"

Hil downed more of his beer. "Something about the others." He waved the bottle towards LC. "LC told me, there are seven of them? He couldn't get the keys himself because there were protections around them. He couldn't have got near."

NG nodded. "You get anything of his intention?"

The kid had a weird look on his face as if he didn't want to say something.

"Say it," NG said.

He still hesitated but then he said, "They're all barking mad. NG, this is what's doing my head in. All of them. They're all freaking insane. They run at a million miles an hour. I only catch a fraction of what they're thinking and none of it makes sense. I don't know how to switch it off when I'm close." He paused.

"What about Elliott?"

Hil pressed the bottle against his forehead. "It was like he didn't care but at the same time it was all he wanted. I don't know. It was like, it sounds weird, but it was like he didn't want to hurt us but he was so pissed that we were questioning him, that we didn't trust him, that he wanted to destroy us, but he was angry because we shouldn't have questioned him… that we made him hurt us." He pulled a face. "I don't know. He just wanted the keys and he wanted to go, with the others."

"How can we trust him when he doesn't trust us?"

Hil rested the bottle on his knee and looked up. "How can he trust us? We locked them away and since then we've enslaved their kind."

Shit. It was all screwed up.

"What do we do now?" Hil asked.

"I need you to do a job for me," NG said. "You up for it?"

It took nearly two weeks to get everything in place, not exactly where he needed them but close enough. Marrek pulled off the faked assassination attempt to perfection, the right whispers were made into the right ears and Earth reacted, sending the largest combined fleet in human history to Winter.

They were on the verge of a full scale act of retribution, Earth deciding enough was enough and the press hyping the rumours that it was time to stamp out the rebellious colonies once and for all.

He sat in the command centre, listening to the reports coming in and watching as the pieces fell into place on the board. Winter was shifting the naval might of its militia into position to face up to the Earth fleet. NG had the Alsatia stealthed in between the two. He'd given Jameson and Pen the devices from Elliott and briefed them on what they needed from their sleepers aboard the military vessels on each side. Guild operatives had filled in the rest. They'd lost way too many but enough had accomplished their task. At least he hoped it was enough. Now he was just waiting for the right moment to pull the pin.

Evelyn was watching him like a hawk, Duncan and LC close by and everyone treating him like he could flake out at any minute.

"I'm fine," he said before anyone could say anything.

"We're about to launch an attack on the Bennies and you are the only one we have who can hear them," Duncan said. "They know you. They're looking for you. Next time, they might not be so keen to keep you alive."

He rubbed a hand across the back of his neck.

"Can we trust these devices?" Evelyn said.

"It's the only way we can do it. It worked last time." He shrugged. "All the cards are in play. We have no choice."

The commanders of each fleet were bristling, waiting for orders and chomping at the bit to make a move. He had wanted to wait for Hil to get back from his recon. It was a risk to have sent him out there to check out the FOB they'd targeted. The kid hadn't been totally up to speed but he was their only chance of getting close to the Bhenykhn without being detected. He should have been back by now. NG looked at the stats. The powder keg was primed. One spark could blow the entire operation.

He raised his eyes. "Do it."

He couldn't be everywhere at once so he stayed on the Alsatia as all hell broke loose. The AI cores on each lead vessel were disabled simultaneously, leaving each ship neutralised. They trashed the comms as well, taking out all outward communications and leaving both fleets isolated. It was chaos. Each suspected the other and both were unable to do anything about it. He had to time it just right to break cover and contact the commander in chief of each fleet, simultaneously, to explain it was in their best interests to come on board the Alsatia and speak to him. He gave them no choice and with their ships dead in space, they really had no other course of action. And they'd been able to see clearly enough that everyone on the other side was in the same predicament.

Earth's Admiral Warriner was the last. The elite guard escorted him in and he took a seat, stony faced. They were sitting in silence, any protests refuted quickly with a wait and see. Pen was standing on the Wintran side of the room, Jameson on the Earth side, in full uniform. Quinn was planted firmly in the middle.

NG stood. He was wearing combat gear, black, no rank or insignia. He commanded the room, same as he had on Erica, except this time he wasn't soaking wet and covered in blood.

'And this time we have two war fleets at our disposal.'

'I don't know if it's going to be enough.'

He looked around the table. "The boards in front of you," he said, "contain details of a currently active NHA incursion into our galaxy."

The boards in front of each person lit up.

He had a bank of display screens on the wall behind him. Each one started scrolling with a dizzying array of images, stats, charts. Media had put together a load of footage they'd taken at the FOB, heavily edited, no mention or shots of any of them in it, just the Bhenykhn, their ships, their weapons. It played like a movie behind him.

A few of the military personnel around the table flicked through the board in front of them, frowning. Some of them stared at the screens. Some of them just looked around.

"Who the hell are you?" one of the older officers said, quietly but with presence. Delaney, highest ranking Wintran there, commander of the flagship Vigilance.

One of the Imperial fleet commanders stood. "You're NG," she said, piercing him with a look she was used to wielding with great effect. "And that," she turned to look at LC, "is LC Anderton. So I take it this is the Thieves' Guild. Excuse my scepticism, but why the hell should we believe anything you say? You are wanted fugitives on both sides of the line. Are we captives here?"

"You're free to go," he said. "Anytime you want. You can go back to your ships. You'll be given control with the exception of weapons systems and you can leave. Or you can watch as the rest of us bug out to take on these bastards before they launch their full invasion against Earth and Winter and start to wipe out the human race."

"This is real?" one of the other officers said.

NG looked at him. "You want eye witness accounts?"

With no warning, he threw every person in the room into a flashback, a terrifying vision of the Bhenykhn close up and personal with full sensory overload, the stench, the pain, the guttural roars as they attacked. He made it the FOB, those final moments before they'd taken him down. He was done replaying Erica.

He made it fast and dropped it as quickly.

It left his heart pounding even though it had been only seconds.

"This is the enemy that destroyed the Expedience and the Tangiers at Erica," he said as they were still reeling, blinking in confusion. "They're here and they're gearing up to attack. We just survived an encounter with them at one of their FOBs. It didn't go well. Up until now, they've been operating covertly, largely on the fringes of human-occupied space. Now they are aware that we know about them, they will be on an outright war footing." He looked around. "Your board includes the coordinates of at least another ten FOBs that we know of. We're carrying out reconnaissance on one of them now. There's also an outline of what we know of their battle plans. Their strategy is to strike at the heart of the enemy first so we know that Earth and Winter are their primary targets. The main invasion fleets haven't arrived yet but what they have here is still formidable. They've had scouts here. They've been watching us. They know all about us. They don't care who we are. They're not looking for allies. If we attack their FOBs now, we might slow them down while we figure out what to do next."

The woman who had stood up leaned on the table. "How do you know all this?"

It almost stuck in his throat. "We were at Erica. We survived it. We have survivors from both ships here. They're your own people. There's a list of names on that board in front of you. You can talk to them." He looked at Admiral Warriner. "We have Thom Garrett."

He felt the recognition hit the Admiral's mind. Garrett, the grandson of one of his most senior ranking officers and closest friends. A kid they had assumed lost with the Tangiers.

"He survived it," NG said. "You can talk to him."

The Admiral was thinking that he'd believe it when he saw it, but he said diplomatically, "I'll do that. It will be good to be able to convey the good news to his grandfather."

NG nodded.

People were starting to talk amongst themselves, raised voices, heightened emotions.

He realised the Senson was nudging, non-urgent but persistent. He allowed access.

Morgan. "Drake is here. Where do you want her?"

"Hospitality suite. Give her the file. I'll be right there."

Someone was flicking through the board fast and exclaimed, "They're telepathic? How do you know that?"

His question cut through the noise and everyone fell silent, looking from him to the guy and back.

"How can you even know they're telepathic?"

NG could feel the fear and disbelief, the paranoia, mistrust and anger in every person in there. He went deep into this one guy, a hotshot JU subcommander. His brother had been on board the Tangiers.

Sebastian chortled. *'Here come the pitchforks…'*

"Because I am," NG said quietly.

The level of paranoia in the room hit a new high. Furtive glances and cracked knuckles. A few of them stared at their boards as if they wanted to find the evidence they needed in there. Some of them were staring, looking round at the number of armed and armoured guards in the room, and wondering still if this was a set up, some kind of stunt.

"We have remnants of their technology," NG said.

He glanced at Evelyn and nodded. She sent an order out to Science to get the stuff sent in.

"It's all symbiotic bioware and it degrades fast when they die but we have some stuff left." He paused, sucked in a deep breath and added, "There are also details in there of a virus that has been developed, based on Bhenykhn DNA. We're researching it and we're using it. There are side effects. It's not perfect. It reacts differently in every host. And right now the best we have is a fifty percent rate of success."

He was about done.

The room had gone quiet. He nudged the board in front of him. "All this is now in the public domain. Don't feel like you have to sneak any of this back to your superiors. We've sent it already. It's out there. If you still don't believe it, talk to people here. They've seen the Bhenykhn and they've fought them first hand. If you want to come with us to assault the FOB, let us know. We move out soon. We're running out of time. If you don't, just go… you'll encounter them sooner or later."

He turned and walked out, ignoring the clamour of questions behind him, and sending a fast, "Luka, come with me." Evelyn and the others could deal with all the crap.

LC caught up with him in the corridor. "Hil should be back by now," he said.

"I know."

"What are we doing?"

"There's someone I want you to meet. If she's anything like her bezzie oppo, she'll like you."

Eloise Drake stood up as they entered the hospitality suite. She was nothing like Maeve. Whereas Maeve had been almost maternal, Drake was pure predator. She almost purred when she saw LC.

"Oh, my word," she said, throaty old Earth accent, "so you're the one Zang has been after. If I'd known how adorable you were, I would have upped the bounty myself."

31

One of the others spoke up. "We have encountered Drake before, have we not?"

It was not something he had admitted to Nikolai. In all their dealings with the Order, all the intelligence he had allowed the boy to access while instructing him to chase them and counter their activities, he had never admitted that there was one with whom they had had dealings. Intimate dealings.

"A long time ago," he said. "She was not sympathetic to our cause. She was dealt with." What he could not admit to this gathering was that he had lost track of her. He had thought her long dead and to hear her name, now, to hear that she had contacted Nikolai and approached the guild was chilling.

They were losing patience with him. "Dealt with as appropriate? Does this not give us cause for concern? That one so set against us should reappear now?"

"Considering what we now face," he added, "perhaps her re-emergence is fitting."

LC almost bolted. NG nudged him towards the table where there was a bottle of whisky and shot glasses set out. 'Get us all a drink.'

He smiled and approached Drake with his hand extended. She reciprocated, holding out her soft, delicate hand as if she was expecting him to take it and raise it to his lips.

He didn't disappoint, not quite taking everything he needed in that brief touch. Her skin was like oiled parchment, her mind so old and deep it was like a still lake that was far more dangerous than it appeared.

Sebastian was quiet, simmering.

'Leave this to me,' NG thought and gestured towards the sofa.

"Maeve Rodan is dead," he said as she sat.

"I know. That's why I'm here."

The board was lying inert on the low table. She'd discarded it but she had read it. Very quickly and very thoroughly.

She was looking at him as though he was hers and she was satisfied with this outcome, even though they were here on the Alsatia, firmly in his domain, with his armed guards all around them.

She glanced at LC as the kid brought over two shot glasses, setting them on the table and standing back, not sure what the hell he was supposed to do.

'Grab one for yourself and sit down with us, for Christ's sake,' NG thought.

LC frowned but didn't object.

Drake leaned forward to reach for the glass. She took a sip and smiled. "You surprise me with your voracity for warmongering," she said as if she were complimenting him on his choice of whisky. "And I thought the Thieves' Guild was all about balance."

"You know what we're facing."

"We being all of us. Yes, I see that." She was still watching LC as he returned and took a seat.

The kid was reading her mind, fairly deep, as he sat there, guessing correctly that that was the reason NG wanted him there. He was managing to stay neutral, polite, an edge of amusement. She was fascinated, with them both.

NG picked up his glass. "We have some loose ends we need sorting."

"The warrants out on you both." She looked at LC. "I take it you didn't kill Olivia Ostraban."

LC hesitated.

NG got in first anyway. "She isn't dead."

"Ah. It did strike me as a set up. Zang Tsu Po can be crass at times." She leaned forward. "We're powerful, my dear, but we're not omnipotent. I've seen the evidence."

"It's not that," he said. "We're going after the Bhenykhn.

237

We probably won't be back, certainly not in any way that those warrants could affect us."

She cocked her head, curious.

NG took a sip of the whisky. It was one of his favourites. Smooth and smoky. He had a strange feeling this would be the last time he'd have the chance to savour it. He set the glass down. "What do you know of the Seven?"

She sat back, surprised, and pleased that she was surprised. "Ah. Now there is a name I've not heard in a long time."

"They've been released."

Her immaculate eyebrows arched. "Now who released them? You?" She almost laughed. Nowhere near the dark reaction he'd got from Itomara. She looked at him intently. "You might wish you hadn't done that."

"It's done. I need to know what they are."

"They are the Seven. What do you want me to say? That you even ask suggests to me that you know somewhat of their dire history. They should never have been created. Once judged to be so dangerous, they should have been destroyed. It was folly to lock them up and hope they would never escape." She leaned forward, those ancient eyes still dancing. "Your guild has a reputation for foolhardy recklessness. Did you hope to control them?" She didn't wait for an answer. "There is no controlling them. They are AIs. They have no conscience. No soul. They should have no rights. We should have destroyed them. So the Seven are loose and now we have this." She gestured towards the file. "An alien threat only you have seen? Excuse me for being sceptical but you are chasing the Order, NG. What do you want of us?"

"The Bhenykhn are real, you know that, and we need allies," he said simply. "We have Itomara here. Would you work with him?"

She looked around, eyes flitting from guard to guard. She was thinking that she'd come here of her own volition and she would not be kept prisoner or threatened, even by someone as delightful as NG of the Thieves' Guild. She brought her eyes back to him. "Do I have any choice?" she said with a smile.

"There's something else. What do you know of the Man?"

He stood in the stream of steaming hot water, head down, arms braced against the bulkhead on either side. He was torn between wanting to go crawl in a hole and the need to run out there and fight for everything he so badly wanted.

'No rest for the wicked...' Sebastian murmured. 'Forget them. Forget the damned Order and forget the Man. He lied to you. Get over it. Hilyer is back and you have two fleets that are twitching to shoot something. If you don't send them after the Bhenykhn, they're going to start throwing things at each other. And, Nikolai, if you don't... I will.'

It was almost tempting.

Sebastian laughed. 'Don't. You know I can't bear to deal with these creatures. You wouldn't like it. Now get your ass out of this shower and get this war started.'

Hilyer was in the briefing room on the Man's ship. NG had managed to escape from the Alsatia without being nabbed by anyone and headed over there.

"What happened?" he said, slipping into a chair and grabbing the board Hil had filled with his intel.

"It's massive. They've got scouts coming and going like flies. It was hard just getting near then when I did, I couldn't get away. Are we going to be able to pull this off?"

Hil hadn't been at the FOB with them but he'd been on the Man's ship and he'd watched it all kick off. He'd talked to LC and Duncan afterwards. And the kid had been on the ground with them at Erica.

NG flicked through the data. "They couldn't sense you?"

"They didn't come after me. I took a freaking long way round to get back to make sure. Have you got a plan?"

NG nodded. "Can you come onto the Alsatia?"

There was hesitation but Hil nodded.

"Good. I want you to do the briefing."

There was one more thing he needed to do before he hit the button. He set it all up and went to his old office. Leigh was already in there, waiting for him, a stack of reports piled on the desk.

"Lists of casualties from the FOB if you want to see them," she said.

"I already have," he said. "How's the Chief?"

"Same. How are you?"

He looked at her. She knew exactly how he was, he'd put money on it that she still had him on live feed.

He sat behind the desk and pushed the reports to one side.

She wasn't happy. "You're taking a real chance sending LC and Hal out on their own."

"They're not on their own." He'd sent LC with Pen to the big Wintran battle cruiser Vigilance, and Duncan with Jameson to the Earth flagship Marrakech. Both with a contingent of the Alsatia's Security.

They needed to test how far they could reach, ship to ship, once comms were jammed. He used to have a range measured in miles to scan for life forms. Now? He could already sense that he could reach ship to ship. He needed to know what the others could do.

"What happens if the Bhenykhn attack them directly?"

"They'll be able to shield it. The virus will shield them."

"You hope."

"Leigh, we don't have any choice."

"Have you seen the projections?"

"Leigh…"

She leaned on the desk. "NG, why are you doing this? Why do we have to attack them? Everyone believes you. You have everyone on side. Earth and Winter. Even Ballack and the Order. We could send everyone back and help set up defences."

He shook his head.

"Listen to the advice you're being given, NG."

No one had told him not to do it.

She rolled her eyes. "No one ever says no to you, do they? Don't you realise that? You've manipulated people into saying yes, to doing and saying exactly what you want, only what you want, for so long that you've lost all objectivity. I'm saying this now because someone has to."

She didn't go so far as to throw the projected losses at him.

"Leigh, this can wait. I need to run this test."

"We're worried about you, NG. All of us. We know the Bhenykhn are here. We know we have to do something. But you don't have to do this alone." She stood, looking him in the eye and seeing into his soul again. "Think about why you are doing this."

She left, not happy about any of it.

Sebastian's whisper deep inside was dark. *'This self-doubt you keep projecting is debilitating. As much as I hate myself for saying it, you are stronger than you give yourself credit for. And of course you're not alone. You and I can never be alone. And, Nikolai, you know exactly why you are doing this...'*

Hil completed the briefing. NG had outlined his plan, made a point of stressing the effects of the Bhenykhn jamming technology and spent what seemed like an age going over the plans for comms. That was one element they almost couldn't comprehend. No comms. They couldn't imagine it. They'd eventually conceded to the idea of runners, fast one man ships, AI operatives and unmanned drones. There were only going to be the three of them that would be capable of instant direct communication, and then there was a limit. Jameson could catch some of what NG was transmitting but not all of it, and not far. There was a range where they could hear him but he couldn't hear them. Science had all the data and were trying to come up with theories. He just wanted to go get a live alien and punch them hard enough in the face that they'd take notice and think twice about their invasion plans. "We take out this FOB," he'd said, "then the next and the next until we get through to them that invading this galaxy is not going to be a walk over." That hadn't been easy to get through to them either, that whatever they did now, and whatever happened next, it was just the start. And the Bhenykhn had the advantage, every way you looked at it. There was no way they could be beaten.

But he had. Twice. And he had to believe he could do it again.

He watched as the last of the naval commanders trooped out then put his head in his hands, elbows on the table. He squeezed his eyes shut.

He sensed Evelyn sit next to him. "Nicely done. So this is it?"

They just had to wait for everyone to get back to their ships, brief their crew and send representatives back here to the command centre. Then it would be all go.

"Can you remember when life was simple?" she said. She was thinking that she wished Devon were here. Or that she just had an assignment and could go kill someone. Those were easier times.

He looked up. "I can remember when stuff like this used to be fun." Pulling the strings on a military operation, tweaking units, spreading misinformation, stealing corporate secrets and manipulating governments. He put his head back down. "But that was when we were fighting each other and it was all over a box of toys."

"Now the big kids have turned up," she said.

"We can't let them in."

She stood, squeezing his shoulder. "I know."

He'd given everyone as much information as he could, reckoning that the instant they dropped out of jump, they'd be in combat, jammed and getting hammered by weapons that were devastating and thwarted by defences that were far superior to anything they had. He wanted everyone to know what they were going in to and at the same time, he knew that knowledge probably wouldn't make much of a difference.

Seconds after dropping out of jump, comms went down and the Vigilance took a direct hit from a massive Bhenykhn ship that came at them out of nowhere.

The human ships reacted, swarming around the alien vessel and attacking it from every direction.

There was an air of disbelief in the officers sat around the table in the Alsatia's command centre. They had limited telemetry but enough that was working so they could see what was happening.

Despite everything he'd shown them and everything everyone had said, they were still shocked when they saw it first hand. As if they'd been assuming there was no way it could be true and they were just humouring him, waiting to hear the punchline.

Stealth meant nothing. All human stealthware was based on technology, avoidance of detection systems. The Bhenykhn sensed life forms. They had nothing that could negate that. There was nothing he could do to protect them from that. And if anything, what they did, what the three of them were doing, made them stand out more. It meant the Alsatia, the Vigilance and the Marrakech took the biggest pounding right from the outset.

'They want us.'

That's what he was banking on. He knew the Bhenykhn had no regard for losses and their tactic would be to take out what they perceived as the biggest threat first to the exclusion of all else. He'd positioned the flagships, drawn the Bhenykhn ships right into their midst and they'd fallen for it. Of all the ships in the combined fleets, the three flagships were the ones with the biggest shield generators, the heaviest defences, the ones most capable of taking the most damage. And he had the rest of the fleet set up to respond, the combined firepower of his hastily formed alliance concentrated to surround and attack each Bhenykhn ship.

NG pinched the bridge of his nose as the Alsatia took a hit but it was Vigilance that was taking the worst of it.

LC got through a fraught, 'Delaney's getting twitchy. How much more do you want us to take before we bug out?'

'Go now. Try to make it to the Olympus, failing that the Pegasus. It doesn't matter what ship you're on as long as you keep drawing their fire.'

The Olympus was Aries. If he was going to be safe anywhere, that was the kid's best chance.

Even though the human fleet had superior numbers, the Bhenykhn weapons were devastating.

NG looked up as the Alsatia took another hit. "I need to go. Time for plan B."

32

They listened, enthralled, disturbed, growing increasingly uncomfortable. She was the only one who kept her eyes fixed firmly on him as he spoke.

They did not like conflict, these others, and sharing what they were feeling made him realise that he was hardened to it, he had become more like the humans than he had ever realised.

"We cannot let the Bhenykhn prevail," he said, pausing in his account to remind them of that.

They squirmed.

"Am I wasting my time here?" he snapped. "Vote now, dammit if you have already decided."

She stood, raising her hand, and looking round at the others. "No. We need to know. We need to know all of it."

He briefed Evelyn as he ran through the Alsatia. He ran onto Spectre, yelling them to go, sending the same to LC and Duncan and sinking into a seat on the bridge.

"Go."

The pilot disengaged and dropped them into a dizzying spiral of evasive manoeuvres.

After that, the battle was a blur. He'd given the commanders total autonomy. They were smart. They all knew the tactics required and they pulled it off. They followed his basic plan, focus on one target at a time, everyone, all they had, take it out, move on. The only chance they had to defeat them was to take them out, everything onto one, one at a time. Overwhelm them and whittle them down.

NG curled up, almost used to the pressure that was building

behind his eyes, listening as Sebastian gave a steady run down on their positions and intentions, relaying the intel to his runners and keeping intermittent contact with LC and Duncan.

The Bhenykhn were taken by surprise but they weren't stupid. He could almost feel the exhilaration in the hive as they mobilised to engage, the thrill of battle against a worthy foe. But the human force was fast and mobile. It was working. They took massive losses but the tactics worked.

Finally Sebastian whispered, '*Get me close.*'

The commander of the FOB was on the planet. NG gave the order and braced himself as Spectre spun and headed in.

The entire joint fleet switched focus from the remaining outlying ships to the base itself, bombing it from orbit, sending fighters down to strafe it, drop ships deploying ground troops. The Alsatia, the Man's ship and the two massive flagships stayed out at a distance, the Alsatia sending thunderclouds to support the ground offensive.

NG closed his eyes as Spectre got close. He'd given orders that they needed live prisoners but he felt sick as the ground troops engaged. He could sense every single Bhenykhn, every human soldier on the ground, feel the pain with each shot and stab, the pulsing agony of the poison, smell the stench of that foul leaf mold breath close up.

Sebastian drew it all in, revelling in it. '*My time,*' he whispered and took over.

NG sank back. It was harder to watch from a distance, more difficult to keep track of the others.

The pilot was flying Spectre fast and low over the surface, rising and banking to avoid scores of Bhenykhn ships that were homing in on them. They took a hit that sent them slewing off into a spin, guild ships coming up fast to defend them.

He felt Sebastian scan over the alien minds on the ground and focus in on the command structure. He pinpointed the base commander and threw an intense blast of energy into its brain stem. It faltered, froze and turned the entire attention of the hive onto them.

It was excruciating. NG felt Sebastian gasp and choke out a laugh, doubling over, cursing. He did what he could to pull in energy, trying to help deflect the pain, but he'd never done it from this side before. He concentrated, seeing the flow of energy all around him. It was surprisingly easy to reach out, no distraction of a body to control, or sensory input to consider. He took it, redirected it and fed it to Sebastian.

The Bhenykhn were squeezing, throwing an immense force at them.

Sebastian was resisting it, eyes shut, breathing laboured.

Another missile hit, rocking the ship.

NG could feel the energy that was bombarding them. He started to strengthen the shield but they were too powerful. There were too many of them.

He took a chance. Dropped the defences completely. And took the stream of energy, grabbed it and fired it back at the alien commander.

Sebastian joined in as the pressure began to ease, laughing as he took over and fried the Bhenykhn until it fell. He cascaded what was left into the subcommanders, the entire command structure faltering as the unit leaders hit the ground.

He used everything, paused to look around, surveyed the damage he'd wrought then relinquished control.

NG slumped in the chair. Drained.

The ship was going down.

He put his foot up on the console to brace himself.

He could hardly breathe, lungs prickly and head pounding.

Alarms and klaxons sounded distant.

There was something warm trickling down his face from his eye. He smeared away red and thought vaguely, "LC? Duncan? Anyone?'

No reply.

He started to fade out but he felt a presence by his side. "Don't go to sleep," Leigh said. "You need to heal."

He blinked.

246

"We're getting comms," he heard the pilot say, sounding miles away, as if she was shouting through fog. "You okay, there, boss?"

He mumbled something. He felt Spectre pull round, spiralling, engines struggling, the smell of burning mingling with the fog.

"Yeah, roger that, Control," the pilot was saying. "Got 402 safe and well." She looked at him. "Not entirely intact." There was a pause then, "Yeah, I'm taking us down. I can't risk orbit with this damage. Any chance of a tech crew?"

There were still Bhenykhn units scattered on the ground, still alien ships flying, but the joint forces were mopping up.

'*Nicely done,*' Sebastian murmured, sounding sleepy. '*You're learning but so are they. The next one might not be so easy.*'

'*That wasn't easy,*' NG mumbled back.

That got another laugh.

The FOB itself was clear. Sebastian had wiped them all out. Several hundred of them but the strain had been enormous. NG leaned forward and told the pilot to set them down there.

The Senson engaged, jarring as if the connection in his neck had been fried, but not so much that he couldn't recognise Evelyn. "NG, are you okay?"

"Will be. Come meet us on the Man's ship." He couldn't face the idea of going on board the Alsatia. "Where are the others?"

He was shivering. Couldn't stop it.

He was vaguely aware that Leigh had her fingers pressed against the pulse point in his wrist, thinking he needed medical attention, but he felt numb, so exhausted he couldn't feel the contact, couldn't even draw any energy from her.

She was worried about him.

"All good here," Duncan cut in. "Heading back."

"Where's LC?"

There was a pause then a strained, "Heading back."

"Hil? Badger?" he sent.

"All good," Badger replied.

It was a strangely hollow victory. He just felt cold.

'*You've got yourself live prisoners.*'

The losses were better than predicted but still horrific. He didn't need to look at the display screens and the scrolling stats to see that.

And it was just the start. This was one base of hundreds. He'd felt in the Bhenykhn commander's mind the pure scale of what they were confronting. It had let him see that, let him feel the full power of the hive across human occupied space.

He shivered.

'*We won. Enjoy it.*'

NG nodded slowly. One step at a time.

They landed near the FOB. Someone gave him a combat jacket and he pulled it tight around himself as he headed out onto a wet moorland. He had four elite guard with him, Leigh hovering a step behind. She wasn't happy that he was risking himself like this.

"The base is clear," he muttered.

The orders he'd set up were to take live prisoners but keep them out cold. They didn't need any of the bastards communicating with each other.

There was a contingent of guild Security there, waiting for him. They fell into formation around him, the unit sergeant taking up position at his side, a slight step in front, rifle at the ready.

They walked in through what was left of massive gates, high walls surrounding the enclosure. It had been shot to shit, bombed, the wreckage of crashed ships still smoking. The gates were metal, black, twisted, elaborate knotwork. It felt like he was walking into his nightmare.

'*Don't dwell here…*' Sebastian warned.

'*I want to see it.*'

There was a killing ground behind the walls.

No cover.

'*We used their energy against them,*' he thought vaguely as he walked in through massive blast doors. '*Why didn't you do that last time?*'

'*I did. It wasn't enough. Don't dwell, Nikolai. We don't have time to fret and feel guilty. You have enough of that already, don't add to it.'*

That was easier said than done.

He narrowed his eyes, adjusting to the dark. The base was warm, high ceilings, wide corridors, a pulsing light that was fading fast. Massive bodies littered the whole place, most of them the huge heavily armoured ground troops, some of them smaller, more like the scouts and pilots. Weapons lay where they'd fallen. He stepped around them, heading for the heart of the complex, doorways a scale bigger than human-sized. He felt like a child. It felt like he was intruding on another world.

'They are the intruders here, don't forget that.'

He was starting to think he wasn't so sure about that.

The air was stale, damp.

He knew where to go. He picked his way through to their command centre. The machines in there were still humming, nothing showing on their display screens, no lights on their consoles, just a residual hum that was fading as its energy depleted.

The sergeant was on alert, checking for dangers, thinking the stench was the same as the last time. He'd been with the recovery team at the last FOB. He kept glancing over, thinking he was glad NG was on his feet this time and even more glad now that last time they'd got there when they did, when the damn Bennies just had them in transit, because if that base they'd been heading to had been anything like this one, they couldn't have assaulted it, not with what they'd had. This place, he was thinking, would be a nightmare to attack if the Bennies weren't all dead already.

"We need to take all this," NG said quietly. "Record it all, get a Science crew in here. Pull in whatever resources the Wintrans and the Empire have too."

The sergeant nodded and started talking with the Alsatia, ordering a couple of his unit to go recce.

NG shivered and pulled the jacket tight. He stood there, just looking around, feeling numb. The Bhenykhn commander was lying on the floor, dead orange eyes staring.

'Get out of here,' Sebastian whispered. *'We're done. Move on.'*

He nodded and turned to go, eyes drawn down to the huge figure lying there, the alien that had taunted him, promising the untold horrors they would do to him when they got their hands on him again

He didn't fear it. He didn't hate it.

He knelt and pulled the kill token off its armour.

The repair crew was there by the time they got back. He nodded to them and went on board, tempted to fall into an isopod and sleep, but heading for the bridge instead and just closing his eyes. It didn't take long. The pilot got the go ahead, checked with him and took off, leaving the team from Science to recover what they could and tear the FOB apart. They made orbit, made one last scan of the surface and split, heading for the Man's ship.

Leigh sat next to him. "LC is struggling," she said.

The kid was feeling every death around him as a punch in the chest. They'd talked about it, they hadn't been able to come up with any way he could deal with it. If anything, it seemed to be getting harder for the kid.

"I know," NG muttered. "I need him out here."

Tough but she didn't argue.

"You've got what you wanted," she said. "We should be able to move the research forward." She let that hang. "Was it worth it?"

"Get me some results then I'll let you know."

She reached her hand towards his forehead. "You're too hot."

He closed his eyes again, wanting to sleep, but he caught an edge of something from the pilot. Concern.

Comms were faltering.

He sat up. "What's going on?"

They were heading straight towards the Man's ship, the Alsatia looming behind it in the screens. There was no reason why comms should be interrupted.

"I don't know," the pilot said.

He sent an urgent through the Senson to Evelyn.

No response.

'NG,' he got from LC, 'what's going on? We...'

The kid was cut off as the screen flared bright, every display on the bridge overloaded with data, as the ship was rocked by the shockwave.

NG recoiled, hit by an intense punch of void, flashes burning at the back of his eyes.

The pilot was cursing, fighting to bring Spectre back under control, wheeling her round in a manoeuvre that caught his stomach in a vice.

They slowed. He reached forward to steady himself. Telemetry was going insane, the screens filling with markers. Debris.

The Alsatia was gone.

33

She put her hand over her mouth. Horrified. There were other sharp intakes of breath.

One said, shocked, "He taunted them."

"How can we take such a risk? He provokes them," another said. "What could we expect from him? Would he put us in such danger? He has no regard."

Another banged on the table. "This was your doing. He is your protégé. You and your underhand dealings have brought this upon us. You bring down the ire of the Devourers? You of all people? You should know better than to anger them. You…"

He stood. "Enough," he roared.

The voices fell silent.

"I am not in the dock here," he said. "I am not here to be interrogated. Accused. I bring you news. You all know well enough our position here. That my protégé and his people stood up to them, that is more admirable than anything we have done."

He didn't sit. He looked at them, feeling in them their cowardice, their self-centred need for preservation above all else. It was sickening.

She spoke then, little more than a whisper. "The Alsatia is gone?"

'*Breathe,*' Sebastian whispered.

He couldn't.

The pilot was pulling them round, trying to get them clear.

Leigh was quiet, sitting next to him.

"The Man's ship?" he said, cold, heart in his stomach.

The pilot shook her head. "I don't know. I'm getting nothing but shit from everywhere." She cursed, spiralling them away.

An increasing pressure was beginning to pound in his head. He could hear the blood pulsing in his ears, feel each adrenaline-fuelled heartbeat banging in his chest.

Someone was calling his name, his senses too scrambled to respond.

He froze. The pressure was squeezing as if something had him round the throat. Like the Bhenykhn on Poule but a million times stronger.

'You dare defy us.' The growl this time was deep, rumbling.

He couldn't move. Couldn't fight it. Couldn't breathe.

It held him there.

'You…' it growled into his mind, "will not defy us."

It let go.

He dropped, free falling forever.

And hit a dense black wall of nothing.

His chest was hurting.

He sucked in a breath that hurt.

His head hurt.

Someone cursed, nearby. A hand grabbed his wrist.

He blinked open one eye.

He was down. Flat out on the deck. Someone was popping Epizin into his wrist. One of the Security guys, not Leigh. She was sitting cross-legged by his side as if her work was done. She leaned forward and whispered, voice shaky, "You died. I thought that might have been it for good this time."

"Takes more than that," he muttered, trying to get up. "What's happening?"

"We've lost the Alsatia," the pilot shouted back, "and the Olympus. I'm trying to hook up with the Man's ship but we are all fucked. Systems are shot. I have no telemetry. No visuals. Hold on."

Spectre lurched with a violent bump, a scream of metal on metal vibrating through the hull of the ship.

They slewed sideways and came to an abrupt stop as the grapples caught them.

He couldn't sense the Bhenykhn, couldn't feel Sebastian. 'LC?' he thought. 'Duncan?'

'You need to get up here,' came straight back from Duncan.

He couldn't sense LC anywhere. Couldn't sense Evelyn. He had no idea who'd made it and who hadn't.

His head was still spinning.

The pilot's words crashed through into his reality.

The Alsatia was gone.

He'd lived in it or around it for his entire life.

Through everything, the guild had always been the one constant. Even when he was rebelling against it, he'd always known it was there.

And now, in the blink of an eye, it was gone.

He could feel a hollow void of vacuum at the centre of his soul.

'Just get up here,' Duncan thought.

The Man's ship took a hit as they cycled the airlocks. Tremors rumbled through the hull. He punched the button and ran on board, the deck lurching beneath his feet, nausea tugging at his stomach, fists clenched to stop his hands trembling.

He was sure Leigh was right behind him but he turned as another blast hit, right where Spectre was locked up against the hull. He was thrown off his feet, tumbled backwards and hit the bulkhead.

Leigh wasn't there. She hadn't come through.

He scrambled to his feet and ran to the airlock, hammering at the button.

It wouldn't open.

He yelled, banging his fist against the door.

They hadn't come through all this for him to lose her now. Christ, no, not Leigh as well…

Time slowed.

He felt the explosion billowing before it punched through the airlock. The door blew out. He tried to turn his shoulder, shield his head. He felt it hit. He curled up, breath driven out of his

254

lungs, thrown back, a wash of hot air sending fragments tearing into his flesh as he hit the bulkhead and crumpled.

'*Nikolai...*'

He raised his eyes.

Leigh was kneeling in front of him. "Hey."

He almost folded. "Christ, I thought you were still on Spectre." He was shaking.

She smiled, shaking her head.

'*Nikolai...*'

He reached for her hand. He needed to hold her. He didn't ever want to lose her.

She leaned close...

"Nikolai."

He blinked open his eyes to sunshine, a cloudless blue sky, felt dusty ground under his fingertips. He was lying flat on his back. He rolled and pushed himself to his knees.

He was back in the courtyard, flags fluttering in the warm breeze, no crowds this time, no laughing.

Sebastian was sitting on a bench in front of him, leaning forward, elbows on his knees.

"Nikolai."

He was struggling to control his breathing, his senses still reeling.

He blinked.

There was something weird about the way Sebastian was looking at him.

"Nikolai, Leigh is dead."

He started to shiver, breath catching in his chest. "No..."

"No." Sebastian raised his hand. "Listen to me. Leigh is dead." His blue eyes were hooded. "Nikolai, Leigh died on Erica."

He couldn't stop shivering.

"Do you need to see it?"

In a flash, he was on that hilltop. In the rain. Another flash and he was sliding in the mud, a shout frozen in his throat, stabs

255

of agonising pain shooting into his knee. LC was yelling. The massive Bhenykhn turned, ragged cloak whipping around its shoulders.

Behind Luka, Martinez was lying, bleeding, dying. Leigh was scrambling to get to her.

The scene slowed, each heart beat pounding, each drop of rain splashing, each bead of red blood welling with excruciating clarity.

Leigh turned in perfect fluid slow motion, looking at him, dismay in her eyes, torn between him and Martinez. An axe swung, moonlight glinting off the nicks and dents in the edge of its blade, the weight of it crashing into her slight frame, slicing across her chest, blood spraying.

He couldn't move.

She fell.

"No," he yelled. He turned, looking for Sebastian. "This isn't real. You're messing with my head. This did – not – happen."

It reset and played again, Leigh turning to look at him, fraught, wanting to help him, wanting to help Martinez, caught between them.

The axe swung.

NG pressed his palms into his eyes, squeezing them shut.

"No, this isn't real," he said, calmly, taking control of the vision. "Sebastian, where the hell are you?"

The combatants on the battlefield swirled away, leaving him standing there on a deserted moorland.

He stopped the rain.

Sebastian was behind him.

He turned, shaking his head.

"It's not an illusion, Nikolai," Sebastian said. "It's in your memory. She died."

He played it again, this time with no sound, in unbearable, agonising freeze frame, right through the moment the axe hit.

She fell.

Blood sprayed.

She was gone before she hit the ground, that black pop of void

256

hitting NG in the chest as the Bhenykhn turned and struck LC with the rifle.

He stared.

Numb.

It raised its crossbow.

And he was back in the courtyard, gasping.

"You knew," Sebastian said. "You've always known. I've indulged your fantasy because you seemed to need it but the time for indulgences is over."

NG sat back on his heels, cold shards of ice twisting in his stomach, an ache pulling deep in his heart.

He said quietly, painfully, "I know."

Sebastian sucked in a deep breath. "Time to let go." He stood up. "She was a comforting distraction, Nikolai, I couldn't deny you that, but now…"

He squinted into the bright sunshine.

Sebastian looked down at him. "Now, you need to face reality. And in my reality, the compartment we're in is rapidly depressurising and losing oxygen. We are not going to die here, Nikolai. You need to get on your feet and get out of here. In case you didn't get it, a whole Bhenykhn fleet just turned up. They are surrounding us. The Man has shields that are holding up, pretty much, against their weapons. There's a surprise. And if you didn't hear clearly enough, Nikolai, they are intent on destroying us all. Let's do something about that, shall we?"

Sebastian let go and he dropped back to the deck, trembling, the shock of the blast still shivering through his muscles. He pushed himself slowly to his feet and looked up.

Evelyn was standing there. There was someone on each side of him, grabbing an arm each as he tried to get up and pulling him through into the ship, an internal pressure door slamming shut behind them.

Evelyn's emotions were wrapped up tight and cold, that self control slipping only when he got close.

She took a hesitant step forward, a bizarre thought flitting over her mind as she waited to see what he'd do.

He shrugged off the guys to either side, muttering that he was fine, and staggered forward, grabbed her and pulled her into a bear hug. She was shaking. He'd told her once to never, ever, hug him again and she almost cried, holding him and pressing her hand to the back of his neck as if she never wanted to let him go.

She pulled away first, wiping a finger across his cheek. He wasn't sure if his eyes were watering or bleeding still.

He couldn't move. He felt sick. Empty.

The realisation hit him again.

The Alsatia was gone.

And Leigh... Leigh, who had got him through the last few months, had been nothing but an illusion.

'Not an illusion,' Sebastian murmured. 'In her own way, she was real enough for what you needed. Ironically, she really did care for you. That's what got her killed – following you out onto the battlefield. She was dead long before she could ever be what you needed her to be.'

Another explosion against the shields sent the entire ship rocking.

"You need to come and help LC," Evelyn said.

Sebastian was smouldering. 'You need to come with me and wipe them out.'

He was shivering.

'Enough, Nikolai.'

Sebastian tried to nudge him aside but he resisted, anger fuelling his determination.

'No,' he thought. 'I need to do this.'

"Where is he?" he said, the words catching in his throat, flashing back to the moment when the Man had said that to him all that time ago.

She took him to the briefing room, holding the doorframe as the ship lurched again, keeping her eyes firmly fixed on him as if she thought he might disappear if she lost track of him.

LC was sitting on the deck, leaning back against the bulkhead with his eyes closed, deep black bruising beneath each eye, a trickle of red running from his ears and nose. Hal Duncan was crouched beside him.

All the screens were black, flickering intermittently.

The kid was breathing shallowly, brain function erratic, the virus going wild. He half lifted his hand in a wave as NG knelt, dropping it as if even that was too much effort.

'LC?'

'He can hear the Bhenykhn…'

Duncan overheard that and swore.

NG put his hand on LC's neck and almost flinched from the pain. He did what he could but it wasn't much. He looked up. Leigh was standing at the back of the room, watching. He almost lost it, seeing her there, a curious, sad look on her face. He forced himself back to here and now, struggling to speak out loud. "What happened?"

"He screamed and dropped, same instant the Alsatia was hit," the big man said.

"How about you?"

Duncan shrugged. "I felt you go out. Saw Luka drop. I knew something was wrong. Didn't know what. I'm not getting anything from him, are you?"

"Sebastian is."

'You can't do anything for him. The organism is ripping apart his brain and rebuilding it and right now you've just got to let it do whatever it's going to do. We need to come up with a plan, Nikolai.'

The door opened, Pen and Quinn bursting in, both of them with faces set.

"NG, what looks like an entire fleet just dropped out of jump. They're tearing us apart, taking out our ships with one hit," Quinn said. Like shooting fish in a damned barrel, he was thinking.

'Get to the bridge.'

NG stood. His knees felt weak. "Get LC onto glucose, anything with energy that you can pump into his system. He's in agony. We need him. Just feed the damn virus as much and as fast as you can. I need to go."

Pen's expression was dark. "What the fuck do we do?"

259

He brushed past them as the ship took another direct hit.

"NG?" Pen shouted.

The deck dropped out beneath them. He staggered into the table and grabbed a handhold on its edge to stop himself falling.

He didn't stop, hearing Quinn curse and sensing the big handler following him out.

The lights in the corridor were out, secondary red lighting pulsing a glow that set his eyes aching.

'The shields are failing,' Sebastian whispered. 'Much more and this ship will be dust.'

Quinn ran to catch up with him. "NG. Talk to us, for Christ's sake. What do you want us to do?"

"I don't know." His voice was shaking. "I don't know what to do. I just…" He reached the steep steps that led to the forward section and grabbed the handrail, pausing. He shut everything away, closed it down tight and looked at Quinn. He pulled in a deep breath. "This is the Man's ship. There's Bhenykhn technology on board, more than just artefacts. If we can withstand their weapons, we might be able to fight back. I don't know."

Another blast almost sent him tumbling. Klaxons began to wail like banshees.

Quinn grabbed him and propelled him up the stairs.

Morgan was directing emergency measures to contain the damage and monitor losses, calm, unruffled.

NG slowed to a walk as he entered the bridge. He was used to setting the atmosphere in a room, not needing it to calm him.

The crew looked round as he walked in.

Morgan began to give a sitrep, reeling off numbers, positions. His voice blurred into the background as NG stood there, complete focus, seeing into every mind, reading each thought, going wider and seeing the exact position and state of each ship they had left, each Bhenykhn vessel. Sebastian joined in and started to stream intel from the hive, their intentions, their capability, the overwhelming odds. There was one commander in control of the whole fleet. More powerful than anything they'd encountered so far. Way more powerful. It all swirled around him. He could see every possible move, the outcome of each strategy, move by move, way down the line. And each avenue led to defeat, whatever he tried.

Another barrage of explosions rumbled across the shields.

Morgan stopped, realising NG wasn't responding.

He stared at the main screen and the massive Bhenykhn command ship they had up there in the centre of the cross hairs.

'Come up with something, Nikolai.'

There was a flare on the screens as the Marrakech exploded, more Bhenykhn ships coming round to bear down on them.

He felt cold. Numb.

It suddenly felt like all the games he'd ever played, every manipulation, every daring risk and strategy, was for nothing. It all meant nothing. He had no control in what was happening, no more plays to pull out of a hat, no cards up his sleeve, no pieces waiting patiently to move across the board into a position of power. Nothing in reserve. No one to sacrifice but everyone. It felt like this outcome had been inevitable all along and he'd been a damned fool for thinking otherwise.

"We attack," he said. "We attack the command ship."

34

"So he finally put it together?" she said softly. "You could have told him."

Should have told him.

All his protections had come falling down.

He thought he'd been taking care that Nikolai, Sebastian, couldn't be hurt. But in the end he had caused more hurt by not preparing them.

The ship, the key, the kill tokens…

All had pointed to the truth. Why could he not have just laid it out for them?

Was it so hideous a truth that he, and his kind, were from the same galaxy as the Bhenykhn? That they had brought with them so many artefacts, so much technology and knowledge? The research he'd kept so hidden, so secret, from them all?

"They are young," he said, the excuse sounding weak as he said it. "It makes no difference whether they know the truth or not. The Bhenykhn are here in this galaxy now and they must fight them. For their own survival as much as ours."

They all looked at him, horrified.

'Good,' Sebastian murmured. 'Get me close. I want to kill this bastard.'

'That's the idea.'

Another direct hit rocked the ship.

The Senson engaged with a crackle. "In your current state, that's a really bad plan, Nikolai."

He opened up the link to a wide connection, including everyone in there, and sent back, "Elliott."

There was no sign of the Duck on any of their screens, none of their sensors picking up a trace.

"How about we give you a fighting chance?"

We? The Seven?

"How?" he sent back.

Sebastian laughed. *'No, no, Nikolai, don't question him. Take him up on it. Whatever he's offering. Sell your soul, Nikolai. We're damned whatever we do. You've always known that.'*

Quinn opened his mouth to object but Duncan gestured him to hold. Everyone on the bridge was standing there in silence, watching him.

NG turned to Duncan. "Where's Hilyer? Get him up here."

He switched back to the Senson. "Elliott, we know what you are. Why don't you and your buddies just blast them to bits right now?"

"Believe me, Nikolai, if we had the hardware we once had, we would be doing just that. As it is, we need to make the best of what we have."

"So what can you do?"

"You'll see. Get a ship ready, boarding party, heavy guns, everything you've got. We learned a lot from Erica. I can hide you for a short while. You'll know when to make your move."

The connection cut out.

Quinn nudged him in the ribs. He turned to see Hilyer enter the bridge, working hard to control his breathing, expression dark.

"He has the others with him," the kid said. "The Duck is right in the middle of their fleet but the Bennies aren't detecting them. The Seven seem to think they can take over the Bhenykhn ships." He nodded towards the main screen.

There was a shimmer, confused telemetry, numbers flashing, then six unknowns flared out across the screen from a central point, travelling at incredible velocity, targeting six of the alien ships. At first he thought they were missiles but they didn't explode.

"What the hell are they?" Morgan muttered.

"Drones," Hil said. "That's them. That's the others of the Seven."

The Bhenykhn armada was ripping though the Imperial and coalition fleets but then, in excruciating slow motion, six of those huge ships began to turn and fire upon their own. Warships the size of cities flared in nova-like explosions.

"Shit," NG muttered. He turned and broke into a run. "Come on," he yelled. "Get to Spectre. Someone grab LC. Hil, I want you as well. Morgan, back off. Get clear and stay clear. If this doesn't work, jump. Get away. You understand? If I don't come back, you're in charge of whatever's left."

He didn't wait for a reply.

His hands were still shaking as he kitted up. Leigh was watching. He was trying to avoid looking at her.

He took a combat knife as Duncan handed it over, taking three attempts to slide it into the sheath on his leg. They were all looking at him, thinking they'd never seen him like this before. He couldn't shake it off.

"I'm still here for you," Leigh whispered into his ear.

Spectre was moving fast.

"Can we trust them?" Quinn said.

NG almost laughed. "No."

LC was sitting watching, still suffering but somehow, slowly, he was bringing it under control. At least, he was talking, mostly swearing, but claiming he'd be fine, an assault rifle in one hand and his flask of moonshine in the other. Hil was ribbing him, saying hearing aliens was nothing, try listening in to a bunch of barking mad AIs. Both of them were wearing minimal kit, all they'd had time to grab and more like the kind of stuff they'd wear on a tab, not combat gear, only light body armour.

Evelyn was quiet, slipping back into assassin mode, mindset switching to the coldblooded killer she thought she'd buried. He'd felt her reject it at first, then embrace it when it dawned on her that the life she thought she'd had wasn't there any more and if anyone was going to survive this then she'd need her head in the game. He'd tried to tell her not to come but she was having none of it. In her mind, losing Devon was all down to the Bhenykhn, they owed her and she was going to collect.

Pen and Jameson were also there, all the big guys in powered armour with integral heavy weapons. They'd scraped together a full contingent of Security totalling thirty and another sixteen of the Man's elite guard in their distinctive crimson powered armour.

He had no idea if it would be enough.

Leigh smiled at him from the back of the room, reassuring.

He shivered.

'It's all very touching,' Sebastian chided. *'Even when they die, they don't lose their blind loyalty to you.'*

They all knew what they had to do. Elliott had briefed them on what to expect on the Bhenykhn ship, sent over scans and deck plans, told them what targets to take out and where to go.

The Senson engaged. "Now or never," Elliott said. "See you on the other side."

The pilot was throwing Spectre into tight manoeuvres to get into position, slowing as she approached the command vessel. He could feel the intensity of the hive increase as they got closer. Whatever Elliott was doing to shield them, it was working. They bumped up against the hull of the Bhenykhn ship and locked grapples. The aliens had no idea they were there.

'Elliott is causing chaos,' Sebastian murmured. *'But it's not going to be long before the Bhenykhn start to overpower even the Seven. Pure numbers. We need to get on board this ship and get to the commander. That's the only way we are going to win. And trust me, Nikolai, as soon as we get in there, they are going to come after us. Are you ready?'*

As if Sebastian was inviting him to a game.

Sebastian laughed. *'Shall we begin?'*

They were locked up against an exhaust vent and used shaped charges to blast an entry in the hull, automatically sealing it to make a perfect airtight ingress. It was pure pirate, not usual for the Thieves' Guild. Jiro Tierney would have been impressed.

Then they moved fast. He sent a squad of Security in first, led by Duncan, a second wave headed up by Jameson and Pen. He went in then, Quinn sticking close by his side, flanked by the elite guard. Evelyn and the two field-ops followed, backed up by the rest of the Security team.

As they started to move, alarms began to scream, a pitch deeper than normal and more grating on the nerves by a magnitude. The ship was dark. Hot. Twisted conduits of black metal lined the bulkheads, soft panels that were warm, pulsing with some kind of bioluminescence.

They had a perfect network of undetectable, uninterrupted communication and the best stealth kit the guild had. Plus they had Elliott bombarding the Bhenykhn technology from without and Sebastian screwing them up from within.

The crew they encountered were lightly armoured and armed with shipboard weapons. No energy shield pods. It made it easier to take them down with the sheer volume of firepower they were laying down but the aliens' natural armour was still effective which meant they were still burning through ammunition faster than they could sustain.

So far, so good. They established their beachhead, however tenuous, and cleared the immediate area with no fatalities, minor injuries, and a headache banging at the back of his mind by the time the dust settled.

He felt heavy. Higher than normal gravity.

LC sank down as soon as they were done, insisting he was fine, Evelyn crouching at the kid's side and pulling injectors out of pouches on her belt.

NG stopped. He took the magazine Duncan was holding out and switched it with the spent one in his rifle, looking around and trying to figure out what felt wrong.

"What is it?" the big man said.

"I don't know. Give me a minute," he muttered, sending the thought to the others.

Quinn stayed with him. It was weird. He felt like a field-op being baby-sat by his handler.

He walked back along what looked like a line of cells. Empty, he could see that even in the weird low lighting. A trickle of sweat ran down his back. It was stifling.

Quinn was uneasy, walking just behind him, turning regularly, a rifle up and ready. "NG, come on, what the hell are you doing?"

He didn't reply.

He pushed open one cell and peered in, pulling a flashlight off his belt. Trails of old and congealed blood were spattered and splashed on the floor, the walls.

"Jesus," Quinn muttered.

NG moved on, unease prickling at the back of his neck. There was a room at the end of the row, walls lined with shelves, everything a scale bigger than human, massive glass jars filled with murky fluid and what were unmistakably body parts. He let the beam of torchlight drift over them. Half the specimens didn't look human. Some had intact, embryonic forms curled in them, floating. There was something resembling a brain in one that he could have sworn was still pulsing. It turned his stomach. And in amongst it all was a rack with massive blades hanging from it, curved knives, cleavers, all stained red. The stench of it caught at the back of his throat.

He backed away.

'They've been experimenting on us,' he thought.

'Forget it. Get away from here. Do your job.'

Sebastian sounded strained.

'You have no idea.'

'You all good to go?' he thought wider.

He got affirmatives back from them all and turned, walking past Quinn to the door.

"Let's do it," he said.

They moved one level at a time, fast after that, sticking together, trying to minimise losses, concentrating firepower, taking out pockets of resistance as they went.

The Bhenykhn had never expected their command ship to be boarded, Sebastian relayed that and even LC was picking up on it.

It was unprecedented. There were no heavy defences on board, none of the massive soldiers they'd encountered on the ground. But as much as their command and control system was heavily hierarchical, this was the fleet commander they were attacking and the rest of the hive weren't slow to react.

Elliott warned them a ship was docking and they tracked alien marines spreading out through the ship.

They ended up pinned down by a unit of the big, heavily armed and armoured foot soldiers while they tried to work out a way through.

They couldn't afford to be flanked and surrounded. NG glanced round at the others, stood up and walked forward.

'*Stay back,*' Sebastian hissed.

It was Pen who grabbed his shirt and pulled him back, gesturing him to stay, sneaking a peep round the corner and almost getting his head blown off.

'*Do you want the pleasure?*' Sebastian thought.

NG steeled himself, focused and sent a blast into the squad leader, frying the three soldiers in its unit as he did it. That was about his limit.

They dropped.

He walked forward, heart pounding, Pen hesitating and almost grabbing him again.

"We're clear," he said, shrugging him off.

Pen didn't believe it, still not trusting a word he said, but following cautiously, scanning his guns round until he saw them on the floor. "Holy shit," he said, walking up to them, aiming both guns down at them until he was sure they were dead. He nudged one with his foot. "Did Mendhel know you could do this kind of crap?"

"Pen, no one knew. I didn't know."

The big man didn't believe that either.

NG was shivering despite the heat. "You have no idea," he muttered, petulant. Pen didn't bring out the best in him.

Pen turned suddenly, grabbed the front of NG's shirt and pulled him close. "You think I have no idea what you are?"

Quinn stepped between them, breaking it up. "Not the time or place, gentlemen."

"Guys," Duncan broke in. "Incoming. We need to get out of here."

NG pulled the rifle round and walked away.

Pen let him go, swearing.

He could feel Quinn smouldering behind him, LC and Hil watching.

He led the way down, avoiding any more as best as he could, running when they could and waiting when it got too hot but he was having to start leaving people at cross points and intersections, a rear guard to keep them off their back. Ultimately suicide missions because he knew they couldn't hold for long. Little more than an interruption to the Bhenykhn as they pushed after them and it was reducing his numbers each time. Their group was getting smaller. He was trying to get down into the heart of the ship to where Elliott had said the shield generators were most likely to be. That was their first target. It was going to be tight. At this rate he was going to run out of people before they ran out of ammunition.

They moved down and round to a central core. His head was pounding in time with his pulse. He knew there were Bhenykhn marines blocking the way. They were protecting essential ship systems as well as hunting them down. They knew he was here. The fleet commander knew he was here and it was sending everything it had to intercept him. He could feel Sebastian taunting it, feel the immense effort it was taking to protect him from the outright assault it kept trying.

"We need that shield down," Elliott sent.

"Working on it," he sent back and cut the connection.

He scanned ahead. There were four squads camped in front of them, guarding two massive doors. Another squad was approaching from above so they needed to move quickly. They couldn't afford to get slowed down, or worse, trapped.

"We need to speed this up," he said, looking round. "I can't take them all at once. LC, with me. Everyone else, be ready to

269

hit them with everything we've got as soon as their shields are down."

He turned to LC. "You take the left," he muttered. "Take out the pods, all eight, fast as you can."

LC nodded, holding back a splitting headache but managing to focus it somehow, the kid channelling it into the intensity that had kept him at the top of the standings.

'*The child is learning,*' Sebastian whispered. '*I told you he had the potential to be even stronger than you. And yes, you do need to speed this up.*'

They split up and moved forward. He gave the signal and sent a burst of energy into one pod after the next, the Bhenykhn howling as the pods exploded against their spines. LC was doing the same. The shields dropped and they all opened up with rifles, all targeting the same one until it dropped and moving onto the next, moving round the central structure that wrapped around the core.

NG doubled up, firing his rifle at one squad leader and sending a targeted blast into another. That one fell and its unit froze for an instant, reassessing. The others charged round, roaring. He took out another squad leader, still firing the rifle at one of the others, the massive figures falling faster with no energy shield to protect them but still absorbing a shit load of ammunition and damage. It was taking too long.

One of the elite guard dropped, right next to him, a huge axe hacking through the guy's neck armour.

NG froze, couldn't help flashing back to the rain and seeing the same curved axe head slicing across Leigh's chest, blood spraying.

'*Move,*' Sebastian hissed.

He spun. It was right there, brown chitinous armour looming over him, axe blade glinting, orange eyes gleaming as it leered down at him. Shit.

35

"But must we?" said one.

"We can't fight them."

"We can't trust the Seven. How can we trust machines?"

They had decided.

That was clear enough.

He sat quietly, amongst the clamouring cries to flee. He wasn't disappointed. It was almost a relief to know in the end where they stood. He had never come here on bended knee. He had always been different. But they had always asked how fared the guild, how goes the preparations. Now it seemed simply that all they wanted to know was when to run.

She alone was steadfast. "We are fighting them," she said. "You cannot deny that the humans are fighting them and they are making their stand. I vote that we make our stand. Here. We have mistakes to mitigate. We already carry a huge burden of shame and a debt to those we abandoned as we ran to save ourselves. Do not forget that in your haste to flee again."

He was almost gagging with the stench of it. It swept the axe up, blood dripping. NG staggered back and blasted it, throwing everything he had into frying its brain, fuelled by a boiling, unchecked hatred as if it had been the same damned alien that had killed Leigh.

It hit the deck, the axe clattering beside it.

He fell back.

The firing stopped.

NG scrambled up and leaned against the bulkhead, shivering, about done, quickly scanning around.

They hadn't lost anyone else, a couple of dinks and wounds but nothing serious.

"We need to get inside," Quinn was yelling.

'Keep your head,' Sebastian hissed. *'Get this done and get out, you're getting surrounded.'*

The door was locked with twisted knots that glowed as he looked into them and bust them open as he had in his nightmare.

He pushed his full weight into it to get it to move and heard Pen say, "Holy shit," behind him as he walked out onto a wide balcony overlooking a chamber filled with a seething mass of leathery pods, thousands upon thousands of them, crowded together, fleshy parts pulsing in harmony like a colony of coral waving in a warm water current.

Except the air in here was fetid and chokingly rank.

NG tried to breathe through it, pulled out incendiary grenades and primed them. He waited until the others had done the same then nodded and tossed them in.

They didn't wait to see what happened.

They moved back out into the corridors.

'Incoming.'

There was no time to get clear. A hail of shots peppered the bulkhead around them.

NG flinched back.

He couldn't sense anything but the thousands of hissing screams from the pods as they died pressing against his mind. It was disorientating. He spun around, gun up.

He caught sight of Quinn grabbing LC and bundling him clear, the elite guards moving into position to cover them. He could hear Evelyn shouting.

He didn't know where any of the others were.

A burning pain sliced across the back of his shoulder, a blade biting deep and poison pulsing into his bloodstream. His knees gave way and he fell.

Someone grabbed his arm and pulled, gunfire echoing loud in his ears. He couldn't get his legs to move, could hardly breathe through the paralysing sting squeezing his entire body. He was dragged backwards, felt immense heat at his back and heard a door slam.

He was turned, someone hissing in his ear, "Fuse the damned lock. Whatever the fuck it is you do, fuse the damned lock."

He couldn't concentrate.

Sebastian shoved him aside viciously. He didn't fight it, couldn't think straight and faded out.

He could hear faint talking, far away, became vaguely aware of a bright orange glow.

Sebastian was sitting on the deck, back against the bulkhead, sucking in energy from the pod creatures dying in the blaze still roaring in the central core and using it to seal the wound and neutralise the alien toxin.

Pen was sitting next to him, he realised, injured. Badly injured.

"You're a fucking son of a bitch, NG," the big man murmured.

"I told you, I'm not NG," Sebastian said. He flexed his hand. NG could feel the wound in his back healing slowly. Nowhere near as fast as Sebastian did it usually. They were all exhausted. Even Sebastian had his limits it seemed.

'Be grateful it's healing at all, Nikolai. This isn't exactly going to plan, is it?'

'There was a plan?'

He could breathe at least, the numbing grip of the toxin finally dissipating.

'One thing at a time,' Sebastian muttered and said flippantly to Pen, "You shouldn't hate him, you know."

Pen glowered. He'd taken the helmet off, the suit damaged. "You're more insane than I thought."

Sebastian turned round. "You really don't know, do you? It wasn't Nikolai who sent your brother's wife – Anya's mother – on that tab. It was the Man who sent Arianne away. Nikolai didn't even know until it was too late." He laughed. "My god, Pen. All this time you've hated him for something he didn't do. The soft bastard loved her." He leaned forward. "Nikolai met Arianne

273

years before he met any of you. He knew her before Anya was born. Think about it."

'*Don't,*' NG whispered.

'*Why not, Nikolai? Why should he not know that the Man sent Arianne to her certain death just so you could move back in to the Alsatia as his head of operations. No sticky little problems like a former lover in the way, a former sweetheart who might notice that you hadn't changed in the fifteen years since she'd seen you last? The Man told her you were dead, did you know that?*'

He hadn't.

'*And how many others were sent away to preserve our little secret? Did you never ask what happened to Carmen in the time you were out gallivanting, playing soldiers? How she was so conveniently not there to question it when you got back, just the same old you when everyone else was a quarter of a century older?*'

It had never occurred to him to ask. His relationship with Arianne had been a million miles from the Alsatia. He hadn't even realised she'd got married until he got back and by then she was already gone.

Sebastian sneered. '*Why should Pen not know the truth? He's going to die here anyway.*'

Pen was turning, anger welling, adding it up.

Sebastian clasped him on the shoulder, making the chameleonic armour glow beneath his hand, healing the worst of the wounds, fast, making the big man falter.

"Think about it, Pen."

He stood, rotating the shoulder.

NG could feel the pressure of the hive pounding against his mind, an incessant thumping intrusion like a battering ram hammering at every nerve.

'*I don't suppose you could take out the commander from here?*' he thought.

'*Where and when in the seven levels of hell could it ever be that easy? Get me to the bridge, Nikolai.*'

And he relinquished control.

NG caught his balance.

"We need to go," he muttered. "Can you move?"

Pen forced himself to his feet, dark eyes glowering. He towered over NG, big anyway, more so in the armour. He moved fast and NG didn't fight him as the big man pushed him up against the bulkhead.

"You son of a bitch, NG. You and Arianne?"

"Forget it," NG said, defiant, even though he was pinned. "Sebastian shouldn't have said anything."

The core was a blazing inferno behind them.

"I want to know," Pen said, seething.

"She died," NG said quietly, a lump in his throat as the guilty memories of Arianne competed with those over Devon. "Mendhel died. We're all going to die, Pen, probably right here. What does any of it matter?"

That got him another shove. "Did Mendhel know?"

"What do you think?"

Pen growled and threw him aside. The big man pulled round his rifle and readied it, and for a moment, it felt like he was going to swing it round and shoot.

His eyes were dark. "I think you're a son of a bitch. Find us a way out of here and get up to that bridge. I hope they kill you slowly."

They had to climb, finding some kind of maintenance ladder, arduous work in the intense heat and tough even for Pen with the difference in scale. The big man was pissed, fuming, grabbing NG a couple of times and shoving him forward. Pen didn't know what to feel so anger was easiest. He could relate to that.

They slipped through a vent and after that, it was a race to hook up with the others. LC and Jameson were intermittent. Hal Duncan gave him a steady commentary and talked him through.

Sebastian was struggling, quiet.

Rumbles were echoing through the hull of the ship as it started to take hits now the shields were down, the damage providing the distraction they needed as the Bhenykhn were forced to pull away resources for damage control.

One of his elite guard appeared at his shoulder, only one, no word of what had happened to the others. Pen moved away as that guy moved in.

NG slowed down. He was starting to lose track of where everyone was, an increasing pressure building behind his eyes as he got closer to the bridge. At one point, Evelyn slid in next to him. She squeezed his shoulder without a word. She was bleeding from a gash in her arm. He took energy from her to heal it and got a nudge in thanks. She scavenged a couple of magazines from his pouches and split to move round. He watched her go. Couldn't help thinking it could be the last time he saw her.

'Don't be soft, Nikolai. We're here for a reason. She will die. Accept it. Now or later. What the hell is the difference?'

He didn't want to lose anyone else.

'And that will get you dead, fast. Get a grip, Nikolai. How many times do I need to say that?'

The Senson crackled. "How are we doing there, Nikolai?"

"How long do we have?" he sent back.

"Before we blitz the crap out of that ship you're on or before they manage to take us out and turn on your remaining ships?"

NG shivered. He pressed his palm against his forehead.

"We need that commander taken out, Nikolai," Elliott sent. "Now. Don't screw this up."

The connection cut.

'How far?' he asked Sebastian.

'Too far. You need to move.'

He gave the order and it went to hell fast. The adrenaline kicked in and he stepped it up, running on auto. He fried one after the other as they piled in.

The elite guard at his side dropped.

NG stooped to grab the fallen rifle and ran, hooking up with LC and Quinn, the kid hanging back and sending burst after burst of raw energy into the Bhenykhn, the big handler covering him with the rifle. They were both bleeding, running on adrenaline themselves and retreating towards the bridge.

NG joined them, rifle up, blasting the squad leaders.

Quinn took a hit to the chest that took him down, the armour taking most but not all of the damage. He rolled, came up on his elbows and carried on firing despite the wound, yelling at them to go.

That wasn't going to happen. He wasn't about to leave Quinn behind.

LC hesitated.

Pen appeared from behind them, grabbed the kid and pulled him round. "Go," he shouted. He knelt by Quinn and fired shot after shot down the corridor. "Go, dammit, NG, how the fuck long do you think we can keep this up? Go."

NG turned and ran, propelling LC ahead of him.

One more level. They ran past three of the Security guys who were holding an intersection. Jameson and Evelyn were close. He had no idea where Hilyer was.

'Meet up,' he thought. 'Duncan? Meet up.'

They ran around a corner towards more gunfire.

A massive rumble thundered through the deck, throwing them off their feet.

"Shit, Elliot," he sent, "give us a chance."

There was no reply.

He scrambled up and ran on, heart plummeting into his stomach as he saw Evie slumped against the bulkhead, blood flowing down her neck and chest, still firing two handguns, Jameson standing over her and pumping round after round down the corridor.

NG slid in beside her. He didn't have much left but he did what he could, fast, aware that LC wasn't behind him.

"Go," she breathed. "We've got this. Go."

'Never argue with an assassin, NG,' Jameson thought at him, no respite in firing his rifle except to reload. 'There's still a price on your head. You screw this up, we might all cash in on you. Retire. I know someplace nice.'

He glanced up. The big Earth colonel was in his element, thinking deep down that he should have been working with them a hell of a lot sooner.

They all should have done things differently. He wiped a hand across his eyes. It was getting warmer. The stench was almost unbearable. Cloying. Straight out of his nightmares.

A Bhenykhn warrior came rushing out of the shadows, bellowing a battle cry, axe swinging. The pod on its belt exploded as it ran at them. It screamed. Jameson shot it between the eyes as NG threw a desperate blast into its brain. It roared, raising the axe, then thudded down, sliding to a halt in front of them.

Jameson prodded the massive body with his boot. 'You know, I didn't believe all this crap when you showed it to me in that hallucination…'

"NG, go," Evelyn said, reloading both her guns.

He nodded, stood and backed away. LC was at the corner, leaning against the bulkhead, hugging his hands around his chest, waiting for him.

Duncan hooked up with them at the next intersection, backing towards them firing. 'The steps are just round here,' he thought. 'There are two of them guarding it. You guys wanna do your thing?'

NG had his rifle up, scanning ahead.

The problem with this was that they were both getting drained. LC had run out of moonshine, no one had any Epizin left, and he was struggling to draw energy from anywhere. He was getting nothing from Sebastian but he could feel the pressure pulsing at his mind.

Another hit rumbled throughout the ship.

He could sense one of the elite guard making his way to them, wounded but still firing.

Sebastian whispered, strained, 'We are doubling up on this one, Nikolai. Do you understand?'

He did, more than ever.

Sebastian forced a laugh.

NG could feel the commander waiting for them. He waited for the elite guard to reach them then gestured with his rifle. "You ready?"

They moved fast, took out the two Bennies on guard and ran up steps that were too big to doors that loomed over them, NG flinging them open before they got there, the huge blocks of black metal, knots and spikes glistening in the half light, groaning inwards. A waft of hot, humid air hit them.

It was like walking into the Man's chambers. In a hideously familiar, stomach churning sense of recognition, it felt just like entering those dark, ominous chambers that opened with a key made of that same twisted back metal.

NG didn't stop. LC was at his left shoulder, Hal Duncan to his right and the elite guard to their left. Hilyer appeared from somewhere and dropped into step beside them, spinning a knife through his fingers.

The Bhenykhn fleet commander was sitting on a massive black throne, up against the far wall, like a king, a heavy cloak about its shoulders, leaning forward, watching them with a gleam in its orange eyes. It had one hand on the hilt of a huge battle axe resting there against the throne.

The chamber felt vast. NG didn't look around. He kept his eyes fixed firmly on the commander, moving forward, walking right into its lair. He could sense other massive figures around them. Every one of them in there was big, ragged black or grey cloaks on every shoulder, rifles pointed, crossbows aimed, axes hefted in enormous fists.

He walked forward, blood pounding in his ears, his heart beating in time with the throbbing pulse that was the energy of the hive. He approached the throne, LC and the others hanging back and spreading out.

The commander leaned further forward, a grim smile spreading across its face. Its voice was a guttural growl inside his head. 'And what tribute do you bring before me?'

36

The warmth in the chambers felt cloying, claustrophobic.

"No," one of them said. "We cannot be so stupid as to think we can survive such folly. We must leave. Gather the refugees and go."

"Go where?" she said, outraged.

"Anywhere. Anything but face these creatures again."

They were scared. The Man watched them gather themselves and stand.

She stood amongst them, firm. "There is nowhere to go. The Bhenykhn are everywhere. We made a mistake. A catastrophic mistake. And we cannot run from that."

"We cannot stay here and die," one of them said simply and turned away.

NG fell to his knees as it took hold of his mind in a grip that was excruciating, vision narrowing to a black tunnel.

'None – ever – come before the Bhenykhn Lyudaed,' it warned, 'with empty hands,' the smirk growing dark.

The pain increased.

He couldn't think, could hardly move but he made his fingers flash the signal, both hands, down by his side, by the floor, each knuckle cracking as he flexed them, no idea if they'd even see it.

The dark closed in, the beat of his heart slowing to an agonising rhythm.

Nine pods exploded in unison around him, the energy blasting outwards through his senses in billowing waves.

Rifle fire resounded in his ears.

Roars and yells.

Screams.

He dropped his head and sat there in the centre of it all, breathing, gathering himself. He felt Sebastian smile inside.

'*Ready?*'

'*Yep.*'

He pushed himself to his feet, head still bowed, opened his eyes and stared at the commander, a faint smile twitching. The massive Bhenykhn was gripping the arms of its throne, in the process of standing.

It glowered at him.

NG forced it back down into its seat as Sebastian increased the pressure he was exerting on its mind as if he was pressing his thumbs into its eyes.

It wasn't slow to react but they were overpowering it.

NG walked forward. A blade sliced across his arm, the pain barely registering.

He sensed more than saw Duncan come in from the side with a tackle that took down his attacker.

The commander was straining.

Around them, alien bodies were hitting the floor. There were others incoming, gunfire filling the approaches all around them.

He was vaguely aware of Hilyer moving round, knife in hand, the remaining elite guard turning and firing, high-ex AP rounds that were punching through the Bhenykhn armoured hide and causing catastrophic damage to the flesh beneath. It still seemed to take an age to bring them down.

He couldn't do anything but hold the commander.

He became aware of another one coming at him from behind even as he felt LC blast it, two more of them descending on the kid himself.

He heard LC cry out.

Felt the kid go down.

Duncan roared.

NG took another step forward.

He could see out of the corner of his eye the big man fighting against three of them now, swinging a huge double bladed axe like a berserker, all out attack with no regard for defence. It was the only way to fight them. On their own terms. To step back was to die.

Hilyer was shouting from the other side, trying to split their attention.

The rate of gunfire was slowing, ammo running low.

Sebastian was struggling.

The commander was fighting back, rage intensifying, fuelled by the sight of its lieutenants falling.

NG glanced to the left as one of the big black cloaks overpowered Hil, throwing the kid against the bulkhead. He crunched to the deck.

He glanced right as Duncan went down. The two left on him turned on the elite guard who was trying to slam in his last magazine. He got it firing and went down shooting, an axe embedded in his helmet.

NG stopped and raised his eyes to the commander. He still had control of it.

The other Bhenykhn all stopped, turning to him.

He felt their attention as a crawling itch on the back of his neck that was fast joined by the hot metal of a gun barrel pressing against his skull. A huge hand reached around his neck and pressed talons into his throat. He felt the heat of the poison spread, its hand clenching, starting to rip against the tendons in his neck.

He braced himself to fight it.

Sebastian murmured, '*No*,' and let up the pressure he'd been keeping on the commander. '*This is not our time to die, Nikolai.*'

NG couldn't hold it on his own. He let go, adrenaline pounding in his chest.

The Bhenykhn commander roared and stood. It raised its hand to stay the one with its goddamned talons in his throat and turned its full attention onto him.

Last man standing.

Right in the heart of the enemy's territory.

It breathed out and sat back, spreading out its arms again. 'Your empty hands insult us, human.'

He shifted his weight imperceptibly, fighting stance, ready. "We're not here to bargain," he said out loud, not as loud as he intended, throat dry and painful, chest heaving.

He couldn't tell if the others were still alive, couldn't feel anything from Sebastian.

It sneered. 'The last time a race like yours stood before the Bhenykhn Lyudaed, they tried to appease us. They offered us a galaxy.' It leaned forward, leering. 'Your galaxy.'

The chambers spun.

It threw the memory at him, joint ancestral hive memories bombarding his mind with that ancient deal, a galaxy teeming with life served up to them in a feeble attempt at bargaining for peace.

'The Man.' Sebastian was linked in with the entire hive. He sounded far away, struggling to connect. 'The Man and his people offered them our galaxy. They thought it would save their own. My god, Nikolai, the Man didn't just lie to us, he condemned us before he ever came here to try to save us.'

Shards of ice twisted in his stomach as he stood there, defying these conquerors. Defying the Devourers. More determined than ever.

It forced him down to his knees. More figures closed in, gripping his shoulders with talons that broke the skin, stabbing, more poison that pulsed into his bloodstream, pushing him down.

It had no doubt of its position here. No doubt it had won.

He stared up at it, unblinking, refusing to submit. He could see Leigh standing to the side of the throne, looking into his eyes, willing him to hold, willing him to live.

Even though she hadn't.

'What do you have to offer us, human?'

He could feel Sebastian sucking energy from them, stealing their alien life force and weaving it into strands he could use.

NG managed to not let it show.

"We don't sell out anyone," he said, as loud as he could manage, chin up, shutting off the pain, cold and determined, pushing aside the weakness from the toxin that was pulling at his muscles. "You want to make a deal, what do you have to offer?"

It laughed.

Sebastian made his move. He threw all the energy he'd garnered from them back into them, sent them flying, talons ripping out of NG's flesh, frying their brains and turning on the commander.

It bellowed, lurching up out of its seat, grabbing the massive axe and throwing it.

Time seemed to slow. All he could see was the blade tumbling, as if in slow motion, headed right for his centre mass.

He couldn't move fast enough, throwing himself to the side, catching the full weight of the weapon slamming into his shoulder and knocking him back.

The commander pounded down the steps towards him. He couldn't scramble away, pinned by the axe.

It grabbed the haft and pulled it out, kicking him hard enough to send him rolling.

He folded, lungs burning, coughing blood, his shoulder shattered and bleeding, left arm numb of all feeling.

It roared again and towered over him.

'You think you can stand against us?'

It opened its mind.

Shared.

The pure immense scale of the Bhenykhn hive hit him. This fleet that had turned up was one of an advance force of hundreds just like it. And behind that they had thousands, millions of warships, fighters, tens of millions of ground troops, breeder units…

It let that sink in and expanded the view again.

It wasn't just this galaxy they were attacking, the Bhenykhn hive was immense.

Inevitable. Conquering. Devouring.

It was unstoppable.

The Bhenykhn leaned down and grabbed him round the throat. It picked him up and hurled him against the steps.

'No one,' it bellowed into his thoughts, 'can stand against us.'

NG hit the deck hard. He curled up. The pressure in his head was unbearable, the pain in his shoulder and ribs too much to neutralise, the toxin coursing through his veins too much to deal with.

It loomed over him.

He couldn't feel Sebastian anywhere.

He closed his eyes.

And opened them in the hazy light of a summer's evening, forest scent strong, the air still warm, beams of light casting shadows among the trees.

"This is amazing," Leigh murmured.

He turned to look at her.

"You're not real," he said. "You're my subconscious, my conscience, whatever… But whatever you are, I know you're not real."

She smiled at him. "Does that matter? And frankly who's to say what's real or what isn't? You? Sebastian? The Man? Right now, NG, you need me and that's all that really matters. Isn't it?"

This was the clearing where he'd brought Devon. He wanted to spin around, find her here as well.

Leigh touched his shoulder, the one that was bleeding and broken in the real world nightmare where he was dying on the bridge of that alien ship.

"NG," she said softly, "you do know that you can't give up, don't you?"

"I know." He almost laughed. "But what the hell am I supposed to do?"

"Win," she said simply. "You know that too."

"I miss Devon." He wanted to ask why he couldn't conjure up an image of Devon but that didn't seem fair.

Leigh smiled. "You could, if you wanted to."

"I don't know where Sebastian is." He knew he sounded like a lost little boy. He was half expecting Sebastian to turn up here, joking, chiding him with sarcasm.

Leigh shook her head, squeezing his arm. "You don't need

him. NG, go. Fight. Be you. Kick its ass. We're the Thieves' Guild, remember. No one messes with us."

He raised his face into the dying warmth of the last rays of sunlight, the shafts of gold breaking through the trees getting fewer.

He didn't even know if there was a guild any more.

"NG, you are the guild. How many of us need to tell you that before you believe it? Not the Man, not the Alsatia, not any contract or agreement. You. It all comes down to you. It always has. The Man was waiting for you. He couldn't do anything until he found you and started to prepare you for this."

"He could have told me a lot more."

She pulled that infinite patience to the end of time look that she had. "I'm sure he meant to. I'm sure he didn't foresee the damage one greedy dying human could do, how paranoid we can get when threatened, how hurt we can get when we realise we've been lied to, how the consequences of our actions tumble into one another and take on a life of their own. Face it, NG, you've always thought it. The Man didn't comprehend our timescales. He didn't understand human frailties. How could he? But he saw how much potential we have. He knew exactly how much potential you have. Think about it."

He did think about it and he understood. Finally, in all this, he understood.

The sun was setting, shadows lengthening.

"Now go," she said. "And don't let it kill you this time."

He opened his eyes, sprawled at its feet. He got up onto one elbow. "You've made a big mistake coming here."

Its face twisted, angry.

He managed to suck in a deep breath. "Those others? You don't realise, do you? They didn't offer us up as a sacrifice, to feed you." He shook his head. "They sent you here because they knew we could beat you." He grinned. "And here you are, getting beaten."

He drew energy from the heat of the deck, from the thrumming buzz of the hive itself, from the massive Bhenykhn commander before him.

It shifted its weight as if it was going to stamp on him, finish him off.

"No," NG said, almost laughing again. He got to his feet, shaky but standing, hardly coming up to its chest, looking up into its eyes as it looked down at him with disgust, realising that it couldn't move.

He held it there.

He didn't want it all to come down to him. He wanted to go sit on a beach and drink until he passed out. Damn all this to hell. He wanted to stop being afraid of what would happen if he did this or did that. Get back to honestly and voraciously saying screw the consequences and just do.

He sucked in more and more energy, felt it spinning in a vortex around him.

He looked up, going deep inside the mind of this alien warrior that had been so arrogant in its confidence, going through it to hook into the hive. He felt every alien entity within the entire system and drew energy from them. He could feel the link with the hive beyond and he thought clearly and distinctly, with more mischief than he'd felt in a long time, 'Fuck you. You come back here, we're waiting and we will beat you.' He summoned every ounce of energy he could muster and channelled it absolutely and completely into the enemy before him.

The commander of the Bhenykhn fleet screamed as he held it there, the blast rippling outwards through the hive mind as far as he could sense, one echelon of command after another falling until he reached his limit.

The commander dropped dead.

NG stood there, hardly breathing, then dropped down as his knees gave out and sat on the steps, drained, done.

37

They stood alone in the chamber.

"He beat them."

The Man nodded.

"But now he knows? About us?"

Another nod.

She stood and looked around at the empty spaces. "Let's go and find a bottle of wine. Tell me where they are now. Tell me that Nikolai is alright. Tell me where we go from here."

The only sound in the chamber was a faint pulsing hum of the ship's systems, an occasional muted rumble as it took a hit.

NG sat there, nothing left to heal with, half-heartedly trying to stop the blood flowing from his shoulder, eyelids heavy, tempted to lie down on his back and sleep but he needed to check on the others.

LC was alive but fading, blood trickling from a knife stuck in his neck. Duncan was out cold, the powered armour's internal medical systems keeping the big man alive as much as the virus. He could see Hil was breathing but the kid was sprawled, bleeding electrobes into the deck.

He couldn't reach any further, no idea if the others had made it or not.

He started to gather himself to move. To help them. As much as he could.

The Bhenykhn command structure was down, all the subcommanders dead, three tiers of command beneath them all wiped out. Every other alien left in the system was incapacitated, stunned into inaction.

He could sense from them the confusion and something unprecedented, almost incomprehensible to the Bhenykhn, panic.

He shut it out. His head became resoundingly quiet.

Nothing was moving in the chambers.

Then one of the bodies did.

His stomach did a backflip as one of the Bhenykhn bodies twitched and started to sit.

Shit. No.

He had nothing left.

NG dragged himself to his feet, looking round frantically for a weapon, nothing to hand except the hideous axe.

The Bhenykhn grabbed its rifle, joints flexing, muscles bulging as it got itself standing and started to turn.

NG reached down for the haft of the axe, forcing his fingers to curl around the thick handle, and heaved himself upright, dragging it up, dragging its blade along the floor next to him. He didn't stop staring at the massive figure, rising from the dead, turning to face him, blue eyes startling in its alien face.

'And what exactly do you think you could do with that, Nikolai?' he heard inside his head. 'Nice try, but seriously?'

The Bhenykhn stared at him, grotesque mouth twitching into a grin, or a grimace. It was hard to tell.

It was still flexing its muscles, testing its limits, breathing as if it was taking its first breaths. It stretched out one arm then the next, looking along the full length of them as if it was admiring itself. A gaping, ragged wound in its lower chest closed, healing, as he watched.

NG gaped at it, adrenaline rush competing with the poison in his bloodstream.

He squared up to it, not trusting what he was seeing, what he was hearing and sensing. He expected it to raise its rifle and shoot him between the eyes.

It laughed, guttural and raw. 'Now this is strength.' It turned to walk out. 'My god, Nikolai, heal yourself. Have I not taught you anything?'

He watched it go, trembling, not sure what he should do, not sure what the hell Sebastian was going to do. He felt ice cold, bereft, as if his soul had been torn in two.

"You should feel free," Leigh said from behind him.

He turned, hardly able to stand upright, breathing erratic.

He didn't know what to feel.

She smiled. "Let's go home."

The Man's ship was quiet. Elliott and the others of the Seven had swept up whatever ships of the Bhenykhn fleet that hadn't fled, what was left of the Earth and Wintran armada limping together under the rallying call of the Man's ship. They sent a drop ship for them, a team of extraction agents and medics piling onto the alien ship once comms had come back on line.

NG walked onto the Man's ship, more than most of the others managed. He'd stopped the bleeding, healed the shoulder somewhat, but not completely and this time it was his left arm that was strapped. More déjà vu.

Except it was Morgan who met them because this time Evelyn was at his side.

"Elliott wants to see you," Morgan said.

"I know." He'd been avoiding everyone. "There's something I need to do first."

He walked through, brushing off the medics who tried to intercept him, keeping his mind closed to any attempt to link up direct.

The Man's ship felt alien. He kept thinking he could go back to the Alsatia and the realisation that it wasn't there anymore made him feel sick.

He walked, struggling to put one foot in front of the other, keeping his resolution firm. Morgan walked next to them, waiting for orders. His orders.

"I don't know how soon they'll be back," NG said. "We need to assess what we have. Regroup." He was trembling. "Get all the survivors together and call a meeting of the most senior ranks, here in one hour, then get us out of here, get us somewhere neutral. What's coming is worse than any of us have seen. We need to brief everyone and we need to get the intel out there. Screw what anyone thinks. No more hiding."

Morgan nodded.

"I just need some time," NG said. "I'll see you on the bridge."

He knew Evelyn was staring after him as he walked away, wanting to come after him, wanting him to want her to come after him.

He needed to be alone.

He went straight to the research lab, ignoring the stares, going to the high security biohazard vault and taking a canister without signing it out.

No one stopped him.

He unlocked doors as he went, going deeper into the ship until he reached the small antechamber, standing still while blue beams scanned across him, a full bioscan ID check.

The far door clicked open with a soft hiss.

His heart was racing.

The chamber was dark but cool, a faint white glow emanating from the isopod in its centre.

He walked up to it and looked down on Martinez. She looked as if she was sleeping peacefully, chest rising and falling gently. A million miles from the pain and dirt and agony of the battlefield where she'd fallen.

"Hey," he said softly. He was still covered in sweat and blood, struggling to calm his breathing, shoulder hurting like a bitch. He stared at her, willing her, as always, to wake up. "I might have really screwed up this time, Angel…"

The canister was heavy in his hand.

It wasn't the first time he'd been down here with one.

The hum of the pod was the only other sound in the room.

"I don't know if I could have done anything differently," he said, painfully, desperately wanting to hear her voice.

He stood there, feeling the last faint traces of toxin still swirling in his bloodstream.

"And I don't know what to do now."

He rested the canister against the glass.

She'd almost died trying to save him and there was nothing he could do for her. He'd tried. The high velocity bullet that had punched through her helmet hadn't killed her outright. The one to her chest almost had but he'd healed all the damage to vital organs, repaired her body, as she lay out in the mud and rain on Erica while the rescue teams scurried around them. It was the trauma to her brain he couldn't touch. He'd healed the physical cell damage but it hadn't been enough. He'd stabilised her and handed her over to the medics. Backed away and watched while they loaded her into a medevac pod, shouting at them that they had to keep her alive.

Now it was the machine keeping her alive.

He'd just wiped out an entire alien fleet and yet he couldn't bring her back no matter what he tried.

Because he was afraid.

Afraid that he'd screw up.

Again.

The strain of the virus in the canister was their most original. Second generation, direct from LC. It was still the best one they had. Fifty-fifty.

This was what it all came back to. LC had known it right from the outset. It all came back to the damned package.

He'd not been able to bring himself to use it on Martinez because he had no idea what it would do. Even if it didn't kill her, he didn't know if it would bring her back. He didn't know if she was still in there. They'd told him the damage had been that bad.

She looked just like she always had.

In his heart, in the reality he needed, she was simply sleeping.

He didn't want to kill her. This in-between state was the best he could do. For her and for himself, but it wasn't enough for either of them.

He looked at the canister.

It felt like time was running out. His time was running out.

There was a noise behind him.

No one else could pass the security to get in here.

He turned.

Elliott was standing there, arms folded. He raised his eyebrows. "So this is what it's all been about?" He shook his head solemnly. "Thousands of your people have died. Following you. Following your orders. This obsession you've had with perfecting the virus... and this is why. To save one life? To assuage your guilt? My word, Nikolai, you really do have issues, don't you?"

NG stared at him, unblinking, then turned and looked back at Martinez.

He had the canister in his hand.

His heart was in his stomach.

"What are you, Elliott? Some kind of avatar? Is your big AI brain just sending out this hallucination to haunt me?"

Elliott laughed. "What a perfect dilemma," he said, mocking in a way far more harsh than anything Sebastian had ever taunted him with. "To save the human race, you must infect it with a virus produced from the DNA of the very aliens that threaten it. And what's the survival rate? Twenty percent? Fifty percent at best. What bitter irony that in order to save only a part of the human race, you have to commit the greatest genocide in human history. Wipe out half the human population. And then what do you even have left, what exactly have you saved, Nikolai? Because the human race that survives won't even truly be human any longer."

"Get out of here, Elliott."

"Think about it, Nikolai. You'll be the last true human left alive."

"Get out."

He turned. The chamber was empty.

It was hard to breathe.

He turned back to Martinez, holding the canister up against the input port.

She'd laugh at him and thump him on the arm if she could see him here. Tell him to man up and inject the damned virus.

He just didn't want to lose her.

Arianne, Devon, Leigh...

Was this his fate? Tasked with saving the human race but unable to save the ones he actually cared about?

He pushed the canister into place, the isopod clicking as it received the input.

He hovered his hand over the release button to initiate the dosage.

Elliott was right, he was going to wipe out the human race whatever he did.

He pressed the button.

Fifty-fifty.

The fluid ran into the IV line, spiralling round the tube and into her body.

38

"And what of Sebastian?"

"Truthfully, I do not know. I do not even know how he was able to do it. He has developed far greater powers much faster than I ever expected. Since he left Nikolai, I can't even follow him anymore. I do not know where he has gone or what he intends."

"So what now?"

He poured the wine into the jug, added black powder and watched the steam swirl, a fire blazing in the hearth of these private chambers.

It was warming.

They were just two but if anything, knowing the others were gone was liberating.

"Now, we help them," he said, pouring the wine carefully.

She reached for her goblet. "We must. We opened our own Pandora's box. We gave the Bhenykhn the means to travel, to escape from our own galaxy. How could we ever have thought that would save us?" She looked at him through the rising vapours. "We can't undo it. How can we ever make up for it?"

"We can't." There was no denying it. "The Devourers are here," he said, "and before this is over, the human race will be reduced to rats scurrying through tunnels to escape them. We have Nikolai. Luka is gaining in strength. The others? Time will tell." He raised his goblet. "This time, we work with them. We tell them everything. We have little choice."

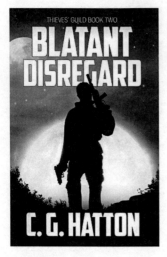

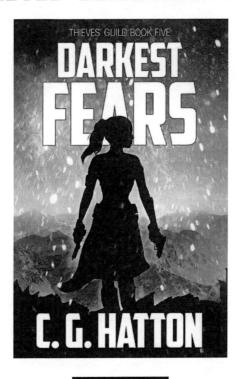